Praise for
The Thirteenth Sacrifice

"One of the most beautifully written and scariest books I've ever read. Samantha, the main character, wrestles with fear and faith in an un-put-downable heart stopper of a supernatural thriller. This is one of my top ten EVER."
—*New York Times* bestselling author Nancy Holder

"Viguié's writing in *The Thirteenth Sacrifice* is so sharp you could cut yourself turning the page. It's got everything—humor, a splash of romance in the air, an undercurrent of magic, and a pure charm that fills every wonderful line of the story. . . . [This] is the kind of book you'll read again. And again. And again."
—Steven Savile, author of *Silver*

THE
THIRTEENTH
SACRIFICE

A WITCH HUNT NOVEL

Debbie Viguié

A SIGNET BOOK

SIGNET
Published by New American Library, a division of
Penguin Group (USA) Inc., 375 Hudson Street,
New York, New York 10014, USA
Penguin Group (Canada), 90 Eglinton Avenue East, Suite 700, Toronto,
Ontario M4P 2Y3, Canada (a division of Pearson Penguin Canada Inc.)
Penguin Books Ltd., 80 Strand, London WC2R 0RL, England
Penguin Ireland, 25 St. Stephen's Green, Dublin 2,
Ireland (a division of Penguin Books Ltd.)
Penguin Group (Australia), 250 Camberwell Road, Camberwell, Victoria 3124,
Australia (a division of Pearson Australia Group Pty. Ltd.)
Penguin Books India Pvt. Ltd., 11 Community Centre, Panchsheel Park,
New Delhi - 110 017, India
Penguin Group (NZ), 67 Apollo Drive, Rosedale, Auckland 0632,
New Zealand (a division of Pearson New Zealand Ltd.)
Penguin Books (South Africa) (Pty.) Ltd., 24 Sturdee Avenue,
Rosebank, Johannesburg 2196, South Africa

Penguin Books Ltd., Registered Offices:
80 Strand, London WC2R 0RL, England

First published by Signet, an imprint of New American Library,
a division of Penguin Group (USA) Inc.

First Printing, April 2012
10 9 8 7 6 5 4 3 2 1

To my husband, Scott.
Every day with you is magical.

ACKNOWLEDGMENTS

Thank you to the incredible team at my publisher, particularly my amazing editor, Danielle Perez. Thank you to my fantastic agent, Howard Morhaim, for all he does every day for me. I also need to thank the incredible people in my life who help keep me sane: Richard and Barbara Reynolds, Juliette Cutts, Ann Liotta, Chris and Calliope Collacott, Traci Owens, and Ken Spivey.

1

Everywhere she looked there were shadows. Somewhere far away a man was chanting in a deep voice, and with each word a new cut appeared on her arms, until she was bleeding from a dozen wounds. The blood rolled down her arms and dripped off the tips of her fingers to land in pools on the floor. She began to shake.

"Turn!" It was one of the grown-ups, the one with the pale blue eyes.

She spun slowly, the blood continuing to drip onto the floor, forming a circle around her.

She stopped when she had gone all the way around. She began to feel faint and the smell of her own blood made her sick.

"It must be unbroken."

She looked down at the floor, at the blood spatters that formed the circle. Except it wasn't perfect; there were three spots where the line was broken.

The man stopped chanting and a moment later several women started a different chant.

"Close it—now."

She stared down in terror at the breaks in the circle. The circle kept her safe. The circle protected her from what was outside, but only if it was unbroken. A sulfurous smell filled her nostrils and she could hear screams nearby.

She began to spin in a circle again, trying to drip blood on the gaps, but no matter how hard she tried, the blood went everywhere but where she wanted it to go.

She started to get dizzy and she thought she was going to fall down, but she had to stay inside the circle and she had to finish it. The screams grew closer and she didn't know what made them.

"You will die!"

She began to scream herself, trying to block out the other screams. She dug her fingernails into her arms, tearing at her skin until the blood flowed faster and fell all around her. Two gaps left.

She heard the sound of claws scratching the ground, running toward her.

One gap left.

Growling and snarling, they were upon her, on every side. She shook her hands, watching her own blood fly through the air, covering her, the ground, the things beyond the circle with red eyes, and then the last gap was closed.

And something hit the circle and sent shock waves through the air and the screaming got louder.

Samantha Ryan shrieked and sat up in bed. Sweat covered her and she could still smell the blood from her dreams. She switched on the lamp on her end table and saw that she had scratched several deep grooves into her arms, and her sheets were bloody.

She wrapped her bleeding arms around herself and began to rock back and forth. "Just a nightmare, just a nightmare," she told herself over and over again.

Only she knew it wasn't a nightmare. They never were. It was another repressed memory from her childhood, bubbling to the surface to haunt her and shatter the peace she had tried so hard to achieve and hold on to.

Finally she got up and made her way to the bathroom and did her best to stanch the flow of blood. The scratches were across the insides of her lower arms. Cat scratches— that's what she'd tell anyone who asked. Scratches from a phantom cat who didn't exist, who got blamed for a lot she didn't want to have to explain.

Once she got the bleeding stopped, she applied Neosporin to the cuts. As her fingers stroked the scratches, she fought the urge to mutter a healing incantation over them. The pain was great but not unbearable. Far better to feel the pain.

She reached up to touch the cross she wore around her neck. It wasn't good to wear it to bed. She risked injuring herself while she was unconscious. Still, she couldn't bring herself to remove it. Her arms began to throb and she said a silent prayer as she swallowed some Tylenol.

She straightened and looked at herself in the mirror. Green eyes that looked far too old to belong to her stared back. Her shoulder-length red hair was damp with sweat and she ducked her head under the faucet, letting the cold water wash away the last clinging tendrils of the nightmare memory.

A few minutes later she toweled her hair dry and walked back into her bedroom, where she looked at the clock. It was almost four in the morning. She knew from experience that she wouldn't be able to go back to sleep, and that even if she could, she wouldn't like what she saw. She stripped her bed, dumped the sheets in the washing machine, and then got ready for work.

Black pants went on first. A gray button-up shirt suited her mood. A small Swiss Army knife she'd carried with her since her first day on the job and her detective's shield went into a pocket. She hesitated only a moment before clipping her holster onto her belt and sliding her gun inside it.

After leaving her house, Samantha drove downtown, parked, and headed to her favorite coffee shop. The city was just beginning to wake up and she savored the sights and sounds. Every city had its own character and Boston was no exception. The city that had witnessed so many historic events had not forgotten its past even as it pushed boldly forward into the future. It felt old and young all at once.

Just like me.

A jogger passed her, throwing an admiring glance her way. She ignored him. Samantha was twenty-eight but often felt much, much older. With her red hair and green eyes betraying her Irish heritage, a gift from the father she had never known, she caught the eyes of a lot of guys her age. It was admiration she found hard to reciprocate because they all seemed so very young and so very, very naive.

She walked into Jake's Eats and settled into her usual booth. Claudia, the motherly brunette waitress who never forgot a customer, appeared with a glass of orange juice in her hand.

"Rough night, huh?"

Samantha smiled at her. "You could say that."

"You're in luck. We've got corned beef hash this morning."

"Sounds like a winner."

Claudia smiled, patted her on the shoulder, and headed back toward the kitchen. Samantha wrapped her hand around the glass of orange juice, feeling the cold of it against her fingers, inhaling the smells coming from the kitchen, feeling the squishiness of the red vinyl uphol-stery, and remembering, as always, her first visit to the restaurant.

She had been twelve and a police officer had brought her. It had seemed like a haven from the horrors of her childhood, and the bloodbath she had just witnessed. It was where she came whenever she needed to remember that the past was the past. *When I need to feel safe,* she thought, briefly closing her eyes.

She heard the chimes on the door and opened her eyes to see a man a few years older than she was, with short black hair, a square jaw, and a brown trench coat, and he was heading her way with a determined stride.

"Morning, Ed," she said in greeting as he slid across from her into the booth.

"Samantha. I knew I'd find you here."

"Did you call the house?"

"Yeah, and, surprise, you weren't there."

"You could have called my cell," she said.

He rolled his eyes at her. "I could have, if you ever had it on."

She resisted the urge to check, but knew he was prob-ably right. Her cell phone spent more time off than it did on. She told people she was forgetful, but deep down she knew that she really just didn't want to talk to anyone.

"I think you must be the worst partner I've ever had," he grouched.

She smiled. "I'm the best partner you've ever had and you know it."

He gave her a defiant look and then grabbed her or-ange juice. "Whatever," he said as he took a swig. She had long before learned not to let his occasional lack of boundaries faze her. He knew she kept secrets from him, but he didn't push. In exchange, she didn't gripe when he mooched her food. It was a tenuous truce at best, but for two years it had worked well for both of them.

Ed was her second partner. Making detective so young hadn't made her popular, and everyone knew that her family was close to the captain. Her first partner had spent more time griping about her age than helping her learn the ropes. It hadn't mattered to him that she had a degree in criminal science, had worked her tail off, stepping up and taking responsibility wherever she could, and earned high praise from her supervisors. The whole partnership had been a disaster. After three months Captain Roberts had assigned Ed to be her partner. Fortunately Ed had been willing to overlook her inexperience, and she had learned a lot from him. But she prided herself on also having taught him a thing or two.

"Why are you here, Ed?" she asked as she retrieved her orange juice.

"Why else? We've got a body—college coed turned up dead in her apartment off campus."

"We're not on duty for another couple of hours."

"Yeah, but there's some local color involved."

Claudia reappeared with the promised corned beef hash. Samantha shoveled several forkfuls into her mouth as Ed grabbed a piece of her sourdough toast and headed for the door. She put money down on the table and followed him outside to his car. They drove for ten minutes in silence before parking outside an apartment complex.

"Local color" was what the other detectives called it when there was anything weird about a call. As soon as they walked inside the apartment, Samantha saw why the phrase had been applied.

A girl was standing, talking to a uniformed officer. Her hair was dyed an unnatural black, and she was dressed like a Goth, in a black velvet dress, black boots, and fishnet tights. Nearby, the crime scene photographer was taking pictures of the body of a young woman dressed in white who had a bloody pentagram drawn on her forehead.

When Samantha and Ed approached, the uniformed officer explained that the live girl was Katie Horn, that she lived there and had discovered the body. The dead girl was Camille. He then moved away.

Samantha turned to Katie and studied her, taking in everything from the pentagram necklace to the crystal ring on her finger. *Wiccan?*

"What's with the getup?" Ed asked.

"I'm a witch," the girl said defiantly.

Wannabe.

Samantha suppressed the urge to roll her eyes. "When is your coven meeting?"

"I don't have one. I'm a solitary practitioner."

"What you are is full of crap," Ed said. "You see, my partner here, she has witch-dar. If you were a witch, I would have known it ten minutes ago."

Samantha sighed and contemplated kicking him, but he continued. "Friend of yours?" he asked, indicating the body.

"My roommate."

"You don't seem too shook up," he noted.

The girl shrugged. "Didn't know her until three weeks ago. I put an ad in the campus paper, and she was the only one who answered who wasn't a freak."

"Good one," Ed said, as if she had just made a joke.

"Was she observant?" Samantha questioned.

"Huh?" Katie asked, a confused look on her face.

"Did she practice? Was she Wiccan? Pagan?" Samantha clarified.

"No, nothing like that. She was like Mormon or something."

"And she didn't have a problem with you being a . . . witch?" Ed asked, choking on the word.

"No, some people have, like, religious tolerance, you know," Katie said, glaring at Ed.

"Right." He snorted.

"Did she have a boyfriend?" Samantha interrupted.

"Yeah, Brad, a real frat brat," Katie said, wrinkling her nose. "They just started going out."

"Did she have any enemies?" Ed asked.

Katie shook her head. "She wasn't interesting enough to have enemies."

Samantha's eyes swept the room. They weren't going to get anything useful out of Katie. The way she stood, all defiant and rebellious posturing, was mostly a front, but if she knew something more, she had no plans to spill it.

Ed continued to question Katie while Samantha inspected the environment for anything of interest. Aside from the bloody pentagram on Camille's forehead, there didn't seem to be any blood on the body or anywhere else in the room.

She walked into Katie's room, which had vampire-themed posters on the walls. Stacks of vampire and witch books cluttered her desk and nightstand. A handful of mythology and comparative lit textbooks teetered precariously on the edge of her desk.

A pentagram had been marked on the floor underneath and around her bed. Samantha raised an eyebrow and wondered if the guys Katie brought home found it as dark and sexy as Katie clearly did.

From there she moved to Camille's room. By contrast, this room was all delicate pastels. A stuffed bear sat lonely in the middle of the neatly made bed. Posters of horses and kittens decorated the walls. If Camille really was Mormon, then Samantha was surprised that she would have tolerated a roommate like Katie. Her parents would no doubt have been even less thrilled.

"Why were you here, Camille?" she whispered to the room. She closed her eyes and could almost feel the younger woman's spirit, her essence.

She opened her eyes and shook herself hard. She moved over to Camille's desk and went through the drawers, finding only school supplies. The textbooks on the desk were neatly stacked and revealed that Camille had been taking biology, chemistry, and French literature.

After gathering all the names and information they could, an hour later they left the scene. Once in Ed's car, Samantha's irritation with him returned. "I don't like it when you do that."

"Get sarcastic with the suspects? You know I can't help myself."

"Not that."

"What, say you have witch-dar?"

"Yes."

"But you do."

"No, I don't."

"Okay, was she a witch?"

"No!"

"Was she a Wiccan?"

"I seriously doubt it."

"I don't know. I think she might have been—after all, there were all those candles around," he said.

She couldn't tell whether he was serious or he was baiting her. "You saw that apartment. There was no place she could cast a proper circle, not easily."

"Maybe she worships outside."

"In the dirt and the mud? Hardly."

"What makes you say that?" he asked.

"Let's just say her boots weren't made for walking."

"Okay, but the candles . . ."

"All black. She's a Goth. You know, darkness, death, tragedy. Wiccans celebrate the whole cycle—birth, life, death. Not just one aspect. Besides, you can't do candle magic with all black candles."

"Witch-dar," he said smugly.

Samantha turned to stare out the window, annoyed that she'd walked into it. She fingered her cross and tried not to think about how her need to touch it to make herself feel better was not much different from ceremonial magic.

"Sorry," he said, growing serious. "What do you think about the dead girl and the pentagram on her forehead?"

Samantha shrugged. "I think it's a red herring. Wiccans take an oath to do no harm. Human sacrifice isn't their thing."

And the types of people who do believe in human sacrifice don't use that symbol.

"Still, it's freaky."

"Do we know what the cause of death was?" Samantha asked. She hadn't been able to see any trauma to the body—no gun or knife wounds, no strangulation marks either.

"Coroner's gotta run some tests. It could be poison or something like that."

"Or she could have had a medical condition. Neither of which points to the supernatural."

"No witches, then? So, all that and it's just going to be a standard investigation," he said, sounding disappointed. "Remember last month it was that fake vampire murder and six months before was that woman who swore the ghost of her dead husband was the one who killed her boyfriend instead of her?"

"Your point?" she asked.

"Mark my words—one of these days there's going to be something supernatural actually going on."

"You really believe that, Ed?" she asked, carefully keeping her tone neutral.

"Where there's smoke there's usually fire. Plus, Vanessa saw a ghost when she was a kid and I believe her."

"It's always a good policy, believing your wife."

"And you don't believe her?" Ed asked.

"Of course I do. She's one of the most grounded, practical people I know. If she says it happened, I take it as gospel."

"So, off to chase down an ordinary killer. Let's go see the boyfriend."

"Frat Brat Brad," Samantha said. "What more did you get on him besides a nickname?"

"Brad Jensen. His name was in Camille's cell. According to Goth girl, he belongs to an honors fraternity. Apparently that's how he and Camille met."

Ed pulled up outside the fraternity house. They walked up to the front door, knocked, and the door was opened by a tired-looking guy with three-day-old stubble and coffee breath.

"We're looking for Brad Jensen," Ed said.

"Come in. He's in the kitchen," the other guy said before yawning.

They walked into the kitchen just as someone picked up a backpack and began to head out.

"Brad?" Samantha asked.

"May I help you?" he asked, open curiosity on his

face. "If this is about pledging, maybe Harry can help. I'm just on my way to class. Sorry."

Samantha looked him over. He was tall and slender with a gentle smile and innocent eyes partially obscured by glasses. He was wearing slacks, a long-sleeved shirt, and a tie and seemed comfortable in them. He didn't look like someone who was into drawing bloody pentagrams on girls after he killed them. Samantha flashed Ed a sideways glance and could tell he was thinking the same thing.

Brad left the kitchen and they followed him into the common room.

"Brad Jensen?" she specified.

"Yes. Why?" he said, turning to look at her. There it was in his eyes, the sudden dawning that something might be wrong. She had seen that look dozens of times. Most people could sense when they were about to get bad news.

"We're Detectives Ryan and Hofferman," she said, flashing her badge. "We need to talk to you about Camille."

"Is she okay?" he asked, going completely white.

"I'm afraid not," Ed said, his voice softening. "She's dead."

"Dead?" Brad asked as he sank down into a green velvet armchair that had seen better days.

Ed nodded. "We understand the two of you were dating."

Brad's eyes had glazed over and he didn't respond. Samantha knelt in front of him and put her hand on his shoulder. "Brad?"

"What? Sorry. Yeah. We had just met, but she was special, you know. We had so much in common." His voice caught in his throat and he looked away.

He doesn't want to cry in front of us.

"I told her to be careful when driving around here, that people were crazy. She wasn't used to all the traffic, and it scared her."

"She didn't die in a car accident," Samantha began.

"She was murdered," Ed finished.

And she watched Brad's eyes as the news shattered him. Grief, pain, and disbelief flashed across his face in quick succession. Rage would come soon enough. It was a critical moment, the one when you realized the world wasn't safe and that those you loved could be ripped from you by evil. It would likely be a defining point of his life. She wondered, as she always did, what it was like to be innocent and then to lose it. Her own innocence had been destroyed when she was too young to even remember it.

"Was she religious?" Samantha asked.

Brad nodded. "Very. She's Mormon. I am too. That was one of the things that was so great. You don't meet as many Mormons out here as you do back home."

"Was she interested in Wicca or anything like that?"

"You mean witchcraft?" Brad asked, looking somewhat shocked.

Samantha sighed. Wicca and witchcraft were two different things, especially in the way he obviously thought.

"Yeah," Ed said, pressing on.

Brad shook his head. "No. I mean, I know her roommate was into some weird stuff, but not Camille. She was only staying there until she could find a better place to live. The fraternity is coed. She applied for a spot in the girls' building. I was really praying she'd get it so she could get out of there."

"When was the last time you heard from her?" Samantha asked.

"Three nights ago. We went out to dinner. We were supposed to go to the movies tonight . . ."

The tears he had been trying to stop started to flow.

"Did anyone ever threaten her in any way?" Samantha asked.

"Who would do that? It was Camille. She was so . . . nice."

The guy who had answered the door and two others had gathered at the far side of the room. Samantha stood and nodded, and one of them moved over and sat down next to Brad, putting a hand on his shoulder.

"If there's anything we can do to help you find her killer, let us know," he said, looking Samantha straight in the eye.

Brad had begun sobbing uncontrollably. Samantha and Ed took the names and phone numbers of the others in the room and then left.

"That got us nowhere," Ed complained when they were finally back in the car.

Samantha wished she could disagree, but Brad didn't know anything. She was sure of it.

"Someone wanted her dead. There had to be a reason, right?" Ed continued.

"Well, we'll just have to keep looking until we find it."

Samantha's phone rang.

"Look at that—it does have an On button."

Samantha grimaced as she went to answer it.

"Let's hope that's the coroner with some good news for us," Ed said.

"And that would be what? 'Oops, our bad—she's still alive'?" Samantha snapped.

Ed looked at her, clearly startled, and she turned away to answer the phone. She could tell by the caller ID that it was George at the coroner's office.

"Do you know the cause of death?" she asked with no greeting.

"Hello to you too," an older male voice said. "No. There's no easily discernible cause. I'll be running a tox screen."

"If you don't have anything, why are you calling?"

"Wanted to let you know that the pentagram was drawn in nail polish."

"Not blood?"

"Nope. Looks like it was applied several hours *after* she was dead."

"Thanks, George," she said and hung up.

"What is it?" Ed asked.

"Pentagram was drawn in nail polish, not blood."

"I think we need to go back to the apartment and do some color checks to see if it might have belonged to her or Katie," Ed said, steering into the right-hand lane and preparing to turn.

"Agreed."

It felt morbid, going through a dead girl's bathroom, looking for her makeup. Three flavored lip glosses, a pale pink blush, and a bottle of clear nail polish turned up in the third drawer Samantha checked. That was it. No eye shadow, no mascara, no liners, not even any powder. The nail polish bottle was nearly full. The blush looked like it had been used only a couple of times.

Samantha searched the other drawers, but she knew she wouldn't find anything else. It fit with the picture of Camille that she had been forming.

Camille's bathroom was the one shared with guests. Katie had the master bedroom with her own bathroom, which Ed was searching. Samantha exited Camille's bathroom and headed for Katie's room.

Katie was sitting on the couch in the living room, arms folded across her chest, clearly upset that as soon as forensics finished their job she was going to be locked out of her apartment for the next couple of days to preserve the scene.

A couple of days on a friend's couch won't hurt her, but a couple of days in prison might, Samantha thought.

Samantha walked into Katie's bathroom just as Ed was whistling and bending over the trash can.

"Look what we have here," he said.

"Red nail polish." Samantha confirmed it as he used tongs to pull the bottle out of the trash can and deposit it in an evidence bag. They returned to the living room and Ed held the bag high.

"Care to explain?" he asked.

"Duh. It's nail polish," Katie said.

"Why did you throw it away?"

"What? I didn't throw it away."

"Then why was it in your trash?" Samantha asked.

"It . . . I don't know," Katie said.

"Did you put it in there, or drop it accidentally, after painting the pentagram on Camille's forehead?" Ed asked.

"What? That was blood, and I didn't do it!"

"It was nail polish, not blood, and you need to start talking to us before this gets any worse for you," Samantha said.

"Worse for me?" Katie squeaked, her eyes widening in fear. "But—but I didn't do anything."

"So who are you covering up for?" Ed demanded.

"I . . . uh—no one. No one!"

"Who are you protecting?"

"I'm not protecting anyone!" Katie said, beginning to sob.

But she was. The question was, who would someone like Katie protect? She seemed more the kind to be loyal to herself first. What would someone have to do to gain her loyalty? What would someone have to be?

Samantha stared hard at Katie. The girl was scared and she was hiding something. "Tell us about your boyfriend," Samantha said suddenly.

"Kyle?" Katie asked, blinking at her in confusion. "Why do you want to know about Kyle?"

"Is he the kind of guy that likes pentagrams a little too much?" Ed asked, gesturing first to Katie's necklace and then mimicking drawing a pentagram on his forehead.

"What? No. He's, like, a normal guy. Anyways, he's not even my boyfriend. We broke up like six months ago."

And yet on some level she still thinks of him as her boyfriend, Samantha thought.

"I mean, he and Camille never even met."

"Are you sure about that?" Ed asked.

"Yeah."

"Do you have any enemies?" Samantha asked.

Katie went pale. "I hope not," she whispered. There was fear in her eyes, a fear that was much deeper, much more primal than her fear of the detectives.

Ed's cell phone rang. After a few seconds he moved several feet away. Samantha turned her attention back to Katie. She wanted to know what the girl was hiding from her, what she was afraid of.

You could make her tell you. It would be easy, a voice whispered in her head.

She set her jaw and tried to ignore the promptings, the urges. A spell of revelation perhaps . . . Samantha shook her head fiercely. She didn't do that anymore, not for years. She took a deep breath, struggling to control herself. It had to be because of the nightmare. Every time she had a nightmare she had to remind herself that she wasn't that person anymore. No spells. But convincing Katie to trust her would be so very easy.

Samantha squatted down slowly, bringing herself to eye level with the girl. She tilted her head slightly and waited for Katie to meet her eyes.

"Look at me, Katie," she said, dropping her voice into its lowest range. "You're going to trust me. You're going to tell me—"

A hand descended on her shoulder and Samantha gasped and nearly fell backward onto her rump. She caught herself with a hand on the floor and took several quick breaths. Guilt rose up in her at what she had been about to do.

She glanced up and saw Ed looking at her with raised eyebrows.

"What?" she snapped, more forcefully than she meant to.

"We need to go. Now."

She stood up.

"Don't leave town," Ed said to Katie. She nodded, eyes wide, still looking at Samantha.

"Joe," Ed said, turning to one of the officers still on the scene, "make sure you drive her to her friend's house, see that she gets settled, and get all the contact info for her and her friend."

Joe nodded his understanding. Ed turned and headed out of the apartment, Samantha trailing behind him. As soon as they were in his car he turned to her. "What was that? Trying to hypnotize her? Watching too much television again?"

"Yes, that was it exactly," she said, letting sarcasm

drip from her voice. "I was just trying to calm her down and get a better look at her eyes when I asked her questions."

"Did it work?"

"I didn't have long enough," she said. *Thank God,* she added silently. "Where are we going?"

"Across town. St. Vincent's Cathedral."

"Can't they put someone else on it?"

"No, we're the go-to guys for this one."

"Let me guess," she said with a sigh. "Local color?"

"Worse. There's a dead nun with a pentagram on her forehead."

2

St. Vincent's Cathedral was one of the oldest in the city. Smaller than some of the newer cathedrals, it held an eerie charm that drew both locals and visitors alike.

When Samantha and Ed arrived they were met by a uniformed officer on the steps outside and escorted in. Unlike many cathedrals in the city, the interior was dark, with the light that streamed in from the stained-glass windows high above rarely reaching the pews or the ground beneath them. It took a moment for Samantha's eyes to adjust, and then she and Ed walked slowly to the front, where police officers were clustered close to the altar. When they were still several feet away, the crowd parted enough for Samantha to get a good look at the body of a woman lying on top of the altar. *Just like a sacrifice.*

Her stomach clenched as they stopped next to the body. The young woman's blue eyes were wide-open, frozen in a look of terror. Camille, by comparison, had looked peaceful. The nun was wearing her habit, but her head was bare. The pentagram on her forehead was bloodred, just as Camille's had been, but Samantha could tell at a glance it wasn't drawn in blood or even fingernail polish.

"What is that?" Ed asked.

"Wax."

"You're sure?"

"Pretty sure," she said grimly.

She glanced around. In addition to the police officers, there were two older nuns and a young priest present. All of them looked deeply shaken. The nuns were talking to an officer, but the priest was sitting alone in a pew, head bowed.

Samantha walked over and sat down next to him. "I'm Detective Samantha Ryan. You okay?"

He looked up at her with troubled eyes. "Not really."

"What can you tell me about her?"

"Sister Mary Ellen had the gentlest spirit of anyone I've ever known. She joined the convent when she was fourteen, after her parents died in an accident. She was truly devoted."

"Did she have any enemies?"

"None," the priest said, throwing up his hands in a gesture of despair.

"Does the church?"

He stared at her like he couldn't believe she had asked him that. "As a whole, I'd say the Catholic Church has many enemies who would like to see harm come to her. If you're referring to this cathedral in particular, there are none that I can think of. We have been blessedly free of scandal and view ourselves as an integral, and welcome, part of the community."

It sounded rehearsed, but she let it go for the moment. "Any friends or family?"

"She has a sister, Jane Daniels. She's in a mental institution—some tragedy a couple of months ago. I'm not sure of the details."

Samantha got out her notepad and jotted down the information. "Do you know which one?"

"No, but I can find out for you."

"I'd appreciate that. Who found the body?"

"I did. I was going to light a candle for my grandfather. When I came in, I saw something on the altar."

Samantha twisted her head to look at the prayer alcove where white candles flickered, representing prayers for deceased loved ones offered up by the devout. Those prayers were supposed to speed the departed souls to heaven. *Candle magic.* She winced as the words came unbidden and then sighed. Candle magic wasn't done with only white candles any more than it was done with only black ones.

And right now I need to find a red one.

She blinked and stood to get a better view. One of the candles in the alcove didn't appear to be white. She walked over and found herself staring at a white candle with remnants of red wax dripping down it. Was it the remains of the red candle that had been used to make the pentagram?

On the floor, a bit of paper caught her eye. She stooped to pick it up just as Ed came over to her side. "Is that what I think it is?" he asked.

She nodded. "Crayon wrapper, from a red crayon."

"And crayons are made of wax."

"Exactly."

"What is that?" the priest asked as he walked up and also noticed the red drips on the candle.

"Don't worry—it's not blood," she reassured him. "It's red wax, probably from a crayon. Do the Sunday school rooms have crayons in them?"

He nodded. "I believe the room for the preschool kids has some."

"We need to check to see if any of the boxes are missing red crayons," Ed said.

Five minutes later they were able to confirm that four of the boxes were missing the red crayons. Together they would provide enough wax to form the pentagram. Samantha pursed her lips. She was willing to bet that pentagram also had been drawn after the woman died. And the killer in both cases had used found items on the premises to make the pentagrams. *First nail polish, now crayons. Sick but creative.*

She watched distractedly as an officer bagged all the boxes, the wrapper, and the remnant of the crayons on the candle.

"The pentagrams seem like a last-minute thing," Ed said quietly to her. "What do you make of it?"

"Someone's trying to stir up fear, superstition?" she guessed.

"Or frame someone."

She thought of the pentagram around Katie's neck and the other one under her bed. "You think someone's got a grudge against little Miss Goth?"

"It would make sense, except I don't get what her connection to the nun could possibly be. The roommate, sure, but the sister?"

"I hear you. Sounds like we need to find out at the very least if Katie knew her."

Ed's phone rang and he answered it. Samantha took the opportunity to walk slowly around the body on the altar. A crime scene photographer was carefully shooting every nuance, every angle that he could. Barricading off an apartment for a few days was one thing; having to barricade off a church would be quite another. Given the details of the crime scene, it was in everyone's best interest to get the entire thing examined and cleaned up as quickly as possible before photos of a dead nun hit the front page and caused an onslaught of curiosity seekers. A murdered coed was a senseless tragedy. A murdered nun was potentially a hate crime and the lead on the six o'clock news. And that was if they all got very lucky and no one uttered the words "sacrifice" or "devil worship."

Ed walked up beside her, finished with his phone call. "This could get ugly very fast," Samantha whispered.

"It already has," Ed said.

The hair on the back of her neck stood up and she turned to him. "Another murdered girl?" she asked.

"Not quite. Katie's ex-boyfriend just turned up dead in his room. Apparently it's not pretty. I called Joe and told him to bring Katie in for questioning. After we check out the new body I think we'll be wanting to question her a little more . . . aggressively."

Samantha turned, eager to be out of the church and away from the sight of the sacrificed woman. As meaningless as the pentagram on her forehead was, as deliberately staged as the body atop the altar was, all seemingly meant to mislead them, she still couldn't shake the feeling that the woman *had* been a sacrifice.

"What's going through your head?" Ed asked when they were back in the car.

"I was wondering how many more times we're going to crisscross the city."

He snorted. "Tell me about it. I think I should have ignored the phone this morning. You know, take a page from your playbook."

"And miss all this excitement?" she asked.

"Gladly. There's such a thing as too much excitement, you know."

"Trust me, I got that message loud and clear," she said, staring out the car window and doing her best not to dredge up memories of her childhood. She should have taken it as a bad omen when she was interrupted at breakfast. She had never gotten to fully unwind from the nightmares that woke her in the middle of the night. "What did they tell you about the dead guy?"

"He was in a fraternity."

"Great. Another one."

"Yeah. This one's more for jocks than geeks, though."

"Even better." She sighed.

"Apparently two of his housemates discovered the body when they broke open his door."

"They broke it open?"

"Yeah. Locked from the inside. They called nine-one-one. When officers arrived on scene, the guys said they were sure his witch ex-girlfriend, Katie, was responsible. One of the officers at that scene was a first responder this morning and figured he'd better call us in."

"Wonderful. So that's two dead who knew Katie. This just keeps getting better and better."

"If we can prove the nun knew her too, then we've got a trifecta."

A few minutes later they were standing outside a different fraternity house, talking to the two guys who had found the body. One was tall, outspoken, and carried himself with a certain amount of arrogance. The other was slightly shorter and seemed genuinely shaken up by what he had seen. His name was Gus. His eyes were red from crying and he kept staring at Samantha.

"It had to be his crazy ex, this chick named Katie," said Jerry, the taller of the two guys. "She was like psycho and into scary stuff. She was a witch, literally. When he dumped her, she came around a few times, and she was totally mental, begging him to take her back, totally stalking him. I think he got a restraining order against her. You should go arrest her now. I can tell you where she lives."

"You're really eager to blame her. Any particular reason?" Ed asked.

"Because she butchered my friend. It was her. I guarantee it," he said heatedly. "She wanted him dead. She threatened him all the time."

Samantha turned to Gus, who had been quiet since their arrival. "Is that true?"

He nodded. "Katie used to scare me," he whispered. "I didn't think, though . . . I mean, they'd been broken up a long time."

"Used to scare you?" Samantha repeated.

He nodded, staring at her in a way that made her uneasy. Did she know him from somewhere? She racked her brain but couldn't place his face. There was definitely a sense of familiarity in the way he looked at her, though, like he was trying to remember who she was. She forced herself to break eye contact.

"So, what makes you guys think she did this?" Ed asked.

"Who else could have?" Jerry said. "I mean, how could something like that happen without anyone hearing anything? The house is old; the walls are thin. You can't whisper without someone hearing you. She cursed Kyle. She's a witch. And you know what they used to do to witches in the old days?"

Samantha jerked her head toward him. His tone was aggressive, threatening, and he was growing more and more agitated. Was he trying to cover up something?

Ed took a step back and raised his hands defensively. "Settle down, guy. I've gotta ask." Although his stance was meant to placate and calm Jerry, Samantha recognized it as the position Ed assumed when he was about to go on the offense.

Everyone needs to just calm down, she thought, wishing that she could whisper a word and make it happen.

Suddenly a girl screamed, high and loud. Samantha spun around and saw a blonde wearing a light blue polo shirt and a white miniskirt, her hair in a high ponytail, wrestling with one of the officers stationed in front of the door to the frat house. "Kyle!" she shrieked. "Kyle! Let go of me! I have to see him!" The girl was stronger than her slender frame would seem to indicate, and the officer trying to restrain her was having trouble doing so without hurting her.

Samantha stepped forward and laid her hand on the girl's shoulder. The girl spun toward her, fists flailing uselessly and landing harmless blows to Samantha's chest and shoulders. Instead of grabbing her hands, Samantha pulled the girl close, crushing her body to her and hugging her tight. The girl's hands pounded a couple of times against her back.

"It's going to be okay," she said, lying to the girl.

The girl slumped in her arms and began to sob brokenly. Samantha glanced up and saw both guys staring, stricken. Jerry started forward and Samantha gratefully handed the girl to him. She leaned against Jerry and continued to cry as he patted her back awkwardly.

Samantha moved back over to Gus. "Who is she?"

"Kyle's girlfriend, Tina. They've been dating for a few months."

Samantha glanced back. Tina was still crying uncontrollably, but occasionally she could make out a word. She didn't like the ones she heard, particularly when Tina screeched "witch" loud enough for everyone to hear.

"Something tells me we're in for an honest-to-goodness witch hunt," Ed breathed in her ear. His proximity startled her and she shied away just for a moment. He shot her a puzzled look and then said quietly, "Tell me I'm wrong."

She prayed he was wrong. She turned her attention back to Gus. "Explain to me about being afraid of Katie."

For a moment she thought he looked embarrassed. Then he said, "Yeah. She's into all that weird stuff. I used to think it was scary . . ."

"What changed?" Ed asked.

Gus shook his head, but continued to stare at Samantha.

"What scares you now, Gus?" she asked softly.

"People like you."

She blinked and then stepped forward until she was in his personal space and looked him squarely in the eye. She saw honesty there and something else. Terror. There was no other word for it.

"You mean police officers or attractive women?" Ed asked, his eyes narrowed.

Gus shook his head but continued to stare at her. "People with . . . power," he said, licking his lips nervously.

A chill danced up her spine. Before she could say anything, one of the uniformed officers hailed them. "Detectives, you want to see the scene while it's still intact?"

She turned with Ed, all too eager to get away from Gus and the way he stared at her. They passed by Tina and Jerry and walked into the house.

"What was that guy saying about you?" Ed asked.

She shrugged. "Who knows? He's probably still in shock. We're lucky he knows his own name."

She could tell Ed wanted to push, but he didn't. "You think Katie finally realized after six months that Kyle wasn't coming back to her and killed him?" he asked instead.

"I'm not sure what to think," Samantha admitted as she climbed the stairs. "By embracing a Goth look and persona she's bound to freak some people out, but I wouldn't think jocks would be afraid of her."

"Maybe they believe in magic and bought that she was a witch like she tries to make out."

"Maybe," she said, unconvinced.

They reached the landing and turned to the left. A police officer outside the room looked pale and nodded his head briefly in greeting.

"Or maybe there's some truth to that whole 'hell hath no fury . . .'"

They walked into the room and he stopped short.

There was blood everywhere—floors, walls, even the ceiling had splatters of it. The body was in the middle of the floor, gutted. Arms and legs were thrown straight out and a circle of blood surrounded it.

"There's no pentagram on him," Ed said after a moment, sounding strangled.

"No, because *he* is the pentagram. His head, legs, and arms represent the five points of the star, and the blood is circled around him." Samantha pointed it out to Ed, anger rising in her.

"Goth chick didn't do this?" Ed asked, clearly hoping she would contradict him. He stayed where he was while she approached the body.

Samantha shook her head. "She hasn't got it in her. Whoever did this was ruthless, cold-blooded."

And a real practitioner, she thought. *Someone with power.*

She knelt next to the body and took a good look at the slash marks on it. The guy's chest had literally been ripped apart and gutted, as though some wild animal had fed on him. The only problem was that in a locked room on the third floor of a fraternity house in the middle of the city there was no wild animal that could have gotten to him.

No earthly one, at any rate.

"Doesn't that make you sick?" Ed said. She glanced up and saw that he had covered his mouth and nose with a handkerchief. The smell of blood was nearly overpowering in the confined space. That smell had been such an integral part of her childhood, though, that she barely noticed it. Just one more thing that made her a freak.

"I don't see the heart anywhere," she said.

"That's because someone either swiped it to use for something awful—though what's worse than this I don't want to even imagine—or someone or something ate it."

"And yet you don't have a problem imagining that?"

"I'm telling myself it was a bear. Bear ate him. Or maybe a wolf."

"You know wolves don't eat people, right?" she asked, trying to keep him calm as she looked closely at the body.

"Tell that to Little Red Riding Hood and her grandmother." He coughed and took a step back. "So, what do you think about the circle?"

She bent closer, looked carefully at the circle, and then straightened and looked at Ed. "It has brushstrokes in it."

"Any chance that's paint?"

"No."

"Someone painted the circle using the blood?"

"It looks like it."

"Maybe they just used something that looked like blood, like with the other two."

"No, that's blood," she said.

"Are you sure?"

"Yeah."

"Anything else?"

"I'm pretty sure it was made after he was dead."

"Why?"

Because it didn't protect him.

She reached up to touch her cross and realized that it was gone.

3

"What's wrong?" Ed asked.

"My cross is missing," Samantha said, working hard to quell the surge of panic that rose in her at the realization.

"Maybe you left it at home."

"I didn't," she hissed, more forcefully than she had meant to. She stood abruptly and began retracing her steps out of the room.

"What are you doing?" he asked.

"I have to find it."

"Seriously? Samantha, look, we've got bigger worries at the moment."

"*You* have bigger worries," she said. "You know that cross is important to me."

"I—"

"Just help me look for it."

"What about the body?"

"Whoever killed the other two killed him to frame Katie."

"Whoa, whoa, whoa. You're jumping to conclusions."

"I'm right," she said, her eyes flashing back and forth on the landing outside the room. She moved slowly down the stairs. She had to find it. When could she have lost it?

She made it downstairs and then finally outside. "Have you seen a cross?" she asked everyone in her path.

Finally she heard Ed's voice beside her. "I'll check the car."

She met him there five minutes later. "Did you find it?"

"No, sorry," he said. "I just called over to the church and told them to keep an eye out for it there. No one's seen it yet."

She swore under her breath and his eyebrows shot up.

"Are you okay?" he asked.

"No, I'm not."

"I'm sure you can get another one."

She balled her hands into fists at her side and forced herself to take several long, deep breaths. "Not like that one I can't."

"Well, if it's not in the car, then it has to be at one of the crime scenes. Forensics will find it. Now, we've done all we can for the moment. How about we go back inside and solve a crime?"

"I told you what happened."

"Great. Now tell me who did it."

He was right and she knew it. She glanced once more at the ground beside the car and then followed him back inside, trying to put the gnawing fear out of her mind.

Back in the room the smell of blood was still strong. She stared at the circle of blood on the floor. There was power in blood. Man had known that since the beginning and it was reflected in art, religion, and myth throughout time. Blood could atone. Blood could protect. Blood could feed. Blood was the perfect sacrifice.

That was why she had had the cross specially made. On her thirteenth birthday she had locked herself in her bedroom and performed the last magic ritual she would ever do. She had put three drops of her own blood into a tiny sealed compartment in the center of the cross. The cross had been specially made for her, a replica of a fifteenth-century piece. It was a birthday gift from her adoptive parents, who hadn't asked her why she wanted it. The ritual was the death of her old life as a witch and the birth of her new one as a Christian. It had been her sacrifice, her way of honoring the sacrifice on the cross. And it had helped her put her faith in the new religion, the new symbol.

For fifteen years it had kept her safe. Without it she felt naked, exposed.

"Sam!"

"Yes?" she asked.

"I need you here, right now," Ed said.

"Sorry. I'm here," she said, starting to look around the room. She was sure that whoever had done this hadn't left any evidence behind for them to find.

A minute later Ed whistled and she joined him at Kyle's desk. There, in the top drawer, was a letter from Katie.

"What do you think?" he asked.

She skimmed it. "*Undying love, connection, do anything to get you back.* Sounds like the kind of letter every confused girl writes to some boy who doesn't deserve her at some point."

"Yeah, but how many of them end up in a dead guy's room?"

"Exactly. This letter is dated three months ago. Why is it here? Why did he hang on to it?"

"As evidence in case he needed to file a restraining order?"

"Do you really believe a jock like him would have thought it through and kept it as the top thing in his desk drawer for three months?" she asked.

He shrugged. "Trophy?"

"And he kept it where the new girlfriend could see it?"

"Maybe whoever killed him found it."

"Left it is more likely," she said.

He stared hard at her for several seconds. It was long enough to make her self-conscious and she reflexively reached for the cross that was no longer there.

"What's going on with you? Usually you're telling me not to jump to conclusions and now you're positive that Katie didn't do this, sure that she's being framed. Why?"

She dropped her eyes and clenched her fists at her side. For two years Ed had trusted her with his life and yet Samantha had never been able to trust him with the truth.

She gestured to the body but kept her eyes fixed on the ground. "I know what it takes to do something like this and I *know* Katie doesn't have it. But I'm willing to believe that at some point she's met someone who does."

There was a silence long enough that she began to squirm. It had been difficult to say the words out loud, but waiting for him to say something in response was worse.

Finally Ed cleared his throat and she glanced up at him. He wasn't looking directly at her, but out the window behind her. "You don't work this town without occasionally hearing things. And before we became partners I heard things about you."

"What things?" she asked, her mouth dry.

"Things. Like you had seen . . . some weird stuff, up close and personal–like."

She knew he liked to tease her about her witch-dar, and about the fact that she knew more about the weird and strange than most did. But he had never asked. He had never had to. They had never seen anything together that would warrant those kinds of questions. She turned and glanced at Kyle. That had changed the moment they walked into his room.

"I've seen . . . things." It was as much of an admission as she could muster. It seemed like such a small thing, but admitting even that much caused a chill to dance up her spine. She stroked the spot on her neck where the cross should have been. She was right. She had lost it and now she was exposed.

Ed licked his lips. "Okay, so you've seen things. Are you telling me that what happened here is a . . . thing?"

She nodded, not trusting her voice.

"And Katie might not be able to do these types of things, but she might know who can?"

She nodded again.

"Okay, then let's go ask Katie a few questions."

"Yes," Samantha said softly, heading to the door.

"Hey."

She turned and forced herself to meet Ed's eye. "We're cool, you and I."

She wasn't sure if he was asking her or telling her. "We're cool," she echoed.

"Good. Now let's get out of here before I have to vomit."

They left the room and headed down the stairs. They didn't speak again until they were in the car.

"Let's hold off on telling Katie about her ex for a while," Ed said.

"Focus her elsewhere and then spring it on her and watch her reaction?"

"That's the theory."

"Works for me."

A couple of minutes later Ed pulled into the parking lot of a hamburger dive they often frequented while working. "Okay, I haven't eaten in hours and neither have you. Swiss cheeseburger and onion rings?"

"Yes, please," Samantha said.

"Be right back."

She took advantage of his absence to take several deep breaths and get hold of her runaway emotions. She was feeling better, stronger, when Ed came back to the car with the food.

"So, you want to play good cop, bad cop?" he asked as he ignored his fries and snagged one of her onion rings. He unwrapped the burger and held it one-handed as he drove out of the parking lot.

Samantha rolled her eyes at him. "No matter how many times you ask, I'm always going to say no. I prefer good cop, smart cop."

"Funny," he said.

His cell rang and he tossed his burger at her as he reached for it. She grabbed it and resisted the urge to take a retaliatory bite out of his blue-cheese-and-bacon burger. A minute later he hung up and made a U-turn. "Katie will just have to wait a little while longer. We located the nun's sister and we have permission from her doctor for a visit now."

Samantha nodded as she handed back his burger and started chomping on her own, forcing herself to focus on the taste of it in her mouth and the feel of the sauce as it rolled down her fingers. It was a trick her adoptive father had taught her. Focusing on tactile impressions helped you be in the moment, not fixating on the past or worrying about the future. She listened to the sound of the car's engine and breathed in the smell of burgers and onions and cheese. Slowly she felt herself beginning to relax.

They turned down a private road that was shaded by

trees on both sides and curved around to the front of a stark white building. A small gold sign that read KENTON PSYCHIATRIC was situated next to the front door. *Like anyone would mistake the hospital for something else.*

"These places give me the creeps," Ed admitted.

"I think they do that to everyone."

"Isn't your dad a shrink?"

"Grief counselor."

"Like I said, shrink."

Inside the building they were greeted by Dr. Matheson, a short, balding man in his early fifties who led them to a small room where the nun's sister, Jane Daniels, was waiting. At the threshold Dr. Matheson turned to them.

"I've already told her that her sister has died and that you want to talk to her about it. I'm not sure how much good it will do, though. We had to give her a pretty strong sedative. I'm afraid it's going to set her treatment back."

"What's wrong with her?" Ed asked.

"About four months ago she was abducted, apparently after one of her classes at the university. After two days she was found behind one of the lab buildings. She had been stabbed and left for dead. Campus police found her and were able to revive her while waiting for the ambulance. She's been paranoid and delusional ever since. As soon as she was well enough to leave the hospital she was transferred here. Last I heard, the police assigned to the case still had no idea who did this to her."

"That's terrible," Ed said.

"Yes, it is."

"Was she sexually assaulted?" Ed asked.

Dr. Matheson hesitated. "The police didn't find any such signs, but there are things that she says sometimes that make me wonder. Whatever happened to her had

to have been traumatic to create such an insurmount-
able disconnect with reality. She had no previous history
that would suggest ongoing mental illness."

"What does she say happened to her?" Ed asked.

The doctor cleared his throat. "She claims that she
was sacrificed."

Samantha focused on her breathing. If what she
feared was true, it was nothing short of a miracle that the
young woman was still alive.

The doctor put his hand on the doorknob. "I'm going
to have to ask you to not agitate her any more than is
necessary by your questions."

They walked into the room and Samantha felt a chill
as she stared at the nineteen-year-old. She looked empty,
somehow hollowed out. It was as though they were staring at a corpse. The shell was there, but the person was
not.

Jane sat in a white gown, slippers on her feet, and
stared at the wall. She had similar features to her sister,
high cheekbones and large, doe eyes. Her skin was un-
naturally pale and her lips were chapped. She was thin,
too thin, and from the looks of the needle marks on her
arms Samantha guessed that she received the majority
of her food intravenously. Her pale blond hair was cut
short, exaggerating her skull. Her left ear had a scar, as
though something had torn the lobe. Her right ear bore
the fading marks of a piercing that had sealed up from
disuse.

No place for adornment in here, Samantha thought,
trying not to stare at the plain white walls, but instead
focus on the girl who practically blended into them.

She and Ed took seats at a table across from Jane.

"Jane, these are the police officers who want to talk
with you," Dr. Matheson said.

Slowly she turned to look at them. She stared first at Ed. Then she shifted her eyes to Samantha and she flinched. She made a whimpering sound deep in her throat that Samantha recognized as terror.

Ed, quick to notice, reached out and touched her hand, forcing her attention back to him. "Jane, I'm Detective Hofferman. I'm very sorry about what happened to your sister."

Samantha watched as Jane took a deep breath and slowly answered. "Thank you." Even the words seemed slightly disconnected, as though the girl herself wasn't sure if she was saying them out loud.

"Was there anyone who would want to hurt your sister?" he asked.

Jane shook her head. "Everyone liked her. Always."

"How about your family? Did anyone want to hurt your family?" he continued.

"No. No family, just her and me."

Ed paused and Samantha sympathized with him. How to ask Jane any more without pushing her over the edge? In her gut she knew, though, that the only way they were going to find answers was to push. She cleared her throat slightly and Jane's eyes swiveled back to her. The pupils dilated swiftly.

Is she afraid of all women or just me? Samantha wondered. Jane made a small motion with her hand and Samantha saw a crocheted cross in it. It was like the kind Samantha's adoptive grandmother used to give out to friends and family every Easter for use as bookmarks. Jane was clutching hers tightly, as if her life depended on it. *I can relate.*

"Jane, who would want to hurt you?"

Jane tucked her legs up and wrapped her arms around

them, making a keening noise in her throat. She began to rock slightly.

"I don't think—" Dr. Matheson began, but Samantha held up a hand to cut him off.

"Jane, tell me who would want to hurt you."

"Bad people."

"Which bad people?"

"The ones who . . . who . . . they wanted my blood . . . knives . . . pushing into me. They sacrificed me."

"I have to insist that you leave now," Dr. Matheson said sternly, rising to his feet. "This is what I was trying to avoid. This girl has suffered enough and she can't possibly know anything."

"Let's go, Detective," Ed said, rising and heading to the door.

Samantha stood her ground. "Jane, look at me!"

The girl did as ordered. "I promise you that you are safe now. They can't harm you in here. Tell me who did this to you and I will make them pay."

"Really?" Jane asked.

"Yes, but you have to say it."

Dr. Matheson was beginning to raise his voice and Ed grabbed her elbow, but Samantha knew she was close to the truth. She knew that even more than she needed to hear it, Jane needed to say it and to have someone believe her.

"They were witches," Jane said, eyes locked on hers.

Samantha leaned close so that their faces were only inches apart. Jane didn't flinch, but Samantha could feel multiple hands pulling at her.

"Jane. You are absolutely right. Witches attacked you and they will pay for what they did."

Relief flooded Jane's face and Samantha could tell

that even through the haze of medication and self-doubt, she had gotten through to the girl. "Thank you," Jane whispered.

"The truth shall set you free," Samantha whispered back.

"They branded me," Jane said, as though suddenly remembering it.

"Branded you? Where?"

Jane turned her head around as far as she could. There, on the back of her head, just at the hairline, was a white scar in the shape of an octagon. One side was jagged, in marked contrast to the almost surgical precision of the rest of it. It was as though whoever did the carving lost concentration. *Or stopped suddenly.*

"You want to tell me what the hell that was all about?" Ed asked once they were back in the car.

"The truth," Samantha said.

"I doubt Dr. Matheson will let us back in for a follow-up without some sort of court order."

"He can bite me," Samantha said. "I don't give a rat's ass about him. What I care about is that girl knows exactly what happened to her. She's never going to find any peace or get out of that damn place until she can come to terms with it."

"Nice theory, but as long as she's claiming she was attacked by witches, there's no way they're ever going to let her go. I think you just did her more harm than good."

"That's a matter of opinion, but the truth is always better, no matter how ugly or unexplainable it is."

"Fine, but if we get blowback for this, you're explaining that to the captain, not me."

"Any time."

A couple of minutes passed while Ed calmed down.

"You were right," he admitted finally as they turned into the parking lot for their precinct.

"I know I was."

"Well, don't expect a medal anytime soon. Let's focus on cracking Katie and getting this thing solved before it gets any stranger."

"We're on the same page there."

They got out of the car and walked up the station steps just as a news van pulled up. They ducked inside the building before the reporter could climb out. "I wonder why the press is here," Ed mused.

"I don't care as long as it has nothing to do with our case," Samantha said. She doubted they would be so lucky as to escape the press entirely, though. Word would soon be spreading about some of the day's events.

When they walked in, Joe was standing on the far side of the room. He held up three fingers and pointed toward the hall. He had put Katie in the third interrogation room. Samantha gave him a nod and then cleared her mind as she and Ed headed there. Once inside the room, she sat down across from Katie. The girl looked frightened but still defiant.

"I told you, I don't know who killed Camille," she said before they could ask her anything.

"Then maybe you can tell us a little about Sister Mary Ellen," Ed said.

"Who's that?" Katie asked.

"A nun at St. Vincent's," Samantha replied.

"I don't know any nuns. I'm not Catholic."

"Just because you aren't Catholic doesn't mean you don't know any nuns," Ed said. "She could be a relative, friend of the family, next-door neighbor."

Katie shook her head. "I told you, I don't know any nuns. Why do you think I would?"

"Because this particular nun ended up dead, just like Camille."

Katie flinched. "What?"

"That's right." Ed pressed on. "Whoever killed your roommate did the same thing to a nun, right down to the pentagram on the forehead."

"I—I wouldn't know anything about that," Katie said.

"Then why are your hands shaking?" Samantha asked.

"I'm exhausted and I haven't eaten anything," Katie said, her eyes on the table.

"Talk to us, Katie, and this will be over faster and we can all get something to eat," Ed said.

"I don't know anything."

"But yet you claim to be a witch," Ed said. "Shouldn't this be right up your alley? Shouldn't you be able to cast a spell and tell us something?"

"I . . . um . . . it doesn't work that way."

"Then why don't you tell me how it does work, because clearly I must be watching too much television."

"It's like, a religion, you know."

"So I've been told. But you didn't claim to be a Wiccan; you claimed to be a witch. Big difference. And the symbol on two dead bodies is the same as the one under your bed. Don't you think that's kind of strange?"

"Lots of people use pentagrams," Katie said, trying to sound tough.

"Katie, do you know any practitioners, any *real* ones?" Samantha asked quietly.

Katie stared hard at the table and didn't say anything, but her shoulders were hunched and she folded her arms across her chest—a protective gesture.

"Katie, if you know something, you need to tell us," Ed said.

"I don't know who killed her. I don't know who would want her dead."

"Do you know who might want someone like her dead?" Samantha asked.

"No!"

Ed turned to Samantha. "I think the lady protests too much."

"I'm not! I don't. I don't know who killed her."

"But what if you had to take a wild guess? Who could have killed her?" Samantha asked.

Katie went back to staring at the table.

"Samantha, let's go get some lunch and let Katie think about who might have done this to her roommate," Ed said, standing casually.

"You can't leave me in here!"

"Actually we can. Sooner or later you have to talk to us, Katie."

He led the way out of the room. As soon as the door was closed he let out a low whistle. "She's certainly scared of someone."

"You think? We have to get her to tell us who."

"Let's grab a picture of Kyle and see if we can't shake a name loose from her with that," he said.

They walked out into the main room. Desks piled high with paperwork were crammed into much of the space. Usually there were half a dozen officers bent over filling out forms, but instead everyone was at the far end of the room, huddled around a television. That was never a good sign.

They walked over and Samantha tapped one of the officers standing on the fringe of the crowd on the shoulder. "What's going on?"

"Witch hunt."

"You're kidding me," she said, praying he was speaking euphemistically.

"See for yourself. Hey, people, clear a path," he boomed.

Several people shuffled a step or two to the side. There, on the television, was a picture of Katie in full Goth regalia.

"How did they—"

She stopped and stared in horror at live images of Katie's room, including a close-up of the pentagram drawn on the floor under her bed. Ed shoved his way over to her, saw what she saw, and immediately began barking orders.

"Martinez, Johnson, and Sparks, get your asses over to that apartment now. Secure the crime scene and arrest every newsperson there who just crossed the police tape. Move!"

Officers began scrambling while Samantha pushed closer to the television to hear what was being said.

"—a self-professed witch who has been linked to the murders of at least three people. The suspect is in police custody now, but no word as yet from the authorities on charges."

"How the hell did they know?" Ed asked.

Samantha shook her head. "Someone called them."

"The real killer?"

She pointed to the screen. There in the background was a familiar blond figure standing in front of a fraternity house. "No. Distraught girlfriend."

"Please tell me we're going to be able to solve this quickly," Captain Roberts said as he walked out of his office.

"We're working on it," Ed said.

"Work faster. I've got a bad feeling about this. I think it's going to turn on us."

"What do you mean?" Samantha asked, studying his

face closely. He looked grim. A shadow hung about him unlike any she had seen there before.

He gestured to the television. "That reporter is crying 'witch' and no one is calling her a liar. Last time something like that happened anywhere around here, a lot of innocent people died."

"This is hardly the sixteen hundreds," Ed said.

"No, but times are tough and people are on edge. And two things never change. People will always blame other people for their problems, and the worse things are, the more zealous people get. That means trouble in any century."

"We're going to have to put her in protective custody," Samantha said.

"Let's hope she gives us something that makes it all worth it," Ed said with a sigh.

"If the real killer doesn't come after her, someone else might."

"You say that like it's a bad thing," he said with a weak smile.

"I think she's a lonely, mixed-up girl who's gotten in way over her head. She doesn't deserve to be in the line of fire."

They walked over to his desk and found a stack of photos from the three crime scenes. They grabbed pictures of each of the three victims and headed back to the interrogation room.

They reclaimed their seats and Ed placed the photos facedown on the table.

"Do you know what's going on out there?" Ed asked, jerking his head toward the outside.

"A cop convention?" Katie asked.

The girl was trying so hard to be tough, but she just couldn't pull it off. Samantha almost felt sorry for her.

Still, it was a good thing that Katie wasn't the seasoned hard case she pretended to be.

"The press is stirring up an angry mob that wants to hunt you down and burn you at the stake, old school."

Katie's jaw dropped open. "What?"

"You heard me. There's a witch hunt going on out there, and by the looks of things, they're going to skip the whole witch trial and go straight to the execution."

"People would do that?" The bewildered look on Katie's face was both sad and comical. "But I'm not a witch, not really."

"You've cried witch so many times that people are starting to believe you, and trust me, they're pissed," Ed interjected.

"They're not going to believe that you didn't have anything to do with all of this," Samantha said.

"But I didn't!"

"But you know who did. You know something. Talk to me, Katie, and we can help you."

Katie shivered and seemed to fold in upon herself. "I didn't do anything wrong," she whispered.

"Tell us what you did do," Ed said, pushing her.

"Look, all I know is I get paid to have a roommate, as long as I screen them special," Katie said, whimpering. "None of them have ever died before."

"Do you know that for certain?" Ed demanded. "Where's your last roommate?"

"I don't know. She just split, and she stiffed me for the rent."

Samantha was watching Katie, a quiet horror creeping over her as Katie's earlier words sank in.

"What are you screening them for?" she asked.

Katie turned to look at her and the girl's eyes were dilated wide with fear. "Purity."

"You mean you're targeting virgins?" Ed asked.

"That's just part of it," Samantha whispered and Katie nodded.

"Total purity. No sex, no drugs, no drinking, no smoking, no tattoos, no piercings, not even ears," Katie said.

"Anything else?" Ed asked, his face turning ash white.

"They have to be religious."

4

"You get paid cash to screen your roommates?" Ed repeated.

"Sort of. Just a little bit. There's other stuff mostly."

"Who? Who pays you to screen your roommates?" Ed asked Katie.

"They're witches. Honest, real live witches," Katie said.

"And how do you know that?" Ed asked sarcastically.

"I met them through a friend of a friend. They're the real thing. They can do all kinds of stuff."

"Did they promise to teach you?" Samantha asked.

"No. I asked, but they said they wouldn't."

"And you didn't think that was strange?" Ed asked.

"No. I'm a nothing, a nobody. I don't have any powers like them."

And since she doesn't have any natural power, there's nothing they could teach her, Samantha realized grimly. *All they can do is use her.*

"You're dealing with scary people," Samantha told Katie. "What did you hope to gain from it?"

"Nothing."

"What was it? Sex, drugs, an adrenaline rush? What?" Ed demanded.

"It was nothing like that!"

Samantha leaned forward. "Look at me, Katie," she

said, lowering her voice slightly and putting as much authority and conviction into her words as possible.

Katie turned and looked her in the eye. "What was it they promised you?" Samantha asked.

"They told me that they would put . . . put . . ." Katie burst into tears.

Samantha studied her for a long minute while the girl cried. Katie had wanted something badly enough that she was willing not to ask questions and to do whatever was asked of her to get it. What could dark practitioners have offered her that she couldn't get elsewhere?

"What spell did they promise to cast for you?" Samantha asked.

"They said they'd curse Kyle for me."

"Kyle?" Ed asked, shooting a sideways glance at Samantha.

"My ex-boyfriend. He dumped me on our one-year anniversary. He was cheating on me with this total skank. She said they could put a curse on him, make it so he couldn't . . . you know."

"Make it so he couldn't what?" Ed asked.

"Make him impotent," Samantha guessed. When Katie nodded she continued. "Start from the beginning. Tell me who this person was, where and how you met her, and exactly what you agreed to do."

"Am I in trouble?" Katie asked. She looked at Samantha with wide eyes, and for a moment it was easy to see the confused, scared girl, barely more than a child, and not the defiant young adult who wanted to embrace the darker side of life.

"Yes, you are. And we're the only ones who can help you," Samantha said.

Katie whimpered. "They wouldn't hurt me, would they?"

"What do you think?"

Katie slunk farther down in her chair and wrapped her arms closer around herself. Samantha wanted to reassure her, but it was false hope and she wasn't in the habit of giving that. Instead she took a deep breath and offered the only comfort she had.

"Katie, if you help us, tell us everything you know, we'll put you in protective custody."

Katie shook her head fiercely. "I don't want to talk anymore."

"It's either talk to us now or talk to the jury later," Ed said roughly.

Katie's eyes widened. "I haven't done anything wrong!"

Samantha cleared her throat. "Your ex, Kyle—is his last name Nelson?"

"Yeah, why?"

Samantha grabbed the picture. "He was murdered last night, killed by magic," she said, tossing the photo on the table in front of Katie.

Katie took one look at it, screamed, and then dissolved into hysterical tears. Samantha sat unmoving, making sure Katie got a good look at what her friends had done.

"How could they do this to Kyle?" she finally managed to ask. "I just wanted him to not be able to sleep with that skank. I didn't want him dead."

"But someone wants to see you get blamed for these deaths," Samantha said. "One of your love letters to him was in the room."

"What? He kept them?" Katie asked. The look of hope that flickered briefly in her eyes was painful to see.

"Somebody did. Somebody who wanted you to take the fall for his death and the others."

"But I didn't even know the nun! How could anyone possibly blame me for that?"

"Who was your last roommate? The one who stiffed you for rent?" Ed broke in.

"Jane. Jane Daniels."

Samantha and Ed shared a glance. "When was the last time you heard from her?" Ed asked.

"Four months ago."

"Do you know where she is now?"

Katie shook her head. "No. I tried calling her cell, but it was disconnected. I got some of her mail."

"Did you keep it?" Ed asked.

"I sent it back."

"Did the witches ask you about Jane?"

"Yes. Just like the others."

"Did Jane ever talk about her family?" Samantha asked.

Katie shrugged. "She wasn't much of a talker. I think she had a sister, but I'm not sure."

"So you never met the sister?"

"No."

"Katie, her sister was the nun that was killed today," Ed said.

"Are you kidding me?" the girl asked, her eyes bulging.

"No, we're not," Samantha said. She put the photo of the nun faceup in front of Katie. The girl took one look at it and then squeezed her eyes shut, as if wishing would make it go away.

"I didn't know."

"Four months ago Jane was attacked by witches who tried to sacrifice her. They stabbed her, left her for dead. She survived by a miracle, but she's locked up in a mental hospital."

Katie began to cry again.

Samantha thought of Jane, remembered the scars on

her ears. It had looked like someone had ripped off one of her earrings. *Her ears were pierced—that's why they couldn't use her. She wasn't completely pure. They didn't know until they started the ritual,* Samantha realized. That meant that whatever this was had started months before.

"You have to help us catch these people," Samantha said.

"They're going to kill me!"

"Not if we can help it, but you have to work with us."

"Is there some kind of witness protection program? You know—change my name and everything."

"That will depend on a great many things. If you help us catch these people you might not have to go into hiding."

Katie bit her lower lip and twisted a silver dagger ring round and round her finger, staring at it as though it would somehow give her the answers she was seeking. "Okay," she finally agreed in a very quiet voice. "I don't know how much I can help, but I'll try."

"You're doing the right thing," Ed said suddenly. "If these people want to hurt you, the only way to be safe is to make sure that they're behind bars."

Katie nodded, clearly wanting to believe him.

Samantha knew better. If the people Katie was involved with were into the things she thought they were, there was no way a prison cell would stand between them and vengeance.

"I don't know how many of them there are. I only ever met the one girl," Katie said.

"Do you know her name?" Ed asked.

"Bridget. I don't know her last name."

"Do you have any pictures?"

"Yeah, we're best friends. We got professional portraits done together," Katie said, her sarcasm returning in full force.

Ed raised an eyebrow. "You can't tell me you didn't snap a pic with your cell, just once?"

Katie looked away. "I tried to and she caught me. She was pretty mad and I was too scared to try again."

"What does she look like?" Samantha asked.

"She has really pale blond hair, like almost white, and it hangs straight down her back to her waist. She has these freaky amber eyes that seem to stare right through you, you know?"

Samantha nodded but didn't say anything.

"She's about an inch taller than me, so she's got to be about five-six. She's thin, but not like skeletal. I think she's my age."

"Where did you meet her?" Samantha asked.

"I met her at a party at this haunted house in Salem a few months ago. I don't know who she knew there; she just sort of showed up. Kyle had just dumped me and I was a mess. I couldn't stop crying. She said that she could help me."

"For a price," Samantha finished.

Katie nodded.

"So how did you contact her?" Ed asked.

"She called me. Her number was always blocked."

"What else do you know about her?"

"I think she lives in Salem. At the party she said she was just a couple of minutes from home."

Samantha blinked. Real witches in Salem? There hadn't been any for years. At least as far as she knew. Most practitioners gave Salem a wide berth. It was one giant tourist trap focused on witchcraft and the town's history. It could get to be a little irritating, but if a person could stand it, it was also a perfect place to hide.

"Do you know where in Salem the party was?" Samantha asked.

Katie nodded. "I don't remember the address, but I could tell you how to get there."

Ed tore off a piece of paper from his notepad and offered it to her along with a pen.

Katie shook her head. "I would have to take you there. I remember what the turns look like, but not well enough to describe them."

"So we'll have to see if we can schedule a little field trip," Ed said.

"Better do it fast," Samantha muttered, thinking about the news broadcast going on. Another couple of hours and it was going to be impossible to take Katie anywhere without someone noticing.

An hour later they were on the road, Katie sitting in the back of Ed's car with an officer on either side of her. They passed Marblehead and into Salem and Samantha felt the hair on her arms stand on end. For years she had avoided Salem like the plague and she had been prepared to never go back.

"Turn left at that light," Katie said.

Ed followed her directions. Katie's memory was a little fuzzy in places, but eventually they turned onto a tree-lined street that Samantha knew well. She reached for her missing cross as panic flared inside her. *Please let me be wrong,* she prayed silently.

"There, that one!" Katie exclaimed. Ed pulled up in front of an old run-down mansion that Samantha recognized from her nightmares.

"You were at a party here?" she asked, her voice barely a whisper.

"Yeah. Amazing, huh? It's creepy even in the daylight," Katie said. "Some guys in one of the fraternities put on a party here. It was like Halloween in April. It made a great haunted house."

Probably because it is *a haunted house,* Samantha thought. *At least it is for me.*

"Bridget said a lot of people died here years ago. Some kind of group suicide, I think. Isn't that freaky? Can you believe stuff like that actually happens?"

"It wasn't a suicide," Samantha said through gritted teeth. Sweat popped out on her forehead and ran down to sting her eyes.

"Are you okay?" Ed asked, so low she was pretty sure she alone heard it.

She shook her head as she began to tremble.

"Katie, you stay in the car with Officer Grant and Detective Ryan. We'll go see if anyone's home," Ed instructed.

Samantha worked to control her breathing as Ed and Oliver got out of the car and approached the front door.

"We're probably going to have to come back with a warrant," Grant said from the backseat.

"I don't think anyone lives there," Katie said.

"Still need a warrant," he said.

Samantha felt like something was trying to crawl its way out of her chest as she watched Ed and Oliver walk up the eight steps to the front door. Ed pressed the doorbell and even though she was too far away to hear it, the sound of it echoed in her memory until it seemed to fill the air around her.

Nothing happened. A minute later she watched as Ed knocked hard on the door. She barely stifled a scream as it swung open. She threw open her car door and sprinted up the steps. She grabbed both men and pulled them away from the door.

"Don't go in there," she pleaded, her voice sounding like a child's in her own ears. "Please, please, please."

"Samantha, let go," Ed said. "What's wrong with you?"

And then, from somewhere deep inside the house they heard a bloodcurdling scream. Ed and Oliver drew their weapons simultaneously and lunged forward.

Samantha grabbed the collar of Oliver's shirt and spun him, throwing him down the steps. He landed at the bottom on one knee with a grunt of pain. "Get out of here!" she shouted. "Go! Now!"

He scrambled to his feet and ran around the car and got into the driver's seat. He hesitated and she pulled her weapon. "We'll call when it's safe to come back."

He gunned the car away from the curb while Ed stood gaping at her. "Stay behind me and do everything I tell you," she said. Her heart was slamming against her rib cage so hard that she winced with every beat. It was a trap. She knew it, but she wouldn't be able to stop Ed from going in if he thought someone was in trouble.

She stepped across the threshold and a blast of air rushed past her. Invisible hands plucked at her shirt as though trying to pull her back outside. She pushed her way through the wind until she was standing in the middle of the foyer.

"You search down here. I'll go upstairs," Ed said.

"No. If there's anyone here, they're in the basement. Stay right behind me."

"Sam—"

"Shut up and do as you're told."

The house caught her words and they echoed around her, sometimes louder, sometimes softer, sometimes in her own voice and sometimes in the voices of others. She heard women, a man, and children repeating her words. She felt dizzy, but she bit the inside of her cheek to have something tangible to focus on and it helped her push through the disorientation.

She turned around and slapped Ed across the face as hard as she could. He yelped in pain and surprise and the house caught that and sent it around the room as well.

"Focus on the pain, no matter what."

She headed for the kitchen. She could hear the floor creaking behind her as Ed followed. Beneath her steps the floorboards were silent, as they had been designed to be. Only those who had never been welcomed into the home caused the wood to groan a warning to the occupants.

They walked into the kitchen and the outline of a woman passed before the window onto the backyard. She turned to look at them and tears streaked down her cheeks.

"Hey!" Ed shouted.

"It's a ghost, Ed. Ignore it," Samantha hissed. The image disappeared, much like a soap bubble bursting.

"Are you friggin' kidding me?"

"Shut up!"

She crossed to the door to the basement and threw it open. She flipped the switch but was not surprised that there was no electricity. The darkness beneath was complete and heavy.

"We need flashlights," Ed whispered.

Without taking her eyes from the doorway, Samantha opened the kitchen drawer nearest her and pulled out two candles and a box of matches. "Light them."

She knew he wanted to protest, could feel it, but he didn't. Instead he handed her a lit candle and she tilted it slightly so the wax wouldn't run over her fingers as it dripped.

She stepped forward into the darkness and began to descend the staircase. The light from the candle sent grotesque shadows dancing over the ceiling and walls, but she ignored them, half shutting her eyes and taking the stairs more from memory than sight.

As she continued downward more sounds assailed her. She heard chanting, wailing, laughter, screams, all mixed together. She bit down harder on her cheek and gradually the sounds faded.

She reached the floor of the basement and stepped away from the staircase. A spectral child ran up it and straight through Ed, almost causing him to fall. He caught himself on the railing, then made it down the rest of the way. The smell of blood filled Samantha's nostrils as memories came pouring back over her.

She was standing in a circle, cutting her arms, and there was so much blood, but not enough to save her, not enough to make the circle complete.

It's not real; none of it's real, she told herself over and over as she stepped slowly into the room, lifting her candle high. *What I'm seeing, what I'm hearing, all of it is echoes only.*

She took one more step and realized that while everything else she had seen and heard might be only phantoms, the pool of blood on the floor was not.

It can't still be here, not fresh, not glistening as though it was spilled moments ago!

She bit the inside of her cheek harder until she tasted blood, but it didn't make the vision go away. She took three steps forward until the light from her candle showed her the source. A young woman in a white gown was on the floor, her eyes wide-open in death. It was her blood that was rippling away from Samantha's shoes as she stepped through it.

With a shout of dismay Ed rushed forward. "I knew I heard someone scream. We should have come faster."

"It was her scream you heard, but she's been dead for at least an hour," Samantha said, wishing that it wasn't true.

"But the blood, it's so fresh. And the scream. That was only five minutes ago."

"Don't let it fool you. She was dead long before we got here. Call it in."

Ed pulled his cell out of his pocket and pushed a button. He waited a moment and then held the candle up to it. "No service."

Need to leave. She heard the words as clearly as though Ed had spoken them.

"Need to leave," Samantha echoed, turning back toward the stairs.

Need to leave.

Need to leave.

"Something touched me!" Ed shouted.

"Need to leave!"

The door at the top of the staircase slammed shut and wind whooshed by her, picking the hair up off her neck. It snuffed the candles, plunging them into darkness.

"What was that?"

Samantha could hear the panic in Ed's voice. It was nearly drowned out, though, by the other voices that were growing louder.

Going to die.

Going to die.

"Going to die," she whispered, her fear choking off her voice.

5

"What's happening?" Samantha heard Ed shout over the voices that surrounded her, the ones that bespoke their death. The harder she bit the inside of her cheek, the louder the voices became until she could feel blood oozing out between her lips.

I'm feeding them with the blood.

"Ed, listen to me—do exactly as I say!"

"Anything! Just tell me what to do," he begged.

"Do you still have the matches? Can you relight your candle?"

She saw a tiny flame as he lit a match. It burned out and was replaced by another and then another until he was swearing steadily.

"What is it?"

"I'm out of matches and none of them would light the candle."

She took a deep breath. They had been snuffed by magic and only magic would light them again. She wished she could teach him a spell to say to light the candle, but with true magic it wasn't about the words but about the spirit and the intent of the practitioner. It couldn't come from him. *It can come only from me.*

"No!"

"What?" he asked, misunderstanding her outburst.

"We will find another way," she said aloud, mustering every ounce of defiance she had left.

Laughter filled the room, creaking and chortling and swirling around her and through her until she thought it might be coming from her.

"What do you hear?" she asked Ed.

"A woman screaming."

He heard something different from what she did. To Ed a woman screaming was terrifying. To her the laughter was far worse. It was playing on their own worst fears, which meant there was no active entity behind it, just a booby trap left for the unfortunate intruder.

"Take a deep breath," she ordered him, trying to do the same herself. "It's meant to scare us, but there's no one else here."

"Then what's making that sound? Some kind of speaker system?"

"I'll explain it to you once we're out of here."

Out of here, out of here, the voices mocked and the laughter kept time.

Fight back; you know how, a small voice whispered inside her mind.

"We don't need the light," she said out loud. "The stairs out of here are to my right about five feet away. And you were what, closer than that to me?"

"Yeah. You're in front of me and the stairs are behind me."

"I'm going to try to touch you," she said to warn him and took a step in the direction she remembered the stairs being. She didn't trust the sound of his voice, as the room caught it and echoed it round and round. It was designed to make sound do strange things and she couldn't believe it.

Samantha stepped slowly, carefully, feeling her way with

hands and feet and praying she didn't trip over something in the dark. She stretched out her fingers toward where she thought Ed was standing. Something wet and cold brushed across them and she forced herself not to jerk away.

No! The word rang in her ears, so loud it made them buzz and ache. She pushed forward, emboldened by the sound until her fingers brushed the cloth of Ed's jacket.

She felt him shy away at her touch despite her warning, and she lunged forward and grabbed his shoulder. She could feel the muscles coiled and tense beneath her fingers and for a moment she thought he was going to turn on her.

"It's me," she said.

"Let's get out of here, please," he begged.

Keeping hold of his shoulder, she slid forward, feeling for the stairs. *You can do this. How many times did you find your way in the dark as a child?* She took a deep breath and focused all her faculties on the task at hand. She blocked out the voices, the chill air, everything that wasn't Ed or the staircase.

Her left foot bumped up against the bottom step and she yanked Ed forward, almost pulling him off his feet. She kept her hand on his shoulder as they made their way up the stairs. As they neared the top she began to move faster, aware that the danger was increasing even as they came closer to escaping the horrors below.

Ed came to a halt so suddenly that she staggered and her foot slipped on the stair. She let go of his shoulder to grab at the railing as she crashed to her knees.

"Listen. She's still alive. We have to go back for her," Ed said.

She struggled to her feet and grabbed a fistful of his shirt and dragged him up another stairstep. "I promise you that she's dead."

He pulled back against her and she slapped him again as hard as she could. "Ed, focus on the pain. Remember what I said. And if you have ever trusted me, you've got to do it now and move!"

She didn't know if it was the pain from the slap or what she had said, but something seemed to sink in and Ed came willingly with her up the last six steps. She grabbed the doorknob, but was not surprised when it wouldn't turn. She threw her shoulder against the door, but it didn't give even an inch. She thought of the gun she was carrying, but she knew that she would be just as likely to injure one of them if she used it. Nothing in the basement was as it seemed and she couldn't risk introducing flying bullets into the equation.

Ed pressed against her, unnatural sounds of fear emanating from him. If he could have, he would have run over her to get out the door. His shirt where she gripped it was soaked with sweat and the stench of fear coming off him was starting to be more overwhelming than the voices that screamed that they were going to die. She slammed her shoulder into the door once more and it still didn't budge.

Then, below them in the darkness she heard the sound of nails clicking and scratching on concrete. Something big began to climb the stairs behind them, its hot breath wafting ahead of it.

"No!" Samantha heard herself screaming.

She grabbed the doorknob again and a surge of energy flashed through her fingers as she shouted, *"Patefacio!"*

The door unlocked at her command and she shoved it open, Ed following with a rush. She slammed the door shut behind them and they raced together to the street. On the porch Samantha spun, hands raised defensively

as she stared at the open front door and waited for
whatever might be coming after them.

She stared, every nerve alive and quivering as beside
her she heard Ed calling for backup. The hair on the
back of her neck rose as something stopped just inside
the front door and stared out at her. She couldn't see it,
but she could feel it and she could hear the heavy breathing of the creature that waited there, daring her to make
a move.

With a flick of her wrist she caused the door to slam
shut in its face and then she collapsed to the sidewalk,
sobbing.

Half an hour later she and Ed sat on the curb as a dozen
officers from the Salem and Boston police departments
swarmed all over the house. She had stopped crying but
was still shaking. She noticed that Ed also looked the
worse for wear, with an ashen face, vacant eyes, and
blood-covered shoes. Fortunately Oliver had listened to
her, and he and Grant had whisked Katie away from the
scene quickly and had taken her to a different precinct
to wait for them while reporters continued to arrive at
their own precinct.

After a while an officer from the Salem department
approached them. He had sandy blond hair and his
name tag read WESLEY. "Sir, ma'am, we've set up some
portable lights down in the basement at the crime scene.
Would you care to come down? We'd like your opinion
on whether this might be linked to the murders in Boston."

Before the others had arrived she had used a few
well-chosen words to banish the beast that had growled
and clawed at the front door, the barrier it could not
cross. Shame still filled her, but she had been able to

think of no other way to dispel the creature and the danger it represented. After that, many of the barriers and protective spells guarding the house had fallen like dust. The barriers were magic; that's all they were, mostly designed to protect the house and its former inhabitants from intruders. Some, like the floorboards that creaked beneath Ed's weight but not hers, were like an alert system. Others, like the sounds they had each heard in the basement, were designed to scare those who did not belong there. The creature had been created to kill those who made it too far into the house and proved resistant to the other spells.

Ed stood up shakily, but Samantha stayed put. It was safe to go inside now. Even if a few barriers remained, they would be of the kind designed to work on the psyches of two or three people, not a dozen. Safety in numbers was an old concept, as old as magic itself. Still, she wasn't going to set foot back in that basement, even if they had managed to drive away all the shadows they thought resided there with all the portable lights in Salem. Some shadows would never leave.

Ed looked down at her, but she shook her head slightly. He didn't argue; he simply trudged into the house after the officer. She knew he didn't want to go, but he was also still not sure what all had happened. If he knew how close they had really come to dying, he would have stayed on the curb with her and looked at photos later.

She sighed as she let her head drop into her hands. The truth was, even if he realized it, he would probably still go. He needed to see for himself that the girl was long dead and that there really had been no way for him to save her. His need to save others was the greatest thing that drove him, was what gave him the strength to go back into that basement. *And I'm still just trying to save myself,* she realized.

So she waited outside while her partner explored the depths of the house and examined the crime scene. She didn't need to see it. Enough of it had been burned into her brain that she would not soon forget. After a while she realized that it had been a long time since Ed had gone back inside. Fear touched her and she turned to look at the house behind her.

It was a gray house, older than those around it by at least a half century. It was large, though. The windows in the attic stared down at her like unblinking eyes and the maw of the beast gaped open. She blinked, forcing herself to see the door as it actually was and not as what it meant to her.

Could she have missed something? Had there been other spells, traps that even now could be killing the officers inside the house? She shook her head forcefully. If that were the case there would be screaming, some whisper of sound. She concentrated, focusing on shutting out all the other sounds around her until she could hear two officers on the main floor talking about meeting at Red's Sandwich Shop the next morning for breakfast.

Finally Ed rejoined her outside and from the look on his face she knew that he had even more questions than when he had gone inside.

"The murders are linked," she said quietly.

"I'm inclined to agree with you. She appears to fit the profile. No piercings, Star of David on a chain around her neck. The killer must have known we were coming, didn't have time to stage the body somewhere maybe," he muttered before sitting down next to her on the curb. "Maybe that's why there was blood this time. You already knew that, though, didn't you?"

"Yes."

"I couldn't find anything else down there—no speakers, no animals, nothing to explain anything. I searched that basement from top to bottom."

"Did you tell anyone what you were looking for?"

"No. That would mean telling them what happened down there when I still don't know myself."

She nodded, staring at his bloodstained shoes and not trusting herself to look at him.

"They don't need us right now. Let's get out of here," he said.

They found a Boston officer who was free to drive them back. They were almost to the precinct when Ed had him drop them off at Jake's Eats instead. Samantha's car was still parked on the street and she moved toward it until she realized that Ed was headed into the restaurant.

She followed him and they slid into the booth in the back. A waitress brought them coffee and menus. Once they'd ordered, they sat in silence until the food came. When the waitress set Ed's steak and Samantha's corned beef sandwich on the table, Ed ignored the potato chips and the pickle spear on her plate and went straight to eating his steak.

Samantha winced and watched him out of the corner of her eye. He usually absconded with her chips and pickle. The fact that he hadn't done that this time made her uneasy. She wondered whether he was just too distracted to think or if it was a sign of sudden mistrust between them. She picked at her sandwich while she tried to decide what to say to him.

When he was halfway through his meal, he finally looked at her for the first time since they had gone into the house. "What are we dealing with here?" he asked.

Samantha shrugged, not wanting to talk about it, and even less sure that he really wanted to know.

"I mean, are those girls being used in some kind of . . . sacrifice?"

Samantha studied the blackness inside her coffee cup and chose her words carefully. "They could also be re-cruits."

"Recruits? Then what happened to them?"

"Maybe they didn't want to join. Or maybe they did and then changed their minds."

"And so these people killed them? What—as a warn-ing, like some sort of gang thing?"

More likely they killed them to keep whatever it was they were doing a secret. She sipped her coffee. "Are we sure they were the first?"

"I haven't heard of anyone else showing up marked with a pentagram, have you?"

"No, but neither of us had heard about an injured girl who was ranting about witches before today," Samantha said, wishing that she had. If only she had known . . .

"Point taken." Ed stared at her hard. "You know there was nothing you could have done for her, right?"

Samantha felt tears stinging her eyes. "I wish I'd had the chance to try."

Ed took a swallow of his coffee and studied her shrewdly. "I'm guessing you did a lot to help her today. What you said to her . . . that it really was witches . . . it was the truth, wasn't it? I mean, not fake witches or wan-nabe witches or delusional psychopaths or some kind of metaphor, but real witches."

She nodded. "They are real witches."

He slammed the rest of the coffee and thumped the mug down on the table. In that moment something sub-

tle changed and he seemed more himself, more in control again.

And the truth will set you free. It had helped Jane and
now it was helping him.

"So, when are we going to talk about the broomstick
in the room?" he asked.

"What are you asking me?" she said, struggling to
buy time. She wasn't ready to talk about it. Not with him.
Not with anyone. *Especially not after what I did today.*

"What is your deal?" Ed asked, leaning in close.

"I don't want to talk about it," she said.

"Unfortunately, that's a luxury neither of us can afford anymore."

She winced. "I don't like to think about my past, much
less discuss it."

"No, really?" he said, the sarcasm thick in his voice.
"I've been your partner for two years. I kind of picked
up on that. Look, I have to tell you I'm really freaked
out about these killings. I know you know more than
you're saying."

She dropped her eyes to the table. "I've never told
anyone."

"No better person to tell than your partner. You
know things about me even my wife doesn't know."

"Lucky her."

He smiled only briefly.

An icy knot settled in the pit of her stomach. He really wanted to know. He deserved to know. And if things
got any freakier, he really *needed* to know.

"I, uh, had a bad childhood," she said, licking her lips.

He leaned forward intently. She glanced up at him
and saw burning curiosity in his eyes. He had known for
a long time that she wasn't normal. He had been more

patient than most people, given her space, but it hadn't meant he didn't want to know. Looking at his face, she could tell just how badly he wanted the truth.

She got it. Being a cop made you a bit of a control freak. Knowledge was power. Knowledge about your partner was life. He had probably wondered for a long time just what baggage she was carrying and when it was going to become a sudden, unexpected problem for both of them. She had heard stories about officers who froze when confronted with something that came a little too close to their own childhood scars.

She took a deep breath. He reached across the table and squeezed her hand. When he tried to pull back, she hung on for dear life. She was afraid and she forced herself to focus on his hand, the look of it, the feel of it, the pressure he was applying.

"I was raised in a coven."

She struggled to gain control of the emotions that suddenly welled up within her, threatening to overtake her. Fear, rage, shame, pride, and a dozen more that made no sense to her.

"Wiccan?" he asked gently.

If only, she thought. Wicca was a religion. Those who followed it were peaceful, taking oaths to harm no one. The coven she had been raised in had nothing to do with Wicca, and its members had taken no such oaths.

"No, this was, um, a group that was into the occult."

She could feel his uncertainty and she didn't blame him. "Occult" meant so many things. It was a word that was thrown around so often that it had lost its meaning, its power.

"They were into very black magic, the bad stuff, you know?"

"What, like sacrificing animals?"

She laughed. She could hear herself laughing, hear the hysterical edge to it, but she couldn't stop. She grabbed her glass of water and gulped, choking on it. The laughter that sounded like it came from someone else ceased as water ran down her chin.

She drew in a long breath of air with a gasp. "No."

A look of relief crossed his face and it broke her heart to say what she had to. "Sacrificing people."

6

Ed didn't have to say anything. The look of horror on his face spoke volumes to Samantha. He tried to yank his hand away again, but she wouldn't let it go. She looked at him, wishing she could make him understand, but knowing that he never could. She waited for him to say something.

"Please tell me you didn't—"

"I did . . . saw . . . a lot of things I wish I could forget. But, no, I was spared from actually delivering a killing blow."

And she knew that he had been on the force long enough to know that just because she hadn't done the deed didn't mean she was completely innocent. Even still, there were so many things she didn't remember, but she clung to the belief that she had never killed a person. She had been too young, and only older, higher-ranking members of the coven did that.

After a long minute Ed cleared his throat. "But I know your father, your family."

"My adoptive family," she corrected.

He nodded slowly. "Your biological family, your . . . coven . . . What happened?"

"They were slaughtered, all of them. I survived." She shook her head, not wanting to describe it, and still not entirely sure how she had escaped it. She remembered the screaming, the blood, the monster that they had raised. And then she remembered walking, feet bare, dress torn, until she found what she was looking for. "Afterward I walked to a police station. I told the first officer I saw that my mother was dead." She licked her lips, shaking at the memory. "It was Captain Roberts, but back then he was a detective in Salem. He went to the house . . . the house you and I were at today . . . and everyone was dead."

Ed swore. "In the basement?" he asked at last.

She nodded.

"And that woman in the kitchen that you said was a ghost?"

"One of them," she whispered.

"Then what?"

"Captain Roberts felt sorry for me and brought me to this place to eat before taking me to see a friend of his, a psychologist named Aaron Ryan. Later the Ryans adopted me and raised me, taught me not to fear the dark . . . and not to worship it either."

They had only half succeeded. She didn't worship the dark, but she had never overcome her fear of it.

"So Ryan's not your real last name."

"It is now. Samantha Ryan. I chose a new name for myself the day they officially adopted me. They gave me Ryan and I chose Samantha."

"What was your name?"

She shook her head. "I won't say that name out loud again. The new one is all that matters."

"Why?" he asked, wrinkling his brow.

"Names have meaning, power. That's why I needed a new one. I couldn't deny what I was, where I came from, but I needed to rob it of its darkness, its hold over me. So

I chose the name Samantha in honor of the witch on *Bewitched,* because she was the nicest, funniest, most harmless witch I could think of. By taking her name I acknowledged my roots while attempting to deny them power over me."

"But why didn't you choose a name with no witch connection?"

"It wouldn't have been the truth and I would know and I would give it power by hiding it."

"That's really . . . weird."

Samantha grimaced. "I even taught myself to twitch my nose like her. How I wished some days that I had been Tabitha and not me. Growing up a witch with Samantha as a mom would have been wonderful."

"Maybe, but you still would have been a witch."

She nodded. That was what she had to remember. A witch was the one thing she didn't want to be, even though she and Ed owed their lives to that part of her that had been able to command the door to open, allowing them to escape.

"How old were you?" he asked.

"Twelve."

"And they were all slaughtered?"

"Yes."

"Care to tell me how?"

"Something they were trying to do backfired on them." That was true, but it didn't even begin to capture the essence of what had happened that day.

"And you didn't have any other family?"

She shook her head. "Not that I knew of. Mom never mentioned anyone."

"What about your dad?"

She shrugged. "I have no idea who he was, or even if he was still alive. My mother refused to talk about him."

"Ouch."

"I figure I'm lucky. If I had relatives, who knows where I would be now. I owe everything to my adoptive parents."

She waited, searching his face to see what his response was going to be. Ed was a good cop, one of the best, and as much as he would want to support his partner, she wasn't sure that after what she had revealed he would want to be partners anymore.

I can barely live with the things I've done. How could I ever ask him to?

"Are we okay?" she asked.

Before he could say anything, her phone rang, startling her. She reached for it, cursing the timing.

"Ryan here."

"Sam, I want to see you in my office as soon as possible," Captain Roberts said without preamble.

"Yes, sir. What about Ed?"

"Make sure he goes downtown where they've got Katie and then come straight here."

"Yes, sir," she said, but he had already hung up. That wasn't good.

"Captain wants to see me, and you've got to see a woman about protective custody," she said, throwing a few dollars on the table and standing up.

"Seems like you're not going to get to finish any meal here today," Ed said as he walked out with her.

"Not in the cards, I guess."

"So, Roberts knows about you . . . your past?"

"Everything."

It wasn't true. Captain Roberts didn't know *everything*, but he knew enough.

A minute later they were in her car, and as she drove she kept trying to get a good look at Ed's face. He spent the entire drive staring out the passenger-side window. He had never answered her question from the diner and she was afraid to repeat it, since she was pretty sure she knew the answer already. She just didn't want to hear that he couldn't deal with her past. Over their two years as a team, Ed had become more than a partner; he had become a good friend. She had been to his house for dinner dozens of times and thought his wife was an absolute saint.

Once they arrived at the precinct, they split up without another word to each other. Ed grabbed his car and headed out for the precinct where they were holding Katie.

Samantha took a seat outside Captain Roberts's office while waiting for him to finish a phone call. He was the one who had listened to her in Salem the night she showed up with stories of witches and demons and death. He had been the lead investigator, and she remembered endless hours spent talking to him in the weeks after the events. She had thought that once he stopped investigating she wouldn't see him again, but he and her adoptive family were close. When he transferred to the Boston Police Department, he had quickly made a name for himself, and by the time she was a rookie, he had made captain. She had always been grateful that once the case was officially closed he had never spoken to her about the massacre again, although she knew that in the end he had believed what she told him. Now, though, sitting, waiting, she knew things were about to change. She had a sick, twisting feeling in her stomach that told her she wasn't going to like whatever it was he had to say to her. At last the door opened and he ushered her inside.

"How are you?" he asked as he closed the door behind her.

"I've been better," she said.

"So I hear. Have a seat."

She sat and waited uneasily as he did likewise. Finally he leaned across the battered desk that he'd been using for years, and fixed her with steely gray eyes that had lost none of their sharpness over the time that she had known him.

"Are we really dealing with witches?" he asked bluntly.

And just hearing him say the word "witches" brought it all back so clearly that it took her breath away. She swallowed hard and forced herself to meet his eyes. "I'm afraid so," she said.

He cursed roundly and she could only nod.

"And I understand the house where you found the last body today was the same house from years ago?"

"Yes," she whispered.

He shook his head. "I should have burned that place to the ground when I had the chance."

"We both should have," she said quietly. "I thought about it a dozen times, but I didn't want to get that close to it."

"No one can blame you for that. Look, there's no easy way to say this. I've been on the phone with the Salem police all afternoon. We all know something big's happening. They were hearing some strange mutterings. Then these bodies. It's safe to say that, for whatever reason, witches have returned to Salem. And we all know what that means."

"More people are going to die. Witches usually avoid Salem," she said.

"Unless they have a really good reason not to. And any reason they have to be here is trouble for us. Look, you know how these groups are—secretive, suspicious.

It can take months to even hear of one, let alone find out anything about them. If they're trying to frame the Horn girl, that means she's already outlived her usefulness for them and is completely expendable."

"We need to make sure she's protected."

"We're already working on that," he said. "What we really need is more information. We need someone . . . on the inside."

"Salem police have someone in mind?" she asked.

"No, but I do," he said, leveling his gaze at her.

"I can't help," she snapped, pushing back her chair and lurching to her feet.

"Samantha," he said, his voice quiet, "you're the only one who can."

"You can't make me."

"No, I can't. But I'm asking you."

"I won't, not even for you." She groaned, wishing she could tear something apart with her bare hands. She reached for the cross that wasn't there. She needed something to focus on. She thought of earlier at the house. She had unlocked the door to save herself and Ed, breaking her vow never to use magic again. And then banishing the creature. She hadn't had a choice; she had to believe that. But deep down inside, she knew she hadn't needed to slam the front door in its face, since it wasn't able to leave the house anyway.

I did it because I could, because I wanted to feel powerful. Rage and shame filled her. She had sworn to turn her back on all of it, and until today she had kept her word. Now everything was falling apart.

She grabbed fistfuls of her hair close to the scalp and yanked hard, needing to feel pain that was external, that was real and tangible. She paced as she pulled on her hair and then finally collapsed in the chair farthest from his desk and began to rock back and forth, shaking.

Then suddenly he was kneeling next to her, pulling her hands away and trying to look into her eyes. She ducked her head, not wanting to see. It was enough that she saw her own pain and fear mirrored on his face. Eyes were the windows to the soul and she didn't want to see his, and she most certainly didn't want him seeing hers.

"Ssh. It's okay. You're safe," he whispered, in the voice he had used once upon a time to quiet her when she was a child. And just like that she wasn't his detective, but a young girl in need of rescuing. He wasn't her captain, but one of the men who saved her from everything, especially herself.

Slowly she stopped rocking and after a couple of minutes she was able to look him in the eye.

"I was there, remember?" he whispered. "I know it was hell. There's only a handful of us that know, that believe, what really happened there. You know I wouldn't ask you to do this if we weren't desperate. The captain in Salem saw that house too, back in the day. He knows what we're dealing with. He doesn't have anyone who can do this."

"No, no, no, no."

He hung his head and nodded slowly. "I haven't seen you like this in years. I'm sorry. If this is what just the thought of it does . . ." He stood abruptly. "I was wrong to ask, wrong to think you could do this."

He turned back to his desk and she sat quietly, wishing she could help him as he had once helped her. She was embarrassed that she had broken down so completely in front of him, but she knew that he understood.

It's just too much. The murders and then the house and talking to Ed.

"If I could, I would, but I can't. Not this. Ask me anything else, but not this," she said.

He turned back to look at her. His eyes were tired and he rubbed them wearily. "Just keep doing what you're doing. We'll come up with Plan B."

She wanted to get up and run out of his office, but she stayed seated, her guilt vying with her fear. "You can't send someone else. If this is a dark coven using real black magic, they'll eat anybody you send alive. These people don't play by the same rules, don't even live by the same code. They don't view life and death the same as everyone else does. They willingly sacrifice their weaker children just to gain more power. You've seen what they're capable of. You know I'm right."

"Maybe we can find someone with experience."

"Where? Whoever you send would have to have spent time in a group like this before and gotten out alive. That doesn't happen."

"We can train someone."

"How? Because I won't do it. I won't teach someone to do the things I've seen . . . and . . . done." She barely managed to say it, her voice a strangled whisper even to her. "I won't spread that evil."

"You wouldn't be spreading it. You'd be helping to stop it."

She shook her head. "It's too dangerous. If I taught someone, and they got out alive, they might not be able to walk away."

But you could, a voice seemed to whisper inside her head. But she wasn't at all sure that was true. Just because she had managed to turn her back once didn't mean she'd be able to again.

She got to her feet. "I'm sorry."

"So am I. Why don't you head home and get some

sleep? It's been a rough day for everyone. Tomorrow should give us all a little more perspective."

She staggered out the door and made it outside to her car in a fog. She couldn't go back, no matter how many people might die. She started to drive home, but images from the day kept flooding her mind until she knew she couldn't be in her home alone. Not yet.

She turned the car toward her adoptive parents' home and prayed that the fears that haunted her would go away, that the uncertainty would cease. Maybe it was all a nightmare. She'd had enough of those, though, to recognize that this was no nightmare. It was living, breathing reality.

It's finally caught up with me, she thought as she pulled up in front of her parents' house.

Her father greeted her with surprise and concern in his lively blue eyes. "Did you get caught up in the witch mess?" he asked after he had closed the door and followed her into the living room, which they had long ago nicknamed the "talking room" because no matter what you had to say it was safe to say it in that room.

"How did you hear about that?" she asked, sinking into her favorite brown leather chair and pulling the purple throw pillow she had made in high school onto her lap. The room was the only one in the house that didn't have a television set. Instead, a large fish tank dominated one wall. She had spent hours staring at it as a child, struggling to find inner peace and marveling at the beauty in the world even as she fought to express herself to parents who desperately wanted to understand her even when they couldn't.

"I may not be a detective, but I still hear things," he said, running a hand through his close-cropped white hair. "Besides, it's been all over the news for hours, to the exclusion of pretty much everything else."

"Oh, Dad, it's awful," she said, pouring out the story of the day's events while staring at the fish as they swam round and round. When she told him about what she had done at the house, she half expected him to chastise her. Instead, he just listened quietly, never judging, always trying to understand. It was one of the traits that made him so good at his job. He was easy to talk to.

"I'm glad you're safe," he said at last.

"Me too."

"Me three," her mom said from the doorway.

The phone rang and her mother moved to get it. She returned with the cordless and handed it to Samantha. "It's Ed."

"Did you turn off your cell phone?" Ed asked.

She pulled it out of her pocket and looked at it. "No. I think the battery died."

"Then grab a charger and head over to the Hotel Salvo, room 415. We're just getting Katie settled in here and I'd like you to help me give the place a good going-over before I leave her here for the night."

"You're going to leave officers with her, right?"

"Yes, but I'd feel better if you'd just come over."

Samantha agreed. She hugged her parents and then made her way to the hotel. It was older and had seen better days but was a definite step up from many of the places she had seen the police put witnesses before. Ed met her in the lobby and escorted her to the stairwell. They began climbing.

"How are you?" she asked.

"They asked you to go undercover, didn't they?" he said, ignoring her question.

"How did you know?"

"Detective, remember?"

"Yes, Captain Roberts asked."

"And you told him no."

"Of course."

"Why?" he asked.

"I can't."

"You'll excuse me, but girls are getting sacrificed. I'm going to need a little more than 'I can't' to make sense of this."

She grabbed his arm, forcing him to turn and look at her. "I can't. It would mean doing things . . . things I swore I'd never do again. I promised God."

"Yes, and you also promised the people of this city to keep them safe."

"I can't act against my beliefs," she said.

"No one's asking you to stop believing in God or to think of yourself as a witch. They're just asking you to be a police officer. Do your job. Save lives. Bring killers to justice."

"I can't."

"Can't or won't?"

"These aren't the kind of people you can just bring to justice like that," she said, snapping her fingers. "This is going to get bloody and they won't be taken alive."

"We can't just do nothing."

"We're not doing *nothing*."

"Yeah, but if the captain wants you to go undercover, I think you should."

"It's not your decision," she hissed.

"Look, police officers helped you. You have a responsibility to do the same."

"Is that why you called me out here? To lecture me?" she demanded. "You have a lot of nerve. You can't even tell me that we're okay when I tell you about the hell I lived through as a kid and now you just expect me to jump back into it because you think it's a good idea?"

And there it was, an undercurrent of power crackling through her and around her. She had learned to block it out, but sometimes she couldn't, and as she grew angrier and angrier, the sense of power grew.

"No, I called you here because I wanted you to check out the room, maybe do something special to it."

"Like magic? I'm out of here," she said, turning and starting back down the stairs.

She was outside and unlocking her car door when he caught up with her. He looked even more tired and disheveled than he had sitting with her on the curb outside the last crime scene. He had lost his tie and jacket at some point and she could see the sweat stains on his shirt. His eyes were desperate when he looked at her and a flickering streetlight cast intermittent shadows over his face that made them look more sunken than usual. "Look, I'm sorry. It's a lot to take in, you know? I'm not sure how you expected me to respond, but I'm scared and I don't understand."

"What don't you understand?"

"All of it, okay? I joked about the supernatural because it got your goat, but I never actually believed in it. How am I supposed to save people and do my job? What happened in that basement . . . I was powerless. But you weren't. You have the ability to do something about all this and that shield you wear means you also have the responsibility to do something. For heaven's sake, you need to at least help me protect Katie."

She couldn't fault his logic, but he didn't know the risks, didn't know how much she could lose. He didn't know how addictive the power was.

"Look, I'll come inside and check everything out, but I won't be doing any magic."

He nodded and she turned once more to follow him.

Once they got upstairs Samantha found Katie pacing in what served as the living room/office area of the suite, threatening to wear a hole in the already thin burgundy carpet. Two officers were sitting on the couch working out what to order for dinner and Ed joined them. Katie rushed over to Samantha, her eyes wide. "What happened after we left? No one will tell me anything."

"It's a long story," Samantha said, really not wanting to get into it with her.

"What do you want on your hot dog?" one of the officers called over.

"Nothing. I want it plain," Katie said.

"Real purist, huh? How about to drink? Soda, water, beer?"

Katie wrinkled her nose. "I'm too young for beer and besides I don't drink anyway. I'll take water."

Katie grabbed Samantha and dragged her toward the bedroom. Once inside, Katie sat down on the edge of the bed and regarded Samantha solemnly. "How screwed am I?" she asked.

"Pretty," Samantha admitted.

Katie sighed. "I'm a good person, you know. I can't believe . . . They put my picture on television. That's what one of the guys said. What if my parents see it?"

"Where do your parents live?"

"Colorado. We moved two years ago, but I came back for college."

"So you're a local girl."

"Yup. My old high school's actually just two blocks from here. I should have stayed in Colorado."

Samantha didn't say anything. Katie sighed and took off her rings and her necklace and put them on the end table. Then she took off her earrings and tossed them down. A chill settled over Samantha as she looked at them. They were clip-ons, not pierced. And Katie didn't drink.

Samantha looked at her sharply. "Katie, are you a virgin?"

The other girl turned scarlet. "Yeah. Why?"

Samantha shot to her feet. They had been wrong. Katie wasn't just meant to be the fall guy.

Suddenly the lights went out and the room was plunged into darkness.

7

"What's happening?" Katie cried out.

"They're coming for you," Samantha hissed.

Lights streamed through the windows from outside, illuminating the room and casting menacing shadows, which Samantha kept scanning warily. A sound was beginning to fill the room, like the rushing of wind.

Katie was going to be the next sacrifice.

"Katie, why don't you have pierced ears?" Samantha demanded.

"I was always too afraid when I was little—what is that sound?"

Samantha yanked her badge off her belt and threw Katie into a wall.

"What are you—"

Before the girl could finish asking her question, Samantha grabbed her ear and in one swift motion punched through it with the pin on the back of her badge. Katie screamed in pain and a few drops of blood bubbled to the surface. The pin on the badge was blunter than was ideal for such a task, but hurting Katie was the least of Samantha's worries. She grabbed Katie's other ear and punched it as well for good measure.

And then the roaring around them stopped. The silence was so profound that Katie's breathing sounded painfully loud in the stillness.

"Why did you do that?"

"I just saved you from being the next blood sacrifice," Samantha said. She grabbed Katie's wrist. "We have to go now."

Katie pulled back. "Why? If you just saved me, wouldn't it be safer here?"

"Oh, Katie, they're going to kill you anyway. At least this way they can't use you."

She heard the girl whimper in fear, but she stopped fighting and went with Samantha into the other room.

In the living room, Ed and the two other officers had their guns drawn and were warily checking doors and windows.

"They've found us," Samantha said.

"Tell us what to do," Ed said.

"We've got to get out of here."

A minute later they hit the lobby and began moving quickly across it. Half a dozen people looked up, their eyes tracking them. Samantha could feel the weight of their stares even as the hair on the back of her neck rose.

"Katie, keep your head down," she hissed.

"Trouble?" Ed asked.

Before she could answer, the man standing near the elevator pointed and shouted, "Witch! That's the witch who killed those people!"

Curses followed his announcement, echoing between the other civilians and Samantha's fellow officers. For one moment it was as though time froze and she could see everyone's faces clearly. The hate on the denouncer's face, the naked fear in Ed's eyes, and the shock in Katie's expression.

And then the bellman lunged toward them. He nailed

one officer on the jaw, shoved another, and was reaching for Katie's arm when Ed threw him to the ground and whipped out his handcuffs. The other spectators surged forward, coming right at them and standing between them and an exit.

"Divert!" one of the officers shouted, drawing his gun.

Samantha grabbed Katie's arm and lurched sideways into an empty room set up with buffet tables, ready for serving breakfast in a few hours. A shot was fired and she winced, hoping no one had been hit. Ed was the last into the room and he slammed the door shut, propping a chair under the doorknob.

Samantha moved to help him secure the door as another officer called for backup. Fists banged on the other side of the door.

"Give us the witch!" she heard one enraged man shout.

"She has to pay," a woman chorused.

"What the hell?" Ed marveled. "They've all gone mad."

"We can't stay here," Samantha said.

"The room isn't secure," Ed agreed.

A sudden rush of wind lifted her hair and she spun around in fear. A sliding glass door onto a patio had been opened.

And Katie was gone.

"Katie!" she yelled, running forward.

"Did someone get her?" one of the other officers shouted.

"Couldn't have," Ed responded. "We would have heard something."

Samantha touched the door and in her panic reached out with her thoughts . . . and felt the memory of Katie opening it.

"She ran," she said quietly.

The other officers except for Ed ran out, shouting for Katie.

"Where would she have gone?" Ed asked.

"Somewhere familiar, somewhere she can hide . . . Her old high school," Samantha said. "She said it was two blocks from here."

"That would be Eastside. Let's go."

She grabbed his arm. "Ed, this is going to get ugly. You're not going to want to be there."

"Uglier than the house? Uglier than that mob trying to break down the door? Forget it. We're partners and if you're going, I'm going."

She nodded. The crack of splintering wood echoed through the room and she realized that with the crowd so frenzied it wasn't safe for him to stay. They ducked out the sliding glass door, and a moment later they were racing down the street, heading for the high school.

"How would she get in?" Samantha asked as they arrived at the fenced-in school, shut tight for the night.

"Girl like her, I'm sure she could find a way. Probably knew it back then. You and I will just have to hop the fence," he said, giving her a boost.

When they were both inside the perimeter, they moved slowly, their eyes sweeping the grounds as they approached the building. Around back they found a door that was slightly ajar. Ed drew his gun and they went in.

Samantha looked up and down the deserted hallways but saw no signs of movement.

"Do you think she's here?" Ed whispered, the sound magnified by the emptiness around them.

She nodded.

"Much as I don't like it, we'll cover more ground if we split up."

"I'll take this way," she said, gesturing to the right.

He stared hard at her. "You got a feeling?"

She hunched her shoulders. "No," she lied.

"Okay."

He started off to the left, calling Katie's name. She watched as he entered and then exited the first room he came across before she turned and headed to the right. Her footsteps sounded as loud as gunshots as she walked, sparing only cursory glances at the rooms she passed. She came to an intersection in the hallway and turned to the left.

Katie's essence lingered in the air almost like perfume, guiding Samantha. She'd worked for years not to notice the impressions people left behind them when they passed through places. Now she was grateful she hadn't lost the skill entirely. The closer she got to Katie, the more her own fear increased.

A ripple like a shock wave suddenly passed through her, forcing a gasp through her clenched teeth. Someone else had entered the building.

She began to run, praying as she did so. At the end of the corridor she took a left and then plunged into the open room on her right.

Moonlight streamed through the large windows, painting everything in a silvery sheen. Lab desks sat silent, and jars of preserved frogs and fetal pigs awaiting dissection sat on the counter that ran along the wall next to her. Katie was at the far end, on her knees, a piece of chalk clutched in her hands as she finished drawing around herself.

"What do you think you're doing?" Samantha demanded.

"It's a protection circle," Katie said between sobs. "They're coming for me and I need to be safe."

"Idiot. You think some chalk on the ground is going to protect you from anything?" Samantha hissed.

"But—it's a circle, and I'm going to ask the goddess to bless it."

"Have you ever asked the goddess for anything, ever? Or any deity, for that matter?"

"Well, I have—"

And then the hair on the back of Samantha's neck stood on end. "Ssh," she said, holding up a hand. She turned and closed her eyes, and then she heard the merest whisper of movement.

Samantha pulled her Swiss Army knife out of her pocket and tossed it to Katie. "Form the circle using your blood," she whispered as she took a step forward and drew her gun. She squared herself so she was facing the door but turned her head so that she could see the opening only out of the corner of her right eye. She focused on her breathing, slowing it down. She stretched her other senses, straining to see, hear, smell everything that she could.

Katie was crying quietly, but Samantha could smell the faintest hint of blood. So the girl was at least doing as she had said. Not that the circle would protect her from a human assailant, but if the thing that had gutted her ex-boyfriend was coming after her, it would slow the creature down.

A breath of wind touched her cheek.

She tensed all her muscles, preparing to move in a moment.

Samantha, a voice seemed to whisper inside her head.

It was coming.

In the distance she heard a shot ring out, then another. Bile rose in her throat as she thought about Ed. Had the witch found him first? By sending him in the opposite direction had she sent him to his death?

Her chest felt constricted, like a giant hand was crushing her rib cage. She could hear the blood pounding in her ears, and her fingers wrapped around the gun were slick with sweat.

I can't do this, she thought, panicking.

She shifted her gun to her left hand and raised her right, energy crackling along her fingertips as the adrenaline rushed through her body.

Samantha! the voice repeated.

The witch knows who I am. It will kill Katie and me and there's nothing I can do to stop it. Waves of despair and hopelessness rushed over her. It was no use fighting—she would lose. Even if she used magic and broke every vow she had made to herself and God, they would still die.

"Samantha!"

The voice was louder, more insistent, and suddenly she realized it was actually coming from behind her.

She twisted her head so she could see Katie, who stood swaying on her feet, her eyes frozen in terror on a cloud of green mist that was hovering just outside the window. And then it was seeping through the gaps in the window casing, sliding down the wall and billowing across the floor toward Katie, who screamed and stepped backward.

Out of her circle.

A howling filled the air and Samantha turned back to see a figure shrouded in black glide across the threshold. She began to shake uncontrollably as images of other witches stirred in her memory. The light streaming through the windows failed to touch the inky figure. In fact, it was more of a shadow than a form in the darkness, something she felt more than saw.

A fragment of a rhyme she had learned as a child ran

through her head. *When witches go to school, little boys cry. When witches go to school, bad girls die.* There was more but she couldn't remember it, didn't want to remember it.

The dark figure was moving, and it stretched out one hand and touched a counter as it passed by. The jars on the counter fell off, smashing on the floor. The witch swept an arm forward as if directing something.

Bad girls die.

"Get back in the circle!" Samantha shouted, not daring to look at Katie but keeping her full attention on the witch. The other moved with a slight, hypnotic swaying motion, coming ever closer.

Samantha was a bad girl. Or she had been but not now. Now she was . . . what was it she was?

Pull yourself together!

A cop. She was a cop.

"Stop! Police officer! Get on the ground! Now!" Samantha ordered, her years of training kicking in.

She might as well not have spoken, for all the effect it had. The witch's arms were extended slightly and the fingertips brushed the sides of desks as she passed. As she touched the first two they erupted into columns of flame, which instantly began to spew dark smoke.

Thoughts collided in Samantha's mind, slipping over one another and scattering. And she wasn't a detective anymore. She was a frightened girl facing down a much stronger opponent. She heard a gasp behind her, followed by a thud. She risked a glance backward and saw Katie on the ground, the last of the green mist disappearing into her nose and mouth.

Samantha turned back and everything suddenly went black. Panic surged through her as she realized the witch had cast a spell of blindness upon her. She had no idea how to reverse it. She froze for a moment. Behind her, Katie was making choking noises.

Sounds. Listen for the sounds.

She moved her gun back and forth, listening for something that would give away the other's location.

Nothing.

Except—there it was—tiny scrabbling, scratching noises. She realized after a moment that the witch wasn't making those noises. She thought of all the jars containing lab specimens that had smashed onto the floor. She had seen frogs, fetal pigs, and other creatures awaiting dissection suspended in the jars. They were dead.

Yet they were moving. She could hear the sounds of the animated corpses scuffling along the floor, animated by the witch, who must also be approaching ever closer.

Something squealed near her foot and then bit her ankle. With a shriek she kicked hard, sending whatever it was flying across the room.

More came and she kicked out again. But for each one she got rid of, two more grabbed her legs. *Stop the witch; stop the attack.*

She didn't have to see the witch to know where she was. She took a deep breath and forced herself to tune in to the swirling energy in the room. She felt the power of the fire, Katie dying behind her, tiny feet scrabbling over her shoes, and to her left . . .

She turned and fired the gun. And she felt, *knew*, that she'd hit her mark.

And in a moment, her vision returned, proof that the spell had been disrupted. Through the smoke she saw a figure crumpled on the ground. She walked over, her gun still aimed, and kicked at the legs.

No movement. She had shot the witch in the chest. She listened, straining, but could not detect any sound of breathing. She kicked the hood back and saw a woman about ten years older than she was, with dark eyes fixed and staring at the ceiling. She was gone.

Samantha took a deep breath. For all their powers and abilities, witches were still human.

And she made a very human mistake. Instead of confusing my senses, blinding me, she should have cursed my gun so it would misfire, Samantha thought. *My mother never would have been so stupid.*

The dead pigs toppled onto their sides. The frogs lay silent. Samantha grabbed a fire extinguisher off the wall by the teacher's desk and snuffed out the flames. In the silence that followed she could hear only her own heartbeat and Katie's labored breathing. She waited for a moment. Were there others? She could sense no other energy spikes in the building, so after a moment she turned to Katie.

Samantha dropped to her knees beside the fallen girl. "Katie! Don't you die on me!"

She looked closely at the girl. Her eyes were frozen open and short, wheezing breaths came from her mouth. Samantha could hear shouts and running steps as Ed arrived with backup.

"It's clear!" Samantha shouted. "Call an ambulance! Girl down!"

In a moment Ed was beside her. She felt a rush of relief that he seemed unharmed. "What happened?" he asked, his eyes traveling from Katie to the dead witch and the animals all over the floor.

"She inhaled poison," Samantha said, cutting to the most important part and leaving the rest of the explanation for later.

"Then we need to make her vomit."

Samantha shook her head. "She inhaled a lot of it and it's spread all through her system at this point, leaching into her bloodstream."

"So what do we do?"

"There's nothing. The paramedics won't be able to do anything."

"Medicine might not help her, but *you* can," Ed said, his voice low and fierce.

Yes, you can, a voice whispered inside her head.

"No," she said out loud, to both Ed and the voice. "I can't help."

"Can't or won't?" Ed accused even as Katie's wheezing breaths stopped.

"You don't know what you're asking me to do," she said, her voice shaking.

The house had been self-defense, reflex. This . . . this would be willfully crossing a line. She couldn't let herself go there. Not even to save Katie.

You'd do it to save Ed. It's not that you won't help; it's that you won't help her. *She's not important enough.*

"Stop it!" she screamed.

Ed grabbed her by the shoulders and shook her, his eyes wide in desperation. "Do something!"

"I can't."

"Look at me!"

His eyes pierced her. "You can and you have to," he insisted. "You saved us in the house and you can save her now."

"No."

"If you don't save her, then it's on your hands. The dead witch might have attacked her, but you'll be the witch that killed her."

She felt like he had just punched her. She hunched

her shoulders and dropped her eyes. Just a few more seconds and there would be nothing anyone could do. It would be over.

"I can't do it alone," she whispered.

"I'm here. Whatever you need."

She nodded. He started to pull away, but she grabbed his hand. She placed her free hand on Katie's chest, took a deep breath, and closed her eyes. Then she shoved energy through her hand and into Katie. At the same time she pulled energy out of Ed.

She felt him gasp and reflexively pull back, but she hung on.

She sent waves of energy into Katie and pictured them rushing through her body, pushing out the toxins. She could feel Katie dying, and when her heart stopped, it was like her own had as well. She ceased to breathe because Katie no longer breathed. She was linking their two systems. It was dangerous, but it was the only way.

There were only moments left. She could feel Katie's mind slipping away to a place where she couldn't follow. The connection was weakening. Fear flooded her. If she pushed too hard, she risked doing catastrophic damage. But if she didn't push hard enough, Katie would still be dead of the toxin.

It had to be expelled, but it was too pervasive to be done quickly or from one source. A flash of insight came to her and she spiked Katie's temperature. The girl's body began to sweat. Samantha took a deep breath and pulled as much energy out of Ed as she dared. She could feel him starting to weave beside her, on the verge of losing consciousness himself.

She sent a sudden rush of energy throughout the girl's body, sterilizing, purifying, just as fire cauterized a wound. Then she pushed the toxins out of each organ, each blood vessel, to the skin, where they began to ooze out of her pores with her sweat.

The stench of something rotten filled the air, and behind her she could hear another police officer arrive and begin gagging in response. Katie's skin briefly took on a greenish tinge and then returned to its normal pallor. Samantha removed her hand with a gasp, forcing air into her own lungs as she broke the connection. Her own heart began to beat again and she felt light-headed.

"She's still not breathing," Ed slurred beside her.

Samantha held her hands together, funneling all the strength she had left into them until she could feel the heat radiating from them. Then she slammed both hands down on Katie's chest and the girl convulsed as the electricity rushed through her.

Samantha watched for a moment, praying she wouldn't have to do it a second time. And then, miraculously, Katie coughed and began to breathe. Samantha fell backward flat on the ground and shuddered with exhaustion. A ragged sob escaped Ed.

Katie was alive. They had succeeded.

But Samantha suspected it had cost her dearly.

8

By the time the paramedics arrived, Katie was conscious but no less terrified. "I could have been killed," she said around her sobs.

"But you weren't." Ed tried to reassure her. "We told you we would protect you and that's what we're going to do."

Katie looked up at Samantha. "And you saved me? How?"

"That's not important," Samantha said, looking away. The last thing she wanted was for Katie to realize what she'd done, who she was.

Who I still am, she thought grimly.

The magic came back so naturally, so effortlessly. It frightened her. And she knew that the closer she got to this case, the worse it would get. She desperately wanted to distance herself, and fast, but she knew that wasn't a realistic option.

"I should have gone on vacation," she muttered.

"Aren't I always telling you to take one?" Ed said. "Bet you wish you'd listened to me now."

She wanted to hit him, but the strength required to lift her arm seemed beyond her at the moment.

They were both sitting on the floor, still drained from what had happened. The stench of formaldehyde hung heavy in the air and she noticed that Ed did everything he could to avoid looking at the fetal pigs. She could feel his relief when Captain Roberts arrived, even though the man's face was like a thundercloud.

"Somebody want to tell me what the hell happened?"

Captain Roberts kicked one of the tiny carcasses, looked down at it, and swore.

"Our location was compromised and we were forced to move the witness," Ed said.

"And?"

"And when we reached the lobby, the crowd recognized Katie from the news broadcasts and decided the only good witch was a dead witch," Ed continued.

The words made Samantha wince. *I'm not a witch. Not anymore.* But Ed had called her one earlier, and she had not forgotten it. He had used the word purposely to manipulate her emotions and get her to save Katie.

Words had power. Names had power. It was true even for people who didn't use magic, and Ed had played the game like a pro.

"And the dead woman?" Captain Roberts asked.

"An assassin," Samantha said. "A witch sent to kill Katie. I suspect that she also put a spell on the crowd, incited them to riot in order to cause confusion so she could get to Katie more easily."

Captain Roberts knelt next to her and looked her in the eye. "And she was a real witch? You're absolutely sure?"

Samantha nodded and he sighed and sat down too, looking suddenly tired and worn.

"Okay, boys and girls, then what's our game plan? We've killed one of their own and they're not about to take that sitting down, I'm guessing."

"We can't let on that we know they exist. These people will go underground and we'll never find them," Ed said.

"What are you suggesting?" Captain Roberts asked. "They'll know she's dead, or at least figure it out eventually."

"We announce it publicly," Samantha said. "Make it sound like she was a bystander who was killed when the riot happened over the alleged witch."

He stared at her like she had lost her mind, his mouth working for a moment before any sound came out. "Are you crazy? Do you know how that would make the department look? And more, we don't want to feed this whole witch thing, especially if it's real."

"That's out of our hands now," Ed pointed out. "Press is going to run with this no matter what we say or do. This plan at least helps us out in the long run, gives us time to catch these people."

"And I think we need to report that Katie was killed in the attack," Samantha added. "We can only protect her if they stop looking for her."

"You think it will work?" he asked.

She shrugged. "It will buy us some time at the very least."

"Okay, we'll play it your way for now," Captain Roberts said with a nod. He caught the eye of one of the paramedics. "Tell me when she's good to travel."

"She's good now," the man said, looking slightly confused. "I'm not sure what's wrong with her—or *was* wrong with her. We can't find anything. They'll run tests at the hospital to check everything."

"No, they won't. She isn't going to any hospital. And I'm going to have to ask for your help," Roberts said, getting back on his feet and moving over to talk to the man.

"You okay?" Ed asked after a minute.

"No. You?"

"Not even a little bit," he admitted. "Don't suppose there's any chance that this is all just a really bad dream?"

"Neither of us is that lucky."

"That's what I was afraid of," he said with a sigh. He hesitated a moment and then continued. "I feel like crap."

"You were the one who volunteered to help," she said, feeling defensive.

"Yeah, about that . . . what did I do exactly? Or, rather, what did you do?"

"Most of witchcraft revolves around the manipulation of energy, electricity. I needed more energy than I had, so I borrowed."

"Borrowed? Does that mean there's a chance you'll give it back?"

She forced herself to smile. "Okay, took is more like it. And you'll feel fine after a good night's sleep. I warn you, though, you'll be out for the whole day if you don't set your alarm."

"That sounds good," he said with a groan.

"But duty calls," she said softly.

"I hear you. Now, any chance can you help me stand up before I decide to just sleep here on the floor?"

"If I had the strength to stand up myself I'd be there for you," she said ruefully.

Ed glanced grimly over at the paramedics. "Hey, fellas, a little help?"

In the morning, when Samantha arrived at the precinct, she found Ed already at work, eyes bloodshot, massive coffee cup in his hand.

"Good morning," she said.

"Nothing good about it. The neighbor's dog woke me up with his barking every hour last night. At four a.m. I seriously considered shooting him."

"The dog?"

"No, the neighbor. He should have let the poor animal go inside so we could all get some rest."

She nodded and sat down, glancing at a few things that had been stacked on her desk.

"Got something for you," Ed said, handing her a file.

"What is it?"

"The police report that was filed regarding the assault on Jane four months ago."

Samantha took it and flipped it open. She skipped the written report and focused on the pictures, which showed Jane, half dead, covered in dirt and bruises. She felt for the girl and prayed fervently that she would find peace. Then she flipped to the last photo and stopped.

It was a picture of the mark on the back of Jane's neck. It was an odd mark, part drawing, part scratch. Samantha looked more closely. Someone had drawn on her in pen and one portion of the skin had been cut, as though someone had traced a pattern and then begun carving it. Blood and inflamed tissue made it hard to see what the pattern was, and part of the ink was smudged, making the original lines unrecognizable. When Jane had shown it to her the day before, she hadn't been able to make out much. She squinted now, staring at the picture. There was something about the placement that was familiar—

Her heart stuttered and she rose abruptly from the desk.

"What is it?" Ed asked.

"Did you see this?" she asked, showing him the picture. He nodded. "Officers couldn't tell what it was supposed to be. They thought it was some kind of gang symbol or something."

"Let's go," she said.

"Where?"

"We have to go talk to the coroner."

Half an hour later Samantha stood staring down at the dead nun as a chill swept through her. "She's got something carved on the back of her neck," she confirmed. The skin was so mangled, though, that she couldn't tell what it had been. She turned to Ed, who was looking down at the body of Camille.

"There's something here too," he confirmed.

Samantha turned to the coroner. "Have you been able to identify what kind of a mark this is?"

He shook his head. "But I can tell you that whatever made it was razor sharp."

"An athame," she mused.

"Pardon?" the coroner said.

"A ceremonial dagger, used by witches."

He raised his eyebrows. "So are we actually going with the press's whole witch theory?"

"More than just a theory," Ed said grimly.

Samantha stood, thinking. Jane had been attacked, nearly sacrificed, four months before. Had it really taken them that long to find a replacement? It didn't seem likely. They would have wanted to sacrifice someone else back then. She thought back, trying to figure out what ritual they might have been performing at that time of year. Practitioners of black arts did not celebrate the phases of the moon and the season in the same way as Wiccans or pagans did. There were, however, a few rituals that were tied to such things. It would have been too early for the summer solstice.

She shook her head. She wasn't going to figure out what they were doing based on the time of year of the first attack. What she needed to figure out was if it had been the only attack until the day before.

"Have any young girls come in during the last four months with something carved into their bodies? It wouldn't just have to be the back of the neck; it could have been concealed elsewhere."

The coroner thought a moment and then moved to one of the large filing cabinets in the room.

"Is that a yes?" Ed asked.

The man didn't say anything, just started flipping through files. Finally he pulled one out and looked at it. Then he turned and looked at Samantha.

"She came in about three months ago. Jane Doe—we never did figure out who she was. Her body was discovered in a park and I estimated that she'd been dead a week. She had a symbol carved on the sole of her left foot."

He held out a piece of paper from the file and turned it so she could see it. It was an eight-sided star cut into her foot with the skin from one section of the star completely removed.

Samantha fell to her knees and began to retch. Terror surged through her and she could feel her world flying apart.

"What is it?" She heard Ed ask it as though from a distance.

She stopped heaving after a moment and looked up at him. "An octogram," she said, her voice shaking.

"What does it mean?" Ed asked.

Wholeness, regeneration, so many things—but only one of them was important.

She wiped her mouth with the back of her hand. "It means I have to go back."

*   *   *

Samantha clutched the piece of paper the coroner had given her tightly in her fist. Captain Roberts's door was open and she closed it behind her as she entered his office.

He looked up from his desk, a mixture of caution and hope in his eyes as he stared at her.

She tossed the piece of paper on his desk and then collapsed into the chair across from him. He picked up the paper and studied the symbol for a moment. "Okay, I give. Other than some kind of star, what is it?"

"Part of a spell to raise the dead."

He stared at her, thunderstruck. "Is that even possible?" he asked at last.

She nodded slowly. "Not easy, not even probable, but certainly possible."

"How?"

"Is that really the question you want to be asking right now?" she said with a sigh.

"That's what all of this is about?"

"I don't know," she confessed. "I'm not sure if that's the endgame or just step one in whatever they're planning."

"Where did you see this symbol?"

"That was from our first victim. Her body turned up three months ago without any type of pentagram, so nobody made the connection right away. The other girls have slightly different versions of the same thing carved somewhere on their bodies. It's all part of the process."

He turned pale. "Do you expect me to go to the governor with this? He'd laugh me out of his office. And if the press gets wind of it, our little troubles are going to escalate far beyond our means to control them."

"I don't want you to tell anyone. It takes someone with experience, someone like me, to understand the significance of that symbol." She took a deep breath. "If the other side discovers that we know what it means, they'll realize we have someone on the inside."

"Inside?" he asked, arching a brow.

She bit her lip and nodded. "I'm going undercover, like you asked me to."

Relief and fear mixed in his gaze and after a moment he looked away from her. "You don't have to do this," he whispered hoarsely.

She stood up and tapped the symbol. "This says otherwise. Unless there are more bodies we haven't found, several more women are going to be killed. Each one is a point of the star. And odds are good that whoever they're trying to resurrect is not a candidate for humanitarian of the year."

"What about Kyle?"

"He's part of this whole mess, but not one of the eight. He wasn't a sacrifice. If I move fast, hopefully there won't be any more sacrifices."

He nodded slowly. "Okay. How do you want to play this? I can let Salem PD know you're coming."

"No. The fewer people who know, the safer I'll be. If you need to reach me, send Ed to Red's Sandwich Shop. I'll check in there most mornings."

"Okay."

"I'll need a day to get some things in order and then I'll be going in."

"Will that give you enough time to stop them?" he asked.

"I hope so, for all our sakes."

"I'll get some paperwork taken care of for you."

"Good."

She turned and started out the door, then stopped. "Do you know anyone who can recommend a discreet tattoo artist?"

"Why?" he asked, startled.

"If I'm going to be a witch again, then there's something I must do," she told him.

"Are you sure about this?" he asked.

"Like you said, someone has to go in and it should be me," she said.

Even if it kills me.

9

Samantha sat down in the chair at the back of the tiny shop and did her best not to betray the powerful emotions within her. The proprietor, a gentleman covered in a hodgepodge of ink ranging from tattoos of tribes he could not possibly be descended from to depictions of animals of prey and the obligatory girl's name on his bicep, sat down next to her.

"Little lady, what can I do for you today? Nice little butterfly, heart maybe?" he asked patronizingly.

Samantha smiled at him. "Actually I had something a little more exotic in mind."

He lifted an eyebrow in surprise. "Really?"

"Really," she said, handing him a slip of paper that showed a series of lines and curves surrounded by a circle.

He took it, looked at it for a moment, and blanched. "I don't think so," he said, standing abruptly and dropping the paper in her lap.

"*I* think so." She contradicted him, allowing her voice to become softer. It had the desired effect. He began to pace and sweat beaded on his brow. Slowly she pulled off her shirt, so that she was wearing only her sports bra. "Right here," she said, indicating a patch of skin near her heart.

He glanced at her and then took a closer look. "You had a tattoo there at some point, had it removed?"

"Very good."

"Lady, look, you don't want this tattoo. Trust me. This is some serious shit, bad juju. I can give you a nice pentagram or something if you want to do the whole Wiccan thing."

"I'm not a Wiccan," she said. "The pentagram is a symbol stolen from the Christians—why would I want to put something like that on my body?"

"Why did you get your tattoo removed?" he asked, clearly trying to work up the courage to deal with what she was asking.

"It was a little hard to hide who I was while wearing it," she said evenly, staring him straight in the eye.

If anything, he grew more agitated. "And who are you?" he asked.

Samantha picked up the piece of paper and turned it around so the symbol was facing him. "This is who I am."

He groaned deep in his throat. "Please don't kill me."

Samantha continued to stare at him. "Do as I say and I won't."

He nodded and then set to work. She watched him closely. The symbol had belonged to one group only, and most of its members were dead; not even the police files held pictures of the symbol. Somewhere, somehow, he had seen one on a living person. Where, though, and on whom? It was possible he had seen one years before, but she didn't think that was the case. The lines inside the circle were an ancient script and when the letters were combined in the pattern Samantha had given him, it meant *I am as god*. It was the epitome of blasphemy, and it pained her that she was having it put back.

He paused and wiped the sweat from his forehead.

His hands were shaking and his breathing was shallow. She frowned, not wanting his hand to slip while he was working.

"Relax," she said, deepening her voice and pushing the words out.

He looked up at her, fear in his eyes. "That's easy for you to say, lady," he muttered.

She reached out her hand and put it on the top of his head. He jerked in alarm, but she didn't move. She pushed energy through her hand until the skin on his forehead was warm, which she knew would produce a calming effect.

"You are doing well," she said, dropping her voice even lower.

He nodded slightly, his pupils dilating, and then returned to work.

When he was finished she nodded her approval even though her blood ran cold to see the familiar symbol once again on her flesh. Everything that was in her rebelled and she wanted to claw it off. She forced herself to smile at him, though. He gave her a tentative smile in return.

She needed to find out what he knew about the symbol. She took a deep breath, and thought about her mother and what she would have done to get the information she wanted.

Samantha grabbed him by the throat and slammed him into the wall. "Tell me where you've seen one of these tattoos," she hissed.

"I can't! She'll kill me!"

"And what do you think I'll do to you if you don't?" she asked, squeezing her fingers tighter around his throat.

It would be so easy to kill him.

She gasped as the thought entered her mind. She

dropped him and he slid to the floor, clutching his throat. She took a step back, shaking herself. This was bad, dangerous. She had no business going undercover, not when after only a couple of hours she was slipping into old habits, deadly habits.

He didn't seem to notice her sudden uncertainty. He raised a hand, begging her. "Please, please. I'll tell you."

She dropped into a crouch so she could look him in the eye. The terror that was there fueled something dark inside that she had tried for so long to suppress. She could feel the adrenaline racing through her body, making her feel strong, powerful, aggressive.

"Where?"

"It was a woman. Long blond hair. She had me give her that tattoo about a year ago. She was bad news. She got inside my head, knew things she shouldn't. She told me she'd kill me if I ever revealed it to anyone else, or even thought of giving someone else the mark."

Samantha studied him. It sounded like he was describing Bridget. If that was true, then the woman was even more formidable than Katie had let on. *Bridget must have done a spell on him to make him so terrified of her.*

"Did she have a name?"

"No. She paid cash. I've never seen her before or since."

"This symbol," Samantha told him, "is who I was raised. The woman you saw does not have the right to wear it. Do you understand?"

He nodded.

"Now, you're not going to tell anyone about meeting me. But you are going to call this number if you see anyone else wearing this tattoo," she said, pressing a card into his hand. "Do you understand?"

He nodded again.

She stood. "And just so you know that *I'm* the one

you need to fear crossing . . ." She waved her hand, and fire appeared on his hands and arms.

He screamed and batted at himself.

The fire wasn't real. It was only in his mind. She had touched him and put the suggestion of his greatest fear into his mind and he had done the rest, imagining what wasn't there.

She leaned down and blew, snuffing out the imagined flames. He collapsed onto the floor, sobbing.

She stood up and walked outside. Once in her car, she leaned her head for a moment on the steering wheel as she struggled to regain control of herself.

After a moment, she left the tattoo shop and headed home. There she packed some clothes and a few other things she would need. She next gathered anything related to her life as a cop and put it all into a box.

Later that evening she drove over to her parents' home, with the box on her car's front seat.

When she walked in the door, her mother took one look at her face and hugged her even as her father grabbed the box to take to his office. Once he had stowed it away he returned and joined them in the living room.

"You're sure you want to do this?" he asked.

"I have to. What they're doing, what they're about to do—"

"We know," her mom said.

She stayed long past the time she'd planned to go home. Fear gnawed at her that she would never see them again, or worse, that when she did she'd be someone they wouldn't want to know.

In the morning she woke, grateful that there'd been no nightmares, at least none that she could remember. Ed showed up at her door looking like he hadn't slept at all and handed her a cup of coffee.

"We've got things arranged for you," he said, handing her a driver's license. The picture was hers. The name was Samantha Castor.

"So that's your original last name?"

"Yes."

"You sure you want to use it?" he asked.

"Names have power. That one is associated with a lot of dark things and if someone does enough digging, they'll figure that out."

"Then why still go by Samantha?"

She followed him out to the car, locking the door on her life, and chose her words carefully. "Same reason. Names have power. I can't risk losing myself completely."

It was only partially true. If someone knew your name, they could cast a variety of spells on you. Knowing her birth name would allow them to do that. And knowing the name she went by now would also allow them to do that. But mixing the two, new first name and old last name, created a false name that wouldn't allow someone to curse her by using it.

She tossed her bags in his trunk and took one last look at her house.

"Okay," he said as they climbed into his car. He handed her an envelope with papers in it. "So, you have an account at the bank in that name and a reservation at the Hawthorne Hotel for a week, although we're all hoping you won't need to be there that long."

"Most undercover operations don't play out overnight," she reminded him grimly. "Not unless they go completely south."

"Yeah, well, this one needs to be finished quickly."

"Any more bodies discovered?"

"Not yet," he said, his voice tense. "But I figure it's early yet. Sure you don't want me to drive you to Salem?"

She nodded. "I don't want you anywhere near unless there's an emergency."

"Then Red's Sandwich Shop. I got the message. One last thing." He handed her a cell phone. "Samantha Castor's phone. Charger's in the envelope. Do me a favor and don't be Samantha Ryan. Keep the damn thing on."

She nodded, her throat suddenly tight as she slipped it into the pocket of her jeans. Ed had no idea how hard it was going to be not to lose Samantha Ryan.

He drove her to the airport. Once there, she retrieved her bags from the trunk of his car and made her way to the taxi stand outside baggage claim. Taking a taxi in from the airport ensured that anyone who saw her arrive would think she'd flown in from California, where she was going to say she'd been living with a distant relative.

If anyone even asks, she thought. It was a house of cards she was setting up. It would hold and look nice as long as no one decided to blow too hard on it.

The taxi driver talked the entire way to the hotel and she let him. It kept her from thinking too much about what was about to happen even as her stomach tightened into painful knots. When they crossed into Salem itself she felt herself stiffen. Everywhere she looked there were memories.

When he pulled up outside the Hawthorne Hotel, it took all of her strength to get out. Bags in hand, she forced herself to march inside. Reprieve was over. She had to be in character now. And Samantha Castor would believe that she owned the place.

She checked in at the tiny front desk to the right of the door. The lobby was as she remembered it, with ornate yet comfortable furnishings.

She went up to her room. It was large and comfortable, with a sitting area and a Victorian look to the furniture.

When she had put her things away she headed back downstairs. She needed to do one last thing before attempting to locate and infiltrate the coven responsible for the human sacrifices.

Downstairs she had the front desk call a taxi for her and she waited in the lobby until it arrived. Once in the car she gave the driver the address for her mother's house in Danvers, which she hadn't set foot in since the day of the massacre so many years before.

The city of Danvers had been called Salem Village before it changed its name in the eighteenth century and became separate from Salem. Many of the events of the witch trials had taken place in Danvers, and many of the sites were still viewable, including the house of Rebecca Nurse, who had been falsely accused of witchcraft and put to death despite an outpouring of public support for her.

When Samantha was seven her mother took her there before her official initiation into the coven. Her hand tingled as she remembered the feel of the place, the history. She'd sliced open her palm with her dagger and offered her blood to the ghosts of the past so that they might help protect her.

It took years after she was adopted and consecrated herself to God before she stopped feeling like she was being watched and condemned by the very spirits whose help she had once implored.

When the driver finally turned down a tree-lined

street, Samantha felt sick inside and began to shake. She had played on this street as a child, though the games she had created were much darker than those of other children. The driver pulled up outside the house where she'd grown up.

It was a colonial with once stately columns that were now sadly in need of repair. Dusty, vacant eyes seemed to stare at her and vines littered the ground and crawled up any structure they could find.

"Are you sure this is the right address?" the driver asked, staring out his window with a dubious expression.

"Very sure," she said, her voice barely a whisper.

"It looks deserted," he noted.

She couldn't argue with him there. It was, after all. Only the dead walked its floors, and she prayed fervently that she wouldn't encounter any of them when she went inside.

"Call when you need a ride back," the driver instructed, handing her his card after she paid him.

She nodded and stepped away from the taxi. The car lurched forward, tires screaming as if the driver couldn't wait to leave the place behind. She didn't blame him. She'd been trying to do the same for years.

She mounted the steps slowly, key in hand. Standing in front of the door, she stared at the tarnished brass door knocker. It was a demonic figure with a gaping mouth. It had always scared her as a child because she had once sworn that she saw it smile at her.

It was unbelievable to her that she was standing in front of the house that she had grown up in. In many ways it was more haunted for her than the house that had belonged to her high priestess, the one where the massacre had occurred. Now within two days she would have revisited them both.

She stood there, emotions colliding within her. Would the house remember her? Would it fail to recognize her because of the ways in which she had changed? Or, perhaps worse, would it recognize her instantly because she hadn't changed enough?

She inserted the key in the lock and then had to turn it hard to get the ancient mechanism to move after years of being frozen in place.

Kind of like me.

The door finally opened and she stepped inside. The stench of dust and decay wafted over her, forcing her to cover her mouth and nose with her hand.

She remembered how surprised her adopted father had been later when she told him that she didn't want anything from her house. She abandoned her clothes, her magic tools, everything. Once the estate had been settled and the house had become hers, people had urged her to sell it. She hadn't done so; she couldn't bring herself to deal with it even though it meant she'd be able to get rid of it. Instead she had let it sit vacant, slowly decaying. She had at one time considered burning it to the ground and salting the earth afterward. Now that she needed some of the things inside, she was glad she hadn't.

She stepped forward through the dust and the memories. Here in her mother's house there were no protections, no alarms, no booby traps. Their house had never been used for a coven meeting. Here they had been able to masquerade as normal people whenever they needed to.

Her mother had always been good at that. She'd been a member of the PTA long after Samantha had been forced to leave school because she kept saying and doing inappropriate things. Most little girls cried when a bully knocked them down. Samantha hadn't cried; she'd blinded him. Things had only become worse when her mother severely punished her for using her powers publicly, though Samantha could tell she was actually thrilled and proud of what her daughter had done.

When witches go to school, little boys cry. When witches go to school, bad girls die.

She'd often thought of that little boy, Marcus, and wondered what had happened to him. She'd overheard her mother talking to another member of the coven about "fixing" the problem. When she'd gotten older she'd prayed that fixing it meant they'd given him back his sight.

She climbed the stairs slowly, still wishing she was miles away. Because her mother wanted to live the appearance of an ordinary life, they had not kept any of the tools of their practice where others might see them. Everything that had to do with that part of their life was stored in the attic.

She reached the second floor landing and moved to a door on the far side. It was locked and the only key she had for the house would not open it. As a child she had taught herself how to pick it magically. As an adult, she knew how to do it manually. She pulled a small case from her purse, and moments later was swinging the door open to reveal a narrow flight of stairs leading up into darkness.

On the wall hung an ancient lantern, and after she had lit it she ascended the stairs, struggling to ignore the leaping shadows that danced in the fire's light. One in particular seemed to take the form of a woman and she struggled not to look at it or think of it as welcoming her home.

Except for the dust, the attic was as she remembered

it. The single dingy window filtered the light as it came through so that even though it was still morning it felt like dusk. Boxes of junk, old furniture, and odds and ends were scattered around the space. She ignored them and moved to the far corner, where she found what she was looking for.

She had come to the house in Danvers specifically for the things inside an old steamer trunk with brass fittings that had been hers. She stared hard at the trunk. On the lid her initials, DC, had been carved, the last in a long line, a line she had sworn to herself would be broken.

Samantha's hands shook as she slowly lifted the trunk's lid and came face-to-face with her past. She felt a chill wash over her as she stared at the black cloak that lay on top. It was just a thing, black cloth cut into a certain pattern in order to hang a particular way. Across the country hundreds of theatergoers, Renaissance fair attendees, and prop houses had cloaks just like it. It was just a thing—there was nothing evil about black cloth, nothing sinister about a cloak. Like so many things in life, it wasn't what an object was that was important, but instead what it was used for.

And the cloak had been used for evil. By her grandfather, by her mother, and by her. She closed her eyes, trying desperately to shut out the flood of memories that threatened to overwhelm her. The smell of blood filled her nostrils, a memory, nothing real. But the cloak was real and as her hand closed on it she could feel that evil washing over her, threatening to smother her.

Tears streaked down her cheeks as she stood slowly, pulling the cloak free of the trunk. She shook it out, dusty folds unfurling, and then with a remembered grace swiveled her wrists so that the cloak swirled about her for a moment before settling onto her frame.

She was two inches taller than she had been when last she'd worn it. It no longer touched the ground, but instead brushed against the tops of her feet. It had been too big on her when she was a child, but it fit perfectly now. Spiritually she had left it behind, but her body had continued to grow into it and it settled around her with a familiarity that chilled her.

She bent over the chest and drew forth a wicked-looking dagger, her athame, which she had forged herself when she was ten. She pulled it free of its sheath and the blade glistened. "Did you miss me?" she whispered, and almost without thinking she sliced open her palm, feeding the blade with her blood. She felt the pain in the wound and the resulting power that surged through the arm that held the blade.

"Careful, Samantha," she breathed. She sheathed the blade and hung it on her belt. She removed a box from the trunk. Inside it were candles of different colors, a dozen different gemstones, and a male and female poppet, which the average person might mistake for voodoo dolls. In the hands of a Wiccan these items were powerful tools for healing, sympathetic magic, and the bringing of light. In the hands of a witch they were lethal. She set the box aside and continued searching in the trunk, pulling out the things that she would need.

Everything that she could remember as being hers was there. After a moment she sat back, lost in thought. She stroked the cloak absently as memories of that last day in the house trickled through her mind. She hadn't taken her cloak or her athame to the coven ritual; that was why they were here, safely stored in the trunk. Why? She racked her brain, trying to remember.

After a few minutes she got up and moved a few feet, to the trunk that her mother had started using for her things on the day she had given Samantha her old one. She opened the lid and her breath caught in her throat.

There, on top of everything, was a picture of her mother wearing her cloak but with the hood folded down, a stern look on her face. Her long black hair was pulled back and her dark eyes seemed to pierce right through Samantha. With a trembling hand she put aside the picture and dug into the trunk. A few minutes later she was able to confirm that her mother's cloak and athame were missing.

She must have taken them with her that night. But why were mine left behind? Samantha wondered.

She didn't know. It was possible that even if she could remember leaving the house that night she still wouldn't know why. If her mother had told her to leave them, she would have and wouldn't have asked questions about it. Her mother had never liked explaining her actions to anyone, let alone to her twelve-year-old daughter.

Her mother had always been stern, demanding. Many in the coven had been that way. And Samantha had been raised to believe that she should take what she wanted and be strong as well. That was who she was going to have to be now, until she could put a stop to the plans of Bridget and the others.

Her mother would have wanted her to be a strong, courageous, fearless witch. And that was the role she had to play. She continued looking through her mother's trunk, but in the end decided to take nothing from it. She didn't want to risk interacting with any residual energy the items might contain. She'd already had enough nightmares about her mother and the coven to last a lifetime without accidentally conjuring a spirit or two.

Finished with gathering what she wanted, she made her way back down the stairs and snuffed out the light.

On the second-floor landing she turned to continue down to the first floor but felt an irresistible pull toward one of the rooms.

A moment later she was standing inside her bedroom.

The room was spartan in its austerity. A simple green comforter adorned the bed. On a shelf were a few weathered books. That was all. There were no toys, no posters, nothing to identify it as a child's room.

As if drawn to the bed, she sat down slowly on it, grimacing at the dust. A memory stirred of hiding something under the mattress. She slipped a hand underneath it and after a few moments of feeling around she pulled out a small journal. She flipped it open and noted that many pages had been torn out, leaving only jagged little bits of paper to attest to their existence. On the first intact page she recognized her handwriting.

I know that I'm going to die.

The words chilled her. She couldn't remember writing them. She skimmed through the rest, but there was nothing else. She hesitated for a moment and then put the journal back where she'd found it. She stood abruptly and left the room, shutting the door behind her.

She forced herself to go into her mother's room next. She didn't want to, but she needed to see whether there was anything in it she could use.

In a shoebox on the top shelf of the closet, she found several old papers, her mother's passport, and three photographs. She recognized one with her grandfather right off. Another was of her, and the third was of a man with red hair whom she'd never seen before. She stared closely at it. He looked muscular and he had a strong jaw and deep blue eyes. She touched her own red hair and couldn't help but wonder if the man in the photo-

graph was her father. A sudden surge of loneliness overwhelmed her and she clutched the picture tightly for a
moment before replacing it in the box with the rest.

As she stood to leave the room, her gaze fell on her
mother's jewelry box. She walked over to the dresser,
lifted the lid of the box, and stared inside. A necklace
with a moon caught her eye and she slipped it into her
pocket, then closed the box.

A few minutes later she had put everything she was
taking with her in a bag and moved downstairs to wait
for the taxi she had called to take her back to the Hawthorne. She knew she was ready. The transformation was
complete.

She was no longer Samantha Ryan, detective and
Christian.

She was Samantha Castor, last of a long line of ruthless witches, and she was pissed.

10

Fire. Screaming. There was blood everywhere, even on her. She clutched her athame in her hand. She had killed . . . who had she killed? Somebody. A woman ran past her, her throat half torn out, and made it a few more steps before collapsing on the floor. Long claws had shredded the back of her cloak and dug into the flesh beneath.

People were running for the stairs, but they never made it. She stood, terrified, watching the chaos. They who had always frightened her were now themselves enmeshed in unspeakable terror.

And there was something she had to do. If only she could remember.

Samantha awoke bathed in sweat but no blood this time. She shook as the horror of the memory took hold. It was just a glimmer, but she knew she'd been remembering the day of the massacre. The images faded, leaving behind only the memory of the screams and the terror she had felt.

She had spent the night before refamiliarizing herself with the tools of the witch. Now, in the pale light of dawn, she steeled herself for what she had to do next.

She chose her wardrobe carefully. Black jeans, a black

scoop-neck sweater, and black boots that she could easily run in if she had to. It was a statement, but she was out to make one. She fastened the moon pendant she'd found in her mother's jewelry box around her neck. It was made of deep blue lapis and had miraculously been untouched for so many years. It seemed she was not the only one who had avoided the house. Despite the obvious signs of decay, there had been no evidence of vandals or trespassers.

She touched the necklace. Lapis gave the wearer strength and vitality. It also helped one tune in to higher spiritual vibrations. She desperately missed her cross. But given the dangers inherent in practicing her Christian faith while undercover, she wouldn't have been able to wear it even if it hadn't been lost. So the necklace she wore in its place seemed to her the only connection she could achieve with God.

She left the hotel and walked the few blocks to Red's Sandwich Shop. Once there, she headed inside. The building dated back to the 1700s, when American revolutionaries had met there. Now it boasted the tastiest, cheapest, most filling breakfast to be found pretty much anywhere. It was also the place to learn just about anything about the goings-on in town.

Tables were squeezed together in the small space. A bustling waitress zipped by with an order of pancakes that flopped over the sides of the plate. It was just like she remembered.

She glanced around the room, noting that all the tables were taken. At a table close to the door a guy sat by himself, sipping some orange juice. She made eye contact and he smiled and gestured to the empty seat across from him. She hesitated for only a moment. Normal Samantha would have preferred to wait. Undercover Samantha needed all the time and information she could get.

With a smile she sat down. "Thanks, I appreciate it."

"No problem," he said. He had short, wavy brown hair and intense green eyes. He wore a long-sleeved button-up black shirt. "I'm Anthony."

"Samantha."

"It's a pleasure to meet you, Samantha," he said, a glint in his eye. "We've got a famous Samantha right here in town, you know."

"Oh?"

"Yeah. Statue of Samantha from the television show *Bewitched*."

Before she could respond, the waitress arrived with a monster omelet for Anthony. She set it down and turned to Samantha. "What can I get you?"

"Two eggs scrambled, corned beef hash, and coffee, please."

The waitress hurried off and Anthony continued to study her. "You should know, it's always this crowded in here," he said.

"I know. Some things never change."

He cocked his head to the side. "I took you for a stranger, tourist, maybe."

She laughed. "I'm not a tourist. I grew up here. Just moved back."

"Good to know," he said, his smile widening. He fished a business card out of his pocket and handed it to her.

She read it aloud. "Anthony Charles, Proprietor. Museum of the Occult."

"That's me."

She tucked the card into her jeans pocket. "I don't remember a Museum of the Occult."

"I opened it about three years ago," he said.

"Because there weren't enough witch museums in town?" she asked drily.

"Most of them are very limited in their view. Mine covers more aspects of the occult, both historic and modern."

"Intriguing," she said. She could sense no power coming off him, but because of his interests, she still had to wonder if he might be tuned in to what was going on in town. She'd been trying to finalize her plan of attack in regard to contacting the coven, and now she made a decision. "I've heard rumors that there are witches back in Salem."

"Despite what we tell the tourists, there are no witches in Salem," he said, his smile faltering.

He didn't believe that.

He picked up his fork and dug into his omelet. She sat for a minute, studying him as he ate. She thought about compelling him to tell her the truth. Something told her, though, that she'd get a lot more from him if she let him come to her with the information.

"It's too bad. I would be curious to meet a real live witch," she said, keeping her tone light.

He looked up at her, his fork suspended in midair. "You really wouldn't," he replied, his voice husky.

Something flashed in his eyes. Fear? Hatred? She looked at him hard and realized that it was both.

Her food arrived and a minute later he paid for his meal and left. "See you around," he said, his smile strained.

"Sure."

He knew something about modern witches; that was for sure. And whatever it was, he had no love for them. Could he be a potential ally?

She finished her breakfast and hurried back to her hotel room, where she sat down on the bed to think. The symbol that she had on her chest stood for something dark and dangerous. That was who she had to be. She couldn't wait for the coven to find her. She had to summon them to her. It was risky and aggressive, but it was what her mother would have done. It was who she had been raised to be. *Who they would be expecting.*

She opened the bag she'd brought with her from her mother's house and carefully pulled out a box of candles.

She cleared the top of the chest of drawers to set up a temporary altar. She placed a white candle to represent herself, seeker of truth, pure of purpose, on the left side. "I name thee Samantha," she said.

Then she carefully selected three candles from the box. She placed the first one, dark blue, on the right side. "I name thee the most impulsive member of the coven I seek." Next to it she placed a brown candle, saying, "I name thee the member of the coven I seek who is most uncertain about the right of what they are doing." Finally she placed the purple candle with them. "I name thee the most ambitious member of the coven I seek who yet is not a leader."

She lit the white candle. "I am immovable, fixed."

Then she lit the other three candles. "They are not."

She let the four candles burn as she selected a final candle from the box, a yellow one. Yellow was the color used when it was necessary to convince someone that they should do something. Samantha set it next to the white candle that represented herself and lit it. "They must come to me."

A Wiccan practitioner would take several days to perform the ritual, each day moving the candles slightly closer to each other until the objective was reached. But the brand of witchcraft she'd been raised with was all about power, brute force, shortcuts.

She waved her hand, feeling the energy crackling from her fingertips, and the three candles representing the other people moved almost imperceptibly. They would continue to do so until they reached her candle. She knew from experience that she had about three hours before the three witches she'd summoned found her.

She picked up her athame and tucked it in the back of her waistband, where she had often carried a gun instead. *An extension of a cop's power just as the athame is an extension of the witch's power.*

She brushed her hand against her throat, missing again the cross that used to hang there.

Finally, she was ready. She left, closing the door behind her. She walked to the Salem Common and then across the street to the beginning of the Essex Street walking mall.

Her first stop was the Witch History Museum. Obvious, but it suited her purposes. She stood on the threshold.

Marking doorways was an ancient practice, done by people of different cultures and beliefs for similar purposes: to claim and to warn. The Israelites had painted their doorframes with lamb's blood to mark themselves as chosen so the angel of death would pass over them. In the Dark Ages the doors of plague victims were marked to warn others and to help identify them. Many Christians used chalk to mark above their doors for Epiphany, welcoming God into their homes.

Witches could leave psychic impressions on doors, marking them so that others would know they had been there. It was something she had learned to do at a young age. Hiding your presence altogether was actually much harder than broadcasting it.

She took a deep breath and then put her hand on the doorframe. She pushed energy through it, into her fingertips, and then out and onto the wood, which warmed perceptibly. And even though she was forcing energy out, she felt the rush that came with using the power. It felt intoxicating and she realized just how much she'd missed it.

She removed her hand and turned away, horrified. She'd worked so hard to give up this life and everything it entailed. It was unsettling how easy it would be to fall back into it.

She moved on, struggling to get a grip on her emotions as they roiled within her. She walked briskly to her next target, a few doors down. It was a New Age shop that sold a complete hodgepodge of materials, but given the extreme range of colored candles and gemstones on display in the window, it would make a good place to pick up supplies. When she put her hand on the doorframe a chill went through her.

Another witch had been there less than a day earlier. Her stomach twisted hard and she realized that despite everything that had happened, she had still been hoping that somehow it had nothing to do with Salem.

She swallowed the bile in her throat and pressed her hand more firmly against the wood, imprinting her energy more strongly than at the museum. Finished, she left quickly.

She walked past a few more doors and then stopped suddenly at an all-black one. She looked up at the sign overhead. MUSEUM OF THE OCCULT. Anthony's museum. There was a crescent moon with a candle sitting on it. There were half a dozen witch museums in town, along with a pirate museum, a shipping museum, and a Nathaniel Hawthorne museum. There was something different about this one, though. She put her hand on the wall away from the door and closed her eyes. Instead of planting her energy, she sought to read the energy that was already part of the place. When she was a child, she had learned to sense power even before she learned to use it to leave an impression.

Power, real power, thrummed through the wood and into her fingers, faint but unmistakable. She opened her eyes, pulled the door open, and walked inside. The door shut behind her and she looked around the darkened interior. Dozens of mannequins in old-fashioned dress reenacted various scenes from the witch trials. Nothing original there.

But something called to her and she allowed herself to drift farther into the building. There were no other customers there that early. The tourists were still lingering over their breakfasts and locals weren't likely to come to the place. Eventually the older displays gave way to objects from the town's more recent history.

And then she found what she was looking for. In a glass case against the back wall was a collection of newspaper clippings and artifacts. A sign in the middle of the display read: UNCOVERING THE TRUTH ABOUT MODERN WITCHCRAFT IN SALEM.

Her gaze fell on a ceremonial goblet with faces carved all around it, and her heart stopped for a moment. From it her eyes flew to a black robe, torn and stained with what she knew to be blood. A wicked-looking athame was displayed beneath a picture of a woman she knew well. It was Abigail, the high priestess of her coven. Bile rose in the back of her throat as she tried to look away. But though the woman had been dead for years, it seemed that even the photograph of her was enough to strike terror into Samantha. It was as though Abigail's eyes were looking straight through her, judging her, cursing her for having turned her back on who she was.

Samantha wrenched her gaze free and next it fell on pictures of two different dead women and a newspaper article recounting the massacre of almost two dozen people.

The room felt like it was tilting and she grabbed the edge of the case to steady herself. At her touch the goblet inside the case began to glow. She yanked her hand away and turned to leave.

A figure blocked her path. Without thinking, she lifted her left hand, prepared to repel him. Just in time she recognized Anthony.

"I'm glad you came," he said with a smile. "Although frankly I didn't expect to see you again so soon." His eyes held open curiosity in them.

She shook herself and stepped away from the case, hoping to lessen her influence on it and its effect on her.

"Well, you know, how could I resist?" she asked. "You made it sound fascinating."

"I see you have a talent for spotting the most important details," he said, glancing behind her.

"What?"

"The display you were looking at. It's the one that's the most important, the one that really means something."

"Oh, and why is that?"

He cocked his head and stared at her for a moment, studying her. Then he nodded to himself as though he had come to some sort of decision. "You see that woman, the one with the long brown hair?"

She didn't want to look, but he expected her to. She

glanced over her shoulder. The woman in question looked out from the photo, her smile wistful, her eyes gentle.

"Yes," she whispered.

"Do you know who she was?"

She trembled. She did, but he could never know that. She didn't know her name or really anything about her. She only knew how she had died.

"Her name was Laura Charles. She was my mother."

She turned to look at him, her heart feeling like someone was squeezing it.

"When I was a kid she was . . . murdered." He took a deep breath. "By witches. That's why I got a little touchy in the restaurant when you mentioned meeting a witch."

"I am so sorry," she said, tears stinging her eyes.

"Thanks," he said, reaching out and brushing her cheek with his finger.

His touch sent electricity through her, but not like any other jolt she had ever felt. She had felt power, fear, darkness, but never this. There was some sort of connection.

He looked at her in surprise and she could tell he had felt it too.

"Do I know you?" he asked at last.

She shook her head.

"We're going to have to change that."

And something sparked between them. She started to reach out to him and then caught herself. She had work to do, dark and dangerous work, and for both their sakes he needed to stay away.

"I'm sorry. I have to go," she said, trying to force herself to smile and failing miserably.

She turned and left him standing there. When she left the building she was careful not to leave her imprint on it. The last thing she needed was to lead the witches to Anthony . . . or to the deadly artifacts he was unwittingly displaying.

On the street she took a deep breath to help clear her mind. She had to focus on her mission. She could do nothing for Anthony's mother, but there were people out there whose lives were in danger as long as the coven was allowed to operate.

She walked up the street, marking three more places, each with more energy than the one before. She was leaving a magical trail of bread crumbs for her targets to follow.

Finally she arrived at the Witchery, a restaurant and microbrewery. She walked inside. The startled employee looked up at her. "I'm sorry, ma'am, we're not open for another hour."

"It's all right," Samantha said, allowing her voice to drop, willing her words to wash away any resistance. "I require the use of your private dining room in the back."

The man nodded slowly, as if that were a completely natural request. "Will you require a menu?"

"No, but in thirty minutes bring four pints for me and my friends."

He went back to his work while she walked past him.

In the back room she chose a table with a commanding view of the room. She sat with her back to the wall, with clear views of the door and windows. Half an hour later the waiter brought her four pints. "Witch's Brew," he said.

"Thanks," she said. "My friends will be along soon. We don't wish to be disturbed."

"Yes, ma'am," he said with a quick bow before leaving.

Samantha felt a ripple in the air a minute later. Within

moments three women appeared in the doorway, eyes wide, faces angry and wary at the same time. Power rolled off each of them, causing slight ripples in the air and energy currents in the room.

"Ladies," Samantha said, gesturing to the table. "I've been waiting for you."

11

The three witches she had summoned, the three she had *chosen*, stood gaping at her. She smirked. So much of magic was symbolic, subject to interpretation. Every once in a while, though, it was incredibly literal. Each woman was wearing a shirt corresponding to the candle color Samantha had given them. She'd exerted more influence than even she had anticipated. And knowing that, she felt her own anxieties about the meeting ease.

To the one in the dark blue shirt, the impulsive one, she said, "Why don't you sit and have a drink? You look like you could use one."

The woman, who was barely more than a girl, took a step forward, but wasn't yet entirely convinced.

Samantha shifted her eyes to the one wearing purple, the one who craved power. She was probably closer to her own age. "That is, if it's okay with your leader here."

"Autumn's not our leader," the oldest of the three, the one in the brown poet shirt, squeaked.

"Shut up, Karen!" Autumn said, flushing.

"No? My mistake, then," Samantha said, forcing a detached, somewhat disinterested note into her voice.

It was just the right tone. The three surged forward and, one by one, took a seat.

The impulsive one reached for the glass.

"Jace, what if it's poisoned?" Karen warned.

Jace looked uncertain for a moment. Samantha smiled and lifted her own glass, taking a deep gulp of the golden brew. It tasted awful, but then beer wasn't her thing. It suited the environment, though, and the atmosphere she had taken pains to create.

She set her glass down. "Ladies, not afraid of a little witch's brew, are we?" she asked, throwing down the gauntlet.

Jace grabbed her glass and downed half her beer before pounding it back on the table, eyes wide as she realized that she might have just made a huge mistake.

"Where's the fun in poisoning someone?" Samantha asked, easing her hand to her back and grasping the hilt of her athame. "I mean, there's only one way to really kill someone. Plunge your blade into their heart and feel it stop beating." She yanked the athame free and lifted it high before plunging it into the heart of the table.

All three women jumped backward, lifting their hands in protective gestures, ready to repulse her with waves of energy if she should come after them.

They weren't raised as witches. They'd have gone on the offensive, not reacted protectively. Now she knew the three were relatively new to the black arts.

"Besides," Samantha said, smiling broadly, like a predator about to devour its prey, "we've all got too much to talk about for anyone to worry about killing just yet."

The three moved back slowly, eyeing her weapon.

"You shouldn't abuse your athame like that," Karen squeaked.

Spoken like a Wiccan and not a witch. Karen had been a Wiccan. What had brought her over to the dark side? If she was Wiccan that explained why she had the

most doubts about the rightness of what she was participating in. Wiccans vowed to harm none and believed
that whatever they put into the world would come back
to them threefold. There had to be a lot weighing on her
conscience. And a compelling reason why she was doing
her best to ignore it. It was possible, maybe even likely,
that she wasn't aware of the coven's true plans. Samantha had a hard time picturing her as a killer.

"You worry too much," Jace said, downing more of
her beer.

And you don't worry enough, Samantha thought. Jace
had low self-esteem, little self-identity, and even less
self-control. It made her a slave to her impulses. And the
impulses of those around her.

Samantha turned to Autumn, who was studying her
even as she was studying them. The girl was smart
enough to realize that Samantha was more powerful.
She was ambitious enough to want to find a way to use
that to her advantage. "So, we found you," Autumn said.
"Since you hit town you haven't exactly been . . . discreet.
Why are you here?"

Samantha looked at each of them in turn. "To take
charge of my coven."

They all stared back at her in surprise and then at one
another.

"What do you mean?" Autumn asked at last.

Samantha stopped smiling and let the mask of jocular
civility slip, revealing all that she was underneath. She
let everything she had ever done shine in her eyes. She
could feel the monster that she had been, climbing out
of the deep dark hole she'd kept her in for so long. It
sickened her, but it terrified them.

"Did you honestly think that a coven could practice
here and I wouldn't know? Did you think you could use

that house and I wouldn't hear? Did you believe that you could dare to use my symbol and I wouldn't feel it?" And the rage that echoed in her voice paled in comparison to that which she felt in her heart.

They stared at her, stunned and speechless. She pulled the edge of her shirt down so they could see the tattoo. They all shrank back with gasps. Karen turned her head away, as if the sight pained her. They knew the symbol, but Samantha was certain none of them was using it herself.

"So, why am I here? *You summoned me.* And now you have to face the consequences of that action. I'm here either to kill you all . . . or to lead you."

They stared at her, dumbfounded. After a minute they began to look at one another. She had made an impact for sure. She took another sip of her brew while she waited for them to say something.

"We already have a leader," Karen squeaked at last.

"Shut up!" Autumn snapped.

She looked at Samantha, who smiled at her. Autumn was weighing her options, trying to decide what would get her power and what would get her killed. She hadn't yet realized that she was in a no-win scenario.

"You'll have to meet with our elders," Autumn said at last.

"Fine. You can find me here tomorrow at the same time."

Samantha stood, yanked her athame from the table, and put it back in her waistband. "And tomorrow the beer's on you."

Samantha swaggered out. When she got to the sidewalk, her knees started to buckle and she braced herself for a moment against the wall. She could feel her blade against the skin of her back and she felt like she was going to be sick. Had the three witches at any point in the conversation decided to pool their power, she would have been no match for them and would have been pushed into a corner where she either had to kill or be killed.

I don't want to kill anyone with magic, she thought, shivering.

She forced herself to straighten up and walk. She wanted to conceal herself and then follow them in hopes that they would lead her to the others. She didn't know if that was what they would do or if they would simply make a couple of phone calls. Without knowing more about the way the group functioned, she couldn't risk it. If she was caught following them, her chances of infiltrating the coven would be pretty much shot. Better to make them come to her; assume the high ground and fortify it.

Politics had been as much a part of the coven she'd grown up in as magic had. She remembered her mother taking five hours to dress for a meeting with their high priestess. She'd agonized over everything in her wardrobe, looking for something that showed respect but not weakness.

The high priestess had been Abigail, a woman with flaming red hair and eyes blacker than night. She'd been old, but not old enough to be weak. She'd been killed in the massacre along with everyone else. One of Samantha's few memories from that night was seeing the witch's face, blood trickling from the corner of her mouth, as she fell backward.

She still had nightmares about Abigail and would wake screaming. The woman had perfected a masterful use of terror.

And now someone else was following in her footsteps, leading a coven that was doing unspeakable evil. Who were they trying to resurrect and for what purpose? She was frustrated because every minute that ticked by meant one minute less to save the next victim. She'd never been patient, never been a fan of waiting, but that was all that was left to her now.

She put the walking mall behind her and headed toward the harbor. She wasn't ready to go back to her hotel room just yet. She didn't think she'd be able to stay cooped up within those four walls for the hours ahead.

She breathed deeply of the salty air as she reached the waterfront. She turned down the street and moments later walked past the house that had inspired Hawthorne to write *The House of the Seven Gables*. The mansion had always fascinated and frightened her as a child. It was rumored to be haunted and she believed it. Why wouldn't she? Her entire life was haunted by specters of her past.

As she walked, the air swirled around her, eddies of energy moving as she passed through. She had worked for years to ignore them and had come close to succeeding. But the energies were always there, just as her powers were. When she was a child she had asked her mother why some, like the two of them, were gifted with abilities that others did not have.

Her mother had laughed the question away, telling her that they were simply favored, "blessed." As she grew older and came to see the evil that so many had done with their power, she realized that it was no blessing but a curse.

She hated feeling the things she did, seeing what others could not, and hearing what others missed. Her father had said more than once that it helped to make her a great cop. She knew that what it made her was a freak.

And with every spell she was performing she could feel herself sliding back into the hell she had once lived in.

She kept walking, trying to calm herself and center her thoughts for the task at hand. It would be difficult to convince the leaders of the coven to accept her quickly, but she had to pull it off. Only from inside would she be able to know enough about them to stop them.

A sudden wave of sorrow hit her broadside and she gasped at the feelings of pain, fear, and anger that accompanied it. She turned and saw a cemetery. Ancient monuments stood, proudly reaching for the heaven that their cherished dead had dreamed of as mortals.

The cemetery was old and Samantha knew that her ancestors were buried there. *Including my mother,* she realized.

As if compelled, she walked through the open gate. She had never known her father, not even anecdotally, since her mother wouldn't talk about him at all. Samantha didn't even know his first name. Castor was her mother's last name. He could be anywhere, anyone, for all she knew. He could even be one of the corpses rotting in the ground beneath her feet. She had spent hours as a child wondering about him, who he was, what he was like. As she grew older she even daydreamed that he would come and take her away, rescue her from the coven and all the things she was being asked to do. She hadn't thought much about him since she had left that life behind. Now she thought of the photograph she had seen, wondered if it was him.

She wandered through the cemetery, picking her way around graves, until she came to the mausoleum that housed seven generations of her family. Someone had added her mother's name to the door when they'd interred her. It hadn't been Samantha—she hadn't even attended the funeral. She reached out a hand and touched the name. Her skin tingled and she pulled her hand away quickly. Even in death her family was still practicing its magic.

All the better to haunt me with.

She turned aside, preparing to leave, but something stopped her. There was power in the cemetery, more power than there should have been. She followed the feeling, twisting farther into the depths of the graveyard. She passed ancient monuments mixed with new. Rich or poor, colonist or modernist, everyone in Salem eventually died.

At last her steps brought her to a grave marker only slightly weathered. A fresh bouquet of flowers was propped against the stone. She bent down to read it and her blood ran cold. It was Abigail's grave. She felt suddenly dizzy and pitched forward. She caught herself with a hand on the grave marker. The stone felt hot to the touch and suddenly the air around her was filled with the sound of laughter, hard and cruel and menacing. Samantha gasped and jerked back, but something tripped her and she crashed to the ground on top of the grave.

She pushed up with her hands and it felt as though the very life was being drained out of her and that in moments she would be as one of the corpses rotting in the ground. Suddenly she froze. There, in the dirt beneath the flowers, someone had drawn the symbol that burned on Samantha's chest.

She scrambled backward even as a terrible suspicion took hold of her. They couldn't be planning to raise Abigail, could they? But why would they want to? Why would they need to?

She pushed herself to her feet, afraid that she was going to vomit. She broke out in a cold sweat. It couldn't be true. Not after all this time. Who would remember, or care? She glanced around wildly but didn't see anyone. Still, she couldn't deny that something had been sucking the life from her while she was touching the grave.

For one terrible moment she wondered if Abigail's power reached beyond the grave.

Get hold of yourself. She's dead and buried. She can't hurt you anymore, she scolded herself.

Something that had been bothering her suddenly jumped to the front of her mind. It had been Abigail's house where the party that Katie had attended was held. But how was that possible? The protections on that place were legion.

Unless someone knows how to take them down and put them back up again. Bridget. Could she have that much power? And is she the one who drew the symbol on Abigail's grave and left the flowers and made it so that it sucked the life from those who come near it?

Whoever it was they were trying to raise, the very fact that they were attempting to do it, thought that they could, was a testament to how strong they must be. Raising someone took an incredible amount of power combined with absolute ruthlessness. It was not for the faint of heart, not something that could be done on a whim.

It would require careful planning. And she was suddenly sure that Abigail's old house was once again truly being used as a center of activity. She should return and examine it more closely, but fear plucked at her heart, urging her to stay as far away from that place as possible.

It wasn't just where Abigail had lived.

It was also where she had died.

Samantha turned and hurried back toward the street, eager to escape the cemetery before it revealed anything else to her.

She quickly began to retrace her steps and heaved a sigh of relief when she finally passed the Seven Gables house again, *When I get back to the hotel I'll just have to perform a calming spell—*

Samantha stopped in her tracks, horrified at what she'd just thought. She'd been back to doing magic for such a short time, and yet her thoughts already turned first to it. *No, not a spell! Pray, that's what I have to do. Pray and meditate. Plan my next move, my next one hundred moves.*

And some of those moves will involve doing more magic. I have to be prepared for it. But please, God, keep me from losing myself in it.

She shuddered suddenly. Someone was watching her. She turned her head slightly, wondering where the observer was.

"Samantha!"

She spun, prepared to defend herself, but then relaxed slightly when she saw Anthony walking briskly toward her.

"Hi," she said.

"Hi, yourself. Listen, I've been thinking. Would you like to grab some dinner?"

"When?"

"Tonight."

She hesitated. She didn't want to bring him into the middle of anything, but he might be able to help her. If he'd managed to get his hands on some of her coven's things, then he had to be resourceful. She'd told the trio of witches that they could find her the next day at the Witchery. She believed there was a strong possibility that members of the coven might hunt her down at her hotel in the middle of the night. But until they reached out to her there was nothing more she could really do except troll for information.

And Anthony might be just the person she needed to talk to.

"Did I ask a difficult question?" he prompted, smiling uncertainly at her.

"No," she said, smiling. "I had some work to do tonight, but I realized I could put it off. So I'm all yours for dinner."

"Great. There's this awesome restaurant called Nathaniel's."

She grimaced. "I'm staying at the Hawthorne and I was hoping to avoid eating there tonight. If I do, it will just remind me that I should be upstairs working." It wasn't true, but in case the witches decided to show early, she didn't want them to see Anthony.

"Then away from the hotel it is," he said. "How about seafood?"

"Fine."

The truth was that at the moment, she felt fine about anything that didn't remind her of the things that she was trying so hard to forget.

The way Abigail could glare and make a person crumble inside.

The fact that it was likely that someone else would die before she could infiltrate the coven.

The night of the massacre.

And most important of all, how much she loved doing the magic.

Because if she remembered that, then she'd truly be lost.

12

By evening, Samantha had gone back to her room, un-packed, changed clothes, and walked to the Whaler's Inn. She met Anthony outside, and moments later they were seated in a booth, waiting for their food. The white tablecloth was topped with a small lantern and a vase holding a single red rose. A fire crackled on the hearth nearby and except for them the dining room was empty. The lighting was low and music played softly in the background. It was romantic.

And for a first date with a guy she didn't know, it was *too* romantic. Especially considering that he had been all too eager to get away from her at breakfast. She looked at him suspiciously. Just exactly what did he want from her on this date?

Don't think of this as a date, she warned herself. *Think of him as a source, just another witness to interrogate.*

But he was looking at her with his beautiful eyes and smiling at her in a way that made her pulse skitter out of control. It was crazy and uncharacteristic of her. Dating had never been her thing. Who would ever understand her, be able to cope with who she was, who she had been?

But staring at his face, lined with its own pain and shadows, she realized that if anyone could understand, he could. That wasn't enough, though. Because of what had happened to his mother, he would never be able to cope, to accept her. And after what her family had done to his, she had no right to lead him on, to hurt him any more than he'd already been hurt.

"I saw you coming out of the cemetery today," he said gently.

She blinked in surprise. "How?"

"I was in the cemetery too. I was checking on my mother's grave."

And the sick feeling was back, knotting itself around her insides. She should never have accepted his dinner invitation. He was looking at her expectantly, clearly waiting for her to share.

"I was visiting my mother too," she said at last.

"I'm sorry," he said. "It's hard to lose a mother."

"Thanks. And I'm sorry about yours."

He shrugged. "It's strange, you know. There are days where I still expect to see her at her favorite coffee shop or walking down the street. Even though it's been years."

"This place is haunted for you."

He nodded. "I guess you could say so."

"Why do you stay?" she asked.

A shadow seemed to pass across his face and his eyes hardened. "The coven that killed my mother, when they were slaughtered, there were rumors that one witch survived. I've spent the past sixteen years searching for that person."

"Why?" Samantha asked, trying to still the sudden pounding of her heart, which no longer had anything to do with how attractive he was.

He smiled. "Let's just say that revenge is a dish best served flambéed."

"As in burning?" she asked.

"As in witch," he said with a nod.

She winced. Had he figured out already who she was? She studied his face carefully as she chose her next words. "It's been years. How do you even know the witch is still alive?"

"I can feel it, in here," he said, tapping his chest over his heart. "If she were dead, I'd feel peace. Someday, though, I will feel that peace. And then—then maybe I can leave this place."

"It seems like you're just punishing yourself by staying here with the memories. Why not move on? I mean, how do you know the witch hasn't done the same thing? For all you know, she's practicing in Oregon or India. Maybe she's not even a witch anymore."

He smiled tightly. "Once a witch, always a witch. But I wouldn't be at all surprised to find out that she had left the state. However, I stay because eventually she'll come back. You see, I have something the witch will want. I figure in time she'll find me."

Is it one of those artifacts in the case? she wondered. *My goblet, for instance?* She took a sip of her water, trying to look nonchalant instead of guilty or too curious. For the first time she felt sympathy for the murderers she had interrogated over the years. They had sat across from her at tables in cold gray rooms, sweating and praying that she wouldn't discover the one bit of evidence that would damn them or that they wouldn't say something that would seal their fate and send them to prison.

"You okay?" he asked.

She nodded quickly. "I was just thinking, that could be incredibly dangerous."

"Some things are worth the risk," he said. He smiled at her. "Like asking you out."

For a moment her heart stopped, thinking that he had

guessed. But then she realized that he was just flirting. She forced herself to smile. "Hardly counts as risky compared to the other."

"But still, a risk. I risked rejection because the potential reward seemed worth it."

"You don't even know me," she protested.

"And yet I feel that I do. You're smart, funny, and driven, just like I am. You're curious and open to things that others dismiss out of hand."

"Very observant of you," she said, working hard not to squirm.

"You're also looking for something. I know what it feels like to be looking for something. It makes me want to see you find it, whatever it is. If you tell me what it is you're looking for, maybe I can help you find it."

"I don't think that's a good idea," she said, forcing a smile.

"I do. It will give me an excuse to spend more time with you. I can't explain it; I just feel like for some reason I *need* to help you."

"It could be very dangerous for both of us."

He laughed. "I think you already pointed out that I tend to rush in where angels fear to tread. Come on. Let me help you."

Samantha leaned across the table and touched his hand with hers. "All right. I too am looking for a witch."

His lips parted in surprise. A moment passed, then another as he took in what she'd said. Finally he asked, "And you're looking for this witch here?"

"I am."

"Listen to me," he said, gripping her hand tight. "Witches—*real* witches—are bad news. They don't live by a code, they don't respect life, law, anything. You don't want to get mixed up with that."

"I could say the same to you."

"But I don't have a choice. And I at least know something about them."

"Yes, but do you know enough?" she countered. "Can you tell a witch from a Wiccan?"

"Of course," he said. "I've met hundreds of Wiccans. There's thousands of Wiccans for every witch. And they tend to be nice, respectful people." He looked at her suspiciously. "How do you know there's a witch in Salem?"

"Haven't you been watching the news? Those women who were killed in Boston?"

He relaxed visibly. "I saw the news. Those women were killed by occultists, maybe a serial killer or a sick college student with a penchant for murder. That's why the pentagrams. No real witch would use that symbol. It used to be a Christian symbol representing the five wounds of Christ—head, hands, feet; the point draws the eye upward toward God. Those worshipping Satan profane the pentagram by instead turning it upside down. It's not a witch symbol. Try telling that to the media, though. They scream *witch* at the first opportunity regardless of the truth. It's dangerous and irresponsible."

"I couldn't agree with you more about the press. I want you to be careful, though, and keep your eyes open. Because, as improbable as it seems, witches are behind those murders."

"How do you know all this?" he asked.

His mind was working on the problem and it would be only a matter of minutes before he came to the conclusion that she was a cop. And that knowledge was too dangerous for him to have. He might accidentally tell someone or unwittingly out her in front of the wrong person. For all she knew, he was working with one of the witches. Better for him to hate her and keep her cover intact than risk blowing it. She made a swift decision.

"How do I know witches are behind it?" she asked softly.

He nodded.

She wrapped her hand around his water glass. Moments later the water began to boil. She let go and it stopped.

His lips moved and he mouthed the word "witch." Then he bolted from the table and out of the restaurant. She got up to chase after him, but when she reached the sidewalk he was nowhere to be seen.

"Anthony!" she shouted.

There was no response. She could tell that he had turned to the left, so she followed. Three more swift turns and she was in an alley. He was hiding, but every instinct she had told her it would be bad to flush him out. Instead she stood in the middle of the space and spoke out loud.

"I didn't mean to hurt you or frighten you. I'm not going to do anything to you, but I could use your help. Please believe me—I'm not your enemy."

There was no response. She waited for a minute and then said softly, "Okay, but I hope you change your mind."

She left and walked slowly back to her hotel, hoping he would catch up to her. When he didn't she was mostly relieved but also somewhat disappointed. She got to her room and sat down with a sigh. She'd made a mistake, revealed herself too fast. But it was better if he steered clear of her, fearing her, than if he knew that she was a police officer. That was the awful thing about deep cover. Nobody aside from the officer's handlers was supposed to know the truth.

She cleared away the candles from the top of the dresser. The flames had automatically snuffed out when the three witches had found her. Autumn, Jace, and Karen. Each of them was going to be useful in her own way. Unfortunately, none of them was highly placed enough to be privy to what was going on in the coven. She had briefly thought of arresting the three of them, but even if they could be made to talk, none of them knew enough to help her stop the others. Especially Karen. She was still surprised that the former Wiccan was involved with the group. There had to be something specific she hoped to gain from the connection. Samantha had wanted to find someone with enough of a moral compass to doubt the rightness of what the witches were doing, and Karen more than met the requirement.

I might be able to reach her, make her see what's happening, persuade her to leave before it's too late.

She shook her head. She shouldn't be so worried for Karen's welfare. She was, after all, part of the coven that was killing girls and trying to raise the dead. Regardless of whether she had a hand in the killings, she was still involved. Still guilty. *Like I was way back then.*

She wanted to talk to Ed, tell him how things were going and see what he'd come up with on his end. Communication was dangerous, though, since it could lead to discovery. And since Ed was one of the officers guarding Katie, communication with the outside world was just as dangerous for him as it was for her. Until she knew how powerful and how connected the coven was, she couldn't risk it for anything short of an emergency.

She prepped her hotel room in case of an unannounced visit from members of the coven. She placed several objects she could use as weapons strategically around the room. Then she carefully staged the rest to make it look like she was a constant, and dangerous, practitioner, right down to building an altar on top of the writing table. Witches occasionally played at mimicking the religious practices of others.

Which was something that worried her, since she could guess the kind of things she would be expected to do if the coven decided to accept her. In many ways it upset her more than the thought of them trying to kill her. She didn't want to think about praying or sacrificing to any being other than God. It would be asked of her, though. She would have to perform dark magic or risk revealing herself and losing all chance of stopping them forever. She wasn't sure which terrified her more—not stopping them or having to do the unthinkable to do so.

Her stomach tightened and twisted. Her hand reached for the cross that wasn't around her neck and she touched the moon instead. She didn't like the way that made her feel.

She looked around the room, working out what more she should do to prepare.

I should put a circle of blood around the bed to guard me while I sleep, she realized. She didn't want to use too much blood and weaken herself, but it was a good idea. She grabbed her pocketknife, sliced open her left hand, and began to draw the circle of blood, being careful to keep it unbroken.

When at last she finished, she cleaned and bandaged the wound and surveyed the room. Everything looked right to her and there wasn't anything else she could think of to do at the moment.

As if on cue there was a knock on her door. It couldn't be a member of the coven—she would have felt the changes in energy if one had gotten that close. She opened the door and was surprised to see Anthony standing there, his features twisted in anger. He pushed past her into the room and she quickly closed the door and turned to face him.

"What the hell did you do to me?" he fumed.

"Excuse me?" she asked, crossing her arms and staring at him.

"You heard me," he said. "I—" He stopped suddenly as his eyes fell on her makeshift altar. Then he turned and took in the other magic tools she had staged around the room. The color drained completely from his face. "It's true. You are a witch."

She raised an eyebrow but didn't say anything in response.

"Why?"

"Why what?" she asked.

"From the moment I saw you I haven't been able to think about anything else."

"Wow, and it's been a whole fourteen hours," she said, letting the sarcasm drip from her voice.

"It's been a lifetime," he flashed, the anger back. "For sixteen years I've had one goal, one purpose. And then you come along and have me thinking thoughts . . . You've bewitched me."

"I've done no such thing," she denied heatedly.

"You have," he insisted.

"If anything, you're the one who's been trying to bewitch me, seduce me," she accused. "Inviting me to your museum, telling me about your childhood so I'd feel sorry for you, taking me out to a romantic restaurant. What was your next move, Romeo?"

Anger poured off him. But something else was there as well, burning inside him. Maybe she could see it because the same fire was burning inside her.

He took a quick step forward and kissed her.

She should have pulled away, but something wouldn't let her. She wrapped her arms around his neck and began to kiss him back. She knew it was crazy, but there was a connection with him. She could feel it, and she knew he felt it too.

He pulled her to his chest, holding her close. Heat flashed through her body. He let his lips drift down to her jaw and then he was kissing her throat. She tilted her head back, reveling in the sensation. Suddenly he let her go and took a step backward.

"What have you done to me?" he moaned.

"Nothing yet," she whispered.

And then he was kissing her again, hard. She lifted her hands and placed them on his cheeks and sent small electrical impulses through her fingers, stimulating the nerve endings. He jerked and looked at her with wide eyes.

"It's just a little electricity," she said. "It won't hurt you. *I* won't hurt you." She leaned forward and kissed him, his lips tingling against hers. She moved her hands to his arms and could feel the hairs there stand on end as she stroked them.

He kissed her harder, deeper, and she matched him in passion, his desire flooding her senses, and she echoed it back to him until she was tearing at his shirt, trying to get it off so she could touch his chest. He responded by grasping her hips and pulling her even closer. She could feel his heart rate accelerating, matching hers. She began to breathe in rhythm with him as their bodies came into tune.

She closed her eyes, wanting to feel more of him, to breathe the air he breathed. She had never felt this way. She was losing herself in him and it felt so right.

And then, suddenly, she felt energy ripple through

the building. She pushed him away with a gasp, staggering as she tried to regain her footing. He was staring at her, confused and panting. The color was slowly draining from his face and he looked as lost as she had felt a moment before. But there was no time to explain, no time to apologize or make things right.

Witches had just entered the hotel and they were coming for her.

13

"What's wrong?" Anthony asked.

"They're coming," Samantha said.

"Who?"

"The witches I'm looking for. There's no time to hide you. Take off your clothes."

"What? No way."

"Do it or I'll do it for you," she snapped. "Dump your clothes at the foot of the bed and get under the covers," she ordered.

She peeled off her own shirt and dropped it on the floor before running to the closet. She grabbed the bathrobe hanging there and put it on. She removed her jeans and threw them on the growing pile.

Clad only in briefs, Anthony was climbing into the bed. She felt her cheeks burning as she moved over to him. He stared up at her. "What next?"

"I won't let anything happen to you," she promised. And then she touched his forehead and put him to sleep. For a moment she considered doing a glamour on him to disguise his appearance and protect him. But if they sensed that she had done that, they'd know she cared if he got hurt.

She shoved hard, rolling him over onto his stomach so that most of his face was obscured by the pillow. It was the best she could do for him besides pretending she didn't care about him at all. Which would be nearly impossible.

Choking down her fear, she stepped around the bed and positioned herself halfway between it and the door and waited. She didn't have to feign her irritation.

Moments later the door opened and three cloaked figures glided into the room, the door swinging shut on its own behind them.

Autumn removed her hood first, looking both excited and nervous. It was a big moment for her, leading the others to the interloper. A second witch removed his hood to expose a sandy-haired man in his forties. She turned her gaze to the third figure, who stood flanked by the other two. Power flowed off her, and Samantha sensed that this was a witch to contend with.

She lowered her hood to reveal long, whitish blond hair. Her eyes were amber and seemed to glow from within. *Bridget,* the girl who had lured Katie in, Samantha realized.

To Bridget she said, "You have terrible timing."

"Did we interrupt something?" Bridget asked, amusement in her voice. She was looking over Samantha's shoulder at the bed and she could tell by the quickening thought in her eyes that Bridget saw not only Anthony but also the circle that Samantha had cast on the floor around the bed. She had drawn it for protection, not to work sex magic as the other guessed, but it worked well.

"Yes, you did interrupt."

"Did you want to have this conversation in front of your lover?"

Samantha snorted. "Him? I don't even know his name. I think sex magic works better that way, keeps things simple. And don't worry, I put him on pause. He won't remember a thing."

The man smirked. "You do sex magic with a normal?"

Samantha turned a scathing gaze on him. "Like I said, it keeps it simple. No competing agendas to worry about."

He looked like he was about to say something else, but Bridget held up a hand. "That's enough, Calvin."

He did as he was told, quickly and without hesitation. Clearly Bridget ran a tight ship and didn't tolerate disobedience.

"Autumn tells me that she found you this morning downtown and you showed some interest in joining a real coven."

"Is that what she told you?" Samantha asked, noting the inconsistencies, particularly the exclusion of the other two witches.

Bridget slid her gaze to Autumn. "Yes."

"So, you're the recruitment officer?"

"Yes, you could say that."

"I want to talk to your high priestess."

Bridget cocked her head and narrowed her eyes. "In time, if you prove yourself . . . worthy."

And even though the evil and the power coming off her intimidated and frightened Samantha, she forced herself to laugh.

"Actually, the real question is, are you worthy of me?"

Samantha flicked her wrist and ignited the candles along the perimeter of the room.

Bridget winked and snuffed them out.

The last thing Samantha needed was a pissing contest with Bridget. And Bridget knew she had already had contact with Autumn, so anything she did to the girl wouldn't be as impressive.

But Calvin was another story. The sight of a spider crawling along the wall triggered a memory, something another witch had done to her when she was a child. Her gaze ticked to her male poppet on top of the dresser. *I name thee Calvin,* she thought. Then with a flick of her finger she dropped the spider onto the poppet's face.

Calvin let out a shriek and fell to the floor, clawing at his face. She knew that in his own mind a giant spider was crawling over it.

"Get it off!" he shouted. "I can't breathe!"

As he thrashed around on the floor, Autumn jumped back several feet, her face ashen. Bridget studied Samantha thoughtfully.

And then Calvin pulled out his athame and poised it to kill the imaginary spider. But the only one he would kill would be himself.

Samantha had not expected him to go that far, but she forced herself to stand immovable, unflinching, though she trembled inside.

"Enough," Bridget said quietly.

Samantha waited a beat, just long enough so that the others would be in doubt about what she would do. Then she shrugged and made a show of flicking her finger again.

The spider fell off the doll. Bridget grabbed Calvin's hand and a moment later he was sobbing with relief. The witch turned back to Samantha. "You would have let him kill himself?" she asked.

Samantha forced herself to meet the other's stare. "If he's that weak, he has no business in a coven connected to my family."

Bridget's gaze sharpened. "What are you talking about?"

Without moving, Samantha slapped Autumn across the face. The girl reeled in shock.

"She told you nothing of import. I'm not just some random witch who wandered into town on a sightseeing tour. Someone in this coven is using my mark. This mark belonged to my old coven and none other. Since I am all that is left of it, someone here summoned me."

Samantha moved the bathrobe just enough to reveal the tattoo. Bridget turned on Autumn with an oath and the girl cringed. "Idiot! The lone survivor lives and you did not think to tell me?"

Bridget turned back to Samantha, struggling to regain her composure. "I'll bring this matter to the immediate attention of my high priestess. I know she will be very interested to meet you. We'll be in touch with you tomorrow."

She bent her head slightly and after a moment Samantha did the same. "Pick him up," Bridget ordered Autumn with a glance at Calvin, who was still on the floor.

Autumn hurried to do as she was told, and avoided looking at Samantha at all.

She realizes how badly she screwed up. And now she has both the stranger and the coven angry with her. It will make her more vulnerable, Samantha thought with satisfaction.

The three witches left and Samantha stood, waiting, until a couple of minutes later she felt them exit the building. Then she staggered backward and collapsed on the bed, her limbs shaking.

She buried her head in her hands and took a deep, shuddering breath. After a minute she looked over at Anthony's still form. She reached out and tapped him, sending a mild shock through his system.

He jerked and rolled over abruptly, eyes wide and disoriented. He turned and looked at her.

"They're gone. It's safe for now," she said.

"What just happened?" he asked, his voice eerily quiet.

"I think the witch I was looking for just found me," she said.

"Lady, I don't know what you're mixed up in, but count me out," he said, swinging his legs off the edge of the bed.

"I wish I could, Anthony. Unfortunately, your timing is as bad as theirs. I can't risk them waiting to pounce on you once you set foot outside. You're going to have to stay here for a while."

"How long?" he ground out.

"The rest of the night."

"That is unacceptable," he said, his face turning red.

"So is your getting killed for sport or tortured to death for information."

"Do they know who I am?" he asked.

"No, and I'd like to keep it that way. I can sneak you out easily enough in the morning. No harm, no foul."

"You can't seriously expect me to stay here . . . with you?"

She smiled grimly at him. "A little while ago that idea didn't seem so unappealing to you."

"I don't know what kind of spell you put on me, but I'm warning you, take it off."

"As I told you before, I haven't done anything to you. That's not my style, not who I am."

"You'll forgive me, but all I know is that you're a witch."

"And what about all those things you said in the restaurant?" she asked, growing irritated. "Funny, smart, searching for something?"

"That was when I thought you were a normal woman."

"Witches aren't made, you know," she snapped. "They're born."

"What does that mean?"

"I was born with these powers. And I was unlucky enough to be born into a family who practiced. I could no more help that than you could help your mother being killed."

She had crossed a line—she could tell it by the way the color drained completely from his face and he began to shake uncontrollably.

"I'm sorry," she said, taking a deep breath. "I'm still freaked out from what just happened, what could have happened. And you seem to bring out the fire in me in all forms."

He didn't say anything, just stood up, taking the sheet with him, wrapping it around himself. He retrieved his clothes and disappeared into the bathroom, and she took the opportunity to put on sweats. There was no doubt about it—Anthony Charles had complicated her life, her job, everything.

Her phone rang and she snatched it up. "Hello?"

"Hey." It was Ed and he sounded tired. "Any progress?"

She lowered her voice. "I just had a close encounter with the recruiter. Bridget."

"I remember the name. Is she as scary as Katie seemed to think?"

"Yes."

"Oh, perfect. Are you in?"

"Not yet, but I think I acquitted myself pretty well. I'll know more tomorrow."

She glanced at the closed bathroom door anxiously.

"Any chance you got something we can move on?"

"Not yet. No proof. Not even the name of the person

in charge." She hesitated. They hadn't ever had a chance to discuss what the endgame would be. Even if she found all the coven members, that didn't mean that any jail on earth could hold them or any jury could remain un-swayed long enough to convict them.

"Great." Ed sighed.

"You shouldn't have risked calling. Is everything okay?" she asked.

"No."

"What happened?"

"If you're asking, then I'm guessing you haven't seen the news yet."

"No," she said, a chill dancing up her spine. "Why? Has another girl turned up dead?"

"Not in the way you think. Turn it on," he said.

She picked up the remote and turned the television on, skipping quickly to the network news. A man with a bushy beard was being interviewed.

"—these are very troubled young women and we should offer them help."

There was a crawl at the bottom of the screen and as she read it her heart plummeted: THREE WOMEN ACCUSED OF WITCHCRAFT KILLED BY OUT-OF-CONTROL MOBS.

"This can't be happening," she whispered.

"But it is," Ed replied. "The first girl was an openly practicing Wiccan. The second was just a Goth."

"And the third?" she asked, her throat constricting.

"Killed at a supermarket where she stopped to buy a few things on her way home from a funeral. Customers saw the black dress, shoes, hat . . . That was all it took."

"I don't understand."

"Neither do we. The guy who threw the first punch was Lopez."

"Sergeant Lopez?" she asked.

"The same."

"I don't believe it."

"I wouldn't either if I hadn't talked to a dozen witnesses and seen the security camera footage. Something's happening. It's making people crazy."

"Like the people in the hotel who came after Katie," she mused.

"Exactly."

"I'm sure the witch who came after Katie incited the crowd."

"But what do they possibly have to gain by these killings?" he asked. "This whole thing makes no sense. I mean, it's like they want witches to get killed."

"No, just people that others mistake for witches," she said, correcting him.

"Yeah, I guess you're right. Anyway, if you've got any theories, we'd love to hear them. Roberts is going crazy. Frankly, so am I. What's worse is I've got guard duty so I'm not even out there trying to solve this thing. Please tell me there's good news on your end soon."

"I at least passed the first hurdle."

"Oh, so the hard part's over," he said drily.

"Don't I wish."

"You holding up okay?"

"I—" She stopped, suddenly feeling eyes on her. "It's complicated. Look, I've got to go."

"What, you got a guy in your room?" he asked.

When she didn't say anything, he said, "Are you kidding me? You? You play witch for like a day and you go totally crazy." He chuckled slightly. "I'm not sure if I should be proud or disappointed."

"It's . . . complicated," she reiterated, fighting the irritation that she was feeling.

"Okay, I hear you. Just be careful, okay?"

"Thanks. You too."

She disconnected the call and turned to see Anthony staring at her. His eyes then shifted slightly and she could tell he was staring at the newscast.

Everything is spinning out of control and I'm not even in the coven yet. I've used magic to harm someone else, I lost my head kissing someone who I should be steering clear of, and now innocents are being hunted down and killed. And this is just the beginning. How much worse is it going to get?

"Three witches killed?" He raised an eyebrow and looked at her. "Friends of yours?"

"No!" she snapped. She shut off the television. "They weren't even witches."

"You want to tell me what's really happening here?"

"I wish I knew," she said grimly. "All I know is something is backward. Seriously, seriously wrong."

He sat down on the chair by the desk, grimacing at her makeshift altar. "I've been thinking the same thing about you."

"Look, I told you, no spell, no nothing. Obviously there's some sort of freaky chemistry between us. So I'll stay out of your way if you'll stay out of mine."

He regarded her for a minute and then shook his head. "Not good enough."

"What do you mean?"

"I saw the look in your eyes when you realized witches were coming here. Now you claim to be a witch—"

She snapped her fingers and all the candles lit again. He jumped and his eyes grew round, but he clenched his jaw and continued. "And maybe that's what you are. But you hate witches."

"I don't know what you're trying to get at," she said. She was torn, struggling with how she felt. It was wrong to endanger him, but she was terrified and didn't want to face everything that was coming alone.

"My point is, if you're on some kind of witch hunt, count me in."

"I thought you wanted to get as far away from me as possible."

"I do, but . . . It's complicated," he said at last with a sigh. "Earlier you mentioned the girls being killed in Boston. Look, I don't like what you are, but something tells me you've got an endgame here that I can get behind. I don't even know why I think that. Just something in my gut, I guess."

"This isn't about revenge or righting old wrongs. This is here and now and very dangerous."

"I don't care. I've been waiting my whole life to stop a witch. Maybe you're right. I might never meet the witch I've sworn to kill. But that doesn't mean I can't stop another witch from taking away some other little boy's mother. Let me do this. I need to help. There was no one to help me and I wish there had been."

Her throat tightened and she felt tears stinging her eyes. She'd been lucky. She'd been raised by adoptive parents who had worked hard to help her overcome the wounds of the past and put them in perspective. If they hadn't been there for her, there was no telling what would have happened, who she would have become. And Anthony didn't have anyone to help him make the same journey.

She swallowed hard and looked away from him so he wouldn't see the emotions she was struggling to suppress.

"Okay, you're in," she whispered.

God help us both.

14

The stench of blood filled the air, along with a thicker, more sulfurous scent. Abigail stood next to an altar inside a ring of fire. On the altar a variety of animals lay dead, lifeless eyes staring right at her. Each member of the coven had brought an animal for the sacrifice. She had been supposed to bring a squirrel, but she couldn't bring herself to harm one. Sometimes she would watch them from her bedroom window, admiring their daring and wishing she could pet their bushy tails. Instead she had brought a rat. Her mother had been furious with her, but had believed her when she lied and said she couldn't trap a squirrel.

At last Abigail picked up the rat and she held her breath. Abigail slit its throat and dumped its body on the pile with the rest. Just as she started to exhale, the old witch spun around and pinned her with her eyes.

"You! Come here!"

And suddenly she was running forward, against her will. It felt like a hand was tightening around her throat, yanking her step by step.

"Do you know why I sacrifice these animals?" Abigail leered down into her face.

She shook her head, terror filling her.

"So that I may be as feared in death as I am in life. Now, I need just one more thing."

Abigail brought her athame up, dripping blood, and tapped it against Samantha's cheek. "The blood of a witch."

And then the blade cut deep, ripping into her face. She screamed and cried, but Abigail kept going. She slashed cheeks and forehead and nose and lips. When she was done, she shoved Samantha back into the circle.

"Next time don't lie," the witch hissed.

Samantha couldn't see through the blood that had dripped into her eyes and she whimpered in fear. She reached out her hand. "Mommy?"

And because she had lied about the squirrel, her mother slapped her so hard she fell to her knees. And in her heart she cried out for someone to save her.

Even though no one could.

Morning dawned and this time it didn't chase the nightmares away. Samantha woke Anthony, who stared up at her groggily. "What happened?" he asked. "The last thing I remember is you had agreed I could help."

"You fell asleep," she said shortly.

She didn't tell him it was because she had put him back to sleep. She had spent hours pacing the room, thinking about what was coming next before finally falling asleep herself.

Bridget frightened her. But she wasn't the high priestess for the coven. The very thought of confronting the witch who held that distinction made her blood run cold.

She also thought about what was happening back in Boston with the murders of the women accused of being witches. It seemed insane. She could hardly believe that the witch hysteria was beginning all over again in the twenty-first century. But Ed had confirmed that the news reports were accurate.

And I saw the mob that tried to kill Katie with my own

eyes, she remembered. They had been unhinged, and they had turned so swiftly and so violently.

Almost like magic.

The more she thought about it, the more convinced she became that the witch—Naomi, she had learned her name was—must have incited the crowd to riot to help cover her own attack.

"So what now?"

She jumped, startled, and turned to look at Anthony as he exited the bathroom. His hair was slicked back and his face freshly scrubbed. He looked so intent, so earnest. She felt herself softening toward him.

And a moment later she silently rebuked herself for it. He was a civilian. One who had already lost far too much to witches.

"Now we get you out of here without anyone noticing," she said, forcing a smile.

"You said I could help and I'm holding you to it," he replied, staring into her eyes.

"I don't want you to get hurt," she admitted.

"Either way, I'm not letting this go. So if you want to protect me, you're going to have to keep an eye on me. Seems like at that point it would just be easier to work together."

"I can't fault your logic. I just don't like it," she admitted.

"So, what are you? A cop?"

"All you need to know right now is I'm someone who wants the killing—*all* of the killing—stopped."

"What can I do?"

"I could use your help figuring out where the witches are meeting, who they are, anything and everything. But you need to be subtle. If they suspect what you're doing, they won't hesitate to kill you."

He grinned. "I own the Museum of the Occult. People get suspicious if I'm *not* snooping around and asking about supernatural things."

"Point taken."

"So, how do I get in contact with you? I mean, besides just showing up at your door again," he asked, looking a little sheepish.

"It's better if I contact you. I have a lot to do today, so let's say sometime tomorrow."

"Nice and ambiguous," he said suspiciously.

"It's the best I can do. But I will be in contact. Besides, as you pointed out, you know where I live."

"Okay, so how do we get out of here?"

"Through the front door. But quietly."

She walked him down the hall and they stood as far from each other as they could in the elevator. She could still feel a connection with him, energy arcing back and forth between them, and she clenched her fists, struggling to control the feelings that he was bringing out in her.

Once they'd stepped out of the elevator into the lobby, she took his arm and they walked swiftly to the front door. She didn't have to worry about the older man at the front desk; he was busy sorting through bills for departing guests and didn't even see them.

At the door she hesitated, stretching out and feeling the air around her. She couldn't sense anything. She touched Anthony's face and the light seemed to bend around it for a moment. It was the closest thing to temporary invisibility she could give him.

"Go quickly and don't stop for anything until you're safe at home," she said.

He nodded, the fear in her voice reflected in his eyes.

Then he slipped outside and, hands in his pockets, made his way quickly up Essex Street.

She watched him until he was out of sight and then closed her eyes and kept track of him for another few moments before his energy was lost to her.

She turned and headed back to her room. She just prayed that no one had connected her with Anthony yet. It had been stupid and sloppy to let him get so close. She was in no mood for breakfast, especially not when she planned on returning to the Witchery in a couple of hours.

She wasn't sure if Bridget would approach her there or not, but it was where she had told Karen, Autumn, and Jace she would be.

She managed to nap for another hour before getting up and preparing for the rest of her day. She was nervous, frightened for herself, for Anthony, and for the unknown girls who might already be on the coven's radar. It was for them that she was doing this and she reminded herself of the girls who had already died.

Finally ready to face whatever was coming, she left her hotel and walked slowly to the microbrewery. She stayed on the opposite side of the street from the Museum of the Occult but was intensely grateful to see that it was open for business. Unless Anthony had employees, that meant he had made it home safe.

The same guy was working at the front of the Witchery when she went in, but this time he didn't even glance at her as she walked past, heading for the back room.

She took the same seat she'd been in the day before and settled down to wait. But within moments waves of energy were rippling through the air, causing her hair to stand on end. The amount of energy they were putting

out guaranteed that it wasn't coming from any of the
three girls she'd met with the day before.

Something was wrong. Before she could make a
move, though, four cloaked figures flowed into the room,
fanning out around the perimeter. Studying them, Samantha realized that Bridget had sent some of the fierc-
est, most powerful witches she had ever encountered.
The door to the room slammed shut and locked itself.
Samantha forced herself to sit still, passive, struggling
not to betray any signs of the terror she was feeling.

Black swirls of mist wrapped around the witches,
spreading out into the room. The lights dimmed and
dark shapes blocked the windows until there was barely
enough illumination to see the hooded figures. Shadows
slid across the floor toward her and she forced herself
not to shudder. Suddenly they were wrapping around
her ankles, binding them to the chair.

Terror flared through her and for a moment she was
a child again, having to face those who would sit in judg-
ment on her. This time, though, the stakes were much
higher. It wasn't a matter of when she'd be initiated into
the coven. It was a matter of whether she would be
killed before she could be.

She placed her right hand on the table moments before another shadow bound her left to the arm of her
chair. She sent out a light electrical pulse with her right
hand, determined to keep it free. The shadow that slid
toward it across the table was momentarily rebuffed.

*We are here to judge you, Samantha Castor, and see if
you are worthy.*

The voice filled the space, though she knew from experience that the words had not been spoken out loud.
There was extra emphasis placed on the name, and she
could feel it pull her. But she was not Samantha Castor,

not truly, and she was able to keep her wits about her despite the spells that were seeking to strip her bare so that her soul would be exposed.

She drummed her fingers lightly on the table, focusing on the sound, the feel, the sight of the rhythmic tapping. It would help to save her.

The air was filled with the sudden screaming of dozens of tormented souls, making her eardrums throb and her heart race. Wind rushed through the room close behind, lifting her hair and plucking at her clothes with icy fingers.

If you are not worthy, you will die.

One by one the others repeated it.

You will die.

You will die.

You will die.

The tallest figure produced a poppet and began wrapping a dark cord around it. *We bind you, Samantha Castor, that you may tell no lies and do no magic while you are tested.*

She struggled with her fear, the feelings of helplessness and despair that crept over her. She reminded herself that they had bound Samantha Castor and that wasn't her, not really. The spell was only partly effective. She sent a small burst of energy out of her free hand just to reassure herself. But she knew she had to be careful. If they suspected it was not her true name, then nothing could save her.

You will tell us who you are.

She could feel the truth and the lies colliding in her brain, the boundaries between them eroding. She opened her mouth and carefully measured the words as she said them. "I am a daughter of the darkness. Born a witch. I was one of the Castors but now I am—" She bit her tongue hard to keep herself from saying the next word and betraying her adopted last name and everything that went with it.

Now you are what?

Sweat beaded on her forehead, dripping into her eyes. Her pulse skidded out of control, more than enough to reveal her as a liar on a mechanical lie detector. But this wasn't mechanical; this was magical. And they were counting on the fact that she would be compelled to tell the truth.

"Now I am the only Castor left," she forced out with a gasp.

The pressure inside her head became unbearable and she choked back a cry of pain.

You will tell us why you have come here.

"I am the summoned. I seek my summoner," she said. "I have the mark of my coven and now someone else has it too."

One of the witches waved a hand and Samantha's tattoo appeared in the air for all to see. The symbol had frightened the three witches the day before, but there was no such flurry of fear now.

We all bear that mark. We honor the coven that came before us in this place and we carry on its traditions.

"Then all of you summoned me."

She tried to close her burning eyes against the pain. She could feel warm liquid leaking from them down her cheeks and realized from the smell that it was blood.

Pain and blood had constituted the majority of her childhood. and now she could feel the part of her that had never forgotten it wanting to curl into the fetal position and sob.

Why have you come now?

"Because you endanger everyone with your carelessness, your stupidity. Those girls . . . they haven't gone unnoticed and it's only a matter of time before the whole world knows who we are and where to find us. The first and greatest rule is that we must protect the secret."

The words came flowing out of her in a torrent and she listened to herself, amazed at how good it sounded, stunned that the truth was still hers alone. She drummed her fingers harder, unable to stop herself from sending up a prayer that the nightmare would be over soon. As soon as she did that, she felt time slow down. Her new religion also believed in power. The power of prayer. They would surely sense that she had done something.

The figure to the far left cocked its head as if listening to some distant song. And then a man's voice spoke the words out loud. "There's power coming off her. She's not fully bound."

And in that moment Samantha knew that she was going to die. Voices screamed in her head. The witch on the right lunged forward, an athame gripped in a strong hand with wicked daggers for fingernails. The slithering shadows rushed her, flowing over her, through her, driving the life out of her.

She felt her heart slow, felt her body spasming in shock as something dug sharp talons into her chest.

Going to die, going to die, going to die!

It was the same voice that had spoken in the house. Panic consumed her. She was still in the house, trapped with Ed. A scream was ripped from her throat and white-hot pain raced down every nerve ending.

She looked down and saw a hand gripping her arm, pulsing with killing energy. Blood was flowing from her own eyes, ears, and nose, running down her face and spattering on her shirt.

She tried to stand up, but her feet were still lashed to

the chair. She tried to jerk her arm out of the witch's grip, but it too was bound.

But her right one wasn't, she remembered. It was still drumming on the table. She slammed her hand down flat and pushed with everything she had in her.

There was a crack and then the table exploded outward in a thousand shards as sharp as daggers. One witch fell silently, a four-inch chunk of wood embedded in her eye. Another was knocked off her feet and hit the ground hard with a dozen projectiles sticking out of her chest.

With a shout, the witch farthest from her hurled an athame at her head. She reached up with her free hand and yanked the woman who was holding her into its path. She fell, the dagger lodged in her throat.

Samantha lifted her hand toward the remaining attacker, but before she could do anything she was thrown backward. Still lashed to the chair, she slammed into the wall behind her so hard she felt bones crunching on impact.

Bridget stood in the doorway, her eyes glowing, her face twisted in malice. An unseen force grabbed Samantha's free hand and crushed the bones. She tried to scream, but something scaly and slithery moved swiftly across her shoulder and clamped itself over her mouth. She breathed in the stench of death and decay and began to gag.

"Enough!" Bridget thundered.

The witch who'd thrown the athame slunk behind her like a cur while the one with a chestful of shrapnel dragged herself across the floor using only her fingernails until she could touch the toe of Bridget's shoe.

And Samantha understood just how desperately she had underestimated Bridget's power.

"Do you yield to me?" Bridget demanded.

All Samantha could do was make a gurgling sound as she struggled to free herself from the things that were binding her.

Bridget snapped her fingers and the unseen serpent slithered away from her mouth.

"Never!" Samantha hissed. She closed her eyes, preparing for death.

And Bridget chuckled.

Samantha opened her eyes and stared at the witch. The light was slowly fading from her eyes and her features were twisted in amusement. "Do you join me?"

Samantha waited a beat and then nodded.

Bridget waved her hand and the shadows retreated from the room. Samantha's arms and legs were suddenly free and she lurched out of the chair, standing on unsteady feet as her starved lungs gulped in fresh air.

"You have proven a worthy adversary, Samantha. It is my wish that you prove yourself an even worthier ally."

Samantha nodded again, not yet trusting herself to speak. The truth spell had dissipated along with everything else, but she was too shaken to chance saying the wrong thing.

Bridget leaned down and plucked a piece of wood from the one witch's chest. She examined it closely. "Inspired. I never would have thought of turning the table into a bomb," she admitted.

"I've never conjured a spirit snake," Samantha said, thinking of the thing that had silenced her.

Bridget shrugged. "Once you learn how, it's as natural as breathing. It's one of the first things my high priestess taught me."

"Are you sure you're not the high priestess?" Samantha asked.

Bridget smiled. "I'm sure."

She turned to the man behind her. "Randy, see to her," she said, indicating the woman at her feet. "And bury them," she said, casting a single glance at each of the bodies.

He nodded.

"Samantha and I are going to get to know each other better," Bridget said.

She extended her hand and Samantha took it, shuddering inwardly at the contact. She felt as if she were holding hands with the devil herself.

15

Samantha walked beside Bridget as they left the Witchery, struggling to control herself every step of the way. Every instinct she had screamed at her to arrest the woman. But they didn't have any evidence to convict her in the girls' deaths. Worse, there wasn't a jail anywhere that would be able to hold her, even if Samantha could succeed in arresting her.

Better just to kill her. Do it quick before she knows what hit her.

The voice inside her head tempted her and the harder she tried to ignore it, the louder it got. The truth was that even if she did kill Bridget, and then ran back inside and arrested or killed Randy and the other witch in there, the coven would still exist. By her own admission Bridget was not the high priestess. Not only would killing her not stop the coven or its plans, but it would make the rest of them that much harder to find.

So, as much as she hated it, she had to walk hand in hand with the other woman and hold her tongue until she could find out enough to take everyone down.

"I was watching you in there," Bridget said as they moved away from the restaurant. "I could tell they hadn't fully bound you. It was sloppy of them not to notice. What I didn't catch, though, was what tipped them off."

Samantha couldn't tell her that she had prayed and the others had felt that surge of power from her. She had to come up with a plausible alternative. She took a deep breath and was relieved when an answer came to her.

"My body started to fight back because of the pain and the damage they were inflicting. It was an autonomic response, but one that used my powers. I couldn't stop it."

"That makes sense."

Samantha was relieved that Bridget didn't question the lie. Although the prayer had functioned much the same way—it had been her soul's response, something she had no control over when it happened.

"So, why the test? It just pissed me off and got two of your coven killed."

Bridget chuckled. "There are always more to take their place. Besides, it was more a test of my people than you."

"So they failed, then."

She nodded. "No matter. Nothing ventured, nothing gained. And now we have you on our side. You're easily worth a dozen of them. It's like getting an entire coven wrapped up in one."

The other woman was deliberately flattering her. Samantha decided to let it go.

"Bridget—one of the names of the goddess. Interesting choice," she said, subtly fishing for information as to whether it was her real name.

"Not really. My mother was a Wiccan. She had a whole list that she was going to name her daughters. I was the only one, though. I heard what you said back there," Bridget said, changing the subject suddenly.

"Which thing?" Samantha asked, instantly on guard.

"About being here because you were worried that we were being careless, stupid."

"Oh."

"We're not," Bridget said, a note of pride in her voice. "It's all part of a plan. A glorious plan."

"Who are you trying to resurrect?" Samantha asked.

Bridget stopped walking and turned to her, clearly startled. "How did you know about that?" she asked, the color draining from her face.

Samantha smiled slowly. "I might have been gone for a few years, but that doesn't mean I don't know when big things are happening in my town."

Bridget chewed her lip for a moment, and that sign of distress in a witch as powerful as she was unnerved Samantha a bit.

"You deserve to know. You should know. You of all people could help us so much."

"I agree. So, tell me who." •

"Abigail Temple."

Samantha began to shake from head to toe as she stared in horror at her.

Bridget mistook the emotion and reached out to grip Samantha's hands. "I know—amazing, right? And so very exciting. Samantha, I cannot wait to meet her. Imagine, your high priestess alive again!"

Samantha could imagine, all too well, the death and destruction that would follow as night to day. The woman she'd feared for twelve years. The ghost who had haunted her dreams nearly every night since. They were trying to resurrect her old high priestess and then she would likely try to take over, restore her way of doing things.

And risk killing them all once again.

"I can't imagine," Samantha whispered.

And from the blissful smile on Bridget's face, Samantha knew that neither could she.

"When?" Samantha forced herself to ask.

"Soon. I promise," Bridget said.

"You're going to need more girls to sacrifice," Samantha said.

Bridget smiled. "Don't worry. We've got that all taken care of."

"I want in."

"Of course you do," Bridget said. "And you will be. But first . . ."

"What?"

"Well, the high priestess wants you to go through a few more tests."

Samantha snapped, "No more tests. I think I've proven who I am and what I'm capable of."

"I agree. But she has a way she likes things to be done," Bridget said with a sigh. "Patience. We're doing some spellcasting tomorrow night and you can join us then."

"Where?"

"At Abigail's old home. You remember it, of course?"

She would never forget it. And after her brief trip there with Ed she was pretty sure the house would remember her too.

"I can't wait," she forced herself to say.

The pain from her injuries was kicking into high gear as the shock wore off. She gritted her teeth against it and willed herself to keep walking. The injuries were extensive enough that doing some quick, minor healing wouldn't help. It was going to take everything she had and she didn't dare let her guard down that much in front of Bridget.

"Several of your coven members are wearing the tattoo that was the mark of my coven without having belonged to it and earning the right to do so. Abigail will not be as forgiving as I am."

Bridget smiled, though there was a hint of uncertainty in her eyes. "We figure that by raising her from the dead we will have proven our worthiness to be her new coven and she will forgive us the premature use of the symbol. Besides, we're raising the dead. Who is more godlike than us?"

Giving life to that which was lifeless was the ultimate act of creation and spoken of in most religions. But what they were attempting could hardly be called creation; it was more like reanimation.

The pain was becoming so intense that Samantha had to concentrate hard just to keep from screaming. "But why my coven?" she asked. "Why even bother resurrecting her? It seems like you have a fully functioning coven on your own."

"Please, you're being too modest. Surely you know that the dark feats of your coven are legendary? Every witch with any shred of imagination would give almost anything to have that type of power. When our high priestess called us together it was clear that she had the power, the will, and the vision to re-create the most dangerous coven that ever walked the earth."

"Power is a double-edged sword. It also cuts the one who wields it."

"Which is why she is so cautious, even with you," Bridget said.

Bridget left her when they reached the Hawthorne. Samantha hadn't been able to glean anything else from her comments.

Samantha made it to her room and then collapsed, feeling sick and exhausted and overwhelmed. Bones in her right hand had been broken, along with a couple of ribs. She had been barely able to stave off the pain while she was with Bridget. Now it overwhelmed her.

She reached deep inside herself and called up the reserves of strength she needed. She screamed into a pillow on the bed to muffle the sound so hotel security wouldn't show up while she was fixing her bones. Healing them by magic was fast but far more painful than letting them heal on their own. It leached the strength and the energy out of her entire body, leaving her shaking uncontrollably. Her body temperature began to drop and she crawled under the down comforter, her teeth chattering.

Though she desperately hoped for warmth, the thermostat on the wall across the room mocked her. She didn't have the strength to walk to it to raise the temperature, nor did she have the magical energy left to push the button remotely.

As she lay shivering and healing, tears ran down her face, washing away the blood that she had forgotten was there and staining her shirt and the pillow.

At last the healing was over and she lay, half conscious, unable to go to sleep like she wanted to so badly and also unable to wake up enough to get to the bathtub. It was the cost of magic, the terrible burden that most people never dreamed of.

I can't do it, she thought. *I was crazy to think I could come back and handle all of this.*

Her thoughts drifted to Anthony. He was different from any man she had ever met. Was she attracted to him because the darkness had also touched his life? He could truly understand her past, her pain. She wished he were with her now, even though he was little more than a stranger.

She drifted in and out of consciousness, battling through the pain and fear. When there was a sound at her door she barely had the ability to turn her head to look at it. A minute later Anthony was sitting on the bed beside her. When had he gotten there? He was saying something and she struggled to focus. Finally she made out the word "hospital."

"No," she forced herself to say, though the voice didn't sound like hers. He was picking her up, holding her in his arms. His body was so warm. She clung to him, trying to feel just a little of that warmth herself. And then, finally, she fell asleep.

"You're lazy," the man accused her.

She whimpered in her throat. She wasn't lazy—she was afraid.

When Samantha woke it was nighttime. She blinked sleepily, the room slowly coming into focus. She heard a sound and managed to lift her head a couple of inches. Anthony was sitting on the foot of the bed, munching away on a burger, a take-out container next to him.

"Hello?"

He turned, a look of relief spreading across his face. "You're awake."

"What are you doing in my hotel room?"

"Watching over you."

"Why?"

He raised an eyebrow. "Because you clearly need it, at least from what I've seen."

She closed her eyes for a moment, trying to summon the strength of will to talk to him. "We agreed I'd see you tomorrow."

"Yeah, about that—I got a feeling you needed me today. When I got here I could see that I was right. What happened to you?"

"Fight."

"Ouch. Sorry."

"I won."

He gave a low whistle. "I'd hate to see your idea of losing."

She struggled to sit up, wincing. Her muscles felt completely weak, as though she had been sick for days. "I got an entrée to the coven."

"Good, I think. Though from the looks of you I'm not sure that's what I should be saying."

She propped herself up and fought to stem the tide of nausea that threatened to overwhelm her. "How about you? Did you find anything?"

He smiled.

"I saw you walking with a woman earlier, name of Bridget."

"Yeah?"

"Moved here a year ago from somewhere on the West Coast. And she was already plugged in before she got here."

"So she was handpicked by the high priestess to be here."

"Sounds as though."

"Did you get a last name?"

He shook his head. "No one seemed to have ever heard one."

"Anthony, you need to be careful talking to people."

"It's okay. Like I said, people are used to my being nosy. Just wait until you hear what I heard about you."

Terror shot through her. Anthony couldn't know about her past. If he did know the truth, it might well destroy both of them. She forced herself to take a deep breath. He wasn't trying to kill her, so that must mean that he didn't know.

"What did you hear?" she forced herself to ask.

"That you're the head of the biggest coven in the south, based out of New Orleans."

Her shoulders slumped as she relaxed. "That's a good one. I've never even been to New Orleans."

He shrugged. "Sometimes you get the facts, sometimes you get the fiction."

"So how do you know which is which?" she asked.

"You don't, not always. But the one thing I've learned is that the truth always reveals itself in time."

She smiled at him even as she was praying that it wouldn't.

He handed her a bag. "I didn't know what you wanted to eat, so I just grabbed you a burger too."

"Thanks."

"I've got to get going," he said, standing up and tossing the remains of his dinner in the trash can.

"Thanks for checking up on me."

"No problem. I just got a weird feeling when I saw you walking by my museum with blondie. You didn't look okay."

"I wasn't. You've got good instincts."

"So, Samantha, what's your last name?" he asked.

She looked away. She didn't dare give him Ryan in case someone else might get it out of him. She couldn't give him Castor because then he might connect her to the coven that killed his mother. "It's Hofferman," she said, silently apologizing to Ed for appropriating his last name.

"Hofferman—okay. Well, it's been a pleasure, Samantha Hofferman."

"Please, don't use my last name. If witches discover it, they could have power over me."

"I understand. Now, you get some rest. My number's next to the phone. Call if you need anything."

As soon as he had gone, Samantha grabbed her cell phone and called Ed. He picked up immediately. "What's wrong?"

"They nearly killed me today," she said, trying her best not to lose it completely.

"Are you hurt?"

"I was. I'm better now."

"Do you need me to pull you out of there?" he asked.

"No, I'm finally in. I'm joining the coven tomorrow night for some rituals."

"Great. Tell me where and I'll have a team standing by."

"Not yet. I need to know if the high priestess is there first. And besides, these people can never be taken as a group. Our best shot is to learn their identities and pick them off one by one."

"Sounds dangerous to me. Both to us and their intended victims."

"It's the only way, though. We send in a team after them and they'll just get killed and my cover will be blown. We're going to have one shot at doing this right."

"Okay, you're the one on the inside. It's your call," he said, sounding very unhappy about it.

"You should know—I had to use your last name today."

"Excuse me?"

"An asset needed a last name and there were reasons why I couldn't give him Castor."

"Thanks, but if people talk, you're the one that gets to explain it to my wife," he said sarcastically.

"She loves me," Samantha said with a smile.

"Is there anything else you need?"

"No. Have there been any more developments?"

"Today has been mercifully quiet, as far as I can tell. But I hate babysitting. I want to go home."

"Someone has to babysit and there's no one I would trust more," she said.

"If Roberts asks, don't tell him that. Tell him to send me home."

She laughed. "I'll tell him you said so."

After she hung up she managed to drag herself to the bathroom and take a shower.

She thought about the magic she had seen performed that day. Some of it had been new to her, the rest hauntingly familiar. She still had huge gaps in her memories from childhood and it was starting to make her nervous. The trick Bridget had done with the invisible snake—should she have known how to do that? Had she known at one time?

She wondered what rituals they were going to do the next night and what they might involve. She had been setting herself up as a seasoned witch, not one with partial memories a decade and a half old. What if they asked her to do something simple and she just couldn't remember how? It wasn't just likely that it could happen—given the gaps in her memory it was probable.

After showering she put on her pajamas and sat down on the bed. What she couldn't remember could get her killed. She dug her fingernails into her palm.

She didn't want to remember. Once that door was open it could never be closed. And if she remembered too much too fast it might turn her into a babbling, incoherent mess.

She crossed her legs and said a brief prayer before she began. She took a deep breath and closed her eyes. She pictured a hallway with a dozen closed doors in it.

"My memories are locked behind these doors," she said out loud. "A childhood lost and forgotten. But the time for remembering is now."

She focused on the door nearest her and imagined herself reaching out, turning the doorknob. She took a deep breath, twisted the knob, and flung the door open.

16

The door in Samantha's mind opened wide. A howling wind came out of it, engulfing her. She tried to take a step forward, but the wind pushed her back. And then it suddenly stopped. Before she could move, a girl walked through the doorway and Samantha recognized herself at about five years of age.

Samantha didn't want to look at the child. She was terrified of what she would see, what she would remember. She could feel herself crying freely.

"Why are you crying?" the child asked.

"I'm afraid of you," Samantha said.

The child shook her head. "You don't need to be afraid of me. You should be afraid of her." She pointed to a door across the hall. The number 12 was printed on it and Samantha's skin crawled just looking at it. She turned away quickly.

The child took her hand. "I can help you," she said. "I can teach you about the snakes."

Samantha knelt so she was on eye level with the child. "Tell me how."

The girl waved her hand and then touched Samantha's forehead. A snake appeared on Samantha's shoulder and she forced herself to stay still. "A person's own fear makes the snake have weight and texture and color. You use their fear to create the snake."

Like making the tattoo artist feel like he was on fire when he wasn't, Samantha thought. She shook her head. "The snake wasn't just a manifestation of my fear. It was there. It was real."

"Of course it was." The girl put her hands together. "You create the energy. The energy is real. It has substance. Then you can mold it into whatever form you want."

As Samantha watched in amazement, the space between the girl's hands turned into a small ball of black fur. It stretched, revealing itself to be a tiny kitten. It hopped onto the girl's shoulder and began to purr, kneading her shoulder.

And Samantha remembered. "Mother wouldn't let us have a pet."

"No matter how much we asked," the girl affirmed.

"So we made ourselves a pet."

"And we listen to the kitty purr. And when Mother is near . . ."

Samantha waved her hand through the kitten, dispersing the energy, and the creature vanished.

"But he's always here in our mind and our heart," she said at the same time as her five-year-old self.

The little girl reached out and dispersed the energy of the snake and it too vanished.

"And he seems real," Samantha mused.

"He *is* real," the little girl insisted.

"Thank you," Samantha said. "What else do I need to know?"

"All magic is the working of energy, fields, magnets, electricity. You know this, but you forget. I can electrocute you or make the iron in your blood react as though it's being pulled by a magnet."

"You know a lot for one so young."

"And you know little for one so old."

They talked together for a while and little by little memories of being that age came back to her. They practiced some magic and when it was time Samantha said good-bye.

The little girl clung to her hand. "I have to tell you a secret."

"What?" Samantha asked.

The little girl glanced fearfully at the door marked 12. "It took all of us to lock her up. And to do it we had to go away too."

A shiver went up Samantha's spine. "Why did you have to lock her up?"

"So that you could be okay."

The little girl let go of her and began to back into the darkness beyond her open door.

"I don't want to lose you again," Samantha said.

"You won't," the girl said with a smile. "This door will be open now. I'll be here when you need me."

Samantha pulled herself out of her mind and slumped, exhausted. There was much that she had forgotten, but it had been such a relief to see that a part of herself still seemed innocent. It was well past midnight when she crawled under the covers and shut her eyes, hoping that there would be no nightmares, just dreams.

But she felt so alone. She wished she could share what had happened, what she'd learned, with someone else. Her mind drifted from memory to memory, some good, some bad, and it was like discovering herself.

She turned onto her side and then put her hands

close together and created a ball of energy. "Kitty," she whispered.

And a moment later a furry black kitten was snuggling against her side, yawning and purring as he kneaded the blanket beneath him.

When Samantha woke in the morning she could feel something swatting at her nose. She opened her eyes and saw the kitten batting at her.

"You're still here, Freaky?" she asked in surprise.

The kitten mewed and jumped on top of her, making Samantha smile. Her phone rang and she reached for it. It was Ed.

"What's happened?" she asked by way of answering.

"It'll be all over the news in a minute," he said, his voice grim. "Two more girls showed up dead this morning."

She waved her hand through the energy kitten, dispersing it even as it tried to chew on the phone, and she sat up. "Where?"

"Both in Marblehead. One just across the city line, and the other close to Salem."

Marblehead was a town between Salem and Boston. The locations of the other murders flashed through her mind and she suddenly realized that like the energy trail she had left for Autumn and the others to find, this was a trail of bodies, leading straight to Salem.

"Any connection to the others?"

"Not that we've found so far. I'm just finishing up here at the second scene. I'll call you in a little bit."

"Okay," she said, but he had already disconnected.

She made her way to the bathroom and splashed cold water on her face. She took her time getting dressed. Every instinct in her wanted to head to the crime scenes, but she forced herself to stay put. After a few minutes she turned on the television and saw that reporters were indeed already at both scenes.

Samantha watched, feeling somewhat numb, as the two murder scenes were described. Reporters recklessly threw around the words "witch" and "sacrifice" until she felt like she was going to be ill. If this kept up, pretty soon any death in the area would be attributed to witches whether it was true or not.

Finally she'd had enough and she turned the TV off. She wasn't doing anyone any good by letting herself dwell on it. Any real clues wouldn't be broadcast on television anyway.

She left the hotel and headed up Essex Street, her mind churning with everything that was happening. She looked intently at every person who passed her, wondering whether they knew who was involved with the coven.

When she got to Red's, she froze for a moment when she saw Ed sitting at one of the tables, staring at her. *What is he doing there?* His hand rested protectively on a manila envelope on the tabletop.

Samantha sat down at his table, glancing around quickly to see if anyone was paying attention. No one seemed to notice or care.

"I'm guessing this isn't good news," she said softly as she picked up her menu and pretended to peruse it.

"The pancakes are bigger than some countries," he noted. Speaking more softly he said, "I brought you pictures from this morning. When you've looked them over you can destroy them."

"It was a risk bringing them here."

"Worth it. Besides, I hear they have great breakfast here."

"What else is happening?"

"People were already going nuts when I left Marblehead."

"How nuts?"

"Looking to burn a witch nuts."

"That's not good," she replied.

"No. No, it's not. But that's not all. Gus, one of the frat brothers of Katie's ex, has gone missing."

"Kidnapped?"

"Inconclusive. Although I have a hunch that wherever he is, he went of his own free will."

"And why is that?" she asked.

"Remember Gus? Remember what he said to you that day we went to examine the body? Gus told you that people like you, people with power, scared him."

"I remember. It seemed very odd at the time."

"To me too, although it's starting to make a lot more sense than it did."

"What about the other guy and the current girlfriend?"

"Accounted for. And they've already moved on with their lives," he said, a look of disdain on his face. "Yeah, they got their fifteen minutes of fame and they used it to scream 'witch' to the whole world."

"What else is going on in Boston?" she asked.

"You're kidding, right?"

"No."

"You really do need to turn on the news every once in a while."

"Spare me the lecture and just tell me."

"Protests, riots. Two more women were killed late last night as they left a concert because people thought they were witches. Now activists on the other side are getting involved."

"How?" she asked.

"There've been calls for people protesting the witch hunt to come here to Salem to do it."

"Here?" she reiterated, the blood draining from her face.

"Yes."

"When?"

"This weekend. They're planning on using Salem and the upcoming Halloween parade as a forum to protest the mistreatment of witches and everyone else. Wiccans, pagans, humanists, Satanists. You name it, they're invited."

"But it's going to be a disaster!"

"I know. That's why I've come to warn you. I think you need to get out. We've been in contact with federal authorities to try to get their help. This thing is beyond all of us at this point."

"There's no reason for them to dump the bodies the way they've been doing," she said. "It would have been easy to just kill them and either hide the bodies or make it look like something else. I can't think of one good reason why they put them on display that way, risking exposure, almost welcoming it. They've been leaving the bodies like a trail of bread crumbs leading right here."

"I know. I can't figure it out either," he admitted. "They must have known it would create an uproar."

Understanding dawned on her. "They didn't just anticipate an uproar—they engineered one!"

"I don't follow."

"Remember when we saved Katie?"

"Of course."

"It took more energy than I alone had, so I pulled some from you."

"I'm not likely to forget."

"If they're actually going to pull off a resurrection spell, it will take an overwhelming amount of energy, more than they have in and of themselves. I should have thought of it before. This is the witch capital of the world, and all these murders have been happening right around here. The Halloween parade always draws huge crowds. This year, with all the attention and the craziness, there will be even more people here, some of them decrying witches, some defending them. Think of all that emotion, all that energy, all those people focused on witches in one way or another. The amount of power they'll generate will be astounding. The coven is going to kill the final victim once people are crowded into downtown when they can siphon off the energy of the crowd, the fervor of the protestors."

"They're going to do what you did to me on a grand scale?"

"Yeah. All those people are going to help bring about a monstrous thing."

"Great. There's no way to stop the people from coming either. Some of them are probably already here."

"Sorry about that," one of the waitresses said, bustling over. "What can I get you?"

Samantha ordered quickly while Ed just sipped his coffee. As soon as the waitress had left, he put down the mug. "How exactly does a resurrection spell work?"

"There's two parts to it. The first part involves the taking back of the soul. To do that requires the sacrifice of eight young women, all completely pure. Think of it as a bribe to the devil, or whatever it is that has the soul, to let it go."

He grimaced. "We know they're at least up to five. Heaven only knows if there've been more. So, what's the second part?"

"The second part is the hardest, the one that requires vast amounts of energy. In order to do a resurrection spell, the body has to be restored."

"Restored? So it looks like the person and not like a rotting corpse?"

"Exactly. Matter is never created or destroyed; it just changes form. So with enough energy, specific matter can be called back to a form it once had."

He stared at her, clearly not quite comprehending what she was saying.

"Say, for instance, that one of the women who was killed this morning was to be resurrected. Any hairs that she had on her head, any bit of skin that was on her neck where the mark is, anything that was a part of her right before she died, has to be called to wherever the body is. So if you found, for instance, a lock of her hair at the crime scene and you put it in evidence, the hair would have to be transported from that baggie in the building to her head in the coroner's office."

"Wow. Okay. But they need enough energy that they have to siphon it off thousands of people to do it?"

"Not in the example I just gave you. But if someone had been dead—say, for sixteen years—parts of them could be scattered everywhere. Drops of blood or saliva that were found at the scene and cleaned up or just left. Any minute particles that didn't get buried with them could be in a number of places. And what has been buried, well, if the coffin has decayed to the point where worms could get at the body, then you're going to have a huge problem."

"Because worms could travel," he said, turning ashen. "They could be eaten by birds or other animals. They could end up on a fisherman's hook and from there get into a fish and then into a human."

"You're starting to see the possibilities, and that's just assuming the dead person was buried instead of cremated with their ashes scattered. Suddenly you've got parts that need to be recalled from all over the world."

He looked down at his cup with a look of disgust on his face. "And that's what they need all that energy for."

"Yes."

"And let me guess—there was nothing neat and clean about the death and burial of whoever they're trying to resurrect."

"Nothing at all."

"I think I'm going to be sick," he admitted.

Samantha picked up the envelope and opened it, peering inside at the top image without taking it out. It was horrific, with yet another bloody-looking pentagram on the girl's forehead. Judging by her clothes she looked like a waitress.

"Waitress?" she asked.

He nodded. "All-night diner. That's ketchup on her forehead. Though I don't know why they don't just use blood."

"Probably because the pentagram's not part of the ritual." Samantha frowned. "But blood is, and I would think they would have been taking blood from some of the victims, although it seems they haven't."

"What does that mean?"

"I'm not sure," she admitted. "But thank you for bringing me these."

"I hope it helps."

She put the envelope next to her on the table. "I just hope I can stop this soon," she said, fear and exhaustion showing in her voice.

Ed reached across the table and took her hands, holding them while he looked into her eyes. "You've got this.

You know why? Because you're the best. And besides, you've got me."

She laughed. "What would I do without you?"

"Let's never find out," he said.

A figure suddenly loomed next to them and Samantha glanced up to see Anthony, his eyes burning with curiosity. Before she could say anything he turned to Ed. "Hello. My name's Anthony Charles. I'm a friend of Samantha's."

He stuck out his hand and Ed let go of hers to shake it. "Ed Hofferman. Nice to meet you."

Anthony looked stricken and turned accusing eyes on her. Samantha opened her mouth quickly to explain, but he cut her off. "See you around, *Mrs.* Hofferman."

He turned and stalked out the door. Ed chuckled. "He's your asset?"

"Yes," she said.

"He also the guy in your room the other night?"

"Yes," she snapped, her irritation growing.

"Looks like you've got multiple people to explain things to."

She glared at him and then got up from the table. Ed threw down a couple of dollars and followed her out.

On the street she looked for Anthony but didn't see him.

"You want me to talk to him? You know, man to man?" Ed asked.

"Stop enjoying this," she hissed.

"A guy's got to find something funny at times like this."

She took a step toward Essex Street and then stopped as ripples of air washed over her and three familiar figures rounded the corner a block away.

Samantha swore under her breath and quickly turned,

pretending not to have seen them. Ed was still grinning at her, enjoying her obvious discomfort.

She shoved him against the building and then kissed him. His entire body tensed and he tried to push her away, but she whispered, softly enough that only he could hear, "We're being watched."

And then he wrapped his arms around her and began kissing her back. "I want you so bad," he said, loud enough to be easily overheard.

"All good things come to those who wait," she said. At last she pulled away and made a show of straightening her dress. "Now, be a good little boy and run along," she said.

Ed walked away. When she finally turned to watch him, she came face-to-face with Autumn, Karen, and Randy staring at her.

"I saw his badge and his gun. There's no doubt about it," Autumn said, as if finishing a conversation Samantha had not been privy to.

"Then the only question left," Randy said, crossing his arms, "is what were you doing with him? He's a cop."

17

"Idiots! Of course he's a cop," Samantha snapped, rolling her eyes. "Someone has to clean up your mess."

"You mean you seduced him?" Autumn asked skeptically.

Samantha laughed. "Of course."

"How?" Karen asked eagerly.

That's why she's here. Wicca forbids the casting of love spells on particular people. And there's someone she wants badly enough that she's willing to break that rule, and more.

Her heart was racing. If they had seen her and Ed just a few minutes earlier . . . The envelope with the crime scene photos was tucked into the back of her waistband, beneath her shirt. She wasn't out of the woods yet. She felt sure she could control Karen and Autumn. She would just have to use that against Randy, who was still somewhat of an unknown in the equation regardless of his participation the day before.

"Has no one taught you, sweet Karen?" Samantha said, dropping her voice slightly.

She shook her head.

"How about you, Autumn?" Samantha said, pinning the other with her eyes.

"No," Autumn said, licking her lips.

Samantha cocked her head to the side. "Are you attracted to me, Autumn?" she asked, making her voice sound husky.

"Of course not. I'm into guys."

"Really?" Samantha asked. She took two steps closer so that she invaded Autumn's comfort zone. Had the girl not been standing with her back to the wall, she would have tried to retreat a step or two. Her discomfort with the closeness was immediately apparent.

"Do you know what . . . lust . . . desire . . . is?" Samantha asked, her voice softer.

"Of course. It's when you want—"

"It's a chemical reaction in the brain," Samantha said, interrupting her. She lifted her hand and stroked Autumn's cheek, letting mild electricity from her fingers tickle the nerve endings in the woman's skin.

"Stop," Autumn said, her voice higher, panicky.

"That's what you say," Samantha said. She took a step closer so that their bodies were nearly touching. "But it's not what you mean," she whispered.

Autumn had begun to tremble. Samantha let her fingers trail down her jaw, then the side of her neck, down her shoulder and arm, and then she took Autumn's hand in hers. She accelerated Autumn's heart rate, forced her lungs to take more shallow breaths.

"Desire," she said, "is just a physical reaction. You, me, our bodies touching."

She leaned closer so that her lips were less than an inch from Autumn's. "Our breath mingling together."

Autumn's pupils had dilated wide and Samantha stared deep into them. "Who do you belong to?"

"You," Autumn whispered.

Samantha stepped back and smiled. Autumn stood, blinking at her, clearly confused and unnerved.

"That's how you seduce someone, Karen."

Karen was staring at her, eyes bugging out of her head. Next to her Randy snickered.

"Problem?" Samantha asked, raising an eyebrow.

He raised his hands. "Not in the least."

He was strong and he was confident. He'd been the last one standing of the four witches that attacked her the day before. And he was the only one unscathed.

"How's your friend with the chest full of table?" Samantha asked.

His face darkened. "She'll live," he said abruptly, then turned away.

Samantha turned back to the two women. "I'll see you tonight," she said.

They both nodded. Autumn still looked dazed. A woman walked out of the restaurant, brushing past Karen. Karen didn't even seem to notice the contact, but instead kept staring admiringly at Samantha.

She wants to learn how to do that to someone.

"See you," Samantha said again, eager to leave. She quickly walked away, heading for the main street, anxious to put the others behind her. As soon as she got to Essex Street, she looked around but saw no sign of either Ed or Anthony.

Ed, hopefully, was on his way back to Boston. She turned right toward Anthony's museum, hoping to catch him there. The street was more crowded than it had been earlier and she couldn't help but think of what Ed had said about people planning to come in to protest the witch persecution.

Finally she reached the museum. A couple of people were inside, looking at the displays in the front. She walked to the back, eager to find him and set things straight. As she worked her way through the museum, though, her anxiety was slowly replaced by anger. He had called her by name in public. She was just lucky she hadn't given him her real last name. Her frustration over his assumption about Ed, the fury she felt at herself for caring what he thought, and the lingering fear about being discovered by the witches added to that annoyance, until when she found him at last, working on one of the displays, she was out of control.

He stood up and looked at her. "What do you want?"

She wanted nothing more than to wipe the scornful look off his face.

She slapped him across the face, shocking both of them.

"What was that for?" he demanded.

"I told you not to use my name in public," she said. "And for jumping to conclusions."

"Sorry—what's a guy to think, though, when he meets a girl's husband?"

"He is not my husband," she said fiercely. "Did you even stop to think that he could be my brother . . . or a cousin? Did you?"

"No, I guess I didn't," he said, blinking in surprise.

"That's right—you didn't. He wasn't supposed to come here; it's too dangerous. But he had information he had to share about the latest victims. And now it's all a mess. Three witches saw him talking to me and they figured out he was a cop."

"So you are a cop!" he said.

"Do you want me to hit you again?" she asked, a note of warning in her voice.

"Not particularly."

"Then just stop. Anthony, I've told you: The less you know about who I am, about what I am, the better . . . for both of us."

"But I can't help myself. I want to know. You're such a pile of contradictions it's driving me crazy."

It had been a mistake coming here. She should have known better. There would have been no harm in letting him continue to think the way he did. In the long run it would have been much safer, much easier. But she couldn't entirely control herself where he was concerned.

She had been devastated when she realized he thought she was married. The attraction she felt for him would have been dangerous, something to avoid at all costs, if she was merely undercover. But coupled with the history they had together that he was unaware of, that attraction made being around him deadly.

"I don't know what I'm thinking," she said. "It's too dangerous for us to be near each other. I have a job to do and you're just distracting me from it. Making me think things I shouldn't."

She turned to go, but he reached out and grabbed her arm. "There's something here—don't you feel it?"

"All too much," she whispered.

She was staring across the room, right at the display case that held her artifacts. And even though she was much farther away than she had been the other day, the goblet was beginning to glow. She spun to face him, desperate that he not see what she was looking at.

"I don't understand you. You're a witch and yet you hate witches. You want to destroy them, but you won't let me help, not really. One minute you seem attracted to me and the next I feel like you hate me. And that's just you. I've got so many conflicted feelings about you. My life has always been simple. I like simple. I understand simple. You are very, very complicated. And I think that's one of the things that fascinates me about you."

She looked into his eyes. "Anthony, I'm too complicated," she said. "Trust me, you don't need what I'd bring into your life."

"Shouldn't that be my choice, not yours?"

He was close to her, close enough to kiss her. He leaned down, but before their lips touched, his eyes grew wide and he jerked.

"What on earth?"

She could tell what he was looking at, didn't need to see for herself. The glowing goblet was reflected in his eyes. He let go of her and moved as one in a dream toward the display case that held it. She turned around to watch but took a few steps back, struggling to put more distance between herself and the cursed thing.

"Do you see that?" he demanded, but he didn't look at her. He just kept walking forward.

Staring at the goblet in horror, she didn't answer. What was worse, she knew the goblet was hers, knew that it was used in certain types of rituals, but for the life of her she couldn't remember what kind.

When Anthony reached the case, he placed his hand on the glass, staring for a moment. Then he pulled a key ring out of his pocket and moved toward the lock.

"No!" she shouted, lunging forward. She reached his side and grabbed his arm before he could unlock the case. "Don't open it!"

"Why? What does it do?" he asked in a hard voice.

"I—I don't know, but whatever it does, it's active right now. Touching it could be incredibly dangerous."

He nodded slowly and then turned troubled eyes on her. "But why now? I've never seen it glow before."

She shook her head, wishing she had an answer she could give him. "Maybe there's something triggering it."

"You're here," he said.

She licked her lips. "I suppose it's possible that the presence of a magic user, the disturbance in the environment, could—"

"But it wasn't glowing when you were here the other day," he interrupted, running a hand through his hair.

So he hadn't seen it that day, she realized as relief swept through her. She chose her next words carefully. "You said that this belonged to the coven that killed your mother."

He nodded.

"Maybe something the coven I'm hunting is doing is triggering this. If we knew what kind of ritual it was used for, we might be able to find that out, even pinpoint the location of the coven."

"I know exactly what it was used for," he said darkly.

"What?"

"Human sacrifice."

She thought she was going to be sick. If that was true, then what did it mean for her? For her past? *What have I done?* And then an echo of a nightmare came back to her. *Who have I killed?*

"How do you know?" she asked.

"Years of research. It's based on a much older design that was used for the same purpose a few centuries earlier in Europe. I've often wondered if it was used in my mother's sacrifice."

"No!" she burst out, louder than she meant to.

He looked at her, startled.

"No," she said more quietly. "You—you can't think like that. You don't know for sure that's the type of ritual it was used for. And even if it was, you can't tie it directly to your mother's death and you shouldn't, for your own sanity."

"I guess you're right. It's just the not knowing that

eats me up inside. They took more than my mother from me that night. They took my innocence, my peace of mind, my future."

"You needn't let them continue to take those things," she said, grabbing his hand.

He sighed. "I just can't fight this feeling, this belief that the two are connected somehow. What's happening now with what happened then."

"You're very likely right to make the connections." She let her eyes rove over the other items in the case. "Tell me about this coven, the older one."

He sighed. "From all accounts, there were thirty members. Twenty-nine perished in a single hour. The official reports never say how, but references are made to rivers of blood and torn limbs. A few years ago I tracked down an Officer Roberts, who was one of the police at the scene. He refused to talk about what he'd seen. And when I pressed, he just shook like a leaf and stopped even looking at me. I can't imagine what would be so horrific he wouldn't be able to talk about it after all these years."

She could.

Anthony pointed to a group of pictures in the right corner of the case that she hadn't even noticed before. "Those were the members I could confirm."

She recognized each face even though she struggled with remembering some of the names. For one of them, though, she didn't need to read the nameplate. It was her mother. She looked young in the picture, younger than Samantha's memories of her. She was wearing a white shirt with billowy sleeves and a low, scoop neckline. Samantha froze, realizing that through the gauzy material she could just barely make out the lines of her mother's tattoo. *My tattoo.*

"As near as I can figure, the coven had been operating here for about twenty years," Anthony continued. "They slowly amassed more and more power, strength. Until slowly wasn't good enough for them anymore. I'm not sure what they were trying to accomplish with the human sacrifices, but my mom was at least the third. She was pregnant with what would have been my baby brother."

The news shook Samantha to her core and wrenched an anguished groan from her lips. He turned and looked at her, eyes moist. "Sorry. I didn't mean to lay all this on you."

"So much pain," she whispered. She just wanted to make it stop. His and hers. She reached up and touched his cheek. He put his hand over hers and the tears began to flow freely down his face. And then they were kissing, trying to lose themselves in each other, trying to hide from the pain and the terror.

She could feel him wrap his arms around her, pulling her close. But it wasn't enough. She needed to shut out the voices in her head, the ones that whispered that she was to blame, that if only he knew, he would never touch her like this. But she was crying too. A lifetime of fear and sorrow needed to be swept away and tears alone were not enough.

"Samantha, I need you," he whispered against her ear.

"I need you more," she reassured him.

Something was happening between them. She could sense the changes. The kisses were becoming more frantic. Her hands roamed over his body and she thrilled to his touch as his did the same to her.

She felt like she was falling from a great height and all the things she'd never said to anyone, never done with anyone, swirled in her mind. And she wanted to say them to him, to do them with him. And by the way he was touching her, the way he kept repeating her name, she knew he wanted that too.

He picked her up in his arms and she wrapped herself around him. Her entire body felt like it was on fire and she sobbed as she tried to hold him closer. "There's something I have to tell you—"

An earsplitting scream came from the front of the museum, followed by an explosion of breaking glass. And then someone shouted, "Witch!"

18

Anthony dropped her and Samantha landed on her bottom. The envelope with the crime scene pictures fell onto the floor and she hastily scooped it up and shoved it back into her waistband as she scrambled up.

Together they ran to the front of the museum. One of the windows had been smashed in and a woman was on the floor, flailing about with one of the mannequins dressed in old-fashioned clothes. The woman screamed again and Samantha realized she was trying to strangle the mannequin.

Anthony bent down to grab her and she kicked at him, hitting him in the stomach. The people who had been in the museum had scattered backward.

"What happened?" Samantha shouted to one of them.

"She came flying through the window," he said, his eyes wide. "She landed on the witch mannequin and started screaming that it was a witch. I think she's trying to kill it!"

"She's crazy!" the woman with him shouted.

Anthony reached for the woman again, but she snapped her teeth at him, as if to bite him, and he retreated to a safe distance. He whipped a phone out of his pocket and called 911.

Samantha focused all her attention on the woman, approaching her slowly, cautiously. "The witch is dead," she said, lowering her voice and willing the sound to wash over the woman, to penetrate the fog that she seemed to be in.

For a moment the woman stopped struggling, cocked her head, and listened.

"You've killed her. You've saved us all," Samantha said.

The woman blinked at her, then turned and looked at the mannequin, as if to check that it was really dead. Samantha took a good look at her and realized she'd seen her less than an hour before when she had walked out of Red's. She had seemed completely normal then, nothing like this.

It's just like the people in the hotel lobby, she thought with a shudder.

"I killed her?" the woman asked.

"Yes. Thank you," Samantha said.

The woman looked up at her. "Really?"

"Yes, really." Samantha could hear a siren in the distance. That had to be the police. She just needed to keep the woman distracted for a few more minutes without revealing to her or the other bystanders that she was a witch.

Samantha pointed toward a nearby chair. "Why don't you sit here and rest a while? You were really heroic and you must be exhausted."

The woman was bleeding from several cuts from the glass window she had leaped through. She seemed to be considering Samantha's offer. She stood up slowly and Samantha nodded encouragement.

Then the woman turned her head and fixed her gaze on a different mannequin. "Another witch!" she shrieked and tackled it to the ground.

Samantha backed up, stunned by her ferocity, while Anthony worked at moving everyone else farther away.

Soon the police arrived and it took three of them to restrain the woman. Samantha had retreated to the back with all the other witnesses. When they finally had the woman who was seeing witches handcuffed and in a police car, another officer came forward to take witness testimony.

With a tiny wave of her hand, Samantha walked right by him without his noticing her at all. She could feel Anthony's eyes on her, but she didn't have time to stick around for the marathon questioning session that was coming. Even if she'd had the time, she had no desire to face Anthony after everything that had just happened.

As she walked toward the hotel she marveled at the feelings that collided inside her. She'd never given much thought to relationships, yet for some reason Anthony now occupied too many of her waking thoughts. A real relationship with him seemed out of the question. But why did he keep sparking something inside her that she had never known was there? Was it guilt? Shared pain? A shared past he wasn't even aware of?

Whatever it was, it couldn't be healthy. And there were too many secrets between them for them to have a shot at anything real. No, the best she could do was try to put him out of her mind. And by the time she reached her hotel room she was prepared to do just that.

She locked herself in before taking the crime scene photos from their envelope and spreading them across her bed. She stared intently at the shot of the waitress with the ketchup pentagram on her head. Then she flipped to the next picture and caught her breath. The octogram on the back of the victim's neck was clearly visible, more so than on the past couple of bodies. Going counterclockwise, the sixth point was filled in on this one.

She quickly flipped through the other photos until she found the one of the octogram on the other girl's neck. It was much more swollen but she could swear the fifth point was filled in.

The drawing the coroner had had of the first victim had shown the first point filled in. Assuming that Katie's roommate and the nun each had a distinct point and that there was an order to the killings, that would make them either two and three or three and four. Either way, there was one victim they hadn't accounted for yet.

And only two more points to go before the resurrection could occur.

Her heart began to hammer painfully in her chest as she reached for her phone. Ed picked up just before her call would have gone to voice mail.

"What is it?" he asked.

"I think we missed a victim. Either before Katie's roommate or after the nun."

He swore. "What makes you think that?"

She explained about the star points and he swore again.

"I'll check with the coroner, see if he got a better look at their octograms. Then I'll put out the word that we're looking for another victim."

"Thanks, Ed. And if we find out which number the missing victim is, it should help us with location too. They've been getting steadily closer to Salem with each death."

"I noticed that too," he said. "I'll see what I can do. Did you get things straightened out with Anthony?"

"None of your business," she snapped before she could stop herself.

"Ouch. I'm not sure if that means you did or you didn't," he said. "Either way, watch yourself."

"I will. You too."

After she hung up, she went back to studying the photographs. The other victim had been a painter, found in her studio by one of her students, with red paint on her forehead.

Two more victims. And if she was right, at least the last one, but probably both of them, would be murdered in Salem. Right under her nose if she wasn't careful.

When she had finally gleaned everything she could from the photographs, she shredded them into tiny pieces and flushed them down the toilet.

She grabbed a late lunch downstairs at the Tavern and lingered over her food, not ready to face what was coming. Finally, when she could put it off no longer, she returned to her room. She changed into black clothes and tucked her athame into the back of her jeans. She debated what other equipment to take with her and finally decided on just her cloak. With it rolled tightly and tucked under her arm she headed downstairs to the lobby.

Bridget hadn't told her what time, but the sun was setting when she hailed a cab. She had it drop her off five blocks from her destination, as she was determined to walk the rest of the way. Autumn leaves crunched under her boots and the air had a bite to it that brought the blood to her cheeks. She breathed deeply and evenly, making sure her muscles got plenty of oxygen in preparation for the work ahead. She resisted the urge to do some small magic as a warm-up, wanting instead to have her full energy available when she was with the others.

When she turned onto the block, she could feel the house. It was waiting for them, for her, calling out. She shuddered and then settled her cloak around her shoulders and put her hood up. The other residents of the block had been trained years before not to notice the passage of cloaked figures.

The house came into view and she stumbled. Furious with herself, she pushed forward. *Don't let it get in your head. It's just a place, nothing more. You could set a match to it and destroy the whole thing within minutes.*

Then finally she was on the sidewalk in front of the house. Memories of being there with Ed just a few days earlier were fresh in her mind. But other memories were coming too, many of them from when she was too young to be an official coven member. But she had watched when the adults practiced magic and she had come here on more than one occasion to celebrate some social event. Her five-year-old self had strong memories of one solstice celebration that had lasted long into the night.

Tonight she was the first to arrive. She could feel it, and although she did not like being here, she was glad that no one else was witness to her first few moments of fear and revulsion. Better to come to terms with it away from prying eyes.

She strode onto the porch and decided to go no farther alone. Better to enter with current practitioners that the house might be more used to. Yellow police tape that had been put up a couple of days before had been taken down by somebody, and only a small strip remained, caught on a nail protruding from the doorframe. Samantha stared at it while wondering how long it would be before the others arrived.

After only a few minutes other cloaked figures appeared on the street. Some walked, while others had driven. Karen was the first up on the porch and she nodded absently at Samantha but seemed to have no desire to go inside either.

"You okay?" Samantha asked, noting that Karen looked worse than she had that morning. Her eyes were slightly sunken and she seemed distracted.

"Fine," Karen said, in the kind of voice people used when they were lying but were in no mood to discuss it further.

Samantha didn't push. Karen didn't belong there any more than she did and she hoped to get the other woman to see that soon. Others joined them on the porch. Some lingered on the steps and a few remained on the sidewalk. Samantha could sense agitation coming off most of the witches present.

Then there was a stir of movement and Samantha realized that Bridget had arrived. The witch walked with her head uncovered, in marked contrast to almost everyone else. Her pale hair shimmered under the streetlights. She mounted the steps and gave Samantha a smile.

Then she pushed open the door and went inside. After a moment others followed. Samantha let about half of them pass before she forced herself to step across the threshold.

The evil that she remembered was still there, practically dripping from the walls. Outside, people had been talking together quietly, but not in here. As they walked through the house toward the door to the cellar, there was no sound except for the occasional footfall.

If the house objected to her presence, it gave no sign. In the kitchen one witch was handing candles to everyone as they filed downstairs. The tiny flames were little comfort in the dark. She took her candle and lit it with a touch, as the others had. As she put her foot on the first stair tread into the cellar, she let out the breath she'd been holding. It was showtime.

She held on to the banister as she descended into the darkness. The young woman whose body she and Ed had discovered in the basement hadn't had the octogram. Her blood had been spilled and, unlike the others, she had been stabbed. On the other women there had been no signs of cause of death and their blood had remained in their bodies. So the body in the basement couldn't count as one of the eight. Had she struggled, fought? Had they accidentally killed her prematurely? So many questions.

Hopefully tonight she would find some answers.

As she reached the bottom of the stairs she took her place in the circle. The candles flickered, but no unearthly wind blew them out. No voices whispered in her mind that she was going to die.

At last they were all together and fear pricked at her scalp. Now she would have to perform, convince them all that she belonged there. And all she wanted to do was to run screaming from the scene of so many of her nightmares.

Bridget stood in the middle of the circle and lifted her candle high. Samantha and the others did the same.

"Welcome, Brothers and Sisters," Bridget said. "Before we begin I must inform you of disturbing news."

Everyone was deathly silent and Samantha felt as though she could hear her own heart pounding in the stillness.

"A couple of days ago an intruder entered this sacred space for the sole purpose of destroying us."

Samantha's heart skipped a beat as people around her began to mutter. *She knows!* Samantha lifted her hands slightly, her mouth going dry, and prepared to attack Bridget before the others could turn on her.

Kill her now, before she denounces you, the voice in her head urged. The blood was pounding in her ears, making it difficult to hear anything. Out of the corner of her eye she saw one of the cloaked figures edging toward the stairs, cutting off the only escape route.

Sixteen years after she had escaped the house, and now it would have its revenge. The last of her coven would die where the others had, a fitting end to a wretched story.

But I won't die alone.

She lifted her hands all the way and felt the energy building between them. She riveted her eyes on Bridget as the woman turned to look at her. Bridget smirked.

Samantha coiled all her muscles.

"But the house took care of her," Bridget said.

Samantha blinked, struggling to comprehend.

"The woman who came here to destroy us is dead."

There was another outburst from those around her. The dead girl that she and Ed had found here in the basement. That had to be who Bridget was talking about. She hadn't been sacrificed — that's why there had been so much blood. *The beast got her,* Samantha realized.

She lowered her hands and closed her eyes, struggling not to send up a prayer of thanks.

"However, she had accomplices," Bridget said. Samantha's eyes flew open and she fought the urge to look around her. Who could Bridget be referring to?

"A man on the outside who knows more about witches than he should furnished her with information and has been continuing to ask questions about us. But not to fear — he's being dealt with even now."

Anthony, Samantha realized in despair. She half

turned toward the stairs. She had to save him. She took a step forward and then stared, startled, as the figure who had been blocking the stairs suddenly spun around and raced up them.

Something whizzed past Samantha's ear and a moment later the witch fell with a cry, toppling back to the bottom of the stairs. Several people screamed in fear and horror, but no one moved to help. Bridget was on the fallen witch in a moment and Samantha realized it was Bridget's athame that had flown past her on its way to bury itself in the fleeing witch's back.

"And so the traitor reveals herself," Bridget hissed, twisting the knife.

"You killed my cousin," the dying witch wheezed. "You knew and you sacrificed her anyway."

Samantha stepped cautiously closer until she could see the fallen woman clearly in the flicker of the candlelight. She bore a resemblance to the pictures of the first sacrifice victim. And now she too was going to die.

And there's nothing I can do to save her, or Anthony, Samantha thought, struggling with the rage and grief that threatened to envelop her. If only Anthony had told her, maybe she could have helped him.

Another cough and the woman was gone. Bridget straightened, a cruel smile playing across her features. "Make no mistake—that's how we deal with traitors."

Her words echoed in Samantha's mind, strangely familiar, except that she heard them in another's voice. Abigail's. She flinched, knowing that she needed to remember but not wanting to.

Bridget strode back to her former place and the coven members again formed a circle around her.

And Samantha's memories slipped away from her.

"Tonight we find a stranger in our midst," Bridget

said, turning slowly so that she looked at everyone. "But she is not a stranger to our cause. She knew the woman we are all here for tonight. In fact, she is the lone survivor of the original coven who worshipped where we do, whose lives and deaths we honor."

There was more stirring around her. With terror for Anthony filling her, Samantha kept trying to pierce the darkness and glimpse faces beneath the hoods of the coven members. She needed to be able to identify all of them before anyone else got hurt. She counted twenty-five besides herself and Bridget. The ripples of energy coming off them bounced around the room, gaining strength only to crash back over the circle like a wave. She had forgotten what this felt like, to stand as part of the circle and feel more powerful for the connection and contributions of every member. She could feel each of the others and their energy, their power, fed her as hers fed them. A perfect circle—no beginning, no ending. It was what the circle was meant to be. For Wiccans it represented the cycle of life and of the year itself. For witches it represented the movement and flow of energy. It was intoxicating and she struggled not to succumb to it.

She forced herself to keep thinking, keep questioning everything she saw and everything that happened in a desperate attempt to keep herself separate from the others.

What was happening to Anthony? Was he still alive or had they already killed him?

Why wasn't the high priestess performing this ritual?

Was it because of her? Bridget had said that she wasn't quite ready to meet Samantha. Was that true? Or was the high priestess there and simply masquerading as one of the others in order to observe unseen?

"You will notice that there are several missing tonight, our high priestess among them," Bridget said, startling Samantha into a brief consideration of whether it was possible that Bridget was reading her thoughts. "They are speeding our purpose."

Samantha felt her heart sink. *They're killing the next victim and I have no idea where they are.*

Bridget continued. "And we must do our part as well. The time is now. The sacrifice is prepared. And we shall stand in for it."

The witch continued to turn in a slow circle, holding the others spellbound.

"Now, as before, one must stand in for the recipient of our sacrifice."

Samantha felt energy ripples around the room and understood in a moment that no one present wanted to stand in for the recipient. A brief look of impatience crossed Bridget's face and then she looked at Samantha and her expression turned to triumph.

"Samantha, as the only member of this original coven, do us the honor of standing in for the recipient. Accept our sacrifice."

She wanted to say no, but knew she couldn't. She needed to be accepted as part of the circle. And she would gain respect by doing that which no one else wanted to do, which would help her if she needed to break the coven in half to take it down. Karen and Autumn were already hers, but she must win others in case the need arose.

She stepped forward. "I will receive your sacrifice in the name of the other."

She could feel the relief spreading through the room and also the respect that she had anticipated. The energy flowed to her from everyone else, and it was more than she was giving out to them. She grew stronger while they grew weaker. That was something that would stay with them unconsciously, so that they would always perceive her as stronger.

And because they did, she would be.

Bridget kissed her on each cheek and then knelt before her. The others took their cue and knelt as well.

And Samantha felt . . . powerful. She closed her eyes and felt her body vibrating with the power.

"Who has the chalice?" Bridget asked.

"I," replied one of the men.

"Then stand in for the sacrifice," she said.

Samantha watched as the man produced his athame and then sliced his palm. He held it out over the goblet and let several drops of his blood fall into it. Then he passed it to the woman on his right.

"Who has the chalice?" Bridget asked.

"I," answered the woman.

"Then stand in for the sacrifice."

The woman sliced open her palm and added her blood to the goblet as well before passing it on.

It continued around the circle counterclockwise. With each new hand holding the goblet Bridget asked the same question and the person holding it gave the same answer. And Samantha struggled to focus on them, their faces, and the ritual at hand instead of Anthony.

Slowly Samantha understood. In order for there to be a sacrifice, blood had to be spilled. Depending on the type of sacrifice, the blood of the practitioner might need to be offered up along with that of the sacrifice. The women who had been marked with the octogram had not had their bodies cut in any other way. No blood had been spilled. While the woman was actually being killed elsewhere, she was being symbolically killed here, her blood spilled, and each person took a turn being the sacrifice. That way only one or two witches needed to actually be present to witness the murder. It was safer.

And that's how they're manipulating and controlling people like Karen. She might not even realize there is a girl out there somewhere being murdered. She might think it's all symbolic.

Samantha shuddered. It was an ingenious way of keeping control of the coven, the victims, and the crime scenes.

When the goblet had progressed all the way around the circle, Bridget took it. "And I also stand in for the sacrifice," she said, slicing open her right palm and squeezing blood into the chalice. "And I stand in for the petitioner," she continued, slicing open her other hand and adding blood from it as well.

"Accept this sacrifice on behalf of the one to whom it is made," she said, lifting the goblet above her head toward Samantha.

Samantha took the goblet from her hand and her fingers tingled where they touched it. She had read in the Bible shortly after her conversion that there was life in the blood of any creature, and it had made complete sense to her. Now, as she stood holding the cup, she could feel the life of each person who had spilled his or her blood into it.

She forced herself to speak. "I stand in for the recipient of the sacrifice and I accept it in their name."

She felt sick inside. She had just declared that she stood in for whatever creature held the dead high priestess's soul. That was who they were sacrificing to.

I am the devil's avatar, she thought with a shudder.

And then she looked down and met Bridget's eyes. The witch was staring at her expectantly.

And that was when the full horror of her situation hit her. She couldn't just accept the sacrifice.

She had to drink it.

19

God, I can't do this! The silent prayer burst from Samantha, desperate and uncontrolled.

A tremor shook the floor beneath her feet.

Bridget's eyes widened in concern. Samantha knew that she had to act soon or lose everything she had worked to gain.

She closed her eyes and tipped the goblet back into her mouth. The hot, sticky blood oozed over her tongue and down her throat and she willed her body not to gag on it even as it started to. The taste of copper filled her mouth and every muscle in her body vibrated in revulsion and agony.

Finally it was done and she lowered the goblet and wiped her mouth.

Bridget took the cup from her and stood slowly. "Our sacrifice has been made and accepted," she said.

The others rose. Then, silently, they turned and began to file up the stairs.

Samantha's legs were shaking, but she hurried to join the others, more than ever determined not to be one of the last ones in the basement. She snuffed her candle and handed it to the witch collecting them in the kitchen, then hurried outside.

She wanted to vomit, but she forced herself to keep it

in. She needed to reach Anthony, but she saw Karen beginning to walk away, her shoulders hunched, and she jogged to catch up to her. "Karen."

The other woman turned, startled.

"Give me your phone number. I want to talk to you about something tomorrow," Samantha said.

As if in a daze Karen recited a string of numbers and Samantha hastily committed them to memory. Then Karen went on her way and Samantha turned back toward the house. Bridget was the last to leave, closing the door firmly behind her. Samantha readied herself to run as soon as Bridget was out of sight, but the witch waved to her.

"Thank you," Bridget said when she got close to her. Everyone else had already passed out of earshot.

Samantha shrugged. "Happy to help."

"The few of the coven with any spine are away at the moment," she said, making a face.

It wouldn't take more than one, likely the high priestess, to murder the latest victim. What could the others be doing? Participating? Cleaning up the crime scene? Or perhaps they were spreading more fear and hatred to keep the witch frenzy alive.

"I'm surprised that there are so many . . . weaker . . . members. Especially given the size of the coven. I would think you would need only to choose the strongest."

"Unfortunately, it's not just about power; it's also about the body count. We need to keep it high. But that won't always be true and then we can afford to thin the ranks."

"By my count we have one more sacrifice to make," Samantha said, deciding to risk revealing how much she knew.

"You never cease to surprise me," Bridget said with a laugh. "Yes, one left."

"So, when are we holding the ceremony?"

"Very soon. I don't know the exact time yet, but I'm telling everyone to be ready with half an hour's notice."

"That's not much time," Samantha noted.

Bridget shrugged. "At least we're local. It's harder on those coming from other cities."

It was so surreal. They might as well be planning a business meeting or an office party, the way they were speaking. Given that lives were being taken, it all seemed far too casual, like Bridget was playing witch and no one had ever told her the stakes were real.

But when Samantha looked in her eyes and saw the darkness there, she knew that Bridget was very much aware of just what she was playing at.

Her stomach lurched and she clamped down on it even harder. She needed to leave, to find Anthony. But it was going to take forever to walk and almost as long to have a cab come pick her up.

"Do you need a ride to your hotel?"

Even though she didn't want to spend another second in Bridget's presence, she was intensely grateful since that would get her there sooner. "Yes, please."

As they drove, Samantha struggled not to vomit up the blood she had drunk and tried to get her fear under control. Anthony was likely already dead and there was nothing she could do about that. But another voice in her mind refused to believe it and kept screaming at her to hurry.

Was he at the museum? If not, where was he? She thought of her candles in her room. Compelling him to come to her would be worse than useless if he was dead or imprisoned.

When Bridget finally pulled up in front of the hotel, it took all of Samantha's willpower to step calmly from the

car. She walked inside the lobby, waited until she saw
Bridget's car pull away, then sprinted back out to the
street.

She raced up Essex, legs pumping, terror spurring her
on. At last the museum came into sight, but it was dark
and locked. She grabbed hold of the door and tried to
feel Anthony. He wasn't inside. *Unless he's dead already.*

She thought about breaking down the door, but she
forced herself to stop and think. If he was already dead,
they could have dumped the body anywhere; they might
even have used it in some way that would draw more
attention to witchcraft. But if he was still alive, they'd
likely kill him somewhere more private, less public.

His home.

But she had no idea where he lived. She yanked her
cell phone out of her pocket and called Ed.

"Come on, come on," she breathed, waiting for him
to pick up.

"Hello?"

"I think they just killed another girl. I don't know
where."

"What happened to you?" he asked, his voice filled
with concern.

"Long story—talk later. Right now I really need you
to get me Anthony's home address. His last name is
Charles."

"Give me a second."

She stood, agony gripping her as she could hear Ed
typing. She was lucky he'd been at the precinct and not
babysitting Katie. She shifted her weight from one foot
to the other, trying to anticipate which way she was going to need to run.

"Got it. Ready?"

He gave her the address and she repeated it hastily,

then ended the call. She spun to her left and dashed off at a sprint. Anthony lived just a couple of blocks from the museum. When she turned onto his street her eyes gravitated instantly to one house, a blue Victorian with white trim. Something dark was stirring inside it; she could feel it. She raced up the steps and shoved open the door, which was already ajar.

"Anthony!" she screamed.

Only the groaning of the floorboards beneath her feet answered. And there was something else. She tilted her head, listening. The sound was coming from upstairs. It was the sound of running water.

She put her foot on the first step of the narrow staircase that hugged the left-hand wall and leaped up the stairs two at a time. At the top, she ran toward the room at the back of the house. She burst into a large bedroom with an antique four-poster bed and flew across it into the bathroom.

She skidded to a stop as her mind froze in fear.

Before her was a monstrous gray dog-shaped creature, similar to the thing that had chased her and Ed out of the basement of Abigail's old house. But this one was fully corporeal. It turned to look at her, blood and saliva dripping from its jaws, a demon from her nightmares made flesh.

Only it wasn't the exact one from her nightmares. This one was smaller, and gray instead of black. She knew from her memories of the one she had seen as a child that when these creatures were in this state, they weren't just so much energy that she could disperse like the snake or the kitten. Rather, what stood before her was a real creature, summoned from the bowels of hell to do its master's bidding.

She looked past the creature and saw the bathtub,

filled with water, and Anthony struggling at the bottom of it, bubbles escaping from his nose and mouth. The creature held his chest down with one massive paw, drowning him. And even as she stared, Anthony ceased to struggle.

"No!" she screamed.

The creature pulled its paw off Anthony and turned fully toward her, its eyes glowing. She couldn't outrun it, she had no time to draw a protective circle, and she had no idea how to banish it.

It must have realized that too, because it grinned at her in the most wickedly human way as it took a slow step forward.

"I will kill you!" she shouted at the creature, more fear than rage making her voice shake.

It opened its mouth and a deep laugh echoed from it. It began to speak in a language she did not know, the words thick and oily and sliding over her. Its hot breath stank of sulfur and the stench drove her to her knees in a fit of coughing. Water spilling over from the bathtub swirled around her on the floor.

Think!

The creature moved impossibly fast for something so large. She threw herself to the side, slamming her temple against the doorframe, to dodge it. Pain exploded behind her eyes and she smelled blood. She glanced down and saw that the beast had slashed her chest with its razorlike claws. In an instant what was left of her shirt was soaked with blood.

The sight was enough to send adrenaline pumping through her body and she could feel a swift buildup of energy unlike anything she'd ever experienced before. She dared not release the energy increasing inside her, though, because she would be electrocuted there in the water.

Water! That's it!

She didn't need to understand its language or figure out how to send it back to where it came from. All she needed to do was kill it.

She yanked her athame free from her waistband and brandished it in front of her. The creature snarled, eyeing the blade warily. As she struggled to her knees, it tracked her movements carefully. Hatred and cunning burned in its soulless eyes. She forced herself to try to stand. Her right foot slid out from under her, though, and she crashed to the floor again.

It leaped for her and she slashed with the athame. As the blade made contact with its hide, the creature howled and jumped back. She seized the moment to gain her feet. With a surge of strength she didn't know she had, she jumped onto the bathroom counter.

She crouched there for a moment, dizzy, as blood continued to flow down her shirt and paint the water pink. The beast coiled all its muscles, readying itself to spring. Samantha brought her hands close together and a ball of energy formed between them, electricity sparking from her fingertips. If there were any chinks in the porcelain of the bathtub, if any part of the metal was touching the water, then she would have no hope of reviving Anthony. His body would fry too.

She shrieked a prayer heavenward even as she threw her hands down, hurling the crackling sphere of energy into the water.

There was an inhuman scream and the creature convulsed uncontrollably as the electric current running through the water entered its body. Finally it collapsed in a smoking heap, the smell of burned hair filling the room.

Samantha turned and looked at the bathtub. She

judged the distance and then jumped, crashing down in the tub near Anthony's body. Pain ripped through her and she struggled to remove the stopper. Finally it came free and the water began to drain.

Straddling his chest, she began CPR, praying that she wasn't too late. She felt a couple of his ribs break under her hands, but she kept going. After thirty chest compressions she hauled Anthony's head out of the water. Slipping and sliding, she managed to twist in such a way that she could give him rescue breaths.

Nothing.

"Don't you die on me," she pleaded in the midst of her sobs.

She did more chest compressions and more breaths. Still there was nothing. No pulse, no sign of life. Tears rolled down her cheeks.

Anthony Charles was dead.

20

Samantha balled her hands into fists, scarcely aware that she was still bleeding from the wounds on her chest. She stared down at Anthony's pale, still face in anguish.

"No!"

He couldn't be dead. Not now, not like this. She slammed her hands down on his chest and sent a jolt of electricity through his heart.

His body arced and when she removed her hands it collapsed again. A shudder went through him and his eyes flew open. He began to gag and cough up water.

With a sob, she clung to him, terrified of what had almost happened and even more terrified that she had cared so much for a man she knew so little about.

Anthony made a gasping sound, followed by more violent coughing.

"What?" she asked, bending close.

"Blood."

She looked down and realized that though the bleeding had slowed, it had not stopped altogether. She took a deep breath, then placed her fingers on her chest and forced herself to start healing.

As soon as the bleeding stopped she struggled to her feet and climbed out of the bathtub. Once she steadied herself she grabbed hold of Anthony and hoisted him to his feet. He made a groan of protest.

"We can't stay here," she said. "We've already stayed too long."

"Can't move."

"You can and you will," she said grimly, picking him up and half dragging, half carrying him into the bedroom.

She eased him down to the floor and took stock. He was wearing a pair of khaki pants and nothing else. He was beginning to shiver from the cold and masses of bruises were springing up on his torso, some from fighting the hellhound and some from her attempts to resuscitate him.

She went into the closet and found a pair of sweatpants and a T-shirt. She touched his hand and gave him a little boost of energy. While he changed, she busied herself with the body of the hellhound.

She had hoped that when she killed it the body would turn to ash or in some other way disintegrate. Instead it lay still, a giant, demonic corpse. She didn't know how to send it back to where it had come from, and she couldn't leave it here. Gritting her teeth, she forced herself to touch the skin, which was rough and covered in tiny hairs that were more like barbs.

She superheated it until it began to burn itself from the inside out. There was nothing mysterious or accidental about spontaneous combustion. It was an old trick used by only the strongest of witches. A living body would fight against it, adapt, and adjust, making it one of the most difficult ways to kill something. With a dead body it was much simpler.

In a matter of seconds the hellhound's body had completely burned.

She turned to look at Anthony, who was sitting with

his back against the bed. He had changed into the dry clothes, but the effort had left him gasping for air.

"What—what was that thing?"

She shook her head. "Their rightful name I don't know. I've always thought of them as hellhounds, monsters summoned to do dark work. They're most often used to kill people."

"Why me?"

"Because you were stupid and careless," she said, her voice harsh even to her own ears. "You lectured me about not knowing what I was getting into with witches when it was you who was the ignorant one."

He was finally regaining his breath and after a moment he asked, "What are you talking about?"

"Why didn't you tell me you were working with someone who was trying to find her cousin's killer?" she demanded.

He looked startled and quickly dropped his eyes. "You have your secrets; I have mine," he said, coughing.

"Well, your secrets just got someone killed."

He blanched. "Serious?"

"Of course I'm serious. This isn't a game we're playing at! They killed her right in front of me. And a few days ago they killed the woman who was helping her. The only reason you're alive is because they said they were killing someone else, and from the description, I knew it had to be you."

He refused to look at her.

"Okay, we have to go," she said.

She bent down and helped him to stand.

"I think I need to go to a hospital," he said in a weak voice.

"A luxury we can't afford. Now, do you have any family nearby?"

"No."

"Okay, new plan."

Half an hour later they were in a motel room a couple of miles from his house.

"This is the plan?" he asked as he sat down on the bed, grunting in pain.

"For now. I can't risk moving you any farther."

"They're going to know I'm not dead."

"Of course. If we're lucky they'll think you got the message and cleared out completely."

"And if we're not lucky?"

"They will find you, and next time they won't fail to kill you."

"You're a very cheery person—you know that?"

"I don't have time to sugarcoat this for you," she snapped. "I'm going to go out and get some food. You don't leave this room until I say it's okay. They could have spies everywhere."

"How long?"

"As long as it takes."

"But my museum—"

"Won't matter at all to you if you're dead," she interrupted. "Now, if you'll promise to be a good boy, I'll take a look at your ribs."

"Fine," he said with a grimace.

Looking into his eyes, though, she knew she couldn't trust him to stay put. Ed had once told her that it was impossible to keep someone alive when they so badly wanted to die. Anthony didn't have a death wish, but neither was he capable of sitting and doing nothing. There was nothing she could do about that, though.

*   *   *

An hour later, after getting Anthony's ribs started on the mend and bringing in a supply of food that he could easily store and eat in the motel room, she returned to her hotel. Her own body was protesting everything that it had been put through and she was having a hard time pushing forward. The nausea she had been holding at bay since the coven meeting had become overwhelming.

Once she got upstairs and into her bathroom, she sank to her knees in front of the toilet and threw up all the blood she had drunk. The smell made her even sicker and it was a good half hour before she stumbled to her feet, shaking and spent. She dumped her clothes unceremoniously in a pile on the floor with her cloak and athame, then fell headlong into bed.

She reached for her phone and put Karen's number in it before she forgot it. Moments later she was asleep.

Blood everywhere. And someone was hurt. Someone was dead. And there was blood on her dress.
"Make no mistake, that's how we deal with traitors."

Samantha sat straight up, screaming, then fell back onto her pillows and sobbed quietly. More nightmares. More half memories. She needed to be able to remember, no matter how much it hurt. It had to be better than this living hell of twisting shadows.

She sat up and took several calming breaths before closing her eyes and willing herself to remember.

In her mind she again saw the corridor lined with doors. The door marked 5 was still open and she could see her younger self lingering just inside the doorway. She gave her a small wave, grateful for her help, fearful for her too. She knew, though, that the little girl had taught her all she could. Samantha set her eyes on the door marked with a 6.

She hesitated as she reached it, wondering what she would find. She forced herself to turn the doorknob. The door swung open slowly on hinges that creaked like the sound of fingernails scraping a chalkboard. A solemn little girl with large, round eyes stared back at her. Her six-year-old self was wearing a white dress with a touch of lace at the neck and sleeves. There were drops of red smeared into the fabric and Samantha swallowed hard as she recognized them as blood.

"What have they done to you?" she whispered.

The little girl looked down at the blood and made a soft whimpering sound. "It's not mine," she said at last in a very small voice.

Samantha didn't want to ask the next question, but she had to know. "Whose is it?"

"Miss Kimberly's."

"What happened to Miss Kimberly?"

The little girl stared at her solemnly. "You don't remember?"

"No," Samantha admitted.

A look of relief flashed over the little girl's face. "Good!" she said before stepping backward into shadow.

"No, wait!" Samantha called. "Don't go. I—I have to know."

"You don't want to know," the little girl warned her.

From behind Samantha the youngest girl said in a voice that trembled, "I liked Miss Kimberly."

Samantha licked her lips, trying to still the pounding of her heart. And then she remembered. She *had* liked Miss Kimberly. A large, jovial woman in her fifties. She always gave Samantha a treat after a coven meeting. Rainbow sherbet. Sometimes Miss Kimberly babysat her and would play games with her. And at Halloween she helped Samantha carve pumpkins. How had she forgotten her?

"Tell me," Samantha pleaded. "What happened to Miss Kimberly?"

"Miss Abigail . . . got mad at her."

"And?"

"You don't want to remember."

"But I have to."

"You don't want to remember!"

But she *did* remember.

She was standing in a circle with the rest of the coven, her mother to her right. She glanced up at her and wished they could go home. She was tired. Miss Abigail was finishing a ritual and she looked very pleased with it.

"Next week we're going to do something amazing," Miss Abigail said. "Once we have made the ultimate sacrifice we will have the power to do whatever we want and no one will be able to stop us."

"We can't." The voice was Miss Kimberly's.

Everyone turned to stare at Miss Kimberly and Samantha was very afraid for her.

"Why not?" Miss Abigail said, her voice full of fury.

"Because it's wrong—that's why. Look at us. How did we get here? Do any of us even remember? Fifteen years ago we were all just looking for a place where we could be ourselves, where we could use our powers, share our knowledge. And now, what? What is it we're trying to accomplish? We've sacrificed animals to gain more power. I didn't think it was right, but I went along. But what have we used that power for? Not to help mankind, but for our own selfish gain."

"I didn't hear you complaining when you moved into your mansion last year."

"You're right. I didn't. But I should have. I didn't let myself think about how I got it, the people who were hurt so that I could have what I wanted. But now, you're talking about sacrificing a human . . . a human! No amount of power, no amount of things or respect or anything is worth that." Miss Kimberly turned in a circle, speaking to all who were present. "Remember how we used to be? Before we decided to follow Abigail?" She began pointing to people in the room. "You just wanted the strength to help cure your mother's cancer and now you want immortality. You wanted the self-confidence to get a promotion and now you won't stop until everyone in the world looks up to you. You wanted people to fall in love with your music so that you might share your gift with the world and now you don't care about the music or the message but just how many people worship you and how much money you make."

Then Miss Kimberly turned and stared up at Samantha's mother. "And you—"

Her mother raised her hand. "Silence! I know who I was and I promise you that I will never go back."

Suddenly Miss Kimberly grabbed her throat, struggling to speak. Her eyes bulged out. Samantha whimpered and tried to move to her, but her mother gripped her hand tight.

"Yes, we have grown, changed, and it is right that we do so," Miss Abigail said. "These powers are ours and we ourselves are gods. It is time we were treated as such."

And then she stabbed Miss Kimberly in the heart. The woman fell and Samantha wanted to scream but no sound would come out.

"Make no mistake, that's how we deal with traitors," Miss Abigail said. *She reached down and retrieved her athame. She held it up before her face and then licked the blood on the blade. She shivered. "We have our first sacrifice and it is more powerful than we ever dreamed!"*

"You see?" her mother asked, staring down at her. Her voice was stern, angry. She grabbed Samantha's chin and forced her head back around. Miss Kimberly lay on the floor, not moving. "That's what happens to witches who disobey."

"No!" Samantha screamed and slid to the floor. Her six-year-old self wrapped her arms around her and they held each other and cried.

In the morning when she woke she could still taste blood from the ritual the night before. She spent nearly ten minutes brushing her teeth and gargling before she felt like she could leave her room.

Downstairs in the lobby of the hotel people were milling about and there was a long line at reception. Samantha lingered for a few minutes listening to visitors and locals alike talking.

Every year in early October Salem hosted a Halloween parade to kick off the season. Normally thousands of people would turn out for it, which was nothing compared to the hundreds of thousands who would descend on the city for Halloween itself. It was the day before the parade and already the town was getting crowded as more and more people arrived from other states and even other countries.

Everyone she heard was saying a record-breaking number would attend this year's parade. Hotels for thirty miles around were filling up.

Ed had been right about the people flocking to Salem to protest the death of witches or just to revel in the spectacle. She hadn't heard anything yet from him and she couldn't help but worry about when and where the most recent victim was going to turn up.

When it seemed that there was nothing new to hear in the hotel, she left. Essex Street was crowded with people and she found herself starting to feel a little claustrophobic after having seen it mostly empty for a few days.

Tourists were cramming into any shop that even looked like it sold anything remotely related to witches. People were wearing handmade T-shirts that had NO BURNING logos on them. She also saw a handful of T-shirts sporting witches' hats or brooms with a circle and line through them.

So both camps were represented by the crowd, those in favor of witches and those against. She shook her head. It seemed so bizarre. When she was a kid, tourists had enjoyed pretending they believed in witches, but no one really had.

And if they had, they certainly wouldn't have come out in favor of them. The times were changing and it made her feel that much more out of control. She noticed several people holding signs with antiviolence slogans outside Anthony's museum. So the crazy woman attacking the mannequins hadn't gone unnoticed. The museum itself was dark and closed.

She felt a brief surge of guilt for not having checked back in with Anthony, but quickly suppressed it. Distance was better for both of them. The more contact she had with him, the greater the chance that the witches would find him.

She still felt unsteady from the night before. She kept experiencing weird power fluctuations, and she wasn't sure whether it was because last night had been the first time in years that she had participated in something like that or if it was because of the blood. Someone brushed past her and then yelped when he got an electric shock.

Finally she turned onto the street where Red's was and then came to a sudden halt. Several hundred people were outside the building, waiting to get in. She stared in amazement at the throng before retracing her steps. She stopped in a cute bakery where she had to stand in line for only fifteen minutes to get a bagel with cream cheese.

She ate it while she walked back toward her hotel. When she reached the entrance she walked past it and continued on to the grassy area next to it. Salem Common was one of the few places that didn't seem to be teeming with people.

She found a bench and sat down. Then she called Karen.

"Hello?" The other witch really didn't sound well.

"It's Samantha. I need to talk to you. Can you meet me in half an hour at Salem Common?"

"Um . . . yeah, I think so."

"Good. I'll see you here."

She settled in to wait, trying not to overthink the coming conversation. She had decided to confront Karen, get her to see the truth of what was happening and encourage her to get out. Maybe they could even use her as a witness if it came to that. Regardless, the Wiccan had no business being involved in everything that was happening.

I can save her, Samantha thought. *I have to.*

Almost half an hour later there was a ripple in the air around her and she swiveled her head, looking for the other woman. Karen was slouching down the street, her head down, hands in her pockets. Something wasn't right.

Karen was weaving slightly as she walked. A man passed her and she bumped against him. A child ran by her and nearly tripped her.

Then Karen stopped in front of Samantha, her eyes still on the ground.

"Karen?" Samantha asked softly, every nerve alert.

Karen looked up and Samantha recoiled as she saw her hollow eyes glowing with an unnatural light.

Is she possessed? she thought. What else could explain the witch's physical transformation?

"What's wrong?" Samantha asked.

Karen dropped her eyes again. "It's nothing," she whispered after a moment.

Samantha reached out and touched her arm, then jerked her hand back as something like an electrical shock hit her. Heat flashed up her arm and a moment later anger and fear flashed through her too.

"What did you do to me?" Samantha demanded, jumping to her feet. *I'm going to kill her for whatever that was.*

She blinked at the ferocity of her reaction.

Karen hunched her shoulders but didn't say anything.

"Answer me!" She wanted desperately to reach out and shake her, slap her—something—but she was afraid to touch her again.

"I don't know what's happening to me," Karen said with a gasp.

Before Samantha could say anything, a high-pitched scream shattered the air around them. She spun and saw the child who had run into Karen on the ground, shrieking and pointing to a nearby tree with skeletal branches.

On one of the branches someone had hung a wind sock with the image of a witch.

"Witch!" the little boy screamed, continuing to point at the tree.

The man who had been walking in front of him turned around. "Where?" he shouted.

The little boy pointed more emphatically.

With a shout the man ran toward the tree and slammed into it, punching at the wind sock and the tree itself.

Samantha stared in amazement. It was just like watching the woman attack the mannequin the day before. What was it Ed had said about the people who were killing those they thought were witches? They seemed to have just gone crazy.

Next to her, Samantha could feel Karen shudder. "There's witches everywhere," she whispered. "Why won't they leave me alone?"

Alarm bells went off in Samantha's mind. "Karen, what are you talking about?"

"I hate them, you know. It's because of them that Wiccans can't practice in peace."

"Then why did you become one of them?"

"They promised me . . ." Karen trailed off, her eyes fixed on something that Samantha couldn't see. "It doesn't matter now. It never mattered. I have to kill them all. They're evil and they must be removed from the earth. They are a scourge upon it."

"Karen, what's gotten into you?" Samantha asked, trying to ignore the emotions that raged within her. The kid continued to scream and the man continued to attack the tree and the witch wind sock. "You're a Wiccan. Wiccans don't kill people."

"I'm not a Wiccan. Not anymore, and it's all their

fault. They're going to have to pay for that. And everything else they've done."

"What else have they done?" Samantha pushed.

The man's shouting grew more frenzied and the child's screaming reached new heights.

Something's wrong with them. They're hallucinating, paranoid, seeing things that aren't there. And they're trying to kill witches. Just like the people who've been killing the women they thought were witches.

Just like the mob that attacked Katie.

Too bad they failed.

Samantha blinked. Her own feelings of hatred were beginning to rage out of control. She had a sudden insane urge to help the man vanquish the tree. After all, what if it was a witch who had glamoured herself to look like a tree? It was slender, about five feet tall; it could be a witch. The boy saw it and that was good enough for her. He was smart—he knew the bogeyman existed.

Karen was muttering to herself and Samantha had the unnerving feeling that she was watching the woman disintegrate before her very eyes. *And so am I.*

She struggled to focus. "Karen, have people around you been seeing witches?"

"Yes," the woman replied, ceasing her muttering long enough to utter the word.

"For how long?"

"Dunno. A week . . . ? More?"

Samantha could feel her shoulders bunching up with tension. "Were you in Boston at the Manor Inn a few nights ago, when that group in the hotel lobby killed those witches?"

Karen nodded. "Naomi said I should go. She wouldn't tell me why. She just told me to touch a couple of people and then leave."

"And you never found out why she wanted you to do that?"

Karen shook her head. "I didn't know Naomi was going to get killed. She was my friend. She promised to help me."

"What did she promise to do?" Samantha pushed.

Karen's eyes suddenly widened. "Witches!" she squeaked.

Samantha spun around, but no one was there. She turned back just as Karen collapsed.

Samantha half caught her and lowered her to the ground. Karen was staring past her at something only she could see. Her lips moved.

"It's her." Her voice was barely audible.

"Who?"

Suddenly Karen's body convulsed and Samantha jumped back as a foul-smelling black liquid began to ooze from her eyes, ears, and nose. She coughed and flecks of it appeared on her lips.

Samantha dropped to her knees next to Karen, her hands fluttering nervously in the air. She didn't know what to do to help her. She hadn't the faintest clue what the black substance was or how to extract it.

Around her the cacophony grew until she wanted to scream at everyone that she needed quiet to think.

"Somebody call an ambulance!" she shouted.

But no one was listening. Instead two guys were trying to pull the first one off the tree. He just kept screaming and hitting at them. And then the three of them were on the ground, fighting one another.

"Everyone's gone insane," she said. "Including me."

She glanced at Karen. *She's a witch. I should kill her.*

The thought came unbidden and filled her with a quiet kind of horror. Karen wasn't the kind of person who deserved to be killed. She was just in love with someone who didn't love her back and had gotten in over her head in a desperate attempt to remedy her situation.

Rip her head off.

"No!" Samantha screamed to the impulses that pushed her to do something to Karen.

This all started when she touched me.

She stared down at Karen and then lifted her eyes to the man and the boy. *And they touched her. And the woman who attacked the mannequins. And the people in the hotel.*

Everyone who's touched her has turned violent against witches.

But she'd seen Autumn and Jace touch her and neither of them had been infected. *It must only work on people who already are predisposed to mistrust or dislike witches. Like me.*

She looked down. Karen was thrashing harder, more of the toxic black sludge oozing out of her body. She was right. The witches had done this to her. She was Typhoid Mary, infected with a mind disease that turned ordinary people into witch haters, witch killers. And now the disease she had unwittingly been spreading had caught up with her.

Karen's entire body jerked once more, hard. Then it went totally slack. Looking into her eyes, Samantha realized that Karen was dead.

But not before she had infected her.

21

Samantha's first instinct was to call 911 and then get out of there before anyone showed up. She took a deep breath and forced herself to try to think rationally despite the heightened emotions that were rushing through her.

Karen's body was still carrying the infection, and if Samantha just left, the chance was great that others would touch her and the madness would continue to spread. She had to try to purge it before the authorities arrived. She squatted beside the body, grateful that everyone's attention was still on the others up the path who were screaming about witches.

She placed her hand on Karen's chest, much as she had with Katie, and began to push, willing the destructive energy out of her. The energy was stubborn, though, and didn't want to leave. It had worked its way into her organs at a fundamental level. Had Karen been alive there would have been no way Samantha could have driven it out. But she was dead and Samantha didn't have to worry about the damage she was causing to the body as she forced the energy to the surface. It came out as more black ooze leaking from the eyes, ears, and nose. It was thick and foul smelling, and it made Samantha sick.

Finally she had pushed it all out. She set the black goo on fire, regretting that it would damage Karen's body. But it was better this way, safer. And a coroner would never have figured out the actual cause of death anyway. Finished, she turned to look at the men and the boy affected by the toxin. She could feel it poisoning her brain, changing the chemicals being released. She didn't know how to fight it in herself or how to drive it out of them without killing them.

The best she could do was to incapacitate and isolate them. She stepped away from Karen's body and moved swiftly to the others. She touched the child on the shoulder first and he crumpled to the ground, asleep. Next she surveyed the tangled mess of limbs of the men, who had begun fighting one another. She swiftly reached out and touched each of them and they too fell asleep.

Then she moved to a gawking woman a little farther away. "Listen to me," Samantha said, deepening her voice and forcing the hypnotic sound to flow over the other woman. "These people have some kind of virus. Do not touch them. Call nine-one-one and tell them that these people need to be restrained and that no one should touch them without protective gear. Do you understand?"

The woman nodded wordlessly and reached for her phone.

As soon as the call connected, Samantha turned and ran as swiftly as she could back to her hotel. She needed to be alone, where she couldn't infect anyone else, while she figured out how to purge the toxin from her system.

In her room she sat down on the floor, forcing herself to breathe slowly and evenly. She took stock of what was happening inside her body, trying to figure out how the toxin worked so she could learn to purge it safely or at

least render it inert. There were spells that could be undone only by the person who cast them, but the great
majority of magic could be undone by anyone with the
skill, knowledge, and power to do so.

It wasn't just energy that had been sent into her system. It had been shaped into something. *It really is like a
virus,* she realized. Hallucinations, paranoia, and violent
outbursts would be three of the symptoms. After a half
hour of trying to analyze it, she gave up. She knew a lot
about physics, and some biology, but this was way beyond her.

And she realized in a flash that whoever had engineered the spell had to be not only a witch but also a
doctor.

She put in a call to the only doctor she knew and
could trust: the coroner.

"Hello?" he answered.

"George, it's Samantha," she said tersely.

"Samantha! Excellent timing! I think I just found
your other victim."

"From last night?"

"What? No. They haven't brought that poor girl in
yet. I'm talking about the missing one."

"They did find the girl from last night, though?" she
asked, racing to process what he'd said.

"Yeah. Didn't Ed fill you in this morning?"

"No," she said, her hand tightening around the phone.

"Oh, well, you might want to give him a call. But first
let me tell you what I found. I went back through my
files and found nothing. So I made some calls. Six weeks
ago a girl was pulled out of the Charles River. Coroner
who looked at her labeled it a suicide. She was listed as
a Jane Doe; clothes she was wearing indicated she was
possibly homeless. Case closed and that was that. Well, it

turns out she did have a mark, on the sole of her foot. I had him fax me a copy of the picture, and I'm sure it was an octogram. I'm having him send me the whole file now."

"Thanks." She was right. That left one more victim before the resurrection.

"Now, why are you calling me?"

"I need to pick your brain about toxins and how they work."

"Sure . . . hold on a second."

She could hear him put the phone down and voices in the background. A minute later he picked it back up. "They just brought in the latest girl. I need to go. I'll call you back in a little while."

"Oh," she said, hearing panic edge into her voice.

"Is it an emergency?" he asked, seeming to notice.

"It can wait a little while," she said. She heard Ed's voice in the background. "But do me a favor and put Ed on," she said.

"You got it."

Seconds later her partner answered the phone. "Why didn't you call me when you found the latest victim?" she asked.

There was a long pause and then he said, "I don't know you."

"What are you talking about, Ed? It's Samantha."

"I know who you are, but I'm not sure I can trust you," he said heatedly.

"Ed, what's going on?" she asked, bewildered and starting to panic even more.

"You're a witch!" he exploded.

"Please, Ed, not you too!"

"I think you need to stay the hell away from me and my case."

"Listen, Ed—listen closely. The paranoia that's going around? The violence against suspected witches? It's being triggered by some kind of magic toxin that messes with your brain. You must have been infected yesterday when you were in town. I was infected today by the person who was spreading it. I'm working on a cure, but you have to trust me."

"Trust you! How can I trust you? All this time we've been partners you never told me you were a witch."

"Because I wasn't. I'm still not. I'm just a cop doing my job," she said raggedly.

"So you say. I think you've been one of them all along."

"I'm not. Please, just try to be calm. I'm going to fix this."

He hung up on her and she stared at the phone in horror. If her own partner turned against her, she was as good as dead. She needed answers and she was running out of time.

Without letting herself stop to think about it, she grabbed a white candle, a yellow candle, and the purple candle, lit them, and then placed them on top of the dresser again. "I am unmoving; I am fixed. I compel you to come to me, Autumn," she said before waving her hand and sending the purple candle on its march toward the white one.

So all she could do now was wait. Wait for George to call her back. Wait for Autumn to show up. *Wait for the toxin to make me as crazy as the others.*

She closed her eyes and prayed for strength. All her fear and confusion bubbled to the surface and she struggled to keep herself under control.

A sudden sound caused her to turn and she saw the purple candle speeding faster than it should toward the white candle until a moment later they were standing together.

A shock wave went through the room and Samantha realized that Autumn had arrived. She couldn't have been very far away to have gotten there so quickly.

There was a tentative knock on her door and with a wave of her hand she swung it open. Autumn stepped inside and Samantha closed the door behind her the same way. It was a waste of energy to use it on such a mundane task, but she had learned from years of watching that the witch who had the energy to waste on such frivolities often impressed upon those witnessing it that she must have greater power than they did.

Autumn looked sufficiently impressed by the display and stopped a couple of feet from Samantha, her head bowed respectfully.

"What do you want?" Samantha asked, hazarding a guess that the other witch must have already been on her way to see her since she had appeared so quickly when summoned.

"I just wanted to tell you that I don't think it's right that you haven't immediately been embraced by the high priestess," Autumn said, licking her lips in distress.

"You speak boldly against your leaders," Samantha said, drawing her words out a little more than usual.

"I speak the truth," Autumn insisted.

Samantha smiled and cocked her head slightly to the side. After a minute Autumn aped the behavior.

"So, what do you think should be done?"

Autumn swallowed. "I think we should break with the coven. I would gladly follow you. I believe there are others who would too."

"And who would they be?"

Autumn hesitated. "I'd rather not say until I know your thoughts on the matter."

"I think it's time you tell me everything you know about what they're doing."

"I don't know!" Autumn burst out. "They won't let me in."

"You seemed pretty cozy with Bridget the other day."

Autumn shook her head glumly and sat down at the desk. "I'm not sure she even knew my name until I told her about you."

"That's okay, Autumn," Samantha said, making her voice soothing. "You're a smart woman. You've been watching, listening. I'm sure you've gathered a lot of useful information. You might not even know how valuable some of it is. So, take your time and tell me everything you can think of."

"I was recruited about six months ago."

"By Bridget?"

She shook her head. "Jace and I are friends, and she introduced me to Calvin. By the way, whatever you did to him was totally amazing. It really got Bridget's attention. Maybe you could teach me?"

"Just tell me more," Samantha said, forcing herself to stay calm.

"It started off with small stuff, pretty boring, really. Then a couple of months ago we did the first one of those blood rituals like you saw the other night. I have no idea how you managed to stomach drinking the blood. Just the smell makes me sick."

Samantha was starting to regret her decision to try to make Autumn relax. The girl was too chatty for her taste.

"What are those rituals for?" Samantha asked.

Autumn shook her head. "I don't know. A lot of us don't. I know for sure that Karen and Jace don't."

"What do you think they're for?"

"I think we're trying to invoke something," Autumn said. "Spooky, huh?"

"What about the people who are getting hurt?"

Autumn looked at her for a moment, uncomprehending. "I don't understand."

"The women who've been killed?" Samantha prompted.

"What women?"

"Do you ever watch the news?"

"I can't afford television and I need to get a new computer. I keep frying them."

Samantha took a deep breath. Autumn, and likely several others, were even more in the dark than she'd guessed. She'd been right to want to get Karen away from the group. She considered trying to steer Autumn in that direction as well.

"Have you ever heard anyone mention the name of the high priestess?" Samantha asked.

"High—" Autumn started to say, then shuddered and collapsed on the floor, her eyes rolling back in her head.

Samantha stared for a moment, startled, and then knelt next to her.

"Autumn!"

The girl was comatose. Samantha touched her and received a mild electrical shock. *What on earth?* she wondered.

She sat there, unsure what to do. The act of saying the words "high priestess" had caused Autumn's mind to shut down. That implied that someone had rigged it that way. There was no reason to do so in a coven, since it would be normal to make reference to the high priestess, either the position or the person.

It had to be something more. Like maybe Autumn actually knew the name of the high priestess.

But why would that be a secret? Her entire coven had known the name and identity of Abigail Temple. She thought back to the ritual she had attended. No one had mentioned the high priestess's name. Most of the coven had never even revealed their faces to one another. She hadn't thought it strange, since performing some rituals fully cloaked was not uncommon.

But what if it was more than that? What if identities were being protected? If the coven was really committed to doing what they were doing, that seemed absurd. What Bridget had said came back to her, though. They needed the extra bodies.

Except for Bridget, the leaders must be unknown to the extra coven members, the ones who could be removed once their purpose was fulfilled. Autumn would seem to fall into that category, but for some reason she had learned a name she was never supposed to know.

And they hadn't killed her because they needed the bodies. So they put a block in her mind to keep her from revealing the name.

Excitement rushed through Samantha. All she had to do was figure out a way to get around the block. She checked Autumn's vital signs and they seemed stable. If they didn't kill her outright but bothered to put in the blocks, it stood to reason that the effects would be temporary.

She got up and paced around the room, running through everything she knew about mental blocks and curses. Figuring out how to remove them would require far more medical and psychological knowledge than she had. She couldn't even remember parts of her past that she had blocked herself, let alone figure out how to remove blocks from someone else's brain that a third party had put there.

Until she could figure out a way to get at the knowledge inside Autumn's brain, she couldn't encourage the woman to leave the coven.

A few minutes later Autumn stirred. She opened her eyes and pressed her hand to her head. "What happened?" she asked.

Samantha briefly debated telling her the truth, but was concerned that even thinking too hard about it might cause her to pass out again. "You fainted," she said.

"Wow, that's never happened before," she said.

"Better take it easy. You know, maybe you should see a doctor just to get checked out. Does anyone in the coven have any medical experience?" she asked. "Nurse, doctor, anyone?" She held her breath, hoping she might also find out the creator of the toxin.

Autumn shrugged. "We don't talk about our jobs, so I don't know."

Frustrated, Samantha tried another tack. "Who is in charge of healings?"

Autumn shook her head. "We've never done any healings. At least not since I've been there."

Samantha wanted to scream. Autumn was completely useless. The only bit of important information she had was locked inside her brain and even she couldn't get at it.

"You might want to ask around anyway," Samantha suggested. "It's better to have one of our kind work on us whenever possible."

"Thanks, I will," Autumn said. "What were we talking about?"

"You had asked me about splitting from the coven."

Autumn colored and then dropped her eyes. "Sorry. I get a bit full of myself sometimes. Forget I said anything." She stood up slowly. "I've really got to get going."

"It's okay," Samantha said, willing to let her go since she wasn't likely to get anything else useful out of her.

"And please, don't tell anyone I was talking like that," she said.

"I won't."

"Thank you."

Autumn left in a rush and Samantha closed the door after her with a frustrated sigh. Moments later she felt the girl exit the building and she allowed herself to relax slightly. It was important for the coven leadership to keep their identities hidden.

That was why she had to make uncovering them a top priority.

Suddenly there was a pounding on her door. It couldn't be Autumn. Perplexed, she went to the door and opened it. Anthony stormed in, his face like a thundercloud. She closed the door and turned to look at him.

"Anthony, why aren't you at the motel? What's wrong?" she asked.

He lifted a gun and aimed it at her heart.

"I just found out who you are. You're a Castor witch . . . the one I've sworn to kill for what you did to my mother."

22

Fear wrapped its icy hand around her heart and squeezed. Samantha had faced down a gun before, but never without one of her own, and never in the hands of someone she knew, someone she cared about.

"Anthony, listen to me," she said, trying to make her voice as soothing as possible.

It served only to inflame him more. "Don't!" he roared, shaking the gun at her. "Don't try to hypnotize me, witch! You might have escaped sixteen years ago, but not this time."

"I was a child when my family was slaughtered. I was adopted by a kind man and he and his wife raised me as their own, taught me right from wrong. I turned my back on the old life, happily, gratefully —"

"Then what the hell are you doing here, and what's all this in your room?"

"I'm a cop. You were right about that. When young women started turning up dead with occult symbols on them, my captain asked me to go undercover, put a stop to all of this."

"All of what? You talk a pretty story, but you still haven't told me what's going on."

She took a steadying breath, "The witches here — they're trying to resurrect somebody."

"Who?"

"The woman who killed your mother."

He jerked and nearly dropped the gun. "It's true," Samantha hastened to say as the color drained from his face.

"Can it be done?"

"Yes. They're close."

"And you're helping them!"

"No! I'm trying to stop them. That's why I'm here. Trust me, the one person that wants her to stay dead more than you is me."

He was staring her straight in the eye, which was good. She tried to keep him pinned with her eyes so that he wouldn't look down and see her sliding her left foot out of her shoe. The rubber sole on the shoe wasn't good for conducting electricity. But his shoes weren't so protected. She put her stocking foot on the floor and began rubbing the toes back and forth against the carpet, building up a static charge that she could use as a jumping-off point for sending electricity to him across the floor, shocking him hard enough that he would either drop the gun or miss wildly when he fired.

She could see the rage that twisted his features, the almost feverish light in his eyes, and for a moment she worried that he too had been affected by the toxin. But as she stared at him, she realized that what he was feeling wasn't enhanced by anything like that. It was the natural result of years of being fixated on revenge.

She was still talking, pleading with him to see reason, but she was only half aware of what she was saying anymore. All of her focus was on reading his body language and preparing for the moment when she would have to strike first.

Revenge against the witch who had killed his mother.

He wanted it so badly. For an instant her heart stuttered as she wondered whether he was actually part of the coven, intent on resurrecting the woman who had taken his mother from him so he could kill her himself.

She quickly dismissed that notion as crazy. Anthony had no powers. And as damaged as he might be by what had happened to his mother, he wasn't capable of killing other innocent women just to try to kill her killer again. It was the toxin, making her see witches where there were none.

No, what he'd said was true—he planned to take his revenge on the only survivor of the coven.

Which was her.

She continued talking and rubbing her foot against the carpet while she watched him. She felt as if all her senses were enhanced as she shifted her gaze from his eyes to his finger on the trigger of the gun and back. She could see the blood vessels in the whites of his eyes, the rippling of the muscles beneath the skin of his fingers.

And then she saw the moment when he finally made his decision, when rage overcame the last shred of reason and his finger began to tighten. She slammed her foot down hard, throwing electricity toward him. It shocked him hard enough that his entire body jerked as the volts raced through him.

And, thankfully, he dropped the gun. She jumped forward, scooping up the gun with her left hand even as she kicked him in the chest with her right foot.

He crashed backward, hitting his head on the ground hard. His entire body went slack and for one terrible moment she thought he was dead. But when she leaned over him, she could see the rise and fall of his chest.

She removed the bullets from the gun and placed the weapon on top of the bureau. She grabbed a length of twine from her bag of supplies and quickly tied his wrists together. She didn't want a fight on her hands when he came to.

She wished more than ever that she knew how the mental blocks worked. She would have loved to give him one so that he could never remember who she really was. Tears stung her eyes. She couldn't blame him for wanting to kill her. Had their positions been reversed she might have done the exact same thing.

She hadn't managed to calm herself down before he woke up with a jolt.

"What did you do to me?"

"Mild electrical shock. You hit your head when you fell," she said. "That's what knocked you out."

"Why not just kill me?" he said, glancing down at his bound wrists.

"I have no desire to kill you. And I didn't kill your mother! I was a child."

"You were there! You let it happen."

She couldn't deny that. She had recognized his mother's face, knew that she had been sacrificed. She had hazy memories of such things, nothing clear, but she knew enough to know that she had been there when his mother died.

"For the last time, I was a kid! I didn't have control over anything in my life back then. What I did, where I was, how I acted—everything in my life was controlled by others. I was made to do terrible things. Things you can't even imagine. I was in hell with no way out until the day I was freed."

She was shaking just thinking about how her life had been. It had been such a relief to be away from it. And the last several days she had been painfully reminded that the power she was wielding didn't come from freedom but from oppression. She remembered how it felt to stand there in the circle, holding the goblet, knowing that she had to drink. No choice. Even if she had been a real member of the coven and not an undercover one, there would have been no choice.

She hated living without choice.

"You should have told me who you were!" he hissed.

"I didn't have time to try to make things okay with you. I had too much work to do. So I just had to hope that you wouldn't find out until everything was safe and I could find a way to tell you."

"That worked out real well."

"How did you find out?" she asked.

"It wasn't hard," he said sarcastically. "I called the hotel to leave a message for you. The operator was quite perplexed that I thought a Samantha Hofferman was in your room. She did, quite helpfully, tell me that a Samantha Castor had that room. You didn't even try to hide who you were! I can't believe you had me eating out of your hand. You were probably laughing the entire time."

"Never laughing," she said. "I felt awful when I realized how we were connected. Everything I told you was true. I just omitted the fact that I was the survivor you were looking for."

"Pretty big fact. I can't believe you kissed me, knowing who you were, what you'd done."

"I didn't want to kiss you," she flared, feeling her cheeks flushing at the memory. "There's something between us. I don't know—"

"You mean my mother's blood?"

She hated him in that moment. She could feel energy surging through her, flowing to her hands. It would be so easy to kill him, to make the accusations and the pain and the confusion stop.

She spun around, wrestling with herself, trying to regain control of her careening emotions. She couldn't believe how she was feeling. She collapsed to her knees, shaking. *I almost killed him,* she realized, struggling to control the energy that was pulsing through her. She could smell something burning and realized that she had set the carpet beneath her on fire.

She put the fire out and dissipated the smoke so it wouldn't set off any smoke alarms, then hunched there, stunned. She was losing control, if she'd ever had it. She was starting to think that when it came to using the powers, to doing anything magical, control was an illusion. *You only think you control it, but it controls you.*

"Um, are you doing that on purpose?" Anthony asked.

She looked up and realized that everything in the room was vibrating, pictures were swinging on the walls, lamp shades were tilting, objects were sliding off the table, and the drawers of the bureau were sliding open and closing.

She was releasing energy in uncontrolled spurts and it was creating havoc in the space. It was probably leaking into the rooms on either side too. *The occupants will think the hotel is haunted,* she thought.

She took a shuddering breath and tried to calm herself.

"Seriously, are you doing that on purpose?" Anthony asked, fear edging into his voice.

"No," she said. She moved so that she was actually sitting down and crossed her legs. She breathed in and out slowly, trying to bring order to her mind.

"Okay, this is not cool!" he said as a candle flew across the room, barely missing his head.

"You're not helping," she said.

"Tell me what's going on!"

"I'm overloaded with energy and I can't focus enough to keep it under control."

"So you need somewhere else to put that energy?"

"That would be helpful since I can't seem to focus."

"My head's killing me."

She looked at him, her eyes narrowed.

"If you've got to put it somewhere, how about you help fix the bump on my head? Or finish patching up these broken ribs?"

"You're making a lot of assumptions," she said darkly. "Like I'm just going to let you go."

His jaw tensed. "Look, I believe you. I don't think you killed my mom."

"I'm not sure if you're telling the truth or if you're just afraid of what I'm going to do to you."

"I admit I'm afraid of what's happening right now," he said as a picture jumped off the wall and crashed on the floor near him. "So, whatever we need to do to stop all this, I'm good with it."

She moved over next to him and put her hand on the back of his head. She could feel the wound, feel the swelling around it. She channeled the energy through her hand, and his skin grew warm to the touch. He jerked slightly. He didn't trust her. And after what she'd almost done to him, maybe he was right not to.

She felt pain in her own head even as she healed his. She next moved her hands over his ribs and sucked in her breath sharply as pain knifed through her side. When she was done he heaved a sigh and she could tell he felt better. After a minute the pain she felt subsided. She pulled her hand back and around them the room started to settle down and soon all was still.

"Does that happen to you all the time?" he asked, open curiosity in his voice.

"No," she said, clearing her throat. "I went fifteen years without using my powers at all. Now in the past week I've had to do so much with them and I'm out of practice. I can't control them like I used to. And for some reason, you upset me even more than the people I'm trying to stop."

"Ditto."

She moved away and sat facing him. "If I let you go, will you promise to not try to kill me?"

"No."

She took a ragged breath. "Will you promise not to try again tonight?"

"Yes."

She moved her hand and the twine binding him snapped apart. He shook it off and rubbed his wrists, staring at her speculatively. "Do you still need help catching the other witches?"

"I'm not a witch."

He raised an eyebrow and glanced around the room.

"Having these powers doesn't make you a witch. It's what you do with them that defines you."

"How long you been rehearsing that?"

"All week."

"Do you believe it yet?"

"No," she whispered.

"So, you need help?"

"Obviously I do. But I don't want you getting hurt."

"We have a strange relationship," he noted ruefully.

"I should warn you, the people who have been going crazy, seeing witches, like the one who attacked the mannequin in your window, seem to have been infected by some kind of magic."

"Okay, what's the deal?" he asked.

"It seems like some sort of magic that's acting like a

toxin, altering brain chemistry and heightening people's fear and paranoia."

"You think I've been infected?"

"No. At least, you weren't when you came in here. But I was infected earlier today and it's possible that when I touched you, you were too."

"How will I know?" he asked, his face growing pale.

"Fear, phobia, paranoia, a desire to kill all witches."

He stared at her for a moment before clearing his throat. "Okay, I'll ask again. How will I know if I've been infected?"

She had the insane urge to laugh. She bit her lip and shook her head. "If you get crazier than you are now."

"Oh good, something to look forward to."

"Tell me about it," she said.

"So how do you fix it?"

"I'm trying to figure that out." She closed her eyes. "Have you ever heard any rumors about medical professionals that link them to witchcraft?"

He frowned. "Like a witch doctor?"

"Very funny. No, like a doctor who also happens to be a witch."

He was silent for a long minute and she opened her eyes. "What is it?"

"Once, a couple of years ago, I ended up in the emergency room. Car accident. The other driver was more messed up than I was and the same doctor saw us both."

"And?"

"It took my broken arm twelve weeks to heal and when I left that hospital I felt completely drained. I was in bad shape for weeks. When I finally got out of the house I saw the other driver in the grocery store. The man had had two broken legs and a crushed arm. And yet there he was, four weeks after the accident and he was perfectly fine, not a scratch on him. He wouldn't even look me in the eye. I heard he moved out of the area shortly after."

"And you think the doctor took energy from you and gave it to him?" she asked.

"I don't know," Anthony admitted. "It always seemed strange to me, and after seeing what you can do with energy, it would explain a whole lot."

"Do you know the name of the doctor?" she asked eagerly. "It's important."

"No, but I can find out," he said.

She hesitated.

"Let me do this. I need to help take these people down."

"What you need to do is go back to that motel and keep your head down until it's safe."

"And what if it's never safe?" he asked. "What if you get killed? Or what if you take this coven down only to have another one spring up in its place? Look, I'm not the kind to just sit and wait and do nothing."

"If something happens, if they catch you, I might not make it in time to save you again."

"I'm willing to live with that risk."

She wasn't sure that she was.

She stood up and then helped him to his feet. He left a couple of minutes later and she locked the door behind him, then moved over to the bed and lay down. Her mind raced.

She tried calling George, but it went to voice mail. She ground her teeth in frustration. It was twenty-four hours until the Halloween parade and she needed to find out how to purge the toxins from her system before then.

Everything was unraveling and she was afraid there was nothing she could do to stop it.

Samantha woke in the dark before dawn with a start. Something was terribly wrong. Shadows oozed down the walls. She sat up, her heart thundering in her chest. It took her a moment to realize they were real and headed right for her.

She threw back the covers and jumped to her feet. Standing in the middle of the bed she could see that shadows were swarming across the floor as well. And she could feel witches present in the building, nearby. The shadows reminded her of those that had bound her in the back room of the Witchery. There was a good chance that either Randy or the witch that had been injured was involved. The way they moved was too similar for it to be a coincidence.

She spun, looking for an exit, but the slithering shadows were everywhere. The ones nearest the bed began to slither onto it. *Like snakes.*

She brought her hands together just as she had done to form the kitten and shaped a ball of energy into a mongoose. It leaped from her hands onto the bed, attacking the shadow snake nearest it. She formed another and another. She cursed while she was doing it. There had to be a better, faster way to banish the shadow creatures, but she didn't know what it was.

I need to remember more magic.

Soon battles were raging all over the room. With the shadows' attention diverted, she was able to leap off the bed and move to the door. As she neared it she felt the energy just on the other side. She braced herself and then flung the door open. She reached out and grabbed the two cloaked figures in the hall and yanked them into the room, slamming the door shut behind them. They spun to face her and she let loose all the energy that had been building for hours and that she'd been struggling to control. The wave swept both of them off their feet and they landed hard on their backs.

"Who sent you?" she demanded as she pressed a knee to the throat of the one nearest to her.

"We're going to kill you," the other one hissed, raising a hand.

"Not if I kill you first."

Four of her mongooses leaped on the witch's face. The witch screamed and Samantha touched her leg, sending a blast of energy to fry her vocal cords.

She returned her attention to the witch beneath her knee. She ripped off the hood and even in the dark she recognized Calvin. "Who sent you?" she asked, putting more pressure on his throat until his eyes bulged in panic. He clawed at her, struggling for air. She let up for a moment.

"No one," he gasped. "We . . . we wanted you dead— what you did to us."

"Tell me the name of the high priestess!"

"She'll eat you alive. She has plans for you," he said.

"Her name?" Samantha said, setting his hair on fire.

"Stop! I'll tell you. Her name is—"

The fire whooshed and suddenly engulfed his entire head, killing him instantly. Samantha snuffed it, stunned. She turned and saw the witch she had severely injured. She had dissipated the mongoose and a snarl twisted her face. Her hand was raised and Samantha realized she had killed Calvin so he wouldn't talk.

The witch raised her hands and made a choking motion and Samantha felt her own air supply cut off. She clawed at her throat, even though she knew there was nothing there to grab.

Calm down! Think! she commanded herself. The remaining shadows began to slither toward her. She had to stop the witch choking her, but she could feel the panic taking over. She needed to think, she needed to . . .

Her thoughts flew to the bullets that were sitting on the desk. She swept her hand and the bullets flew through the air and embedded themselves deep in the witch's chest.

The woman's eyes opened wide in surprise, blood began to trickle from the corner of her mouth, and then she collapsed. The shadows disappeared from the room and the invisible hands released their hold on Samantha's throat.

She collapsed on her side, gagging, and closed her eyes. *I killed her with magic. Even though I used bullets, I still killed her with magic. Dear God, what have I done?*

23

It took Samantha an hour to clean herself up. Afterward she called her captain and told him what had happened. He wanted to send in officers, but she talked him out of it.

"If I was who I'm pretending to be, the police would never find the bodies," she said. "I can't have anyone bag and tag these bodies and take them out of here."

"Then what do you want to do?"

"I'm going to hide them for now. I'll preserve them and we can figure out what you want to do about them later," she said.

"There's nothing natural about any of this," he said in a strangled voice.

"My world. Welcome to it," she said with a bone-weary sigh. "Have you heard anything from Ed or George?"

"They've been working hard. It turns out the latest victim had a sister who's also missing."

"The final sacrifice."

"That's what we're thinking. It's the most we've had to go on, so I've got everyone working overtime on it."

"I've left a couple of messages for George. I need to talk to him in a medical capacity. I've figured out how they're causing the rioting. It's magic that's infecting people like a toxin, making them delusional and provoking them." She hesitated and then continued. "Based on something Ed said to me yesterday, I think he might have been infected."

Captain Roberts swore. "Can you undo whatever this is?"

"Not without talking to George."

"I'll see that he calls you back as soon as possible," he said.

"Thanks."

She hung up and stared at her phone. The battery was all but dead. It had had a full charge when she went to bed, but all the magic had drained it. It was why many witches had trouble with technology. With a sigh she plugged it in to charge. She had to do a couple of things and she just hoped she didn't miss George's call.

First she stacked the bodies in the bathtub and put a light spell on them to keep them from starting to decay.

Just as she was finishing that task, the phone rang. She picked up, relieved to find that it was George.

"Hi. Thanks for calling."

"Captain said it was urgent. I don't have anything new yet."

"That's okay. I had another question for you," Samantha said, sitting down on the bed. "I need to discuss how viruses can be transmitted by touch."

"Okay. Well, most diseases, such as the flu, are actually transmitted by droplets. A person coughs or sneezes and droplets end up in someone else's nose or mouth or breathed into their lungs. These droplets can travel up to six feet to infect someone else. By the same token, common items such as doorknobs that have been touched by someone who has sneezed may then be touched by a healthy person who then rubs their eyes or nose or eats without washing their hands, and the disease is transmitted."

"What about ways other than droplets?" she asked.

"Other transmission of disease through physical contact is usually incurred through touching of bodily fluids during kissing, sex, sharing of utensils, or touching weeping blisters from diseases such as shingles."

"And what about cures for viruses or toxins?"

"Do you think you've come across some kind of outbreak?" he asked sharply.

She hesitated, not sure what Ed or Captain Roberts had shared with George about the nature of witches and magic. "I just need to know. I can't explain at the moment," she said at last.

"For something like a toxin, or poison, you would need an antidote, something that would render it inert. Toxins are something you can absorb right through your skin. The skin is permeable and will absorb what's placed on it. Some kinds of poisons and even drugs are meant to be absorbed through the skin."

"Can confusion, hallucination, erratic behavior be attributed to poisons or toxins?"

"Yes, all of those. Those kinds of responses are often seen in hospitals in patients who are allergic to certain medications."

"How do antidotes generally work?" Samantha asked.

"They're used to counteract. Something that is particularly acidic, for example, can be neutralized by a base. Charcoal when swallowed can absorb several types of poisons. For many types of poisonous bites, like those from snakes or spiders, antidotes have been created by injecting small amounts of the poison into lab animals. Their bodies create antibodies to fight the poison and we use those antibodies to create antidotes."

"Thank you, George."

"Is there anything I should know?" he asked.

"Not right now."

"If you need anything else, call," he said, sounding worried.

"I will," she promised, then hung up.

She put the phone down and stared at the battery-charge light for a minute while she thought. Her five-year-old self had taught her that energy could be shaped into whatever form the magic user wished. Instead of a snake or a cat someone had found a way to shape energy into a toxin. Physical contact imparted a bit of the charged energy to the next person, who was then infected, and so on. It was brilliant. Instead of putting a spell or curse on a single person, you could use a single person to spread that curse to dozens. But there had to also be a cure. Almost all magic could be reversed. And there was no way the coven would have risked putting something so dangerous out into the world if they didn't also have a means of controlling it if that became necessary.

But the mechanics of it were beyond her. It would take a strong, experienced witch to even hope to pull something like that off. A working knowledge of biochemistry would also be a huge plus so they could know exactly what parts of the brain they were targeting. It was so elaborate it seemed insane. But if you needed a way to cause hysteria in mass quantities of people, it was brilliant.

She stood up. She would find no answers sitting there. Finished with what she needed to do to secure the bodies, she locked the room and left her phone charging.

The lobby was filled with people and she had to shove to make her way outside. The Halloween parade wasn't until evening, but the streets were already filling. She gaped in amazement as she walked toward Essex Street.

Throngs of people lined the streets, many carrying signs either condemning witches or condemning the killing of witches. Every couple of blocks a fight broke out among the protestors.

Samantha's whole body was tingling, overloaded by the passion and energy of the spectators. She had been present when there were massive crowds before, but this was different. The energies were focused instead of scattered.

Her own paranoia was building to impossible levels and no amount of prayer or cleansing spells seemed to help. She was toxic, just another victim of the fever that Karen had unwittingly spread to so many.

Police officers, some on horseback, struggled to keep the crowd under control, but some of them were also falling victim to the toxin. As she hurried toward the Museum of the Occult, she saw one officer trying to arrest an old woman and yelling, "Witch!" She wasn't one, but given the way she looked and dressed, she certainly wasn't discouraging this interpretation.

Samantha hurried past. It was taking all of her concentration to move through the crowd unnoticed. She wanted to check on the museum, make sure no one, especially Anthony, was there. Sooner or later she was going to need to remove some of the artifacts he had in the building. They were just too dangerous to be left there. Then she needed to check on Anthony, make sure he was okay and knew to keep away from the crowd.

She was near the museum when she felt a wave of energy rolling toward her. She half turned as it crashed against her. She flailed wildly to keep her balance and then staggered backward as an undertow sought to pull her in the direction the wave had come from.

She spun to face it, gritting her jaw in determination, but another wave knocked her down and the resultant undertow dragged her six feet across the pavement, scraping her hands and arms.

She was being summoned, but unlike her summoning of Autumn and the others, there was nothing subtle about it. And whoever was doing it had more power than Samantha could ever dream of. There was no way she could fight it, and to try would only delay the inevitable and risk exposing her to the crowd, which was already staring in fascination.

She staggered to her feet, feeling their eyes upon her. She pointed with a shaky hand to the fake witch the policeman was trying to arrest. The woman had dressed in a pointy hat and was wearing her long, straggly gray hair free for a reason. She wanted the attention. Samantha shouted, "The witch did this to me!"

And just like that all attention swiveled away from Samantha and to the old woman and the policeman. Samantha began to run in the direction the wave was pulling her, guilt nearly crushing her. There was a very real chance that she had just given those infected with the toxin a target.

Now that she was heading in the direction she was meant to go, the energy didn't crash against her violently, but rather flowed around her, gently pulling her in the right way. She expected it to take her to the old house where they had performed the latest ritual. She was surprised when instead of leading her to the end of Essex Street, the energy led her to the right.

She ran past her hotel, and as she came to the harbor,

she tried to slow to a walk. The moment she did, though, the energy smashed against her, and she staggered to keep her feet. She began to run again. It wasn't enough for the summoner that she arrive at the desired location. Time was clearly an issue.

As she ran past the House of the Seven Gables, a terrible suspicion filled her mind. As she approached the cemetery she could feel waves of power rippling through the air and others came into sight, also running from several different directions. They were all converging on one place.

The grave of Abigail Temple.

She didn't want to go. She was terrified that whoever was summoning her had the power to compel her to participate in the resurrection against her will. Tears of rage and fear stung her eyes, but still she ran through the open gate, flashing past rows of headstones. And then she arrived at the grave of her former high priestess.

The earth had been dug up, the coffin opened and emptied. The wave of energy that had compelled her forward ceased, and she spun to her left to see that an altar had been erected among the graves and on it lay the skeleton of Abigail Temple. Bile rose in Samantha's throat as she stared.

There were others present. A few were cloaked, but the vast majority, like her, had been summoned in what they were wearing at the time. One young girl, wearing nothing more than a towel, was quaking and ashen. Her feet were oozing blood into the grass, having been cut when she was forced to run barefoot. An overweight man collapsed onto the ground, wheezing and grabbing at his left arm. Samantha took a step forward to help him and then stayed her hand. She might not have any control over what happened in the next few minutes, but he was one witch she didn't have to save.

She looked around to see the faces of the others. A few wore looks of triumph, but far more wore looks of fear. They were accustomed to being asked to join, not forced to. Autumn stood a few feet away, refusing to look at Samantha. *She's afraid they'll find out what she said to me,* she thought.

Jace was hugging herself, a look of excitement on her face. As the others showed up, Samantha counted thirty. All of them were staring openly at the skeleton except for Randy, who had been looking steadily at her. She couldn't read his expression and it worried her.

Ten minutes passed slowly. Samantha took a couple of experimental steps backward only to feel the wave of energy threatening to pull her back, so she stopped. It hadn't been meant just to bring her; it was also meant to ensure that she stayed.

Finally Bridget stepped up to the altar and raised her hands. Silence fell. Even the birds in the trees ceased their chirping, and though Samantha could see the wind pushing the trees, she could not hear the leaves fluttering together. It was the most complete, most disturbing silence she had ever known.

"My brothers and sisters, the day we have been working for is finally upon us. We are gathered here to resurrect Abigail Temple, high priestess. It was she who led the coven who once occupied this place. It is she we have sought to honor with all of our actions. And now, after we call her back to this world, with her help we will gain the ultimate power and be ourselves gods and goddesses of this world."

Glancing around, Samantha saw a few skeptical

looks, but the vast majority of those present believed. The light of fanaticism illuminated their faces and they nodded their heads eagerly just as she had seen many people do in church during a particularly moving sermon.

Her hand touched her throat, tracing the outline of the moon necklace she had been wearing in lieu of her cross. She glanced over at Randy and found that he was still staring at her. And for just a moment, she thought he might not be the enemy.

He turned away and the moment was gone.

"Remove your shoes and socks so that we might form a connection with the earth," Bridget commanded.

Reluctantly, Samantha pulled off her shoes and socks, carefully placing them beside her. She could feel the grass beneath her toes, the energy of the earth and the creatures in it. She closed her eyes. The sensation, the connection with the natural world, and the enhanced abilities in the presence of others of power were overwhelming, addictive. It was one of the reasons so many with the power were drawn to nature-based religions and why others shunned religion in favor of viewing themselves as gods.

"Form the circle."

The ground itself pushed up against her feet, forcing her to move forward. She looked around and saw fear touching a few other faces, those who were aware that their will was no longer their own. And then they were in a circle ringing the altar. Bridget and those who were cloaked formed a smaller circle inside the large one, each with a hand on the altar.

Samantha's mind worked feverishly, trying to find a way to put an end to all of this. Her phone was charging back in her hotel room. She couldn't have called for backup even if she'd wanted to. She was convinced that the presence of other officers would only result in their own slaughter at the hands of the witches.

Thirty people were present. Only one was under her sway and together they weren't enough. Autumn had ambition but was unskilled in combat. Samantha reached out, sensing the life of everything around her, the energy of the animals, the people gathering throughout the nearby streets, even the other witches. If she could pull energy from all of them, it might be enough.

She closed her eyes and felt a surge of power rush through her.

And then rush *out* of her.

She opened her eyes in panic and saw from the stricken looks on other faces that it wasn't happening just to her. Bridget's skin was actually glowing with luminescence as she and the other cloaked figures together pulled the energy from all those in the outer circle.

We're feeding them.

She tried to stop pulling energy from the animals and people that she had connected to through the ground and realized with a shudder that she couldn't stop. All of them were chained together like a battery and they were going to be used to animate the dead witch.

She could feel so much and it hurt. She could feel the pain and confusion of the people downtown as their energy, their very life force, was being drained from them. Tears streaked her cheeks. Bridget was hurting them by bringing life to Abigail and there was nothing Samantha could do to stop it.

Several others were crying openly, and she could feel their panic, their misery. They had all come to the coven like Karen, seeking something. They hadn't signed up for what was happening.

"They're dying!" Jace burst out, confusion and guilt in her voice.

Samantha watched as a witch to her left moved her hand with great effort and raised an athame, which she plunged into her own chest.

Samantha cried out as she felt the woman die, her own heart stopping for a moment before painfully resuming. The woman's body crumpled to the ground and began to mummify even as what remained of her energy was sucked out by the group. The woman who had been standing next to her began to sob uncontrollably, but her grief only added to what she was sending toward the altar.

Around the circle several who had shown no doubts about being there shouted in triumph as the energy rolled through them and bloodlust took them over.

Maybe they'll kill one another, she thought with a surge of hope. And then a moment later realized that if they did, it would just aid in what Bridget was trying to accomplish.

As more energy poured through her, all her muscles tightened and began to vibrate. She screamed in pain and heard other voices joining hers. Around her the ground started moving, pulsing. A small funnel cloud formed over the skeleton. Dirt and debris from the open grave behind her flew past her head, sucked up by the tornado.

A bird fell out of the sky at her feet and exploded. Pieces of it flew into the tornado and the rest evaporated as the energy was ripped from it. The trees nearby shuddered and bits of bark flew to join the twister. The girl in the towel fell to the ground, writhing in pain and vomiting blood. Samantha couldn't see but could feel the tiny molecules of matter that were separating themselves from the rest of the girl's body, called to rejoin the witch.

The rush of wind continued and more bits and pieces, most too small to be seen, flew past until the tornado above the body was dense and dark. And then Bridget shouted something into the wind and those touching the altar jumped backward.

The tornado dropped down, engulfing the altar and the skeleton and a roaring sound filled Samantha's ears. Around her, witches were shaking with the exertion, bleeding from eyes and ears. Across the circle Jace collapsed and was subsumed. The woman to her left fell next and Samantha cried as she felt herself pulling the woman's body apart, draining the energy and sending it on.

The tornado became less dense and she began to see muscles forming over the skeleton. Everything that had made up Abigail Temple's body in life was returning to her and Samantha watched in horror as the body rebuilt itself. Blood vessels and nerve endings re-formed. Skin, hair, nails, eyes, teeth returned last.

And then the body was complete. Abigail Temple, just as she had looked in life.

And suddenly the rush of energy stopped. Samantha crashed to her knees along with the others in the outer circle. Autumn had fallen facefirst in the grass and lay unmoving. Samantha wondered if the exertion had killed her. Three witches some distance away from her clung to one another and cried. She could feel their grief, their sense of betrayal. She wanted to reach out to them, to connect, but she didn't have the strength left.

She was too weak even to pull energy to help herself. Next to her Randy was moaning softly, his eyes glazed with pain. She hated him and the others. Murderous thoughts bubbled up within her.

God, help me!

From somewhere she found the strength to rise to her feet. She stood, swaying slightly, feeling like she was going to pass out. But at least she was standing, and no one else in the outer circle was.

But she didn't have the strength to do anything else. Bridget stripped the cloak off one of the inner circle to reveal a young woman, clearly hypnotized. She wasn't one of the witches. She was the final sacrifice.

While Samantha watched, helpless to intervene, one of the other cloaked figures slashed the young woman's wrists. She started to collapse, but they held her up as she bled out into the same ceremonial goblet that Samantha had been forced to drink from.

She had no tears left to cry for the dying girl. She tried to take a step forward, but her knees buckled and she barely kept herself from falling. It was too late anyway. The girl was dead. Bridget raised the goblet to the sky and then took a drink of it before turning and pouring the sacrificial blood over Abigail's body.

"Accept this final sacrifice in exchange for releasing Abigail Temple!"

The earth shook but Samantha managed to keep her feet. Thunder clapped overhead and a screaming sound echoed it. And the dead witch sat up.

Abigail Temple was alive.

Samantha wanted to run. She wanted to scream.

But most of all she wanted to kill.

The remaining hooded figures surrounded Abigail. They put a cloak around her and then she was lost to Samantha's sight.

After a moment Bridget separated herself and came toward Samantha, a spring in her step, and a smile on her face.

I'm going to kill her.

Bridget stopped and glanced down at Randy. "Don't just lie there," she said with a laugh.

Samantha watched as Randy dragged himself to his feet and knew what it cost him. He was shaking from head to toe. His athame was in a sheath on his waist and the hilt swung back and forth as he tried to gain his balance.

Bridget turned to Samantha and gave her a small pout.

"I'm sorry you weren't with me," Bridget said. "But the plans were laid long before you arrived and disturbing them would have caused more problems than I needed to handle."

"You should have included me anyway," Samantha said, forcing herself to stand tall and growl disapprovingly. "At the very least, you should have asked my permission before using me that way."

"I'm sorry about that," Bridget said with a grimace. "I know it had to be unpleasant."

"Unpleasant?" Samantha asked, rage rushing through her. "Being forced into something against your will isn't unpleasant. There's a much more appropriate word for what you did."

"Oh, come on, aren't you being a little melodramatic?" Bridget asked.

Samantha grabbed Randy's athame and before either he or Bridget could act, she stabbed Bridget in the throat with it.

Bridget fell without making a sound, her blood spilling onto the ground, washing over Samantha's toes. And Samantha let it. There was energy in the blood and she needed all she could get.

She handed Randy back his athame and he took it, a

strange look on his face as he stared at the blood on it.
Then he wiped it on his pants before resheathing it.

Samantha heard a chuckle and looked up.

Abigail Temple was standing before her, a smile on
her face. "I'm glad to see, child, that you have grown into
the kind of woman I can be proud of."

24

Samantha stood, Bridget's blood coating her feet, her old high priestess smiling at her, and she felt something inside her shatter. She had failed. All those girls had still died and evil walked the earth even though she had tried to stop it. Breaking her vows, using magic, turning into someone she didn't want to be—all had been for nothing.

Abigail looked down at Bridget and nudged the body with a bare toe. "A useful tool, but in the end no more than that." She looked back at Samantha. "I'm proud of you for seeing that."

The old woman turned and surveyed the rest. She raised a hand high and Samantha knew better than to try to stab her in the back. The first lesson she had learned about Abigail as a child was that the woman had eyes in the back of her head. Just hearing her voice served to unlock more memories that swirled around her, threatening to overwhelm her.

And deep inside, a spark of joy flickered. Abigail had said she was proud of her. Standing there, Samantha felt like two people, like she was literally splitting in two. Darkness clawed at the corners of her mind, scratching, wanting to be let out.

Her hand reached to her throat but found only the

moon necklace that was there. Her mother's. And even though the gemstone in it was designed to help her focus her energies on higher things, it made her feel no closer to God. If anything, it was moving her closer to being like her mother.

She ripped it from around her throat and flung it away in disgust.

Abigail began to speak. "I am Abigail, high priestess of an old and powerful coven. I have heard you call for me and I am here now to help lead you. And with the assent of your high priestess, I will share that role with her."

The cloaked figure who had been the one to kill the final victim gave a brief nod. *The high priestess, at last.* Samantha needed to know who she was. She took a step forward, but Randy reached out and grabbed her arm. She turned to look at him and he shook his head ever so slightly.

She narrowed her eyes, wondering again what his story was. He turned his eyes back to Abigail and as soon as she forced herself to relax, he let her arm go.

She didn't know why he had stopped her, but he was right to do so. Despite the energy she had absorbed from Bridget, she was still shaky from everything that had happened. She wasn't even sure she'd have been able to walk the steps needed to reach the witch.

"And now we will retire to my home, so that we might gather our strength for what is to come. As should the rest of you. Return to your homes and prepare yourselves. There is much work ahead."

Samantha looked around. Two dozen witches remained and they were exhausted, battered, but they were listening. Abigail's voice held a certain resonance to it that never failed to mesmerize lesser witches. In the normal world she would have been described as charismatic.

To Samantha she was just plain evil. And there was the age-old dilemma with which man struggled. Evil at its very heart held a strange fascination, attraction. She could feel its pull, calling to the dark parts of her own soul. She glanced over at Randy and could tell that he was consciously fighting it as well.

Abigail moved back to join the cloaked witches, and as a group they moved away. Samantha couldn't let them escape. She might never have them all in one place again. She had to try, no matter how drained she was.

She stepped forward and something hit her in the chest and pushed her back. She glanced over at Randy, but he was kneeling, looking at Bridget. It hadn't come from him then.

She tried to move again and again was pushed back, this time hard enough to knock her to the ground. She lay there for a moment, struggling to catch her breath.

You will join us soon enough. She heard Abigail's voice echoing in her head. She was not welcomed into the inner circle, but left outcast with the others. She gritted her teeth in frustration.

I know where they're going at least, she thought. She just needed to let them get there and then maybe she could follow. She sat up slowly, pain knifing through her. She was spent. She rolled over so she could push up off the ground with her hands and feet. She straightened with difficulty, still winded.

She glanced around and saw the anxiety on the faces of the remaining witches. They were sitting in a graveyard with an open grave and a fresh corpse. They were feeling exposed and vulnerable but most of them were still too sapped to move.

Randy stood slowly and looked after the retreating group. Then, without a word, he turned and limped out of the graveyard, heading in the opposite direction.

Samantha looked down at her feet. Bridget was dead. But with Abigail alive it seemed such a hollow victory. Autumn had rolled over and was lying on her back staring blankly up at the sky. She was alive.

I should kill her. I should kill them all.

The thought came to her and she held it in her mind, examining it from every possible angle. It made complete sense. As she had told her captain, no jail would be able to hold the witches, no jury would have the clarity of mind to convict them after they worked their magic on it. And even attempting to arrest them would get a lot of good officers killed.

Besides, they deserve to die for what they've done.

She didn't have the strength to do it. But even if she could kill just one or two more, that would be one or two she wouldn't have to face later.

Her eyes swiveled to Autumn. Tears were flowing down the girl's cheeks. Whether they were from the pain she was experiencing or grief over the loss of her friend, Jace, was impossible to tell.

Or it could be fear. Or guilt over what she's done.

Samantha knew that at least until this moment Autumn had been completely naive about what was really going on. But now—now she had witnessed the high priestess killing the girl.

Samantha looked around slowly, wondering how many of those who were still there had had their eyes opened to what was really happening and might be looking for a way out.

She hobbled very slowly over to the altar, feeling their eyes upon her. She could feel their fear, their uncertainty too. If ever there was a time to sway them, it was now.

"I can tell that not all of you knew what you were getting into today. Now you do. And having been a member of Abigail's coven since birth, I can tell you that it will only get worse from here." She turned slowly in a circle. Her body ached in protest, but she forced herself to move, to make eye contact with everyone who wasn't afraid to look at her.

"You think today was terrible? You think watching them sacrifice a girl, raise the dead, and use you, your magic, essentially raping you, was hell? I'm here to tell you that you haven't even begun to see hell. But now that your eyes are opened, now that Abigail Temple walks the earth, I'm telling you that you *will* see hell.

"That woman raised a demon that slaughtered my entire coven, including her. I alone escaped. I am bound to this coven, but none of the rest of you is. You are not part of their inner circle. If you leave now, leave Salem, they are not likely to hunt you. And for everyone who does leave, I will dig an extra grave when I bury these," she said, pointing to the bodies around them. "That will assure that no one will ever come looking for you. Not even me."

She straightened and forced her voice to resonate as she continued. "This is my only act of compassion. For any who choose to remain, I will bind them from speaking of your leaving to anyone; they will suffer death at my hand if they do. I have killed Bridget, whom you all feared, as easily as breathing when I was weakened and she was not. Imagine what I would do to any of you. To *all* of you."

She paused to let her words sink in. She could see the struggle on many faces. In the end she had been able to kill Bridget not because she was more powerful than her but because she had managed to take her by surprise. That wasn't how they saw it, though, and she could see just as much fear of her on their faces as fear of staying in the coven. Finally she finished. "I offer each of you a chance at life, a chance to walk away and save yourselves. Who will take it?"

"I will." A young girl with flaming red hair spoke up quickly. Samantha walked to her. She leaned down and took the girl's hand. She closed her eyes and reached deep inside herself, pulling energy from the air around her and the earth beneath her. And then she passed some of it to the girl. She opened her eyes and helped her to stand.

And the girl's eyes brimmed with tears. "Thank you," she whispered.

"Go, and do no more evil," Samantha whispered for her ears alone.

The girl began to walk and then she ran, fleeing the cemetery as though the very hounds of hell were on her heels. The others watched her go and then turned admiring and fearful gazes upon Samantha. They knew she had found the extra power to grant the girl enough energy to run when none of the rest of them had enough even to stand.

"Who else?" Samantha demanded.

Two older women who were sitting together with clasped hands nodded. "Us."

Samantha moved over to them, took their hands, and gave them the strength to stand. They did and embraced each other tearfully. Then they turned to Samantha. She could do nothing to alleviate the horror and the pain in their eyes.

"Help each other to heal, but do not let each other forget," she whispered.

They nodded and then they too hurried from the cemetery. Samantha's knees wanted to buckle, but she forced herself to turn, trying to pull more energy from her environment, though she was so exhausted that her ability to do so was badly impaired.

"Who else?" she asked.

A man lying on the ground, too weak to move or speak, grunted. She walked to him, working hard not to show her own pain and fatigue. She leaned down and touched his hand. After a moment he sat up and took a deep breath. He had been on the verge of death. Slowly, he stood.

"Forgive me," he whispered.

"There are others you must ask that of, not me. Make sure that you do so when you can say it and they can hear it."

He bowed his head and then limped slowly away.

Before she could ask the question again, an old woman and a young man raised their hands. Samantha moved to them, took each by the hand, and raised them to their feet.

"I wanted a better life for my grandson than I had," the old woman said, tears shimmering in her eyes.

"Then give him the love you never had."

Samantha turned to the boy. "And give her the hope she needs."

They both nodded and they held each other up as they left.

"Anyone else?" she asked the remaining ten.

Silence greeted her. She turned and looked at Autumn, silently willing her to go, but the girl turned her head away. *She's sealed her own fate,* Samantha thought.

"Last chance," she said.

She turned slowly. The remaining ones were staying.

She could see it in their body language, though none dared to meet her eyes.

"Very well. Those six that have left—they are dead to all of us. And if I hear a word that anyone said otherwise, that anyone sought them out, then I will end that person. Understood?"

Every head nodded.

"Good."

Samantha turned and walked away, head held high, refusing to show any sign of weakness. The others she left lying on the ground. It would be hours before they recovered strength enough to move on their own. Until then they could sit with the dead, including their recently fallen comrades, and contemplate the consequences of their decisions.

She made it past the cemetery and slowed slightly, forcing one step at a time. She stumbled a couple of times, but forced herself to keep walking. There was so much she needed to do, but she was helpless until she could heal and regain her strength.

She gritted her teeth against the pain. Every step sent shock waves through her bones, jarring them. Her nerve endings flared, on fire. She could hear her body creaking and groaning, threatening to fly apart at any moment. She was completely drained. She was so dehydrated that despite the pain, no tears could form.

Her muscles began to cramp and spasm. Her fingers contracted, curling into her palms, and the pain robbed her momentarily of her vision. Her body was beginning to shut down. She had drained it of everything it needed to sustain itself. She needed to find some place of safety, where she could get off the street and hide. She would never make it back to her hotel room, and the farther she walked toward it, the more protestors and revelers she would encounter.

I can't die, not like this, she thought, her mind flailing about for a solution. She took one more step and crumpled to the pavement. Her vision started to fade and she could feel her heart slowing, slowing.

"Samantha!"

Someone was calling her name, but she didn't know who. *I should answer,* she thought. But she was too tired.

"Samantha!" Someone was touching her, but she didn't know why.

And then she didn't know anything.

Samantha woke with a start, her heart pounding. She opened her eyes and had no idea where she was. It was an old-fashioned bedroom and she was lying on the bed. She turned her head and saw Anthony sitting in a chair, watching her quietly.

She tried to speak, but her mouth was too dry.

Most of her childhood she'd heard the voices of the others of her coven in her head at one time or another. And trapped with Ed in the basement of Abigail's house, the voices there that had said she was going to die had also been internal. She had forgotten how to put her words into another's mind, but the knowledge came rushing back suddenly. *Where am I?* she thought, reaching out to touch his mind.

He jumped, startled, and stared at her for a moment wide-eyed.

"The Turner-Ingersoll Mansion."

She blinked. The name sounded familiar, but at the moment everything seemed hazy.

"The House of the Seven Gables," he said.

How?

"I found you on the street just outside. I could barely feel your pulse. They know me pretty well here and as a professional courtesy to another museum curator, they allowed me to bring you up here. Don't worry, we won't be disturbed."

How long?

"Going on two hours now." He flushed and looked away. "I tried doing that thing you did to me, you know, pushing energy into you. Not sure it worked."

It did. You saved my life. Thank you.

He nodded, but didn't say anything.

Water?

He got up and disappeared, then returned a minute later with a bottle of water.

He helped her sit up and put it into her hand, steadying it as she tilted it to her lips.

The water flowed into her and she felt her parched body absorbing it before it even passed down her throat. She drained the bottle and then blinked at him.

"Oh, okay. Be right back."

He returned a minute later with three more bottles and then helped her as she drank them one after the other.

When she was finished she looked up at him. She tested her voice, which was scratchy, and said out loud, "Thank you. Really."

He shrugged, clearly conflicted. "I just gave you back what was yours."

It was her turn to nod. He hadn't given her much energy, but it had been enough to sustain her, allow her body to restart.

"So, you going to tell me what happened?"

She shuddered and dropped her eyes. "I failed."

25

"What do you mean you failed?" Samantha heard Anthony ask.

"She's back, from the dead. And there was nothing I could do to stop it." She buried her face in her hands. "I wasn't strong enough."

He was silent for so long that she thought he had left. She finally lifted her head and saw him sitting there, emotions colliding on his face as he clenched and unclenched his fists.

"I guess the real question is, what are we going to do about it?" he asked. "What's the new plan?"

And looking at him she realized that as exhausted as she was, as much as she needed to fall apart, she had to hold it together for him.

She took a shuddering breath. "Did you find out the name of the doctor that treated you?"

"No, I was on my way to the hospital to find out when I saw you."

"Now would be a good time to go. He won't be there. All the members of the inner circle left with Abigail after the event and are having a private meeting."

"I see you weren't invited."

"No. And none of them will live to regret that."

"I like the way you're thinking."

"I need to find the name of that doctor so I can confront him when he's alone and make him tell me how we can purge the toxins. Otherwise, by the time night falls, the number of people that are out there, with emotions running high, there's going to be a bloodbath. We have to secure the environment and I have to recover my strength before we can make a move against Abigail and the others."

She stood up. She was unsteady on her feet for a moment, but better than she had been at any point since the resurrection. She reached out and grabbed his shoulder for support, trying not to unconsciously siphon energy off him as she did so.

"I need to get back to my hotel room. Get me the name of that doctor as soon as you can."

"Okay. Do you want me to take you to the hotel?"

"No, I can manage," she said, wincing. "The walk will do me good."

A minute later they walked downstairs and out of the mansion. On the street he headed to his car while she turned her steps back toward the Hawthorne. It seemed hard to believe, but it was only noon. Still, the people had packed themselves in even tighter, and around her she could feel tensions soaring. Many sat on the curbs lining the streets and she knew that most of them had been there a few hours earlier when their energy had been used to fuel the resurrection. The people crowding in behind them were more restless, many of them newer arrivals. She had to push past them on her way to her hotel and as she passed through the crowds, she leached a small amount of energy off everyone she touched—not enough that they would miss it, but enough to do her some real good.

By the time the hotel came within sight, her strides

had regained their strength. She took slightly more energy from the last dozen people, and when she reached the door of the hotel she felt stronger, better than she ever had. She thought of how Bridget had looked when she was funneling energy off everyone and she wondered whether her own skin and eyes were glowing.

She crossed the threshold into the hotel and uttered a sigh of relief, which caught in her throat as a wave of energy slammed into her. Abigail was there.

Samantha turned her head to the left, where a small staircase led downstairs to a meeting room called the library. It had a cozy, cavelike feel and shelves filled with books.

She went downstairs and entered the room. Abigail was sitting in a chair, her hair freshly washed and braided, wearing a black dress that Samantha remembered all too well. She glanced around the room but didn't see anyone else present.

"You always loved this place as a child," Abigail said, sounding amused.

Samantha's blood ran cold. The woman knew more about her childhood than she did. She would have to be alert to keep from giving herself away.

Instead of answering she just smiled and sat down in the chair next to her. Abigail was taller than she was. Time had not changed that. Samantha forced herself to sit still as the witch reached for her.

Abigail's clawlike fingers grabbed her chin and she peered into Samantha's eyes.

"I understand you go by the name Samantha now, child," Abigail whispered.

"Yes," Samantha said, raising her head defiantly, hoping that Abigail had not revealed her birth name to the others.

Abigail chuckled. "It's wise, not to let others have your real name. A practice I myself adopted a long time ago. Fortunately, they did not need my name to bring me back, just my bones."

Samantha forced herself to keep smiling even as despair ate at her. Growing up, she had never dreamed that Abigail Temple was not the woman's real name, though she shouldn't have been so surprised.

"I know what you did in the cemetery, after we left," Abigail said, still smiling. "It was very, very clever. You found a way to rid our coven of the weaklings, those without the heart or stomach for the work they do, without making extra work disposing of the bodies. Clever girl. And they'll be so terrified of us, and so grateful to you, for the rest of their lives, that they will never tell. You've won their loyalty as well. I imagine they'd do just about anything for you if you asked."

Samantha couldn't tell if Abigail suspected her real reasons for letting them go. Fear coursed through her, but she forced herself to stare into the old woman's eyes. "In many cultures when you save someone's life, you own their life. Those people were far more valuable owing me than feeding the worms. Someday when I need something from one of them they'll have no choice but to give me anything I ask."

"A dangerous plan," Abigail mused. "But very, very clever," she added with a slight smile.

"I had an excellent teacher," Samantha said. She tried hard not to give any indication of her fear for those she had let go.

"And you were my best student. I had such dreams for you, such plans. I'm sorry I didn't live to see them fulfilled. But now all that is changed. They told me how you found them, and I must say, I would have expected nothing less from you."

Samantha didn't know how to respond. She sat quietly, though her mind was racing.

"You know why they raised me?" Abigail asked at last. "Because of the secrets I took to my grave."

"What secrets?" Samantha asked. It was a good question. Both she and the witch she was pretending to be would want to know.

The old woman cackled. "I left a book of my knowledge, spells, but one spell I left only half complete on purpose. That's the one they're after. That's the one they want to be able to perform and so they needed me to do it."

"Which one?" Samantha asked, her heart beginning to hammer in her chest.

"How to raise the demon, of course," Abigail said, a look of triumph in her eyes.

Samantha shuddered. "No," she whispered, unable to stop herself.

Abigail cocked her head and looked at her sharply. "What do you know of it, child?"

Samantha looked back at her, studying her, and realized that Abigail didn't remember.

The most important night in both of their lives and neither of them remembered it.

She fought the urge to laugh hysterically. It was so unreal, so ironic. She stared at the old woman and forced herself under control. She chose her words very carefully. "I know that trying to raise the demon is what killed you, what killed everyone."

"How?" Abigail asked, sharp eyes probing her features even as Samantha had just probed hers.

"I don't remember."

"Nonsense!"

Samantha shook her head.

Abigail put both hands on her face, pinning her eyes with hers. "Tell me, child!"

Samantha whimpered. She could feel Abigail pulling at her mind, trying to dislodge the memories. She tried to jerk back but the old woman held on. Samantha began to scream. She could feel fire and smell blood. It was a flash of memory. But that was all there was.

Abigail released her and pushed away in her chair, swaying for a moment as she regained her equilibrium. "You don't remember," she said thoughtfully.

"I told you I don't."

Abigail smiled. "You know, neither do I. We're going to have to remember together."

Abigail stood swiftly, startling her.

"I look forward to it," the old woman said.

She turned and swept out of the room, leaving Samantha stricken. She continued to sit for several minutes in the library, long after the witch had left the hotel. Finally she stood and made her way upstairs.

Once in her room, she grimaced as she glanced at the two bodies in the bathtub. She grabbed her bag filled with the tools of magic that she had taken from her mother's house and began to inventory everything in it. Halfway through she stopped, fear gnawing at her. She wasn't prepared to take on Abigail and the others. There was too much she didn't know.

She sat on the bed, crossing her legs. The room itself was vibrating with weird energies, all the residue from the events of the past few days. She was going to have to do some serious work to clear them before she left or someday teams of ghost hunters would be passing through with EMF readers and other equipment looking for ghosts when all that would be there would be the echo of her tenure and the battles she had fought.

She worked to clear her mind so she could focus. After a few minutes her breathing slowed and she again pictured in her mind the corridor lined with doors. The door marked with the number 5 was open, as she had been promised it would stay, and the little girl stood just inside it, waving solemnly. Samantha smiled at her before looking toward the other doors. Door 6 was open also, but she caught only a glimpse of the girl inside.

She stood for a moment between doors 6 and 7 before reaching out her hand and turning the knob of door 7. It opened slowly and frightened green eyes peered out at her from the darkness beyond.

"Why are you here?" the little girl asked cautiously.

"To remember."

"You don't want to do that. I know."

"I have to," Samantha said, feeling the girl's sorrow in her own heart. "Even if I don't want to."

The phone in her room rang, snapping her back to the present. She reached for it. "Hello?"

"You know, you really need to give me your cell number," Anthony said.

"I'm told it wouldn't help," she said.

"Okay. Anyway, I've got the name of the doctor who worked on me. He's not here today. John Lynch. He lives here in town. Got a pen?"

She grabbed a piece of the hotel stationery and jotted down the address he gave her. "Got it," she said when he was finished.

"I can come pick you up," he offered.

"No. I need you to get out of town. Things are going to get really bad."

"I'm not leaving and if you try to make me I'll likely do something foolish." In her heart she knew he wasn't bluffing. He wanted to see justice done even more than she did. "Okay, go back to the museum. Dig up everything you can for me about the original coven—papers, artifacts, whatever you've got. Abigail mentioned something about leaving a spellbook behind."

He frowned. "I've never seen one."

"But someone got hold of it. If I can figure out how or who, that might help."

"That will take very little time. What's not on display I keep in my safe."

"Perfect. I'll meet you there in about an hour. Be careful. If anyone sees you—"

"I know the risks," he said softly. "It's just not in me to be on the sidelines. Especially not now, not with my mother's killer walking the streets."

"Be careful," she whispered.

"You too," he said before he hung up.

She knew the street the doctor lived on. If Abigail had separated from the others, with any luck he had gone home and she could catch him there. She pulled a small vial out of the bag she had brought with her from her mother's house. Very carefully she dipped the tip of her athame into it. Then she let it dry and placed the dagger in a sheath that she belted to her waist. Her shirt fell over it, hiding its presence. She hurried downstairs, noting that the lobby was even more packed than it had been half an hour earlier.

Fifteen minutes later she had turned onto John Lynch's street. She didn't need to look at the address; she could sense the house as she approached it. She steeled herself as she mounted the steps to the porch. She could feel the witch inside, which meant he could feel her as well. It was dangerous to attack him in his own home, but she didn't see that she had much choice, especially since he had gone to such efforts to protect his identity from the majority of the others.

She knocked on the door. A moment later he cracked it open. He was tall, with a shock of white hair and blue eyes that were crinkled in concern.

"Abigail sent me," she said shortly, pushing past him into the house.

It had the intended response. He closed the door and turned to her, arms folded defensively across his chest. "What does she want?"

"She wants to congratulate you, John, on the success of the toxin you engineered to start the witch riots."

Pride flashed across his face. "It took me months to get that just right."

"It's worked brilliantly," she said, smiling conspiratorially at him. "Now she wants to discuss phase two."

"Phase two?" he asked, suddenly unsettled. "What phase two?"

"Let's sit and talk," Samantha suggested.

"Sure." He led the way to a living room and motioned her toward a seat on the couch while he took a chair. She glanced around, casually looking for anything she, or he, might be able to use as a weapon while she debated how far she could take the conversation without tipping her hand.

At a moment like this she wished Ed were with her. She'd seen him play it cool for a long time, stringing people along and questioning them without their once realizing it.

"Abigail wants to know how long before we can spread this virus globally."

"Globally?" he asked, his eyes bulging slightly. "I didn't realize her ambitions reached that far."

"The one thing you should know, Doctor, is that there is no constraint on Abigail's ambition."

"I see. Well, it loses potency after it's passed to the fourth person in any given chain. With some help I could boost that, which would considerably speed the spread. I could work up some time frame estimations for her, with and without modification."

"That would be excellent. She'd also like your assessment on potential roadblocks to dissemination."

He smiled again. "There's no way to guard against the toxin. Anyone predisposed to mistrust or dislike witches is automatically infected."

"And as we know, that's most people," she said with a smile. "Abigail also has plans to maintain close ties with a few normal people in key strategic positions both here and abroad. These are people who might be swayed to her cause without trusting her completely. She doesn't necessarily want them destabilized, so she wants to know about immunization."

He shook his head. "There's nothing that can be given prior to exposure. However, there is, of course, a cure that can be passed. I can easily teach her how to administer it through a simple touch."

"An antidote. That's fine, but does it carry the risk of itself being spread through touch, just like the disease?"

"Yes. That's why she'll want to be extremely selective about who she administers it to and when."

"Of course. We wouldn't want to undo all your good work."

Something flickered in his eyes and she realized that somewhere she had pushed too far.

He moved but she was faster. She threw her athame and it nailed him in the leg. She followed it, slamming her hand into his chest and yanking all the energy from him.

"What are you doing?" he shouted.

"What you and the others did to me," she hissed.

His eyes bulged. "Something's wrong."

"I should say so. I painted the tip of that knife with death adder venom."

"You're insane!"

"No, just highly motivated. Now, you tell me how to cure the toxin or I'll sit here and watch you die."

"You wouldn't."

"You saw me kill Bridget. What do you think?"

"Abigail will have your head for this," he said, wheezing.

"She and I have a very complicated relationship. But don't you worry, we'll work it out in the end," she said. "Now tell me how to reverse it or I'll help speed that venom toward your heart. And trust me, with the amount of energy I've just taken from you, you'll never be able to heal yourself if it gets there."

"I can give you the cure," he said, lifting a hand toward her.

"Just tell me how to do it."

"You can't administer it to yourself. It doesn't work that way. Someone else has to do it for you."

She debated briefly, but there was no one else she could trust to do it for her. She was just going to have to take a chance. "If you try *anything*, I'll make sure you die in the most agonizing way possible," she promised him.

He lifted his hand. He touched her arm and she could feel something flash through her, like blinding light. For a single moment she could feel every atom of her body and it was beautiful and terrible all at the same time.

And then she could feel the fear and paranoia releasing their grip on her.

She looked down at him and he nodded. "It's working. The energy I released into your body seeks out and binds to the toxin energy and together they become inert. They cancel each other out."

"What side effects?" she asked.

"None."

"And if I touch other infected people?"

"The cure will spread to them, just like the original toxin. You won't have to do a thing. And then they'll spread it to the people they touch, and so on."

"And what if the cure spreads to someone who's not infected?"

"They'll be high for a week, like they're living on air. And eventually it will fade and they will return to normal. It really is ingenious," he said.

"Yeah, you should win the Nobel Prize," she snapped.

"Okay, I helped you. Now it's your turn."

She yanked her athame from his leg, wiping the blade on his shirt before reholstering it. "Sorry. I'm not going to help you."

"But you promised!"

"I promised to kill you if you didn't help me. No, I've left you just enough energy that you'll be able to heal yourself if you're half the doctor you think you are. But I wouldn't want to be you for the next twenty-four hours. And you're most certainly going to lose that leg."

She headed for the door and stopped as he shouted after her. "You won't be so smug in a few hours!"

She spun. "Why? What happens in a few hours?"

"All your games, all your machinations, and you don't know?" he said. "You should ask your friend at the museum. Oh, wait — you won't be able to do that because by the time you get there he'll already be dead!"

She turned and ran out the door. She hit the sidewalk and ran at a full sprint for the Museum of the Occult. Anthony had been right. He had something the witches wanted. And they knew that he was alive. She had known she wouldn't be able to keep that secret for long, but she had hoped to at least protect him. Instead she had sent him into a trap.

She had to reach him before the others did. She hit the wall of people as she neared Essex Street. With a shout she sent a wave of energy ahead of her, shoving them out of the way before she reached them. She was less than a block away when she heard an explosion.

Fear gave her more speed and she vaulted over a woman who had tripped in front of her. Samantha had gone only a few feet when she staggered to a halt.

The museum was gone. Only a pile of rubble marked the spot where it had been.

26

Dust and debris still drifted down from the sky and Samantha screamed. Up and down the block bewildered bystanders were picking themselves up and brushing themselves off. She was too late. The witches had what they had come for. But what of Anthony?

"Anthony!" she shouted as she pushed away the debris. She tried to calm down, to reach out and feel and see if she could sense life under the rubble, but her mind was racing so fast with fear that she couldn't.

She moved one chunk of wall to the side and saw a leg, a bone jutting out of it. Her hands flew to the remaining rubble on top and she began to dig. She was dimly aware of others gathering behind her. Someone else crouched down nearby and also began digging. In the distance she could hear the wail of a siren.

In a couple of minutes they had unearthed Anthony completely. He was unconscious but still breathing. He was bleeding from a dozen cuts, including a nasty one on the side of his head. His left hand was completely smashed and turning the color of dead flesh.

She grabbed him and with a sob sent a mighty pulse of energy through him. She moved her hands over his cuts and stopped the bleeding. The man beside her jumped back with a shout as he saw her do it.

Then paramedics were pulling her away while others bent over Anthony. Tears streaked down her face and her mouth was coated with dust. She began to choke on it as she tried to suck air into her lungs.

She knew she should go after the witches who had done this. What could it be that they had taken? And then, in a flash, she knew. Her ceremonial goblet. They had taken that. It had glowed in the case when she approached it because it was still connected to her. But in a flash she understood. It had belonged in the display case for a special reason. It had been used in the ritual to summon the demon. She had to get that goblet away from them. She knew it, but she was rooted to the ground in fear. What if she left and Anthony died? She would never forgive herself.

At last they loaded him on a stretcher and put him in the ambulance. An oxygen mask covered his face and IVs were hooked up to his arms. People were speaking around her but she heard only snippets of conversations.

Screams punctuated the air and she spun to look. A few feet away protestors were fighting one another. The ambulance pulled away from the curb and she marched forward, touching everyone she reached with grim determination. She could feel the cure passing out of her and into each of them. Each combatant that she touched stopped fighting immediately and looked around, bewildered, as if they weren't entirely sure where they were or how they got there.

She had to keep moving. She had told Anthony that they had to save the people amassed in downtown Salem, get them to safety. Now that she knew Abigail was going to try to raise the demon again, she realized there was nowhere safe to send the people. But she could at least stop them from tearing one another apart.

She picked up speed, zigzagging in and around the crowd, heading toward the hospital, where she knew they were taking Anthony.

When she finally found herself free of the crowds, she sped up. The hospital was only a short distance away and a few minutes later she stood in the waiting room, a cup of cold coffee in her hand, which hadn't helped in cutting the taste of the dust in her mouth. A doctor appeared and she jumped to her feet to meet him.

"You're here about Anthony Charles?" he asked.

"Yes. Is he—?" She couldn't bring herself to say the word.

"He's a very lucky man. He lost a lot of blood and has multiple broken bones. Otherwise he's okay. It's a miracle, frankly. We gave him something so he could sleep."

"He's not in a coma, then?"

"No. Like I said, he's very lucky. I would advise against trying to see him until tomorrow, though."

Tomorrow could very well be too late, she thought as her throat constricted.

"I hear he has you to thank for saving him," the doctor continued.

Samantha shook his head, tears stinging her eyes and threatening to fall. "No, I didn't save him," she whispered. If anything she was the one who had put him in danger. "I will come back tomorrow," she finished, ready to end the conversation.

He gave her a puzzled look and then nodded. She turned and left, hurrying to get out of the building. Now that she knew Anthony was going to be all right, she could focus on finding the goblet and stopping them before they could use it.

Outside she grabbed a taxi, which ultimately had to drop her off four blocks from her hotel because of the crowds jamming the streets. She ran inside and when she saw the line for the elevator, she skipped it in favor of the stairs.

Once in her room she raced to assemble all the tools that she would need, filling her pockets with things while she tried to prep herself mentally for what was coming.

Her cell phone rang and she snatched it up. It was George again.

"George, please tell me you have good news for me."

"It's about the second victim."

"Okay," she said, feeling exhausted. The identity of the second victim wouldn't help them bring down the coven or stop them from raising the demon. But knowledge was power and she wouldn't pass up either at this point.

"Turns out they only ran the girl's fingerprints through missing persons. But no one had ever reported her. I got creative, ran it through every database I could, called in a few favors, but I've got the name of victim number two and you're not going to like this."

"Why, who is she?"

"Katie Horn."

For just a moment time seemed to freeze as Samantha processed what he had just said. *Katie.* The girl they'd been hiding from the witches, the girl whose life she had saved. If that girl wasn't Katie Horn, then who was she?

Samantha nearly dropped the phone. "Did you call Ed?" she demanded.

"I've been trying, but I haven't been able to reach him. That's why I called you."

"Call Captain Roberts. Tell him to send officers to wherever they're keeping her and to call me with the location."

"Will do."

She hung up with George and immediately called Ed. It rang several times and just went to voice mail.

"Ed! Katie is an impostor! I don't know who she really is, but you have to get out of there. Call me and tell me where you are."

As soon as she disconnected she saw the indicator telling her she had voice mail. Five messages, all left within the past hour. The first one was from Ed. Every time that he had lectured her about keeping her phone on flashed painfully through her mind.

Her phone had been on, just not with her.

Her hand shook as she hit the button and then brought the phone to her ear.

The first message began to play. "Samantha! Help! They've found us. We're moving Katie, but there are too many of them. I— What? Martinez! Get your ass out of there! Sparks! Sparks!" There was an explosion and then the message ended.

She stood there, shaking in shock as the next message started playing. "It's Captain Roberts. Call me—"

She exited voice mail and dialed her captain's cell phone number. After three rings he answered.

"Captain! It's Samantha-"

He exploded in a torrent of profanity.

"What's happened?" she asked.

"Witches snatched Katie. Our boys never stood a chance. They took her an hour ago, blew up half a hotel doing it. Martinez, Johnson, and Sparks were killed."

She sank down onto the chair, gripping the armrest with her free hand. "Ed?"

"I'm sorry. Doctors are working on him now, and they're saying he's not going to make it. Catastrophic damage to all his major organs."

"Captain . . ."

"I know. What's happening on your end?"

"They pulled off the resurrection. I killed Bridget and incapacitated the doctor who engineered the toxin after he gave me the cure."

"Well, at least one thing went right," he growled.

"But a whole lot more's going to go bad. I think they're going to try to raise —" She stammered to a halt.

"Raise what?" he demanded.

"Remember the night I came into the police station?" she asked.

The silence on the other end of the line spoke more than any words could. "Are you sure?" he asked at last.

"Yes."

"I'll send everyone I have to back you up. They'll be standing by, waiting for your call."

"I'm not sure where it's going down yet. It might be at the same house. But then again, it could be somewhere completely different."

"Could you make it harder to back you?" he asked.

"Not if I tried," she whispered as reality came crashing down around her. What good was it if she saved the world but lost everyone she cared about?

The phone slipped from her fingers onto the floor and she buried her face in her hands, sobbing uncontrollably. She had let everyone down. Anthony and Ed were both in hospitals because she had failed to protect them.

Samantha staggered to her feet. She had to get to Boston and see Ed. Maybe she'd make it before he died. *Maybe there's something I can do to help him.* She shoved the cell phone into her pocket and ran out of the room.

She hit the lobby and shock waves rippled through her. She stopped and stared as Autumn entered from the street. *Not now!*

"Good, you're ready to go," Autumn said in a tight voice.

"Go where?"

"No one's told me, but it's important," Autumn said. She was frightened.

Samantha felt the anguish welling up inside her. This might be her only chance to take the coven down. But if she went, Ed would die. And if she tried to save Ed she might ruin her one chance to take down the coven and save countless lives, perhaps even Katie's. She knew what Ed would tell her to do.

She forced herself to smile at Autumn. "Let's go."

The woman had parked behind the hotel and a minute later they were in her car.

"Where do we go if you don't know?" Samantha asked.

Autumn looked worried. "They said I'll just know."

A chill touched Samantha. *They had put a summoning spell on the witch. Why not put one on me as well? Why have her come get me?* She didn't like it. She purposely left her seat belt off in case she would need to launch herself from the car without warning.

They drove in silence for several minutes. Finally Samantha broke out. "You should have gotten out while you had a chance."

"I thought about it," Autumn admitted. "But there was this voice inside my head telling me that if I tried to leave I'd die. And there was another voice that said not living an extraordinary life was not an option."

Samantha shouldn't have been shocked. After all, when she had first called Autumn to her she'd been looking for the most ambitious witch who had no power. Autumn still had all that ambition and with nowhere else to focus it, of course she wouldn't leave.

On the outskirts of town Autumn turned down a long driveway that wound through a stand of trees and finally ended at a mansion. "Who lives here?" Samantha asked as she cautiously exited the car.

"The high priestess," Autumn said. "At least I think she does."

Samantha moved forward and approached the door with Autumn right behind her.

The door stood open and both light and power flowed out of the building. Night had finally fallen and Samantha couldn't help but feel anxious. She thought about all the people she had touched, praying that there had been enough of them to spread the cure. Chaos in the streets, fighting, and bloodshed would only strengthen whatever evil the witches chose to do.

Samantha stepped up to the door.

"Only those who come with purity of purpose may pass," a shrouded figure intoned from just inside. "All others must turn back or risk perishing."

Samantha swallowed. It was the moment of truth. She fought to suppress the paranoia she was feeling, the fear for Ed, the guilt over Anthony, everything. She struggled to focus solely on her goal.

I am pure and single-minded of purpose, she thought. That was the trouble with such spells—they couldn't detect when that purpose might run counter to the hoped-for one.

She walked through the doorway and nothing happened. She heaved a sigh of relief, which was not half so audible as Autumn's.

"Take the staircase to the top floor," the cloaked figure instructed.

They did as they were told and entered an observatory with a giant telescope. Whoever owned the house was definitely a moon worshipper. She looked at the gathered number of witches and realized that they must be the last two to arrive.

Her eyes gravitated toward the far end of the room, where a permanent altar had been established. And there she saw a familiar figure standing in front of the altar. She was dressed in ceremonial robes and flanked by two witches, each of whom gripped one of her arms.

"Katie!" Samantha shouted, running forward.

"Samantha, help me!"

A witch stepped in her path and Samantha backhanded her and kept running. Ahead of her one of the witches who was holding Katie lifted an athame high into the air. Samantha screamed in fury as two others reached for her. She spun out of their grip and kept going, eyes focused on the witch who was about to sacrifice Katie.

The dagger started to move and Samantha threw herself forward, colliding with the witch and sending the athame skidding across the floor. Both women tumbled to the floor and with a shout Samantha snapped the neck of the witch beneath her.

She could hear screaming around her, but she forced herself to focus. The details mattered.

She stood up and came face-to-face with Katie, who was holding the athame.

And then Samantha noticed the most important detail of all, one she couldn't have felt before because of all the other witches present. She felt power flowing off Katie.

"No."

"Very good, Samantha," Katie purred. "You finally found the high priestess of this coven. Surprise."

27

Horror and disbelief flooded through Samantha. How could this possibly be? She had felt no power in Katie before, but now she was flooded with it.

"It's impossible," Samantha whispered as she stared at Katie. "I felt you. You had no power. How?"

Katie smiled wickedly. "It turns out that just as spells can augment our powers, they can also strip them away for a time. That's what we did in order to get close to you, manipulate you into joining the coven. We stripped our powers, but only for a few days. Did you know that magic could do that?"

Samantha hadn't. If she had, she'd probably have stripped her own years before. But what concerned her more was the use of the word "we." Who else had been stripped of their powers to get close to her? Could it have been Anthony?

Katie made a *tsk*ing sound. "There's so much about magic that you don't know. It's a shame, really. You would make a powerful witch if you only let yourself."

Samantha just continued to stare at Katie, her mind racing.

"That's why I kept pushing you and pushing you. I needed you to use your powers. I needed you to come here. That night at the school, I didn't expect you'd kill

Naomi. I was sad to lose her. She was one of my best. And it made what I was doing that much more dangerous."

"You were dying," Samantha said.

"Yes, and without Naomi there to save me if she had to, it was quite frightening. But you came through in the end, just like I knew you would. After that, it was a simple matter to put my babysitters to sleep when I had to slip out and perform a ritual. Except for today, of course. This morning another witch took my place, disguised as me. We couldn't risk having any of the police contact you, tell you that I was gone until I was ready for them to do so. Then, at the appointed hour, she slaughtered them."

Samantha lunged forward and with a wave of her hand Katie sent her flying back. She landed hard on her side and felt a rib crack. She shoved her hand against the floor and unleashed a wave of energy that made the floor buckle. She saw several witches swept off their feet, but Katie just chuckled and absorbed the energy.

Samantha pushed herself to her feet, grunting with the pain. "Why did you do this to me?" she demanded. "No one could have stopped you. The police were never a real threat."

Katie smiled wickedly. "Because unlike you, dear Samantha, I learn from the past. A few years ago my mentor gave me Abigail's spellbook and personal journal. I studied them, read them until I had them memorized, especially the parts that related to raising the demon. Abigail left that spell incomplete, but even though I knew I couldn't work the spell without her, I did eventually figure out what went wrong so many years ago."

"What?" Samantha whispered.

"It takes the blood of a witch to raise the demon. Abigail tried to use the blood of one of her own coven, sparking a rebellion when her plans were revealed. I'm smarter. I lured in a witch who wasn't one of my own to offer as a sacrifice. No one here will care if I kill you. It's all very exciting, really. I had to sacrifice to earn my mentor's respect and be worthy to see Abigail's book, sacrifice in order to take Katie's place, sacrifice to strip my powers, sacrifice the girls to raise Abigail. So many sacrifices, but you . . . you, Samantha, will be the greatest. My thirteenth sacrifice, a real witch."

"Why do you even want to raise this demon? Are you crazy? You'll never be able to control it."

"Why did Abigail want to raise it so many years ago?" Katie asked with a smirk.

And Samantha realized that she didn't know. She stared back at Katie and hated the smug look on her face, the air of superiority.

"I want what she wanted back then," Katie said.

Which was what? Samantha wondered desperately.

"But why all the games, the pretending?" she asked.

"I needed you to embrace your powers first. You needed to be a practicing witch. You know, when I met you, you were pathetic. I could barely feel any power in you. But look at you now. A worthy feast for the beast. And I must say, killing Bridget? I didn't see that coming. You know, I actually considered for a minute trying to sway you to our side instead. Abigail thinks it's possible. But in the end I realized I just don't have the time."

Samantha looked around the room, searching for allies. There were none, but both Randy and Autumn bore looks of concern. She turned back. "You've failed," she told Katie. "I found the doctor you tried so hard to hide, and I have unleashed the cure to the toxin."

"A mild annoyance at best. Really, after tonight, we won't need the toxin."

"You're very sure of yourself," Samantha said, fighting for time to think, to work out a plan.

"No, *we* are," Katie said. And at that, the witches flanking her lowered their hoods. Samantha recognized one woman as the owner of the store that sold all the candles downtown. The other was Gus, the fraternity student who had talked about people with real power and who Ed had said had disappeared.

"You knew the real Katie," Samantha accused.

He nodded. "But really, I like this version so much better."

"Drop the glamour," Samantha said to Katie. "Let me and your followers see your true face."

Katie laughed. "This is my true face. The real Katie Horn already looked a bit like me. After I sacrificed her it was easy to tweak the memories of others so that mine was the face they thought of when they thought of her."

"You killed Katie!" Autumn cried out, stricken. "She was my friend!"

That was why they had put the mental block on Autumn. She had known the real Katie.

Autumn raised her hands, her face contorting in fury, and hurled an athame toward Katie. It stopped in midair, spun, and shot back, embedding itself in Autumn's stomach.

She collapsed with an unnatural wailing sound that made several witches cover their ears. Samantha took advantage of the moment and leaped forward. She grabbed Katie's head and slammed it into the edge of the altar.

Blood gushed from the wound, but before Samantha could slam it again, something sharp punctured her back between her shoulders. Her hands dropped, momentarily useless, and she spun to face Abigail.

She could feel the blade in her back and she dug deep, sending waves of energy through her muscles, and pushed hard enough to dislodge it. The weapon fell to the ground.

Katie, blood trickling down her face, began to chant and Abigail joined in. The words were familiar; Samantha had heard them before. Then came the sound of nails scrabbling on the ground and for a moment she was a child again, hearing the thing that was going to come and kill her. She sliced open her arms and spun in a circle, dripping blood onto the ground to create a circle of protection.

Howls, screaming, just like in her nightmares. And she knew, deep inside, the hellhound that was coming. She'd dreamed about it the night before she met Katie.

She'd dreamed about it when Katie had sent it to gut Brad inside his locked bedroom at the fraternity house.

She'd dreamed about it even as it was killing him.

Which meant she was connected to it.

She finished the circle just as something slammed into it, snarling as it was rebuffed.

She turned slowly around and saw it. The thing that had clawed and growled in her nightmares. Not a demon, but a creature just as terrifying. It was similar to the hellhound that had tried to drown Anthony, only larger by half. It was roughly dog shaped, with a mouthful of fangs several inches long, glowing black eyes, and quills like a porcupine flared next to its spine. Saliva dripped from its fangs as she stared in fascination. It was the one she had seen as a child. She recognized it and she felt sick to the bottom of her soul when she realized that it recognized her as well. Beyond it she could see Abigail and Katie at the altar. They had her chalice and were dropping things into it, preparing to summon the demon while their pet monster kept her at bay.

But what if she could control their monster? What if she was the master? It was an insane thought, but something about it felt true. It was more connected to her than Katie. She gathered her energy, preparing to make her move. She raised both hands, and then Randy lunged toward her, grabbing her left hand in his, and she felt his energy mixing with hers. "What are you doing?"

"I'm on your side!" he shouted above the rising wind. "But you're stronger. Use me!"

"The circle won't protect you!"

"Just do it."

She chained their energies together and then stared the monster in the eye, forcing the energy to wash over him. The hellhound's head cocked slowly to the side.

"Who do you belong to?"

The creature blinked. And then it turned and attacked Katie.

The witch didn't realize it was coming until it was too late. She twisted with a cry and then it was on her. Its jaws snapped shut on her throat and it shook her, hard.

Then it dropped her limp body and turned to Abigail, who was better prepared.

The witch hit it in the face with a blinding flash of light. The creature roared and flailed blindly. It staggered into a cluster of onlookers and when they screamed it slashed with claws and fangs, piling up bodies in its wake. Others exploded into action, trying to form their own protective circles, but it was too late.

Samantha turned away from the carnage and reached out to Abigail. But instead of slamming her with energy, Samantha took a page from what had happened to her the day before. She still clutched Randy's hand, and together they began to pull the energy out of Abigail's body.

The witch fought back, but every wave of energy she sent they absorbed and she was left weaker. Finally Samantha let go of Randy and stepped forward, put her hand on the woman's chest, and yanked as hard as she could. The life force streamed out of Abigail and into her. She could feel the wound on her back heal in an instant.

Abigail fell to her knees with a cry, and as her features began to shrivel and wither before Samantha's eyes, Abigail looked up at her and a flash of memory sparked across her face.

"I remember," the old witch said, eyes wide. "It was you."

And then her eyes rolled back and she fell to the ground, dead again. With a sweep of her hand Samantha knocked the chalice off the altar and its contents spilled across the floor. The wind that had been whipping through the room ceased instantly.

A scream erupted behind her and she turned to see the monster bite Randy nearly in half. And then she was shouting in Latin, words she didn't know that came from somewhere deep within. A burst of energy pulsed out of her and surrounded the monster and in a flash of light it disappeared.

The door crashed open and Samantha spun to face the new threat, but lowered her hands as she saw Captain Roberts in full tactical gear and several others she knew swarm into the room.

The three witches who were still alive threw a wave of energy at them, but Samantha raised her hand and diverted it to herself. Moments later the three were cut down in a hail of bullets.

"Clear!" she shouted when the firing had ceased.

The officers fanned out through the room as she

dropped to her knees next to Randy. He looked up at her with pain-filled eyes. He was dying. Given the amount of damage his body had taken, there was nothing she could do. "Why did you help me?" she whispered.

"It's my job. Just wish I'd known sooner we were on the same side," he wheezed. "Randy Turner, FBI."

"Samantha Ryan, Boston PD."

He nodded. "This isn't our first witch hunt. Been trying to stop Bridget and whoever was behind her. They're dead, but it's not over. Salem was just one of the front lines. There are others."

Not for me, she thought.

He shuddered and then he was gone. She bent her head over him and wept for him, for herself, and thought she might never stop.

After a while Captain Roberts pulled her away and took her downstairs, far from the smell of blood. She sat at the kitchen table, dimly aware that someone put a blanket over her.

He shoved a cup of coffee into her hands and she clutched it but drew little comfort from its warmth.

After what seemed like a lifetime she looked up and saw him staring at her. "How did you find me?" Samantha asked.

"The GPS in your phone. I'm just grateful that you actually had it on you."

"Ed will be so happy," she said numbly.

"Did they raise the . . . the thing?"

The demon. She had stopped them from raising it. She shuddered and couldn't contain the sob of relief that escaped her.

"What now?" he asked.

She shook herself. There was work still to be done. She couldn't collapse just yet.

"Now we tear this place apart. We're looking for a spellbook and journal that used to belong to Abigail. If it's not here, check her house next. There's a doctor you're going to need to pick up. He's a witch and a dangerous one at that. I'll give you the address. Also, there are two dead witches in the bathtub back at my hotel room."

"It's a hell of a mess," he said.

"I know. But one that has to be cleaned up. While you're at it, search Gus's room at the frat house. And tell everyone to be on the lookout for a cross necklace."

He raised an eyebrow.

"It's mine. I think Gus might have taken it off me the day we were at the fraternity. It could be anywhere. Have everyone keep an eye out for it."

"Done. Where are you headed?"

"To the hospital. If he's still alive, I have to see Ed."

An hour later Samantha walked into Ed's room in the intensive care unit. He was hooked up to so many machines, and lying there with his eyes closed and face pale, he looked so fragile.

She reached out and took his hand. She felt the cure flowing into him. Then, a few moments later, she poured her energy into him as well. As her body synced with his, she struggled to get breath and keep her heart beating. Her kidneys shut down, along with her liver. She could feel toxins escaping into her bloodstream. Her legs gave out and she fell on top of him and lay there, writhing in agony.

And slowly his body began to heal. When his kidneys started functioning again so did hers. Same for the liver. Her breath came easier and her heartbeat regulated. Slowly she was able to stand as the bones in his legs knit. She was weak, exhausted, but otherwise okay.

Ed opened his eyes a slit and she forced herself to smile. He closed them again and then sank into a deep, healing sleep. Samantha turned to go and saw his wife, Vanessa, staring at her through the glass window in the door.

Once she was outside the room, Vanessa hugged her tight. "Thank you."

"He'd have done the same for me," Samantha said.

Together they walked to the waiting room. "He told me everything. You just saved him like you saved that girl, right?"

Samantha nodded, not having the heart to tell her that saving Katie had been a huge mistake.

"Is it over? Everything that's been happening?"

"Yes."

"I'm so glad. Why don't you go home and get some rest? Then you can come back and see him tomorrow."

Samantha nodded. "You're right."

And she felt her heart lighten slightly. Because there would be a tomorrow.

28

She was standing in the corridor. The door marked with the number 5 stood wide-open. Her five-year-old self stood in front of it, stroking the small black kitten. Two other doors, numbered 6 and 7, were open as well, and slightly older versions of her were poking their heads out and watching her with the same solemn green eyes, tinged with shadows. There were nine other doors, all shut, and she looked at them slowly. When she finally turned her eyes to the door marked 12, the three girls whimpered as though in pain.

"Don't," they begged in chorus.

"You mustn't," the youngest girl insisted, reaching out to take her by the hand. "You won't like what you find in there."

"And if you let her out, we might never get her put back," the other two said in unison.

But curiosity burned in her along with the nameless fear. What if the children were right? She continued to stare at the forbidden door. She became aware that it was glowing, dimly at first and then more brightly until red light poured out from beneath it, reaching toward her.

She stepped back, away from the creeping light as the children screamed at her not to look. I did this, she realized. The beast would escape and it would be all her fault.

*   *   *

Samantha sat up shaking and looked around. It took her a minute to recognize her home. She hadn't been gone from it that long, but so much had happened that it felt different. *She* felt different.

Around her the shadows pressed in, calling to her, whispering. They wanted something from her. And she couldn't let them have it, no matter what. Her hand stroked her neck, missing the comfort of her cross more than ever. But it was gone, lost before her pledge not to use magic again had been broken.

She forced herself to lie down again and told herself that she couldn't hear the echo of children's screams in her mind. She turned on her side and squeezed her eyes shut, trying to pray, trying to find comfort in anything. The words came haltingly and when she was done only a little of the anxiety was gone.

She moved her hands and before she realized what she was doing she felt energy flowing out of her, vibrating between her hands, taking shape. She felt a soft body press against her hands and a low purr rumbled. Freaky, her little kitten. She swallowed hard, trying to fight back the tears of frustration and confusion. Freaky was the product of magic, which was dangerous. But he was nuzzling her hands and he was so warm and fluffy and felt so real. She needed the companionship. Even if he was magic. With him licking her fingers she fell asleep.

It was nearly noon when Samantha awoke again. She opened her eyes and Freaky yawned and stretched his tiny body on her pillow. She knew she should banish him, but she couldn't bring herself to do it just yet.

She got up, showered, and dressed. When she was ready to leave she dissipated Freaky with a sense of sorrow. On the way to the hospital she stopped at a small jewelry store and bought herself a new cross, a silver filigree one. It wasn't the same, but she still felt a sense of relief as she clasped it around her neck and it settled into place against her skin.

By the time she reached the hospital, she felt a little calmer. She made her way up to Ed's room. Vanessa was visiting. She got up and gave Samantha a quick hug before exiting the room.

"So, I heard someone in this room has been very stubborn and not listening to the nurses," Samantha said, trying hard to tease him.

Ed gave her a weak smile but didn't respond to her humor. "I was told you caught all the bad guys."

"I couldn't have done it without my partner," she said, sitting down next to him.

"Yeah," he said, his smile fading.

"What's wrong?"

"I wanted to talk to you about that."

She felt like she was going to be sick, because in her heart she knew where he was going. Some things were just too much for other people to handle. Some burdens couldn't be shared.

"You did the right thing."

"Then why do I feel like I'm on trial?" she asked.

He cleared his throat. "Sometimes, even when you do the right thing . . . it changes things."

"Our actions have consequences," she acknowledged.

"Yeah."

"Come on, Ed. We've always been able to level with each other."

He lifted his head and looked her in the eye. "That's what I thought."

"You know why I couldn't tell you about my past. And it was just that—my past."

"I know. And I know that I pushed you to do everything you did."

"But?"

"But I'm not okay with it."

Even though she'd known it was coming, his words cut her to the bone.

"Okay, we can talk about that, or not," she said, forcing herself to sound calm. "In a couple of weeks we'll be back on the job, catching bad guys, and we can put all this behind us. After all, we're partners. I've got your back."

"Not anymore. Not after everything. I know I said some terrible things to you."

"It was the toxin, but it's gone now. Don't worry. I forgive you."

"And I really do appreciate that, but I can't forgive you. Nor can I forget. You're one of them. I've shared my concerns with Captain Roberts and put in for a new partner."

She stood. "Then I guess there's really nothing left to say."

He shook his head.

She walked out the door, reeling from the betrayal. She had been hoping that Ed would be there for her, help her as she tried to recover and rebuild her life. Vanessa was just outside the room. She looked at Samantha with tears in her eyes.

"He'll come around. Just give him some time," Vanessa said. She rubbed Samantha's back. "It will work out—you'll see."

Samantha gripped her hand. "You need anything, you call me."

Vanessa nodded.

Samantha turned and walked away. She made it out

to the parking lot, barely registering anything around her. She got in her car and drove to the precinct in a fog.

When she entered the building all eyes immediately focused on her. The weight of their stares made it hard to breathe, let alone keep walking. She sought out the eyes of those she knew. People she worked with, men she counted as friends, all refused to meet her eye.

She walked into Captain Roberts's office and closed the door. He quickly drew the blinds and she crumpled slightly. "I did what everyone wanted me to do," she whispered.

"You saved countless lives."

"But not my own."

"I know that it feels like the end of the world. A lot of cops coming off undercover assignments struggle with many of the same things you're going through."

"But they don't get ostracized," she pointed out.

"No," he said with a weary sigh. "Look, I know it's bad."

"Is it as bad as I think?"

"Probably worse. Now, as I see it you've got two options. You can sit right here and weather the storm. I'll find someone willing to partner you even if I have to bring them in from the outside."

"Or?"

"I know the chief of police in San Francisco. I put in a call and he's willing to have you transfer out there. No one will know anything about your past. We managed to keep your name out of the media here, so you'll have a chance to start fresh."

"What do you think I should do?" she asked.

"Personally, I think you should hightail it west. It will be better for you."

"Better for me or better for everyone else?"

"Both."

"I see." She stood up and offered him her hand, which he shook. "Sir, I believe I'll take you up on your offer."

"If you need a few days to think it over—"

"We both know that a few days isn't going to change things. If anything, the longer I'm here, the worse it's going to get."

"I'm sorry to lose you," he said.

You should have thought about that earlier, she thought bitterly. She handed him her badge and gun, then turned and left. She stopped briefly at her desk to grab the few things that belonged to her and then she walked out, head held high, refusing to let the staring onlookers see her cry.

She drove to her parents' home and they helped her work out the arrangements. When all was said and done, she decided that the sooner she left, the better. She spent the next week packing up her life. She dumped most of her stuff into storage and arranged with her dad to ship the rest once she had found a place in San Francisco.

The day she was leaving, all her tasks had been completed except one. So, with her car trunk packed and ready to go, she found herself driving into Salem. She parked the car and walked the familiar downtown area until she reached Red's.

She walked into the restaurant and, like the first time they'd met, Anthony looked up and their eyes locked. She sat down opposite him. He tried to smile, but the misery on his face overwhelmed it. His left arm was in a cast and so was his right leg. But his obvious physical discomfort seemed to be overshadowed by something greater.

"So, what's good here?" she asked.

"You are," he said seriously.

Her breath caught in her throat. He wasn't going to make this easy on her. And part of her didn't want him to.

"So, the witches?" he asked.

"Dead."

"So once again you're the sole survivor?"

She shook her head. "There were no survivors this time."

He looked at her sharply. "What do you mean?"

"I was never part of the coven. Officially, all the witches are dead." It was true. When officers had gone to pick up the doctor, he'd resisted arrest and they'd been forced to shoot him.

"Unofficially?"

"I'm pretty messed up," she admitted, reaching for the new cross necklace she was wearing. She still missed the original and part of her felt like there was a piece of her missing as well—a part that she'd give anything to have back.

"I can imagine," he said softly.

"How about you?"

"The same."

"What are you going to do now?"

He shrugged. "The insurance covers everything at the museum, so I guess it's just a matter of deciding what I want to do. For so many years I chased the phantom of my mother's death, driven, because I felt I had to. That's done now, behind me. I could rebuild the museum, but I'm not sure I want to. I just know that whatever I do now, it's my decision, my future."

She wished things could be that clean for her. But officers had never found her cross or Abigail's spellbook and journal. There were just so many questions still left unanswered. Katie had mentioned a mentor; who was it, and how had they come into possession of Abigail's things? "That has to be freeing," she said with a wistful sigh.

"More like terrifying," he admitted. "I'm starting to wonder what I want to do with my life."

"I'm sure whatever you decide to do, you'll be great at it," she said.

"How about you?"

She took a deep breath. "I'm leaving."

"Salem?"

She shook her head. "Salem, Boston, everything. I'm going out to San Francisco. My former captain is friends with the captain there. He offered me a job."

"But your friends here?"

"I don't have any friends. I thought I did, but it turns out not so much."

"I'm sorry."

"Thanks. I'll never be able to put my life back together where people know me, where they know what happened to me and what I did last week."

"I can understand that."

"I kind of figured you would."

"So, where does that leave us?" Anthony asked.

"I don't know."

"Yeah," he said, voice tinged with regret. "It is a good story, though. Boy meets girl. Boy falls for girl. Boy tries to kill girl."

"Good story, but not a nice story," she said.

"It needs a better ending," he suggested, lacing his fingers through hers and smiling.

She hesitated. They both knew there wasn't likely to be a happy ending, especially with all they both needed to sort out.

His smile faded. "How about this for now? Boy waits for girl."

"I think it's the best ending we can hope for," she said.

She got up to leave, but he held on to her hand. She looked at him questioningly.

"Do me two favors?"

"What?" she asked.

"Call when you get where you're going."

She nodded, not trusting herself to speak.

"And stay in the city, away from some of the other areas. They say Santa Cruz is full of witches."

A chill shot up her spine and she nodded again. He let his fingers slide from hers and she left quickly. When she got back to the car she turned to take one last look at Salem. The city that had raised her and ultimately destroyed her life. It was the second time she was leaving it and this time she swore she wouldn't return.

Mew.

Freaky rubbed against her ankles and she looked down at him in surprise. She didn't remember conjuring him again. Had she done so when she left the restaurant? She reached down and picked him up and cuddled him under her chin. "Well, boy, I guess it's just you and me."

She climbed into the car and set the kitten on the passenger seat. "San Francisco, here we come."

Don't miss the next thrilling novel in
the Witch Hunt series
by Debbie Viguié,
coming from Signet in 2013.

Samantha sat up with a scream. She was shaking and drenched in sweat. Beside her, Freaky Kitty was blinking at her with great, round eyes. He mewed and she reached out to cuddle him.

Freaky wasn't a real cat; he was an energy creation she had learned to make when she was a young witch and had only recently remembered how to do so. In the important ways, though, he seemed real. He had weight and warmth and was incredibly soft. He was inquisitive, mischievous, and loving. He licked her finger and she could feel the sandpaper roughness of his tiny tongue.

There was a knock on her door and she waved her hand and dispelled the energy that made up the kitten. The great thing about his not being completely real was that he didn't need feeding, he never got sick, and she could hide him with a flick of her wrist.

"Come in," she said as she swung her legs over the edge of her bed. She reached a shaking hand up and fingered the cross around her neck.

The door opened and a blond head poked inside. Her roommate, Jill, who was even now staring at her with wide eyes as though she was some kind of monster.

But I am. I'm a witch.

She gouged her fingernails into her palm, anger rising

to the surface swiftly. *I'm not—that's not who I want to be.*

"Everything okay?" Jill asked.

"Fine."

"Sounded like a nightmare. Want to talk about it?" Jill asked, sitting down next to her and putting a hand on her shoulder.

"No!" Samantha said, jerking away.

"You've got real trust issues," Jill said. "Especially when it comes to women."

"Tell me something I don't know," Samantha snapped, instantly regretting her tone.

"It would make you feel better if you talked about it," Jill said, looking at her grimly.

Samantha squeezed her eyes shut. "Look, I get that you're trying to help. And I'm sorry that my nightmares are waking you up. But I really, really don't want to talk about it."

Samantha's phone rang and she jumped. She looked pointedly at Jill, who gave her a perky smile and left the room.

"Hello?"

"We're up."

It was her partner, Lance Garris.

She glanced at the clock. "It's three in the morning."

"Crime waits for no man. Besides, what did you expect, coming to the big city? Everyone else is already on something else."

She gritted her teeth. Lance knew she was from Boston, but he kept acting like she was some hick from a small town. It wasn't the only thing about him that grated on her nerves.

"I'll pick you up in five."

"Ten," she countered.

"Seven and I won't look if you need to change in the backseat."

Samantha hung up and clenched her fists, forcing herself to breathe. A moment later she stood swiftly, threw on a pair of black pants and a white shirt. She tucked her gun into the back of her waistband and clipped her detective's shield to her belt. Then she put on a heavy jacket. It was mid-January, and while that didn't mean snow in San Francisco, it didn't mean it wouldn't be cold.

In the kitchen Jill handed her a cup of coffee and a bagel.

"Thanks," Samantha said, forcing herself to smile.

She headed downstairs to wait for Lance.

It had been three months since she'd moved from Boston to San Francisco following an undercover investigation where she'd taken down a coven that was murdering young women. She'd hoped that getting some distance would help her forget, but it just seemed like every night more memories from a childhood best forgotten bubbled to the surface.

Samantha had been raised a witch, and only the massacre of her entire coven had allowed her to escape. After being adopted by a kind couple, she had turned her back on her old life and embraced the Christian faith of her adopted parents. She'd studied hard, joined the police force, and made detective. She'd spent a lot of effort building a life for herself only to have it torn apart again.

She took a sip of the coffee and grimaced. Jill always dumped a lot of crap into coffee and this cup was no exception.

Is that cinnamon? she wondered.

Having a roommate was strange and dangerous. She was constantly on edge and aware of everything she did. Which in its own way was good. Her last case in Boston had been a nightmare. It had required her to go undercover in a dark coven and use magic. Being undercover and having to use magic made her backslide quite a lot into her old ways. But having someone else in her apartment ensured that she couldn't use magic often. She never wanted to use magic, Freaky Kitty being the one exception. She'd grown to need the little ball of fur more than she should.

Of course, she hadn't planned on having a roommate, but it was so much more expensive to rent a place in San Francisco than it had been back home. A roommate had been a necessary evil.

And it's just a bonus that her presence keeps me from doing actual evil.

She went outside, and a silver car pulled up to the curb. She got in, rubbing her hands briskly. "Morning, Lance."

He grunted in reply and pulled away from the curb.

Lance was thirty, just two years older than she was, but his dark hair was streaked with gray.

Her phone rang and he swore.

"You need to have that thing on all the time?" he asked.

If only my old partner Ed could hear you say that, she thought sadly. She never used to carry her phone and it had nearly gotten him killed. Now it was like it was a lifeline.

She checked to see who was calling.

Anthony.

Her heart stuttered. She couldn't deal with talking to him, not right now. She declined the call and pocketed the phone.

"The guy back home who won't let you go?" Lance said.

"Something like that," she replied with a sigh. The relationship with Anthony was far too complicated to deal with, especially at three in the morning.

"Want me to tell him to get a life?"

"No, but thanks for the offer."

"You know what they say: 'Protect and serve.'"

She smiled. "So, are we going somewhere or did you just miss me?"

"Someone called in a disturbance at the Natural History Museum. By the time officers got there, there was no disturbance, just a body."

"Lucky us."

With little traffic on the streets, they soon arrived at their destination. Officers had already cordoned off the scene and one of them met Lance and Samantha at the car.

"What do we have?" Lance asked.

"Winona Lightfoot, local historian, dead."

"How?" Samantha asked as she moved toward the building.

"That's one for the coroner."

"Any witnesses?" Lance asked.

"Nah. Call about a disturbance was anonymous and there was no one outside when I got here."

"No one? Not even the homeless?" Lance asked sharply.

"Not a living soul."

"So where's the body?" Samantha asked.

"Inside."

"Was the alarm tripped?" Lance asked.

"No, and when we got here a side door was unlocked."

Samantha paused and turned to look at the officer. His name badge proclaimed him to be Zack. "Zack, what made you go inside?"

Zack looked sheepish for a moment. "My boy and his scout troop are having one of those overnights at the African hall exhibit. When I realized the one door was unlocked . . ."

"You didn't feel you could not investigate, just in case."

"That's about the size of it," Zack admitted.

"Sounds like it's a good thing you did," Lance noted. "None of the scouts heard anything?"

"No. Not a sound."

They entered the structure and headed straight back toward the area known as the Swamp, which housed alligators.

"Someone didn't feed her to a gator, did they?" Lance asked as they got closer.

Zack shook his head.

Samantha had been through the museum complex, the California Academy of Sciences, once since she'd moved there. She'd gotten sick of having everyone she worked with suggest she see it, so she'd gone one Saturday.

Now, with the sound of their footsteps echoing eerily and darkness reigning over much of the area, it was a completely different experience.

The body came into view and Samantha caught her breath. The woman was well dressed, wearing a business suit. Her eyes were frozen wide in terror. And her arms were lifted straight up, hands clenched into fists that looked like they were clawing at something Samantha couldn't see.

"What the hell?" Lance said, stopping abruptly.

"We found her like that," the officer said. "Took us a minute to realize she was actually dead. I've never seen a body do that before. It's like she was frozen."

"I've never seen rigor mortis like this," Lance said.

Samantha grabbed a pair of gloves and slid them on. She knelt down on the ground and touched the body. The skin was warm to the touch.

"She's still warm. She can't have been dead more than a few minutes, so this isn't rigor mortis and she isn't frozen."

She pushed gently on the arms and then on the woman's stomach and finally on her cheeks. Then she sat back, head reeling.

"What is it?" Lance asked, kneeling down next to her.

"She's been petrified."

"Come again?"

"Like a tree. She's warm to the touch but everything is hard as wood. There's no give in her skin at all," she said.

Lance put on gloves and touched the woman's cheek. "She feels like stone," he said, marveling.

Samantha stood slowly and backed a few feet away from the body. Something wasn't right. She walked away, leaving Lance with the officers who had discovered the body.

She swept the ground with her eyes, looking for something, anything, that could tell her what had happened to the woman.

You won't find anything, a voice inside her head mocked her. *Nothing natural, nothing rational.*

She hissed to herself, trying to silence the voice. She walked away from the African hall. If the kids and their leaders hadn't seen anything, then there probably wasn't anything to find over there, and it was best to leave them alone anyway.

She stepped lightly, straining her senses to hear and see whatever she could.

Whoever had killed Winona must have left just as Zack and his partner arrived.

Unless they're still here.

She came to a standstill and struggled with herself. It would be so easy to reach out with her senses, see if she could feel anyone nearby.

But that wasn't going to help her fight the desire to use magic. And if she found something, she'd have to find a way that didn't sound supernatural to explain it to her new partner.

Her last partner hadn't been able to handle the truth.

She forced herself to keep watching and she reached the rain forest biosphere. She let herself in and then stood for a moment, letting her eyes adjust. It would be the perfect place to hide and it would be easy to slip out in the morning after the academy had opened.

She took a step into the darkness and felt a growing apprehension. Another step and the birds that lived in the rain forest exhibit fell silent.

And suddenly she wanted nothing more than to be out of there and to be *anywhere* else.

She backed out slowly.

It felt as though the trees were actually whispering her name.

The trees.

She had seen a petrified tree once when she was younger. People thought it had been hit by lightning but she'd been able to tell that lightning hadn't killed it; magic had.

What killed Winona?

She began to sweat and her heart sped up.

She didn't want to know the answer.

She made her way back to the Swamp, feeling like there were eyes watching her the whole way.

Lance was talking to a man who looked like he was shy several hours of sleep and a gallon of coffee. He had the look of shock people exhibited when they were awoken in the middle of the night with bad news. He was wearing a name badge on his shirt.

He must be one of the people in charge of the academy, she realized.

"Nah, she worked in the city, but she commuted in. She lived in Santa Cruz," the man was telling Lance.

Samantha gasped and reached for her cross.

"Is that a problem?" he asked, turning empty eyes in her direction.

It was a huge problem. Because what had happened to Winona was unnatural. There was nothing Samantha knew short of magic that could have caused the petrification. And before she left Salem, Anthony had warned her that Santa Cruz was home to witches.

Also Available

Sean McCabe

UPRISING
VAMPIRE FEDERATION

A gruesome ritual murder has stained the Oxfordshire countryside. It's just the first incident in a chain of events awakening Detective Inspector Joel Solomon to his worst nightmare—and a dreadful omen of things to come. Because Joel has a secret: he believes in vampires.

Alex Bishop is an agent of the Vampire Intelligence Agency. She's tasked with enforcing the laws of the global Vampire Federation, and hunting rogue members of her race—a tough job made tougher when the Federation comes under attack by traditionalist vampires. They have a stake in old-school terror—and in an uprising as violent as it is widespread.

Now it's plunging Alex and Joel into a deadly war between the living and the unliving—and against a horrifying tradition given new life by the blood of the innocent.

**Available wherever books are sold or at
penguin.com**

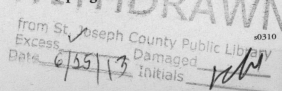